CLARA

Haunted by a tragedy in her past, her life is a constant struggle between guilty memories and hidden desires.

ADELINE

The victim of a cruel man's desire for revenge, she seeks refuge in hard work, trying to bury her lingering hopes for happiness.

LILLIAN

Seduced by the glittering silver screen, she transforms herself into film star Lily French ... but the secret behind her success turns her life into a nightmare.

JOANNA

Torn between a happy marriage to a flyer and a desperate passion for a war correspondent, she must search her heart and soul for direction.

The Dreamers

LOUISE O'FLAHERTY

BALLANTINE BOOKS • NEW YORK

Library of Congress Catalog Card Number: 83–90556

ISBN 0–345–30690–2

Manufactured in the United States of America

First Ballantine Books Edition: May 1984

For Helen and Carl Wilde
A token of remembrance

If there were dreams to sell,
Merry and sad to tell,
And the crier rang the bell,
What would you buy?
—THOMAS LOVELL BEDDOES

Part One

1904–1910

I have spread my dreams under your feet;
Tread softly. . . .
　　　　　　　　—W. B. Yeats

Chapter 1

It was at the fair, the great Louisiana Purchase Exposition, that Sam Fritsch, for the second time in his thirty-four years, fell deeply in love. He would always consider this an uncanny coincidence, because St. Louis was also the place where he'd once found Clara, then made her his wife.

For Sam to have returned to St. Louis just at the time of the fair was pure chance. All over the country that summer of 1904, people were singing the catchy new song, "Meet Me in St. Louis, Louis, Meet Me at the Fair," but he hadn't dreamt of attending. Not go all that long way from California, and him with a livelihood to make for Clara and the girls! But it happened that St. Louis was his hometown, and when he got word that his mother was very ill he'd boarded the train at once, despite his considerable misgivings at leaving his business.

His mother, thank God, was much improved by the time he arrived. This was evidenced by her asking the same old bitter questions about his marriage, and it was partly to escape from her recriminations that he walked with his father over to the fairgrounds.

As soon as they entered the gates, Sam's heart began beating faster. The huge fair was a spectacle, all right, more than 1,200 acres, shaped like a fan with wide paths radiating out from the high-domed festival hall. In between lay blue lagoons, rippling white cascades, and sunken gardens in a rainbow of bright colors, all a breathtaking background for the endless variety of exhibition buildings. One would need days and days to explore all this—and Sam had thought their own Chutes Park, back in Los Angeles, was impressive!

His father said, "Do you mind if I leave you here? Lately, the livery stable's had to run itself . . ." and Sam, hardly hearing, nodded. Alone, he began to stroll, gaping, as he told Clara afterward, like a regular country bumpkin.

3

He watched Tall Cloud, a grizzled old Sioux in beaded deerskins with an eagle feather in his headband, display incredible horsemanship on a pinto pony. He was shown, in the Palace of Electricity, the newest electromagnetic inventions, including one which, it was claimed, could make the deaf hear! Then, outside again, he was witness to a furtive, sad encounter, in which an elderly man sold his pet beagle to a group of small dark-skinned natives from the Philippine exhibit. These so called Igorrotes, were hungry, it seemed, for their accustomed food, and word had gotten around among the St. Louis poor that they paid well for dog.

Sam sauntered on, and just outside a gleaming white replica of the Taj Mahal he found a number of spectators gathered, craning their necks to gaze upward.

The object of the general excitement hovered just overhead, an enormous, elongated, shiny balloon, shaped like a lemon and bright yellow in color. Suspended beneath it was a narrow gondola, nothing more than an open framework of metal spars with a motor-driven propeller turning steadily at the rear. A stocky young man, dressed in a tweed coat, knee britches, and billed cap actually was riding in this contraption. Back and forth on the fragile platform he ran, pulling on lines and throwing his weight to left and right, obviously trying to trim the balance as the great balloon continued to glide upward on a steep slant. Then suddenly the front end dropped, and with the propeller still churning, the craft plunged to within a few feet of the ground, heading at top speed toward a high brick wall.

The crowd gasped. But the pilot coolly tossed out an iron weight, the balloon rose, and he skimmed safely across the barrier. He turned and bowed, as unperturbed as if he hadn't narrowly missed crashing.

"What is that thing?" Sam asked. The man he addressed stared at him in disbelief, and was forced to shout his answer as a wild cheering broke out.

"It's a dirigible! Surely, sir, you've heard of the *California Arrow*? That's Roy Knabenshue up there, the first man to fly a powered airship in these United States!"

"Where did he go?" The dirigible was becoming smaller in the distance, finally disappearing from view in a grove of trees. "Will he be back?"

"Not today. Probably landing somewhere 'cross river, and it'll be a big job for his crew to load up. But he's scheduled to go up again tomorrow. Along with all the foreign aeronauts. They're all hoping for some prize money."

Sam sighed with the wonder of it. He rambled on, but all he could think about was that graceful yellow balloon gliding through the sky.

He and his father ate supper together that night, talking companionably as they hadn't had a chance to do in many years.

Sam told him about the *Arrow*, and his father said, "These are exciting times. I never imagined men would fly like birds, but last year two brothers named Wright kept some sort of light wood contraption up in the air for almost a minute. Just a novelty, of course, but still it makes you think."

"I heard about the Wrights, yes. But to actually *see*..." Sam shook his head.

"How are things out there in California, Sam? Clara and the children—they're fine? And you're happy, are you?"

"Couldn't be happier."

"I'm glad I went to see you two married. Before I couldn't imagine why you'd want to give up everything here for a girl like that. A girl who did what she did every day! But after I saw her, it was clearer to me. She wasn't only so amazingly pretty, there was something about her, I don't mean just her— well, appeal—but a kind of sweetness."

"Yes." Just hearing about Clara made Sam homesick.

"Your mother doesn't understand, though, and never will...she's out of danger now, Sam, but you'll stay and visit with us?"

"I'd like to, for a few days." He felt guilty. He did want to stay longer, but not because of his parents. Because of the dirigible.

The *Arrow* completed three more ascensions in so many days, even though the hazards of the sport were only too apparent. Accidents abounded. The most famous of the Frenchmen, Monsieur Santos Dumont, crashed against a building; he survived, but his dirigible was considerably damaged and his pride, too. Only the American, Knabenshue, surmounted every problem. On one occasion his ship broke free from its moorings with him on board and drifted for miles, but he brought it safely back to earth. Consequently, Sam was as outraged as any of the fans when it was bruited about that on some technicality or other neither the airship's owner, Captain Thomas Baldwin, nor his pilot would receive any prize money.

After the rumor was confirmed, Sam, astride one of his father's horses and riding at a gallop, managed to reach the *Arrow*'s landing spot at the edge of a stubble field, a little in advance of Knabenshue's ground crew. He slid from his terrified horse as the airship hovered a few feet above the ground.

Knabenshue, having thrown an anchor out, jumped from the gondola. Together he and Sam tied the trailing ropes to a tree.

Sam said hotly, "You and the *Arrow* deserved the prize!"

Knabenshue glanced at him. "Thanks. I agree." He started to turn away, then his eyes narrowed. He studied Sam's small, wiry figure.

"Interested in dirigibles, are you?"

"Yes, although I never even heard the word until I came to the fair. Now I believe—to be an aeronaut must be the greatest thrill in the world."

"It is." Knabenshue's granite expression softened. "But the thrill isn't all. There's a kind of peace up there. A feeling, well, of contentment. Like sitting before a fire and stroking a cat's fur."

Sam understood perfectly, even though he'd never been aloft.

The young man then said to him abruptly, "You're right for it, you know."

"Right for it?"

"You're small. Light. I tell you, Mr . . ."

"Fritsch. Sam Fritsch."

"Mr. Fritsch. Someday a man's weight won't matter in airships, but right now it does. How do you think I got my chance here at the fair? Captain Baldwin owns the *Arrow*, although I helped to build her, so he had the right to take her up in competition himself. But when we tested our ship, we could see he was far too heavy and the job fell to me."

"Each ascension, I've been trying her out, finding what she'll do, and getting experience myself at the same time. The prize money, while I could use it, isn't so important."

Sam, overwhelmed by these unexpected confidences, said diffidently, "Then you'll continue anyway?"

"No. We're finished here. Captain Baldwin is too angry with the committee. We'll be taking the *Arrow* back to California."

"California?" Sam's spirits rose. "Then I may be able to see the *Arrow* again. I live in Los Angeles."

But Knabenshue was looking out over the rough stubble in the direction of the city. A heavy wagon, drawn by four horses, was nearing them, jouncing across the furrows. He asked absently, "What sort of work do you do?" Sam told him about the carousel in Chutes Park, but the aeronaut couldn't have been listening. He was waving his arms at his crew, directing their approach.

Sam mounted his horse. He took a long last look at the yellow balloon swaying gently above, tugging at its ropes. Then he rode away, and the next day boarded the train for home.

Chapter 2

Clara loved festive occasions. Her husband's return from a long journey certainly could be classed as such, and she happily made her preparations.

Meeting the train, Clara and her daughters would be dressed in their very best. The night before, instead of reading a novel or painting with watercolors, a skill she was assiduously teaching herself, she'd dust and scrub, put the house in order, and early in the morning she'd bake a big chocolate cake, Sam's favorite. Written on top in white icing would be the words: *Welcome Home!*

These plans duly carried out, she and the three girls arrived at the Santa Fe station and were waiting on the platform well ahead of time. The train, unfortunately, turned out to be running late, and the little group gradually splintered.

The youngest child, Joanna, being only five, contented herself with adventurous little forays into the station and back, clutching Clara's hand and lingering a while on each return.

However, Adeline, the oldest, paced up and down at a distance, now and then sending her mother a look of reproach.

In Sam's absence, Adeline, called Dell, had done a fine job of keeping the family's park concessions going, actually taking charge when the man Sam had hired quit without notice. Clara well knew that she would have much preferred remaining at the park today, a twelve-year-old martyr, impressing Papa with her diligence.

Lillian, the middle girl, clearly wouldn't have missed coming along. She was amusing herself by strolling about, observing the various people waiting on the platform. Her sapphire eyes bright with curiosity, she would be memorizing the way they walked and talked, the fashionable and correct as well as the eccentric, and later on she might entertain Clara with her imitations—some funny, some sad, but all surprisingly true.

Clara herself was content merely to wait.

Shortly before the train was due, two young men, mashers by the admiring looks they gave her, walked past several times, the second time raising their hats and greeting her as though she and they were acquainted. Clara good-naturedly murmured a good morning, but then called her girls to her, and their noisy arrival had the usual desired effect of dampening the unwanted advances. Not only was she a married woman, she was clearly three times a mother, despite her youthful appearance.

She and her daughters were all still together when the train, belching smoke, iron wheels screeching on the track, chugged in slowly and stopped. Sam, the first passenger to descend the car steps, saw them, and their waves and smiles made him ask himself how he could possibly have stayed away so long.

He kissed them all, one by one, Clara first—decorously of course in this public place, but his eyes searching hers with special meaning. After Clara, it was the turn of the littlest one, and Joanna clung to him, arms tight around his waist. Next was Lillian, who hugged him fondly but a bit absently while her interested gaze continued to roam. Last of all came Adeline, who studied him anxiously, saying, "Papa, you look tired!"

He supposed he did. After so many days of riding in a hot and dusty day coach, he was. He said only, "A long trip, Dell, honey. I'm glad to be home." Taking Joanna by the waist and swinging her up to ride on his shoulder, he added, "Nothing like pretty girls to perk a man up."

"Oh, Papa!" Dell protested, an unbecoming blush settling on her pale skin. She was the least pretty of the three and Clara wondered if she were aware of the fact. But still their daughters

did make a picture, all together like this. Stairsteps in size, all
fair like Clara, and all beautifully if inexpensively dressed.
Clara might not always be the most diligent housekeeper, but
she was skillful with a needle. Today the girls' dresses were
made of a soft blue-and-white-striped gingham, delicately
smocked at the neck, with the full skirts at differing lengths
according to the wearer's age—Dell's modestly to her ankles,
but Joanna's showing ribbed white stockings well past her
chubby knees.

The family rode the streetcar out Los Angeles Street to the
corner of Washington, where they could disembark immediately before their own house, just a few short blocks from the
wide, arbored acres of Chutes Park. At that point, Sam, who
had been describing some of the wonders of the great fair,
interrupted himself. "Wait a minute!" he exclaimed. "The park's
open now, so who's tending to business?"

"It's all right," Clara reassured him. "Aunt Flossie's ferris
wheel broke down yesterday and it can't be fixed until later
this morning, so she offered to help us out for an hour or so."

"But even Flossie has only two hands—"

"I wanted to stay behind, Papa," Dell said, gazing at her
mother resentfully. "I could have stayed and sold tickets at
least. You always tell us, if we want something done right, we
should do it ourselves. Taking in the money is so important."

"Goodness, child," Clara interrupted, "it was more important for all of us to be at the station. Surely you trust Aunt
Flossie!"

"Of course I trust her," Adeline said sullenly, adding, "just
the same, she might think it was all right to *give* some tickets
away."

"That will do, Dell," Sam said sternly. He was realizing
there'd been more than a little friction while he was gone. That
last remark of Dell's had been pure spite and directed at her
mother. Miss Florence Mendenhall, no relation but called Aunt
Flossie by everyone in the park, had made a good living with
her ferris wheel for quite a few years now. A generous woman
in her way, she was still not at all the sort to be unbusinesslike.

Adeline obediently fell silent, but her mouth was pursed
and she was eyeing Clara as if to say, "It's a good thing I don't
tell Papa *everything*."

Not that any telling was needed. Sam was well aware of
Clara's soft side, and could visualize what had caused their
eldest daughter's outrage. He'd seen a similar occurrence him-

self one time at the small deer enclosure which accounted for a share of the family's income. The deer were all tame and for a nickel could be approached and petted. Occasionally a boy or girl without money for admission would approach the fence and gaze through wistfully, and Clara, pressed unavoidably into service that day, hadn't been able to bear it. She'd furtively lifted the latch, and with finger to lips to enjoin secrecy had let the children sidle in through the gate free of charge.

Sam hadn't really minded, that once. He loved children himself. But if word got around, all the customers, young and old, would want to come in free as well. And now it seemed Clara had been caught red-handed by conscientious Dell. The episode only confirmed and justified Sam's deep-seated reluctance to let Clara work regularly in the public park. A wife had her own duties. And Joanna was still so young—she needed Clara's full attention, surely!

He saw that Adeline was opening her mouth to defy her mother further, and he said quickly, "Come on, girls, let's go over and get to work. Yes, Joanna, you can come, too. And will you fix a picnic lunch for all of us, Clara? There's no reason we can't close down for a few minutes at noon today. I want to celebrate being home."

"I'll bring it in an hour or so. We can eat by the lake," Clara agreed, her face clearing. She was thinking she'd bring the big cake—surprise him.

Sam and his daughters hurried and a few minutes later were in the park. This late fall day in Los Angeles was oppressively warm, but there, because of the large shimmering basin at the center, dotted as usual by a number of small rental rowboats skimming the surface like colorful water bugs, the air felt cooler, less dry and dusty. At one end of the lake, rapids continually churned and gushed down two wooden chutes, and on their way to their own concessions, Sam and the three girls paused to watch the big flat chute boats, filled with laughing people, come sliding and splashing down.

Sam felt Joanna's small hand tighten in his, and suddenly it occurred to him that he'd brought not a single present home to any of them.

He suppressed his eagerness to get to his carousel and said, "Let's take a ride ourselves, shall we?"

Adeline, of course, protested, "Papa, we haven't time now." But Joanna was looking up at him, her blue gray eyes—Clara's eyes—shining, and Lillian, never loath to postpone her work, was urging, "Oh, Papa, let's!"

So he paid his money, only half-price for his family because he too worked in the park, and they climbed in, all sitting together on one wide seat. Hauled by a cable, their boat chugged its slow clanking way to the top, poised there for a breathtaking moment so the riders could look out over the labyrinth of shaded walks and water, then went flying down in a shower of spray. It came to a floating stop in the lake.

"Oh, thank you, Papa!" Lillian cried as they disembarked onto a small platform at the side. She added with her saucy grin, "Now I won't mind so much feeding all the deer or cleaning up after them. Ugh!" In another moment they had arrived at the scene of her daily chores, and the little animals, recognizing her, crowded to the fence, nuzzling their soft noses through the bars.

But neither Sam nor any of his girls had eyes for the deer now. They were all gazing at the family's most important and valuable possession that stood midway between the deer enclosure and Aunt Flossie's ferris wheel. Even as they watched, the carousel platform began to rotate, the brightly painted animals rose and fell on their turned brass poles, and the loud pipe organ music filled the air, happy brassy music that drew still more people from all corners of the park. A line of customers already had formed, waiting a turn to ride.

It was no wonder, Sam reflected, that his carousel was so popular. Admittedly there were many finer, far more magnificent merry-go-rounds scattered across America. The St. Louis Fair had featured a huge, glittering machine with four circles of gallopers abreast. He'd even heard of a marvel back East somewhere that was two stories high, one platform atop the other. But this little carousel had a special charm because the wooden animals following each other endlessly round and round had been carved by a true master. They might have been alive, actually leaping as they moved up and down, their flowing manes lifted by the wind, their eyes gleaming with expression, not menacing like some, but friendly, seeming to share the enjoyment of their riders. Even the little figure of a black boy, which had moving hands to feign the playing of the organ, was often remarked on for his happy and beckoning smile.

Indeed, to its very top, this carousel was distinctive. The graceful peak, including what appeared to be a long and stream-

ing pennant, was not made of the usual sun-faded canvas, but
of wood, painted a bright Chinese red. The effect of the vibrant
color, enhanced by music and rows of glowing light bulbs, was
one of cheerful liveliness.

Sam muttered fondly, "Pretty gaudy for an old lady." It was
far from the first time his daughters had heard the remark, and
the two eldest already had drifted away, Lillian to station herself
at the gate of the deer enclosure, while Adeline ducked under
the counter into the ticket booth.

Sam circled around his carousel to where a big woman of
perhaps fifty years of age was standing by the operating lever.

"You're back, are you, Sam? *Sehr gut!*" she greeted him,
her deep voice rumbling out over the blare of the pipe organ.
Her command of English, after living so long in America, was
as good as his own, and the occasional German word that crept
in was only for emphasis or out of old habit. Her accent,
however, was heavy and unmistakable, and always would be.

"I certainly do thank you for helping us out, Aunt Flossie.
You're a real friend," he said, smiling.

When he'd first met this middle-aged spinster, owner of the
ferris wheel, he'd considered *Flossie* an absurd name for someone of her stature and plainness. But by now the broad face
under an unruly pile of thick chestnut hair, the slight mustache
shadowing her upper lip, and the heavy square figure which
towered over his small one—all were as familiar as her name,
and no longer noticed.

"Wasn't any trouble at all. Glad to do it." She handed him
a leather sack. "Here's what I took in already this morning.
Business was good."

"Hope you didn't lose out yourself on my account."

"Wish I could say I did, but my wheel broke down again,
so I have to wait around anyhow for the handyman, Ralph
Wilson."

"Isn't there somebody else can fix it? Want me to take a
look?"

While he was talking, he'd been watching the carousel turn.
He pulled out his pocket watch, but experience had already
told him time was up, and he took over the lever from Aunt
Flossie. The platform slowed gradually and stopped. The customers dismounted and reluctantly began to straggle down the
ramp on the far side, while he opened the white picket entrance
gate to admit the next group. This time the carousel wasn't
quite filled.

"Want to ride, you girls?" he called to his daughters, and with a shout of delight Lillian dashed away from the deer pen to climb on, claiming for herself a big horse on the outermost ring.

Sam glanced over at Dell, inviting her too, but his eldest, looking only a little wistful, shook her head. She was grown up now, her expression said, and her responsibilities were more important than mere amusement.

"I want to, Papa," Joanna said firmly, looking up at him.

"All right. There's still the swan car, the one you usually ride in with Mama."

"I see a little lion."

"But I can't be with you."

"Oh."

She was torn, he knew. The gilded white swan was so beautiful, but one could only sit inside and glide slowly around with the turn of the platform. The lion's back went up and down. She'd have to hold onto the pole for dear life, and he wouldn't be beside her.

"Which will it be? Hurry, honey."

"The lion," she decided bravely.

They ran up the ramp. He lifted her onto the saddle and fastened the safety strap. Then he returned to his post at the lever.

This moment, when the carousel started to turn and all the animals, rising slowly, came to life again, was one he never tired of. He chuckled with pleasure, seeing the littlest riders clutch their poles with so much wide-eyed excitement and trepidation. In contrast, Lillian and the others on the outside, while circling and leaping faster and faster, would lean sideways and boldly reach for the brass ring, which hung on a pole almost out of reach, tantalizing them all. Lillian it seemed to tantalize most of all. Sam marveled at that look of determination on such a pretty, schoolgirl face.

Joanna, on her little lion, waved to him once or twice as she passed, and after that, not at all frightened, she gazed straight ahead, her face glowing with dreamy pleasure, her mind somewhere faraway. What did such a little girl have visions of? her father wondered.

"Don't bother with it, Sam." He realized that Aunt Flossie, though there'd been no interruption in their talk, was answering him. "She's downright cranky, that wheel. Ralph is too quiet for my taste, but he does have a way with machinery."

"He's able," Sam agreed. Secretly he was amused by her comment on Ralph. The young mechanic wasn't much of a talker, it was true, and Aunt Flossie, with her old-world upbringing, would expect a little more sociability and manners.

She went on, "I don't mean to be unfair to the young man. Lord knows he's honest enough. Ran the wheel for me one whole week. Remember? It was just before *lieber Vater* died— he was feeling so poorly, I couldn't get away. He was only a little over seventy, did I tell you that?"

"You did. Such a hearty man, I'd have expected him to live to ninety," Sam responded politely. To his mind, her *dear father* had been a tyrant.

But Flossie said, "I miss him. That old house is mighty big since he's been gone. Well, Sam. Your family must be glad to see you back. I know Clara was lonesome, even with her three girls. You came back at a good time for another reason, too, Sam."

"How's that?"

"I remember you saying once you figured the ice cream stand was a good business and you wished you had it along with your other concessions. Of course, then it wasn't for sale. But now it is. Or will be in a few weeks. I heard yesterday, Jake's wife wants for them to move back East."

"Is that a fact? I appreciate your telling me. But why don't you buy it yourself?" Sam spoke casually, but his mind was racing, thinking about his savings, wondering if he could get enough money together. There was only one ice cream salesman allowed in the park—one of anything was the rule—so business at the stand was excellent.

"What would I want with something else to run?" Aunt Flossie snorted. "A maiden lady like me, all on my own? No, Sam, I've got plenty to live on. But you, with three daughters to raise and find husbands for, you've got to hustle."

"That's so. There's a problem though—aside from the cost."

"What's that?"

"I'd be so short-handed. It's hard enough as it is to run two businesses. An ice cream stand would take a lot more of my time, and who would do everything else? I kept the girls out of school while I was gone, had to, but—"

"Those are fine girls," Aunt Flossie interrupted, "and hard workers. Especially your Adeline. Last week the boiler went out, and she got it going again all by herself. The *Liebchen* did everything herself! Worked the carousel lever, buckled up the young ones, even took in the money. Some of the grown folks gave her funny looks at first, as if she might let the platform run away and somehow kill them all, but when they saw she knew as much as a body twice her age, they stopped worrying."

"What about Lillian?"

"Um . . . for a nine-year-old, she did fine . . . Sam. . . ." Aunt Flossie hesitated. "Sam, little Joanna will be starting school in January. I know you don't want Clara working in the park, she told me so, but there were a couple of days when Lillian got sick and Clara had to take charge of the deer. She didn't mind at all. Now, with her littlest about to be gone from the house, she'll have time on her hands. Sam, why not have Clara sell the ice cream?"

Sam didn't answer at once. He pulled the lever again and went off, busy with the customers. Then, when he returned, he stood thinking. His eyes were on the young faces circling past, but for once he didn't see them.

Aunt Flossie said, "You'll need to tell Jake right away, if you think you can spare the money. If he doesn't know, he might promise someone else."

Sam said, "A man should be able to support his wife. She shouldn't have to work. See here, Aunt Flossie, you know Clara pretty well. She hasn't got a head for business. She'd likely give all the ice cream away. Or if not that, she'd be daydreaming and the customers would steal her blind. People don't cheat children very often, but a grown woman who'll let them cheat is fair game, if you see what I mean."

I do see, Sam Fritsch, Aunt Flossie was thinking. If any of them but Clara had let those children in free, you'd have given her a talking-to and that would be the end of it. But with Clara there's something more. You want to keep her all snug and protected, and I'd guess it's because you haven't got confidence in her. Why, instead of asking less of a woman, a man ought to ask more. What you ask for you get, *Vater* used to say.

But it wasn't possible, even for a blunt old friend, and her a spinster, to meddle in a marriage, so she merely said gruffly, "Well, I think Clara would manage . . . oh, there's Ralph at last! When I think what it cost me to shut down that wheel all morning—"

She hurried away, arriving at the ferris wheel just as the mechanic did. Although Sam couldn't hear a word because of the blaring loud music close to his ear, he could see them conferring, Aunt Flossie with her stout arms akimbo, palms planted on her wide hips, explaining the breakdown, and Ralph, tall, dark-haired, handsome, not saying anything but listening intently. Ralph soon gave a brief nod. He'd fix whatever was wrong.

Sam sent Joanna over to help Lillian with the deer. Not that the little girl would be much help, but she'd be safe there and out of the way. He went on pushing his lever and pulling it again, at first keeping a close eye on Adeline, who was selling tickets and making change. But Dell made no mistakes, not one. Feeling his gaze, she looked up at him happily. Now she and Papa were partners, her smile seemed to say. We work together, Papa and I!

His mind wandered back to St. Louis. Would he ever watch the *Arrow* make another ascension? Probably not, but just now it didn't seem to matter very much. He was tired, and he wished Clara would come.

Then he saw her approaching, graceful and lovely, but laden with such an enormous picnic basket it made him laugh. His fatigue forgotten, he ran to help her.

Chapter 3

At last the park closed for the night, and Sam could be alone with Clara. They were at home, the three girls were sleeping like angels, the older ones exhausted, poor children, with all the work he'd put on them.

He and Clara sat on the porch swing, listening to the chirp of the cicadas. Some people didn't like late September in California. But on a night like tonight, when there was none of the usual chill coming in from the sea, Sam enjoyed being able to sit outdoors of an evening, just as people did back in the Midwest. The swing moved gently to and fro. Both of them comfortable in the warm balmy air, Sam put his arm around Clara.

She said, "I'm glad you're back, Sam."

"I'm glad, too." His arm tightened, and he kissed her. She kissed him back with fervor, and St. Louis was very far away indeed. All he could think about was Clara.

Although she never initiated lovemaking, even in bed, she had always responded to him warmly, and he remained as grateful as he'd been when they were first married. His experience with women was very limited—Clara was his first and she would be his last—but he'd heard other men talk, and knew that some wives made no bones about finding the marital act repugnant and shameful, insisting on total darkness and never seeing their husbands undressed. Clara always welcomed him in the most natural way, and her continuing affection for him, the small nondescript man he acknowledged he was, was cause each time for fresh wonder.

He had found Clara some thirteen years before, when he was twenty-one and she only fifteen, in a setting which to staid, respectable St. Louis was tawdry at best. She'd been a dancer, performing almost nude, at a small traveling carnival.

Sam had been working at his father's livery stable, expecting some day in the distant future to inherit the family business and lead the same well-off existence his parents had. In a leisurely way, he was courting a neighbor girl named Sue, and what spare time he had left was spent fishing and boating on the river with his friends. He couldn't recall being in any way restless with his life or with his prospects.

Then the carnival came to town, and instead of going fishing on Saturday Sam went, that sultry summer day, to stroll the sawdust lanes between the small booths and tents. He shied baseballs at pyramids of rubber bottles and finally won a sailor doll which he decided to take home as a present for Sue. He paid to see a fire eater, and a freak who was half-man, half-woman, and a show of performing dogs. Then, ready to leave, for it was late in the afternoon, he heard a barker extol the beauty and talents to be found in the *Paris Revue*, and with the last of his money he bought a ticket.

Inside the airless tent, before a tiny dingy platform lighted by kerosene lamps, he sat alongside a sparse sprinkling of other men on a bench and waited. When the barker outside decided the paying audience was large enough, the tent flap was closed and three young women pranced onto the stage from a curtained area at the back.

Each girl wore a G-string, from which hung strands of beads

that swayed with her hips. Above their waists, shocking to
Sam, there was only bare skin, except for circlets of glitter
pasted on the tips of each breast.

One of the dancers, who must have been a country girl
newly recruited, blushed painfully, keeping one hand spread
across her bosom in a futile effort to cover it. In contrast, the
middle performer, older and brassier, assumed a heavy pose
meant to be alluring while she stared vacantly at the nearest
patron.

It was the third girl who drew all eyes and the loud appreciative whistles. Her hair, fine and yellow white like new corn-
silk, was arranged in a coronet of braids seeming almost too
heavy for her neck and her heart-shaped face, which was small
and dominated by large eyes tilting faintly upward at the outer
corners. Her young body was slender, not voluptuous yet firm
and rounded and, to Sam's mind—an opinion evidently shared
by those around him—quite perfect.

He had never before seen a woman display herself. He
stared, spellbound.

The barker, a burly man whose rolled-up shirt sleeves revealed hard muscles under elaborate tattoos, took a seat at the
upright piano. He began to pound out a tune, which set the
girls in motion. The dancing of the first two was perfunctory
at best, the country girl merely galloping about, her jaws set
in a grimace of embarrassment, and the seasoned trooper striking crude poses and now and then obliging with a few bumps
and grinds. But Sam's attention was riveted on the girl with
the flaxen hair.

She too moved her hips in the provocative routine she'd
been taught. The steps were elementary but she did them well,
seeming to flow with the music. In response to the shouts and
whistles of the audience, she smiled, and there was a hint of
genuine friendliness on her lips and in her eyes.

The performance lasted only a minute or two. Then the
pounding of the piano ceased, and the dancing abruptly ended
as well. The three girls did not wave or even glance back as
they walked away, to disappear behind the canvas serving as
a curtain.

The audience shouted after them, and several men jumped
up to follow, but the barker, anticipating this, had already
stationed himself in their path. One look at his massive bulk
and they contented themselves with muttering. Slowly they
filed from the tent.

All but Sam, who said politely, "I'd like to speak to the young lady with the blond hair."

"Out, buster."

"But I only—"

"Out. Do I have to tell you twice?"

The barker was grinning. What his audiences never knew was that he made it a point to eject with force at least one patron a day, purely as a come on to the marks outside. His show of dancing girls must surely be worth seeing if some fool refused to leave!

Sam might not have insisted—but he made the mistake of hesitating. So the burly man, without further warning, clamped Sam's shirt in one meaty hand, pulled him up close, then slammed a fist against his chin, sending him flying through the tent flap.

He landed heavily outside in a shower of sawdust.

The barker strode to where he lay sprawled and dizzy, and remarked to the crowd with a genial chuckle, "You see, boys? Just keep in mind, them girls is sacred. But they're beauties all." The circle of men, all strangers to Sam, licked their lips. Sam managed to get to his feet and lurched away.

"Next show in only ten minutes. Buy your tickets here," he heard the barker chant behind him. "See the most beautiful dancers in the whole wide state of Missouri. They drive men wild. . . ."

Searching for the horse he'd tethered in back some hours before, Sam staggered behind the tents. When he came upon his chestnut mare, peacefully grazing in the weeds, he stood for a time resting his forehead against her withers, waiting for his vision to clear.

"I'm awfully sorry, mister," a soft voice said, and he straightened.

Beside the tent ropes was a girl. She was modestly dressed in a white, high-necked bodice and sweeping calico skirt, but he recognized her. In the late afternoon sunlight her flaxen hair had glints of gold, and he could see now that her eyes, framed in surprisingly dark long lashes, were blue gray, like a catbird's egg.

"You forgot this," she was saying. "It dropped, I guess, when Pa hit you."

She handed him the little sailor doll.

"Thanks." Then, in amazement, noticing again her willowy look of fragility and remembering the hulking, coarse body of the barker, he burst out, "That terrible man is your father? He can't be!"

She shook her head. "Big Fred is Ma's last husband. She had three after Pa died. He's my stepfather but I don't like him."

"I can understand that!"

"Can you? It was all right while Ma was still here, but she was killed last month falling from the trapeze and since then he . . ." Her voice trailed away.

"He hasn't tried to—he doesn't—" Sam stammered in horror. That gross brutal man surely hadn't forced himself on her?

"Doesn't what? Oh, I see. No. But he beat me last week. He said I gave one of the marks the eye. He made me strip down, said he wanted to be sure I felt it, and then he took his belt to me."

Sam was outraged by this disclosure, yet at the same time he could not help feeling pleased that she was lingering here and confiding in him. How strange, he thought, that so quickly they were like old friends.

Before he could say anything more, however, she looked quickly, anxiously, over her shoulder and began to back away.

"Oh, my, I've stayed away too long. The next show will be starting and he'll catch me out—"

"Wait—please! If I come back tonight, will you meet me here again?"

"I guess so. You're nice, I could tell by your voice in the tent. But—not till after ten." She caught up her skirt and turned and ran, unaware, he was certain, of how gracefully she moved.

The blow to his head had worn off, but he rode home still in a daze. The sailor doll was clutched under his arm, and as he cantered up the familiar elm-lined street, on seeing a small neighbor child playing on a front lawn, he reined in, beckoned her over, and gave her the doll. He was no longer interested in making a present of it to Sue, and surely, *she*, the girl at the carnival, had all of them she could possibly want. *She?* What was her name? He hadn't thought to ask!

When he returned that night to the rendezvous spot, he was more than a little early, and he waited, leaning against one of the thick ropes and listening to the muted voices and laughter. He found he was eager but not impatient. He was savoring his anticipation, certain somehow that she would not fail him.

And at a few minutes past ten, her light figure appeared,

this time accompanied by a hunchbacked man who slowly propelled himself on crutches.

"This is my uncle Paul—Paul Perkins," the girl explained to Sam.

Perkins was squinting in the pale darkness, studying Sam. He said, "I remember you. You won a sailor doll at my stall. What's your name?" He had a strangely cultivated voice, more befitting a schoolmaster than a carney.

"Sam Fritsch, sir."

Perkins hesitated. Then he said, "All right, Clara. But fifteen minutes is all I can promise."

He swung his crutches around and hobbled off into the darkness.

"He's going to keep my stepfather busy for us," the girl said.

"Good . . . so your name is Clara. I like it."

"I like Sam, too." She seated herself on the ground, arms hugging her knees. "Please, Sam. Tell me about where you live and what you do there every day."

It wasn't as tall an order as it sounded. He'd been very few places outside St. Louis and had led an ordinary, perhaps dull life. But he could hear a kind of hunger in her voice, and it occurred to him that while the carnival moved constantly from place to place, little town to little town, she must seldom have left the confining circle of the tents.

So he began to talk, evoking as best he could his family's two-story brick house, the school he'd attended for so many years, his father's stable with its familiar coolness and the strong pleasant smell of clean horses and baled hay piled to the rafters. He even described the Methodist church where each Sunday morning his father, solemn and dignified in black frock coat, collected the offerings.

She listened, sighed once, then finally gave a start and jumped to her feet. "Oh, it's late!"

"Tomorrow night again?" Sam asked eagerly.

"Yes, tomorrow—"

"Goodnight, Clara," he called, but softly and to himself because already she was gone.

Four more times they met so briefly and talked. Or rather he talked. Clara mostly listened, her wide eyes distant and dreamy. Her uncle did not appear again, and Sam assumed

Paul Perkins was still forestalling interference by her stepfather.
These trysts were so pleasant and sped by so fast that Sam
began to wish all the evenings of his life could be spun out in
this way, he and Clara together, remote from the rest of the
world. Then abruptly, the world made its intrusion.

Clara was about to take her usual hurried departure, when
a portly St. Louis man, a crony of Sam's father's, strode around
the end of the tent.

"Why, hello there, Sam," he said, surprised. "Seen my horse
anywhere? Left him grazing and the old devil's strayed."

"Evening, Mr. Meade. No, sir, I haven't."

That was all. After a quick sharp look at Clara, Mr. Meade
had hurried on, and Clara, hardly noticing the exchange, had
slipped away into the darkness. But Sam felt a certain disquiet.
Mr. Meade was not, he knew, one to hold back if he felt he
had a duty to perform.

Sure enough. The next afternoon, as Sam approached the
livery stable, Mr. Meade was striding out the big double doors,
and when Sam entered the tackroom that was his father's office,
Pa was waiting for him.

"I want to talk to you, son."

Pa lit his pipe, taking some time about it. Finally he said,
"I wonder if Jim Meade got it right. He said he saw you with
one of those cheap girls from the carnival."

"Cheap?" Sam swallowed because his throat was suddenly
so tight. "What cause does he have for saying a thing like
that?"

"He was certain he recognized the girl as one of the dancers
in the sideshow. Said you couldn't miss the color of her hair,
or the shape of her face, or—well, never mind. Did he make
a mistake?"

"So proper old Mr. Meade was at the sideshow himself,
leering at the girls," Sam answered angrily. "Who is he to talk,
I'd like to know!"

"Jim Meade's morals aren't my concern, son. Yours are.
Was he right about you and that girl?"

"Yes! I was talking to her! Is that a crime?"

"Sam, listen to me. We've raised you right. You've been
a good boy, gone to church regular—we're proud of you.
Always have been. And someday you'll be the owner of the
biggest stable in St. Louis. It would break your mother's heart
to have you take up now with trash."

"She's not trash." Sam's face was white to the lips.

"I'll say it again, son, it would break your mother's heart. She could never hold her head up again. Not in this town."

"I don't see why not, Pa. Clara is a good respectable girl—"

"A good respectable girl doesn't prance around in a G-string and some little pasties. I heard all about it. Sam, Sam. Think. Don't do something you'll be sorry for all your life. St. Louis is straitlaced. People expect a man to have good judgment, good morals, if he's to amount to anything. Now, hanging around a girl like that—"

If Pa could have his mind so made up, Pa who loved Sam and had always been so easygoing with his only son, then Sam had to concede that the crazy idea he'd gotten in the back of his mind was just that, a crazy idea. He couldn't possibly ask Clara to marry him. Clara would never be accepted in St. Louis. Not by Sam's parents. Not by anyone.

But the carnival would be moving on in another two days. She would be leaving with it. Lovely, lovely Clara. How could he just let her go? Say goodbye for always?

That evening as he gloomily rode out to the carnival grounds the prospect facing him was such an unhappy one that he almost dreaded seeing and being with her. He rounded the back of the tents, and to his surprise found the hunchback, Paul Perkins, waiting. There was no sign of Clara.

Perkins said, "I told Clara not to come for a bit. I want to talk to you myself."

Consumed by disappointment, and able to think only that they were wasting what little remained of his precious few moments with Clara, Sam said nothing.

"Our last day here is tomorrow." The hunchback's gaze on Sam's face was intent.

"I know that!"

"Then—you're willing to let Clara go? I'm sorry to be so blunt but there is no time left to be otherwise."

"What else can I do?" Sam could not prevent anguish from sharpening his voice. "I was hoping—I know it sounds foolish when I've known her such a short time—but I had hoped she might marry me."

"Then why not ask her?"

"Because I can't! She'd never be happy in St. Louis. They're all so hidebound, so narrow—"

"Not really narrow," Perkins said calmly. "Just conventional. So you sounded out your parents? They'd naturally think as they do. It's what I expected."

"You expected?" Sam gaped at him, and added bitterly, "I suppose you knew I'd fall in love with Clara?"

Perkins smiled. "How could you—or any normal man—given the chance to know Clara, not love her? So you do, and I'm glad. Just one thing—and because you yourself come from that same hidebound St. Louis world you were describing—I must say this. Clara, I do assure you, is still a child, in spite of being fifteen and earning a living the way she does. An unawakened child. She knows nothing. About men, that is. My sister, her mother, was a little free and easy herself, I admit it, but she did her best for Clara and protected her. Do you understand what I'm saying?"

"Yes, sir." He told himself that he hadn't needed to be assured of Clara's virginal innocence.

"But," Perkins continued, "while she's still pure as the driven snow, I have seen her stepfather, Big Fred, looking at her, and with my sister gone, well, he won't hold off much longer. The prospect, to be frank, repels me.

"Understand, I wouldn't give my niece away to just anyone, and not this fast, but Fred will only swat me like a fly if I try to interfere, and you seem a decent young man. Clara likes you. So I suggest you marry her, and quickly."

"I don't understand. Didn't you just agree she'd never be happy in St. Louis?"

"I did," Perkins said impatiently. "But surely there are other places. For example, a cousin of mine out in California operates a carousel—"

"A what?"

"In these parts, I guess you'd call it a merry-go-round. But there are a lot of names for it—flying horses, steam circus, carry-us-all. Take your pick, they all mean carousel. Anyway, my cousin makes a good living from his, but I happen to know he wants to sell out. You could buy his carousel and take Clara to California."

California? To Sam, California was the other side of the moon. As for what he'd seen this week of carnival life . . .

He said with distaste, "I don't know anything about carnivals."

"Nor want to, I suspect. I don't blame you. But my cousin isn't a carney. He works in a fine big park in Los Angeles."

Perkins added dryly, "A place, I suspect, even your parents would approve of."

"I see." Sam sounded as dubious as he felt. Even if Perkins were right about the park, how did he imagine that Sam, a man just turned twenty-one and living at home with his parents, could possibly pay for anything as expensive as a merry-go-round?

"I've practically no money saved. Pa doesn't pay me much more than he pays the stable boys. I'm still learning the business."

"Well, of course. Again, you don't surprise me. Carousels are expensive, but my cousin and I are very close—I did him a favor once. Also, Clara is dear to me. So something can be worked out. Well, you think about it, Sam. You still have a day left to think about it."

Paul Perkins went away then, and Clara came, but only to say that Big Fred was getting suspicious and she didn't dare linger.

"May I still come tomorrow night then?" He added, surprising himself, "Maybe I'll have something to say to you. After I've worked some problems out in my mind."

She said warmly, "I'm going to miss you when we move on. Please do come once more."

And he did. He had never considered himself very rash or daring. He had never dreamed of leaving St. Louis. Yet despite his mother's shock and her subsequent rage and tears, despite what was far worse—his father's quiet disappointment at his desertion of the livery stable—he'd done just as Paul Perkins suggested. He'd hurriedly spirited Clara away to an itinerant preacher in the Ozarks, married her, and taken her on the train to California.

In all the years since, he hadn't had an instant's regret.

Throughout those years, Clara had often surprised him by guessing his thoughts. Sitting on the porch swing in the dark, she said, "Going back there, you must have felt you'd gone home again. You must have been remembering how we met and wondering what would have happened to you if we hadn't. Were you sorry this time to leave St. Louis?"

"This is home," he said quietly. "No, I wasn't sorry. I won't ever be sorry. I missed you, Clara. Will you come upstairs with me now?"

Chapter 4

"Clara—"

He had made up his mind to buy the ice cream stand. He'd spent some evenings calculating, and decided his savings were sufficient. But it was clear that in the beginning at least, he couldn't hire anyone. Until there was money coming in he would be needing Clara's help.

For several days though, he couldn't bring himself to broach the subject. His reluctance was too deep-seated. He didn't want Clara working in the park. Never had. And he could give himself the best of solid reasons. Her place was at home, reading her books, designing and making clothes for the girls. Doing those little sketches of hers—some of her pictures were mighty good, in his opinion. She shouldn't need to do more. Leisure time was a gift he was proud to give her.

But at last he had to say, "Clara, I think I should make an offer on the ice cream stand. It's too good an opportunity to miss. But if I do, would you mind very much doing the selling? It would only be for a while, and I hate to ask you...."

"Of course I don't mind, Sam."

"It's too bad, though. Luckily Joanna will be starting school in January. But the work will keep you away from the house. And I'm sorry."

"Oh, I'll be glad to get away from the house."

"You will?" Why was he so disturbed by this easy acquiescence?

Clara looked at him, puzzled. "Sam, while you were away, I often had to help out over there. The girls couldn't have gotten along otherwise. And I liked it. The park is lively. I like the crowds. Staying home all day I get lonely."

"But we're only a few blocks away. The girls and I come home often during the day. How could you be lonely?"

She didn't answer. She was sewing, and her head was bent.

26

He said, "Then it's just as well you have a taste of what the grind of that work is like, day after day. You'll find out. It gets tiresome." He couldn't help himself. He was resentful, and beneath the resentment was the same old uneasiness. "All right. I'll make the deal with Jake then. You'll start selling, maybe next month."

"I'm so glad! And Sam, please don't worry that your home will be neglected. I can easily manage everything, with the girls' help. Even the sewing. I'd never want to give up making our clothes. There's always time in the evenings . . ." She paused. "Another thing. I will do my best. I know Dell was annoyed with me because I let some little children in free to pet the deer. But I did think it out and I couldn't see that we lost anything. Those children had no money, so we wouldn't have been paid anyway, would we? Now, ice cream's different. If you give away ice cream, you give away something you've had to buy and you can't stay in business long that way."

The reasoning did make sense, and he laughed and hugged her, his disquietude fading. Early the following week, he struck a bargain with Jake, and soon after that the gay little stand with its green-and-white-striped awning was moved from the opposite end of the park to a position close by the carousel. Now the whole family left the house together in the morning.

Until she started school, Joanna came to the park, too, apparently as happy playing in and around the stand as she had been at home. When there was enough of a lull between customers, Clara might read to her from the well-loved *Heidi*, by Johanna Spyri. Or again, Clara would say, "Invite Mrs. Merriweather and Miss MacIntosh to a party, why don't you?" and the two rag dolls, invited and accepting with pleasure, were seated along with Joanna and her mother at the tiny table in back. Four dishes of ice cream were set in place, polite party conversation was carried on, although Mrs. Merriweather, something of a braggart, had to be banished for rudeness, and Joanna ate her portion.

All was going well with the family enterprises. Even though Lillian happily abandoned her chores to resume her education, Sam, with Adeline's devoted help, was able to manage. Between those two, Lillian's work was done as well as their own.

Once Sam had asked his eldest daughter if she didn't want another year of schooling herself. But the girl reassured him: "Papa, I know how to read and write and figure. I can add up what we take in without a single mistake. What else do I need?

No. Going back to school would be a waste of time for me.
I'd hate it."

"Lillian likes school. She says it's fun."

"Then let her go! I shall stay here with you."

Sam did wonder if he wasn't being selfish. At present his
Dell was enjoying all the responsibilities he gave her. Later
she might tire of them and miss her classmates. But perhaps
not. She wasn't a girl who made friends easily.

As for education—his own mother had had no more book
learning than Dell, and enjoyed a pleasant life. And take Clara.
Clara's only teacher had been Paul Perkins. Yet she read a lot
of novels and could play well enough on the upright piano Sam
had bought her. So formal education for a woman wasn't so
important.

The easiest course was to accept Dell's devoted help as the
blessing it was, and indeed he would have been hard pressed
without her.

He was not as pleased by his wife adapting so readily to
the work at the park. Contrary to his warnings, she didn't seem
to find the long hours tiresome, even after Joanna left to begin
school. Nor could he complain about her competency. At first
she made a few mistakes in giving the customers their change,
but she soon grew familiar with the various transactions, and
the correct amounts became automatic.

No, it was quite another aspect of her working that disturbed
him. She was, from the first day, a drawing card for their end
of the park.

Clara was undeniably lovely to look at, even in her long
concealing apron with the matching cap to restrain her bright
hair. Lovelier as a woman than she'd been as a girl. She had
some quality that Sam had never defined, some attraction that
made male customers, old and young, suck in their breath.

Then there was the snatch of conversation Sam overheard.

"Notice the woman selling ice cream?"

"I'm not blind."

"Any chance there?"

"She's married, and he keeps an eye on her. Although I
don't see him about just now—"

Sam for an instant was immobilized by a sick fury. He was
about to stalk forward when the last speaker added, "He's the
man who runs the carousel," and the other answered, "Jesus!
That nondescript little man? How did he manage to get her?"

Sam didn't mind the aspersions on himself. How could he?

He wasn't tall; he wasn't much to look at. But it infuriated him that Clara should be ogled and spoken of in that way. It was almost, he thought, as though she were back in the side-show at the carnival.

Tight lipped, he said to her that night, "Clara, I'll arrange for someone else to take over the stand from now on. You've put up with enough."

But he hadn't anticipated her dismay. "Oh no, Sam! Why? Please—I don't believe I've ever been so happy."

"Some of the customers—men—aren't respectful to you. They think because you sell ice cream—"

"They're just customers to me, Sam," she said more calmly. "What harm can they do? After all, you are always there with me, or close by."

He wanted to insist, but he couldn't decide what reason to give her. While he hesitated, she added, "The family is working so well together. Even little Joanna helps when she comes home. And Dell seems to think more highly of me now. Have you noticed? Not that we'll ever be close, she and I. . . . There's Lillian, too. We don't want to interfere with her schooling. She loves it so. She can hardly tear herself away from school in the afternoons—and without me, she'd be needed."

What could he say against such arguments? The matter was dropped temporarily, and the situation remained unchanged. But Sam told himself that just as soon as there was money enough, they'd get back to what he wistfully thought of as the old days. Meanwhile, he assured himself that with his constant presence at the park, Clara could never come to harm.

Then one morning, as he was firing up the steam boiler of the carousel, he looked up to see a short stocky man observing him from just outside the barrier fence.

"Remember me, Mr. Fritsch?" the stranger asked.

For an instant, he didn't. He hadn't thought about airships for a long time. Then he exclaimed, "Mr. Knabenshue!"

"That's right."

"How surprising—that you'd happen to be in Chutes Park and recognize me!"

"Not so surprising. You told me you ran a merry-go-round in Los Angeles. I inquired, and this is the only one anywhere around."

"You inquired? You were looking for me?"

"I was. But perhaps you've lost your interest in dirigibles?"

"No, although I'd lost hope of ever seeing you or the *Arrow* again." Sam beamed. "This is wonderful! Say, I'm early this morning. I'd be honored, sir, if you'd come across to my house and let me offer you coffee, or breakfast if you haven't eaten."

Knabenshue agreed at once. Afterward he would admit to Sam that before making the proposition he had in mind he'd wanted to know Sam a little better, and how better to judge a man than in his own home?

The two passed Adeline hurrying to the park, and Sam called to her, "Open up for me if I'm late getting back."

Dell answered importantly, "I will, Papa."

"My oldest girl," Sam explained to the aeronaut. A few moments later he was introducing Clara. She was dressed in her gay striped uniform, ready to see Joanna off for school and then make her own way to work.

"Now you've met all of the family, except my middle girl, Lillian," Sam said proudly. He continued to gaze after the pleasing sight of his wife and smallest daughter, hand in hand, diminishing along the sidewalk.

"You're a lucky fellow. As am I. I have four children myself," Knabenshue said, further amazing Sam, who had always envisioned this daring young man as a totally free spirit, unencumbered by family or responsibilities. "Matter of fact, it was because I needed to make extra money for them all that I first entered Captain Baldwin's employ. I started as his mechanic."

Sam, bemused, invited his unexpected guest to enter the house and soon was pouring him a cup of coffee. Knabenshue took the steaming cup and wandered to the window. He stared absently out to where the arc of the ferris wheel was just visible over houses and trees.

"Mr. Fritsch, perhaps I'd better come to the point at once. As you might expect, in my career I've encountered a great number of admirers and would-be aeronauts. But none impressed me quite as you did."

"I was sincere," Sam said. "From the first flight I saw, I wanted more than anything in the world to be up there."

"Even so"—Knabenshue was pursuing his own train of thought, undeterred—"I would probably have forgotten all about you but for the fact, which I remarked on at the time, that you have a fine physique for an aeronaut. Wiry and strong, yet light. Lighter than I, which brings me to the reason for this visit.

"Captain Baldwin, who owns the *Arrow*, is a man of means—

fortunately, as I am not. We've built another smaller, very experimental dirigible, and I think you'd be a good man to fly it for us, as even I am too heavy. What do you say?"

Knabenshue had chosen well. Many men, no matter how enthusiastic before, on being faced with this astounding offer might have been thinking of excuses. But there was no ambivalence in Sam's mind. He knew what he wanted to say.

So, standing there in his small, cluttered home, in the familiar parlor which seemed to echo still with the voices of his family, he fought temptation.

Flying would take a great deal of time, time he didn't have. Already he was stretched so thin there were barely enough hours in the day. He should refuse. He must!

He remained silent.

Knabenshue, frowning, added after a moment, "Of course there'd be a little money in it for you—not much, but enough to pay for someone to do your work at the park."

And with that, hope began to stir in Sam's breast. With extra money, even a little, he could hire old Mr. Brundage to take his place on weekdays. And with Lillian filling in in the late afternoons and weekends—yes, it might be possible.

Yet what had Clara said? About all of them working together so well? There was a good feeling of solidarity now. He'd felt it himself.

Most important of all, Clara needed him. He must not forget her trusting words, "Sam, you're here with me."

"I don't believe I'm the man you want," he had to force himself to speak. "After all, I've no experience—"

"I'm well aware of that," Knabenshue said, brushing the objection aside. "The skill is easily learned. Myself, I had done some ballooning before, but you witnessed my very first dirigible flight. Did you realize that day that I was only a novice?"

"Good heavens, no! You seemed entirely confident."

"I was confident, sir. I am. Confidence is essential, and I am convinced you will attain it. Mr. Fritsch, I assure you, if a man can only keep his head in an emergency, the ascensions are quite safe. Safe as a horse and buggy ride. I've no intention of leaving my own children fatherless."

Sam had to smile. He'd seen hair-breadth escapes aplenty at the St. Louis Fair, and only by a miracle had no one been killed. The sport could hardly be classed as safe!

Knabenshue must have noticed the smile. He said coldly,

"Well, then, Mr. Fritsch, I won't press you. Not everyone has the heart for such adventure." He consulted his pocket watch. "I must leave. I've another gentleman I can interview."

He was going away! Taking with him Sam's only chance to realize an impossible dream, a dream he'd put aside but which he would never forget.

Surely something could be arranged. Just for a short time. Just long enough for him to fly once. Once was all he asked.

"Wait, sir! You misunderstand. My hesitation is not because of fear, believe me it is not. But there are a few things I must work out—in my business—before I can commit myself. Give me a little longer, please. . . ."

Knabenshue paused. Turned back.

"Very well. I will wait a week. As it happens, I'm scheduled for an ascension from this very park next Sunday, in which I intend to set a record for the longest flight ever made in lighter-than-air craft. A rather historic event, if I do say so. So historic that there'll be a motion picture taken, the first such film ever made of a flying object. Afterward, if you are interested in my offer, come and tell me."

The longest flight ever . . . motion pictures taken . . .

To Sam, all such heady words! A week earlier, and he might not have known what a motion picture was. But by chance he'd recently walked past a nickelodeon, and curious but rather shame-faced, for he'd heard such places were seedy and disreputable, he'd bought himself a ticket.

The Great Train Robbery was what he saw. A flickering one-reeler, over almost before it started, dark in spots, light in others, and the motion so fast and jerky it hurt his eyes. But the people in the picture were real people. They ran, shot guns, even prayed, and the train was a real train, pounding toward him on the track. Sam sat on in the small grimy room seeing the performance through twice, oblivious of the hard seat and the hot closeness of the air. To him, the film was pure magic.

And now Knabenshue and the *California Arrow* soon would be soaring on the screen as well as in life, admired by the whole world.

A further thought came and humbled Sam. Roy Knabenshue had come here seeking him. This famous man believed Sam could pilot a dirigible, had offered him the chance. Sam owed it to him to make every effort.

Knabenshue did not leave the house immediately, after all. He stayed to talk, not pressing Sam for his answer, but discoursing in a general way on dirigibles, how they were made, what made them rise and descend. All of which Sam found so fascinating he forgot the hour, and for the first time in his life was very late arriving at the park.

Chapter 5

Clara leaned out over the linoleum-covered counter, washing away sticky pools of melted ice cream and shooing away the clusters of buzzing flies. At home in the quiet empty house she'd dreaded the boredom of scrubbing, but out here at the stand she actually enjoyed it. She liked the warmth of the late afternoon sun on her face and she liked having to work fast and hard when there was a crowd of customers.

In a way, this little stand of hers reminded her of the old days at the carnival, back in the Midwest. As a child, she'd hung around Uncle Paul's cramped little stall, picking up the baseballs that rolled onto the sawdust floor and being a real help to him, or so he always said. She'd been contented, playing at his feet, just as Joanna had played here at hers for the short time before starting school.

When there weren't any customers, she remembered how Uncle Paul had read to her, or put her through her times tables. She was the only person in the whole carnival who could do the times tables up to twelve. But she hadn't liked numbers really. She liked the stories. Being read to and then learning to read them herself.

Dear Uncle Paul. She wondered where he was and how he was. There hadn't been a letter from him for a long time.

Briefly she was very busy, putting ice cream into cones or little cups and taking the money. Then the crowd of customers dispersed and once again, Clara plied her soapy rag.

As her firm smooth arms, in short, perky red-and-white striped sleeves, moved vigorously, and her breasts beneath the modestly cut bodice swung with the movement, she realized suddenly that she was being watched.

She always knew, and the feeling she'd get was much like the one she remembered from long ago in the sideshow tent. She hadn't particularly enjoyed being caressed by all those hot and lusting eyes, and yet she hadn't hated it either, not the way Sam assumed she had. To her, the eyes were like some harmless little mice, running softly all over her bare skin.

She'd said something about this once to her mother. Ma was the one person she could talk to always. Uncle Paul loved Clara very much but, like Sam, he expected her to be perfect, so when she'd had a queer thought like that she'd kept it hidden. But not from Ma. Ma had just laughed her loud throaty laugh that Clara found so comforting.

Ma said, "That's right, like little mice, though I never would think to put it that way. Well, let 'em look all they want to, honey. That's what they pay their money to do." Then her voice sharpened. "But touching is something else, remember. Keep their hands off of you. I married just about every man I let take me to bed, and I didn't raise you to be a slut neither . . . ah well, Clara, you don't have to worry. Fred's a good stepfather. He'll watch out for you, and the other girls, too, never fear."

Then one terrible day Ma was killed in the little tent where she performed alone. She lost her grip on the trapeze bar and fell to the hard ground. After that, it wasn't the customers Clara had to worry about, but Big Fred himself. The time he'd stripped and beaten her, the heat of his hands on her body had made her skin crawl, not with the little mice but as if she were in a pit of snakes. When he let her dress again, she'd gone out back and been violently sick.

If it hadn't been for Fred and her fear of him, she'd have probably gone on just as she was, dancing in the sideshow. But then Sam came, and she liked him and was comfortable with him. After Uncle Paul explained in no uncertain terms what would happen to her, what her future most likely would be if she stayed any longer with the carnival, she'd been happy to marry Sam and go far away with him.

She was still being watched, but she didn't look up. Carefully she finished scrubbing, then stood leaning on her elbows at the counter, her gaze on the checkered oilcloth. With half of her mind, she thought about Uncle Paul again. Now that she was older, she understood why he hadn't really fit into carnival life. He wasn't a carney by choice. His crippled body must have been the only reason he'd stayed, to be close to his sister who was so strong and vital and sure.

"Afternoon, Mrs. Fritsch." The words were respectful, but she knew immediately whose stare she'd been feeling. She'd noticed this man's somber brooding eyes more than once in the fifteen months or so she'd been working the stand.

"Sam around?"

"No." Clara smiled politely. "Sam's gone up in the airship again today. Over in Pasadena. He'll be back this afternoon later. Should I tell him you asked, Mr.—?"

"I'm Ralph Wilson. I fix the machinery around here."

"Sam's mentioned you."

"I was here a few weeks back, working on the water pump for the chutes. Don't you remember? I bought some ice cream from you."

"Is that so?" She felt a flush rising in her throat. She was ill at ease, and annoyed with herself because, though she'd never admit to it, she did remember. Indeed, she'd been vividly aware of the long muscular male body clad in close-fitting trousers and an open-necked shirt, the lean tanned face, and the curly black hair cut shorter than was usual.

"Anyways…." He paused. "I wanted to make your acquaintance."

Anyways. That was bad grammar. One of Uncle Paul's pet peeves, in fact. Clara's composure returned.

She said firmly, to close the conversation, "Nice to meet you, too, Mr. Wilson."

"Yes, but you see I've been wondering. I'm thinking all the time I saw you somewhere before. I just can't—"

He was interrupted by a large family with children, pushing up to the counter. Clara concentrated on serving all the different orders, and when she was finally free again, Ralph Wilson was gone.

To her delight, at home there was the long-awaited letter from Uncle Paul. But before she could open it, Sam came in from the stable behind the house.

"Where's Lillian?" he asked, passing a tired hand across his forehead. "She used to rub down the horse for me. But lately it seems she's never here till suppertime, which means paying old Brundage still more to watch the deer pen. I don't like to see such flightiness in a young girl, Clara."

"Lillian's only growing up, I guess."

"Growing up? She was more grownup last year when she was more willing."

"I mean..." Clara hesitated. "She's gotten a mind of her own lately. After all, she's turned eleven. Ma used to say when girls began to fill out with a bosom, they're becoming women and they act strange for a while."

"Clara!" Sam was incensed. "Why is it whenever you mention your mother, I hear something coarse?"

Clara's lips pressed together, but she did not allow herself to answer angrily. There was truth in what he said and she was at fault for mentioning Ma at all, knowing Sam's feelings. He had liked Uncle Paul, but he never wanted to hear anything about Ma. Clara had asked him why once and he'd only said that he thought a woman who would marry four times wasn't someone he'd have had much in common with.

"But you never knew her!" Clara had protested.

"I admit that. I just happen to believe that it's wrong to make light of marriage. Three divorces she had. Three!"

"Just two. My own Pa died," Clara corrected. "Anyway, I loved her." This last sentence, though, she said only to herself, trying once again to ignore the resentment that always rose in her when Sam spoke so of Ma. Ma had been courageous and honest, hadn't she? Surely, being a trapeze artist wasn't something to be ashamed of. But Sam was her husband. And he had his mind made up. She said, "I'm sorry. I didn't mean to be coarse. But you asked me what I thought was wrong with Lillian and I told you."

Sam's face cleared. He said ruefully, "I'm a great fool, aren't I? I love you as you are, natural and open. Why, anyone would think I wanted you to be the image of my mother!"

Clara did not comment. How could she—after chiding Sam for critizing Ma when he'd never even met her? She, Clara, had never met Mrs. Fritsch. Sam's mother had stayed away from the small wedding ceremony. At the last moment Mr. Fritsch had attended and had even kissed her afterward and wished her happiness. But not Sam's mother. Like Big Fred, as Uncle Paul put it, she'd sulked in her tent, and never had she written a line to Clara in all these years. She acknowledged her granddaughters, sent them gifts on their birthdays, and always a particularly nice one to Adeline who was named for her. But for Clara there was nothing. She did not exist.

The thought of letters reminded Clara of the one she still

held in her hand and hurriedly she tore it open.

The news was not happy, although as always Paul Perkins was not one to complain. It was only because he mentioned that he'd had to cut back the hours at his stand that she gathered his crooked back had become even more painful and troublesome.

"He's still with the carnival?" Sam asked, observing her troubled expression.

"Yes. And he doesn't sound well. He's never been strong."

"Why don't you urge him to come visit us? I would make him welcome, you know." Sam was atoning for his harsh words about her mother, words that had surprised even him in their intensity.

"Thank you, Sam. It's difficult to write to him because the carnival moves around so. But I'll try again."

"Good."

"Sam, don't worry about Lillian."

"No, I really don't, though I hope she marries a rich man." He essayed a small joke. "She was well named, wasn't she? As I recall from my church lessons, it says in the Bible, about lilies, that they toil not, neither do they spin, yet Solomon in all his glory was not arrayed like one of these."

"She is pretty, isn't she!" Clara said. "And you'll see, she isn't lazy. I've an idea she'll work till she drops if she finds something she's interested in. Like school. As for lilies"— Clara pleased him by continuing his metaphor—"they're hardy. Our own lily will survive."

He laughed. But contemplating his daughters that evening, he felt a twinge of guilt. Was he doing all he could for them? Lillian—lazy or not—he cared about her. And Dell, hardworking and devoted Dell, who by rights should have been his favorite, although somehow his heart warmed most to the youngest, Joanna. That was because he always saw Clara in Joanna's fine-boned face and widely spaced gray blue eyes.

Ah, he loved Clara so deeply!

And while it seemed he'd been wrong to worry as much about her as he did—she'd had no problems at the park after all; indeed Aunt Flossie had mentioned several times what a dignified way Clara had with the customers, and how well respected she was by everyone else working there—all the same, he'd intended to give up the dirigible ascensions long ago and he certainly would soon.

Even though he was the only one light enough to pilot *Little*

Blue Star, as Captain Baldwin had dubbed the newest member
of his fleet, and even though Sam enjoyed flying her even more
than he had ever imagined he would, soon, he resolved, soon
he'd resign. He'd come home to stay where he belonged, at
Clara's side.

Chapter 6

Lillian did do well in school. Having quick comprehension and
a fine memory, she made an excellent record with only a modest
expenditure of effort. Far more modest than her parents realized.

Now that Papa was no longer waiting for her each afternoon,
his observant eye on his pocket watch, she was remaining away
from the park as long as she could and thus avoiding much of
the loathed work with the deer. It was easy to fool Mama, who
believed very readily that she was staying late each day to
study. Mama would probably have done just that. Even Adeline, who no longer thought about school and its routines, was
not suspicious, merely annoyed. Lately Dell had become a
regular scold. But after all, Dell loved the park and was doing
what she liked. Papa certainly was doing what he enjoyed, off
somewhere in Pasadena. So why shouldn't Lillian please herself, too?

She spent these precious free hours at the home of a new
friend, Olive Sengstacken.

Olive's father was an attorney, not only for various businesses in town but also for the Santa Fe Railroad, and the
Sengstackens were people of wealth. Their large, imposing
white house, with its many round turrets and the lovely ornate
trim of carved balls and curliques, deeply impressed Lillian.
She no longer stared openly at the oil paintings in gold-leaf
frames, or at the thick Persian carpets, or even at the pink plush
settee in Olive's bedroom, a room which unbelievably belonged
to Olive alone. No, Lillian did not stare; she'd learned that

staring was ill-bred. But she was naturally observant, and could have described for Clara every knickknack in the glass-fronted cabinets, had she wished. She did not, but instead hugged to herself this secret lingering in a life of luxury.

Olive's mother had been born in England, and frequently referred to her girlhood home there, an estate called Bedlington Hall. She also made a point of continuing her native customs, and one of these, teatime, Lillian found a delight.

Seated at a polished oak table in the big pantry, Lillian and Olive wolfed down innumerable small cakes and sandwiches, and between bites they giggled, all too conscious of the male company sharing the table. They did not mind being more or less ignored by the two boys opposite, who were so much older, being all of seventeen. One was Eddie Sengstacken, who bore his sister a strong facial resemblance and therefore stirred no dreams in Lillian's breast. But the other, his friend Charles Gold, blessed with regular features, broad shoulders, and a quiet confident manner, caused her to behave with as much silliness as Olive. When Olive suggested they send him a note, unsigned but announcing in flowing script: *I love you*, Lillian agreed enthusiastically. The girls were disappointed but hardly surprised when the young man never mentioned the matter. Merely to have written the exciting adult words satisfied them both.

In the beginning of their close friendship, Olive had occasionally asked, "Shall we play at your house today?" Lillian was quick to refuse as an image of the Fritsch house, plain and square, its only ornament a common stone-pillared porch, flashed into her mind.

"Oh, I'm not allowed to bring friends home when Mama isn't there."

"You always say that," Olive complained. "And where is your mother, if she isn't at home?"

Lillian replied loftily, "My mother spends all her time taking baskets to the poor and caring for sick people who have no money for a doctor. People bless her on their deathbeds."

Out of the corner of her eye, she watched Olive uneasily. Olive seldom read books, Lillian well knew, but Louisa Mae Alcott's *Little Women* was still very popular, and anyone familiar with the story would at once recognize this description as that of Marmie, the saintly mother of the March family.

But Olive said with envy, "Really? My mother is too busy here at home, giving parties and managing servants."

"I think your mother is splendid anyway," Lillian declared. In fact, she quite adored Mrs. Sengstacken, who was always so beautifully dressed and who was, unlike her daughter, a remarkably handsome woman.

So Olive let the matter drop. She was eager to please, being deeply grateful for Lillian's companionship. Olive was plain. She had mousy hair, uneven front teeth, and sallow skin on which prominent red pimples were wont to appear. Being bosom friends with a girl like Lillian was so important to Olive that when Mrs. Sengstacken had originally asked a few pointed questions about the Fritsch family, Olive, who was by no means stupid, had done a little improvising of her own.

"Yes, her father is in business."

"What sort of business?"

"The entertainment business." That much Lillian had said. Alarmed by her mother's expression, Olive added, "But lots of other kinds, too. He's a very important—"

"Entertainment?" Mrs. Sengstacken was not easily distracted. "My dear child, that can mean anything. The stage, or worse, one of those dreadful nickelodeons. What sort of entertainment?"

"I think—she mentioned the Opera House." Olive had quickly considered and discarded several less genteel possibilities. "Isn't that interesting? You and Papa go so often to the opera."

Her mother replied with a sniff. "Being a patron of the arts does not mean I care to associate with artists—or singers."

However, she had noted how poised Lillian was, and how becomingly dressed, a fact which suggested an expensive dressmaker. Mr. Fritsch must, she decided, be well-to-do. Perhaps among his other enterprises he managed the Opera House, or more likely still, was the backer.

In any case, prudence told her not to probe further, because it was, after all, delightful that poor Olive had such an attractive companion. And if it seemed a trifle odd that Lillian could never be with Olive on weekends, for that Lillian herself offered the explanation. Her great-aunt was an old, crotchety lady with bad eyesight. Lillian was expected to spend Saturdays and Sundays as a companion to her Aunt Susan, running her errands, reading to her, and just being helpful.

"I don't know why, but I'm her favorite." Lillian's eyes were downcast modestly. "There's even been talk of her taking me with her to Europe. Wouldn't that be exciting?"

Mrs. Sengstacken was satisfied. She was no better acquainted with *Little Women* than her daughter was.

The long days of summer, when the family enterprises were at their busiest and Lillian's attendance at the park would be absolutely required, were still months away. Lillian gave them little heed. If necessary, when the time came, she could always be taking a Grand Tour of Europe with the imaginary aunt. Much more worrisome, and preying constantly on her mind, was the possibility of being discovered at the park some weekend, either by Olive or by one of those gossipy girls at school. There she'd be, hard at work, not caring for old Aunt Susan but a herd of messy deer!

Her fear was well founded. Olive was eager to visit Chutes Park, and on one occasion had even arranged for her mother to take the two of them there after school. Lillian had managed to look bored at the announcement, and said with perfect truth, "Oh, thanks, Olive, but I'd really rather not. I've been there so often!" and the plan was abandoned. But Lillian, munching on a hot buttered bun at the pantry table, faced the fact that her days as a welcome member of the Sengstacken family were numbered. Eventually she'd be found out.

Sure enough, in April, the dreaded moment came.

Another dirigible ascension had been scheduled for early Sunday morning at Chutes Park. Because of the fame of the aeronaut, Mr. Roy Knabenshue, as well as an unusual aspect of the event, newspaper coverage was extensive and public interest ran high.

The evening beforehand, Sam explained to his family the reason for all the excitement.

"There's a man named Hancock who's been bedeviling Captain Baldwin to race one of our dirigibles against Hancock's fancy Pope-Toledo motorcar. The poor fool is convinced the automobile is faster! Baldwin's finally agreed, and the course will be from Chutes Park to the site of the Raymond Hotel in Pasadena, with Captain Baldwin riding along in the motorcar to make sure there's no cheating. Although how Hancock might cheat beats me. He'll have enough trouble trying not to blow out his tires or let the engine boil over."

"Only a year ago," Clara observed, more coolly than she'd intended, "you were keen for a motorcar yourself. Perhaps Mr. Hancock will win, and to be truthful, I almost hope—" She stopped, appalled at herself.

"You hope he does?" An incensed Adeline finished the

thought for her. "Mama, how can you be so disloyal?"

But Sam said sternly, "That will do, Dell. Have you no respect? Goodness, girl, your mother worries about me. Quite naturally, she believes dirigibles are dangerous and dislikes them. I wouldn't call that disloyal." He smiled at Clara, who found it difficult to meet his gaze.

In fact, it hadn't occurred to her to worry. The one time she'd gone with him to the little field where Captain Baldwin kept his airships, and she'd waited in the buggy while Sam soared slowly, sedately above her head, she'd been filled at first with awed amazement, finding the bright silk of the balloon a pretty sight against the blue of the sky. But nothing had happened that was frightening or even very exciting. Indeed it seemed to her that after the novelty wore off, rising in the air and gliding about would prove to be just a little boring.

But how right he was that she wanted him to give up dirigibles! She wanted her husband back with her at the park, within call, keeping Ralph Wilson at a distance and in his place. Not that Mr. Wilson ever said a word anyone could object to; he didn't even approach her very often. But when he did, when his dark deep-set eyes held hers so she couldn't look away, she could almost wish she was back in the safe dull confines of her house.

"Papa—" Dell, at the mere idea of her beloved father being in the slightest peril, had turned pale. "Papa, I didn't think. Is it really—"

"Of course not! An ascension is as safe as walking down the street," Sam said firmly, but he appeared relieved that just then there was an interruption. They could hear the sizzling of a pot boiling over on the iron range. Clara, noticing that Lillian's abstraction had survived even that arresting noise, said sharply, "Lillian, our supper!"

The girl jumped up guiltily and ran out.

Sam said, "Now, about tomorrow—"

"Wait, Sam—" Clara had to risk his displeasure. "I really must ask. I thought this work of yours with dirigibles was to last only a short time. When are you going to be finished? We need you at the park. I—Dell has far too much to do. Oh, Sam," she finished, "we miss you!"

"I haven't too much to do," Dell put in resentfully, but Sam ignored her.

He said to Clara, "I'm glad you miss me, and even yesterday, I might have given you a different answer. But now I'm afraid it will be some time before I can stop flying. You see, my dear, there's a splendid opportunity which I only learned of yesterday. Roy and Captain Baldwin have been thinking of offering regular sightseeing excursions—taking passengers, that is—and to that end they are developing a very much larger machine. But there, you don't care about details. What matters is that they want me with them and I can hardly say no. There would be good money in it. Enough that my family would no longer need to work in the park at all."

He paused, but no one spoke. Dell and Joanna as well as Clara were staring at him.

"Here now—what's the matter? Surely you'd like to give up scooping ice cream, Clara? As for you, Dell, you could stop being a slavey to a carousel. No more strapping little children onto the jumpers, eh? No more pulling that heavy lever, selling tickets—"

"But I like pulling the lever, Papa," Dell said. "And I like selling tickets." Even she, for whom his every wish was law, sounded bewildered. "What do you mean? That someone else would run our carousel?"

"Well, I don't know. I haven't thought . . . I'd sell it, I suppose."

"Oh, Papa, no!"

The sudden wail was Joanna's. The little girl ran to Clara and threw herself down, face buried in Clara's lap, her body shaking with sobs.

"Hush, hush," Clara soothed. "Sam, you've upset her terribly! Tell her, Sam. You didn't mean what you said—"

"But I did. About the passenger service anyway. Lordy, woman, business is business, you know that. I must do what's best for us all. But about the carousel. I suppose I . . ." He was shaken. For Joanna to carry on so, she who was usually so sunny and even tempered! "Well, you all know I'm fond of the old thing myself. No, all right, I won't sell it. Don't worry, any of you. I won't sell it."

Dell jumped to her feet. "Don't be such a little silly, Joanna! You heard Papa. The carousel will still be ours. Nothing is going to change."

But Clara understood forlornly that no such promise had been given about the ice cream stand. One day soon, she would be relegated back to the house. Even then, life wouldn't be as

it was before, when Sam had been busy at the park nearby,
coming home often during the day. Sam would be nowhere
around.

Clara shivered.

"Now, that's settled," Sam said. "I've something to tell you
about the plans for tomorrow. There'll be hundreds of spectators, but Captain Baldwin has arranged for a few rows of
chairs for the important people. And my family is numbered
among them. You'll have reserved seats. Now what do you
think of that?"

"Papa," Lillian said. She'd returned and was standing in
the doorway. "I really should study tomorrow morning and not
go. There's reading I haven't done. . . ."

"It will wait. I reserved four chairs for the four prettiest
ladies in town and I want them all filled."

Lillian sighed. "Yes, Papa."

So early the following morning, when dew was still sparkling on the grass, Clara and her three daughters were shown
to their folding chairs in the front row. There, for some time,
they and the throng of spectators waited while the yellow airship
was filled with hydrogen. Gradually the *Arrow* came alive,
growing big and round, and straining harder and harder against
the strong tethering ropes.

Lillian watched, twisting her fingers in her lap. How conspicuous she was, sitting in the very front row! Yet at the same
time she could not help feeling proud that it was her own father
who was ordering the ground crew about so competently. She'd
been so wrapped up in her own dilemma of late that she had
hardly had an idea what it was Papa was doing, away from
home so much. She'd never expected him to play such a prominent part today.

The *Arrow* was ready. Mr. Knabenshue stepped into the
long open gondola which now hovered a foot or so above the
ground. The aeronaut was dressed in a black frock coat, ruffled
shirt, and oval-crowned beaver hat. He looked, Lillian thought,
brave and stalwart. The crowd thought so, too, and gave him
a cheer which he acknowledged with a majestic wave of his
hand.

Nearby, chugging noisily, a gleaming motorcar rested on
the grass. Seated in it were two gentlemen, both arrayed in
long white dusters, motoring goggles, and leather gauntlets.
As exhaust smoke poured from the car's rear, the smaller man,
in the passenger seat, raised his arm for silence. He wet a finger

at his lips and extended it upward to test the wind.

"Mr. Knabenshue! I suggest an altitude of five hundred feet. Can you hear me?"

The aeronaut continued his last-moment adjustment of lines and small levers, but he was visibly annoyed. "Captain Baldwin," he called back, "as pilot, I shall have to use my own best judgment."

"I expect your best judgment. Bearing in mind my greater experience, your judgment will tell you five hundred feet. . . . Ladies and gentlemen, Mr. Sam Fritsch will give the signal. All right, Mr. Fritsch. When you are ready, sir."

Sam gestured to one of his assistants, who formally handed him a fine teakwood box, the lid open. From the gleaming folds of white silk inside, Sam took a silver-handled pistol, gave the ropes holding the dirigible one last inspecting look, then pointed the gun in the air and fired.

The restraining lines were released, the balloon jerked the gondola upward, and at the same time the shining Pope-Toledo automobile clashed its gears and charged away down the park path. Several unwary spectators were forced to leap to safety.

Calmly, Sam and his crew began loading their equipment into a heavy wagon.

"Good morning, Mrs. Fritsch."

Clara, who had risen, intending to hasten away to her stand, turned slowly and said, "Why, good morning, Mr. Wilson."

She pulled her daughters forward, as if making them a barricade between herself and Ralph. "I think you know my girls?"

Dell snorted. "Of course he does, Mama. Mr. Wilson's fixed the carousel lots of times. I asked him to myself just last week and he was ever so quick to help me. There isn't anything you can't fix, is there, Mr. Wilson? Even a dirigible, I bet!"

Ralph answered her with indifference. "On one of them, the engine's simple enough."

"But even if it wasn't simple, you could do it. I know you could," Dell insisted, and at her excited tone, Clara's attention was drawn to her daughter's flushed face. She put a restraining hand on the girl's arm, but Dell impatiently pulled herself free.

Ralph, whose eyes had not left Clara, said, ignoring Adeline, "I'm going to be away. Going up to Frisco. Did you know I'm thinking of buying a roller coaster? There's a place up there that builds good ones."

Clara answered, "No. I didn't know." He's just talking big,

she assured herself. Why, he's only a handyman. He hasn't any money.

"A roller coaster!" Dell said excitedly. "That'll be a fine thing for the park."

"It ain't settled," Ralph muttered, shaking his head. He said pointedly, finally looking at Dell, "Not going to open the carousel today?"

"Yes, of course. I always open it." For once though, she wasn't hurrying to do so.

Clara said, "Mr. Wilson is right. We can't stand here talking—the customers are already arriving...." Pulling Joanna with her, she began to move away. Ralph Wilson, with no further words, took himself off in the opposite direction, an abruptness which was lost on Lillian, who had heard none of the conversation anyway. But Dell stood staring after him until she was recalled to herself by a jostling throng of children.

"Well, Lillian, come on!" she said then.

Her sister surprised her. Lillian answered in an anguished voice, "You go—I'll come later. Please, Dell!"

Not far away, just as she'd been expecting, were the Sengstackens. Olive was waving to attract her attention, and running toward her. Mrs. Sengstacken was also approaching, trailed by her portly husband.

Olive, panting, reached her side. "What fun, Lil! Lil, that man, Mr. Fritsch—Mama was wondering, too—is he your father? Really? Oh, my! Imagine being the starter of such an important race!"

Lillian, who had only nodded in a dispirited way, suddenly began to take heart. But before she could speak, her sister, Dell, not waiting to be introduced, said, "Papa isn't only the starter, miss. Good gracious, no! He flies dirigibles himself."

"That's right," Lillian affirmed, although until now, having paid so little attention to what was said at home, she hadn't realized this important fact.

Olive was studying Dell with avid interest. "You are saying—he's *your* father, too? This is your sister, Lil?"

Lillian sneaked a look beyond Olive. Thank goodness! The elder Sengstackens had paused to speak to some acquaintances. Now if she could only get away before her sister mentioned those awful deer.

"Olive, I've got to leave. I'll see you at school tomorrow."

"But where are you going? I thought we could visit the park together, maybe ride the carousel."

"Not now, she can't. We're late." Dell grasped Lillian's arm. "Come *on*, Lillian, Mama's stand is already open for business and I see people waiting at the pen."

Lillian, stricken, jerked away from her sister. "Go ahead then, Dell. Go on! If you don't go right now, Dell Fritsch, I'll—I'll run off. I won't be here the whole livelong day!"

Dell's mouth had fallen open. She closed it with a snap. "Very well! Joanna can take your place. But only for a couple of minutes, mind." She rushed away, calling back, "Only for *one* minute!"

"What is all this?" Olive asked, bewildered. "What does she mean about the pen—and your mother's stand?"

"She means—that's what my family does. We work in the park." Although her face was flushed and her voice was high and tight, Lillian spoke calmly. "I have the deer pen, my sister sells tickets and runs the carousel, and my mother"—she drew a deep breath—"sells ice cream."

"Oh!" Olive looked away. She said, "Oh," once more and then was silent.

"Your father is so rich and everything, I didn't think your family would want us to play together if they knew."

"I guess not. No, they wouldn't."

"Olive." Mrs. Sengstacken finally came up to them. "Hello, Lillian dear. Your aunt doesn't need you today?"

Lillian hesitated, then quietly said, "No, Mrs. Sengstacken, I guess she doesn't. Not today."

"No doubt she knew you'd want to see the ascension. Was the starter your father? Fritsch isn't a very common name so I thought he might be. My, that was very exciting for you, I'm sure."

"My father does ascensions himself."

"Indeed? How daring." Mrs. Sengstacken glanced with a slight frown at her approaching husband's sedentary figure. "But I'm surprised he has the time."

"The time?" Lillian stammered.

"With all his business interests."

"Oh, I see. No, it isn't easy for him to fit in anything more."

Papa's business interests! Lillian had to struggle not to go off in fits of laughter. Or was it that she wanted to cry?

"Now that you girls are here together at the park," Mrs. Sengstacken said, "what would you like to do? I know Olive always loves a carousel."

The two girls exchanged a long glance.

Then Olive said, "Not any more, Mama. That's for children." She turned away from the enticing scarlet top with its streaming pennant. "I'd just love to ride the chutes though. Wouldn't you, Lil?"

"Oh, yes!" Lillian breathed.

So things were going to be all right after all. She could manage the man at the chutes if he greeted her by name—some lie or other would get her by that. And she could count on Olive to keep the Sengstackens away from the other end of the park.

Wasn't it grand to have a loyal bosom friend like Olive!

Chapter 7

April was almost gone, but what a profitable month it had been. In the days following the dirigible—motor car race (won by Knabenshue, by a hair), it seemed everyone in Los Angeles wanted to visit Chutes Park. And today was another warm sunny morning, unusual for this time of year. The park by rights should be crowded.

By noon, Clara was mystified. She hadn't had a single customer; even the pleasant walks around the basin were deserted. Dell in her ticket booth wore a disconsolate, bored expression, and over at the chutes the owner sat idly, tipped back in his chair and chewing impatiently on a cigar.

What could be the reason for this strange quiet? Clara would have liked to consult Aunt Flossie, but the ferris wheel operator had not yet appeared, and this was also mysterious. Aunt Flossie never was late or missed a day at the park.

Then Lillian came, dismissed early from school and full of excited importance at being the bearer of such devastating news.

"Mama! Dell! Joanna's already at home, and you needn't stay here any longer. There won't be any business today."

"Why in the world not?" Clara asked. "Is it some holiday I've forgotten?"

"There's been an earthquake, Mama!"

"Yes, I did feel a small tremble just before dawn, but hardly—"

"Not a small one, Mama. Not here, up in San Francisco. It was terrible up there! The worse ever! Our teacher says big cracks opened up, buildings have fallen, and the shaking broke gas pipes and water pipes. If people weren't killed by their walls caving in, they've lost all their possessions because of the fires. Oh, it's a real calamity, our teacher says. Maybe the whole city will be gone."

"People have been killed?" Clara spoke numbly.

"Hundreds. Maybe thousands . . . Mama, why are you looking like that?"

Clara rubbed her arms. She felt cold, even in this warm sunshine. "Because . . . people dying—"

And then Dell, who had come running from the booth, for once leaving it wide open, cried, "Mama, Mr. Wilson went to San Francisco! He's there now! Don't you remember, he said—"

"Yes, I remember." Clara began to rub the oilcloth with a rag, although the counter, unused today, was perfectly clean.

"Now, Mama," Lillian went on, "you and Dell have to close up and go home. Our teacher said we weren't to come back this afternoon, there's too much for all of us to do. Committees are being formed to send relief and we are all to bring clothing and food to the train station—one trainload of doctors and nurses and bandages has already gone. Just about everyone in town is helping . . . oh, Mama, isn't it thrilling—dreadful, I mean?"

"Dreadful, yes." Clara was suddenly galvanized into activity. She was covering the ice cream, pushing the containers deeper into the straw.

She would not think about Ralph, wonder if he was still alive. She would not. Yet walking home, her resolve crumbled. Visions of what must be taking place, where he was, crowded her mind. She had only been in San Francisco once, and that brief visit was long ago, but Sam had taken her up there on the train, during a week when the chutes had had to be shut down for repairs and the owner simply closed all the park at the same time. She and Sam only had Dell then, and the three of them, Clara and Sam and the baby in her wicker carriage with a parasol top, had explored the city daily, starting from their modest hotel on Leavenworth Street. Clara had loved the steepness of the hills, and the blue haze over the bay, and sipping a hot cup of chocolate at Ghirardelli's when they ventured as far as the wharves. Surely this news couldn't be true, couldn't be as bad as Lillian said? That lovely city in flames, the buildings reduced to rubble . . . people dying?

Lillian, glancing triumphantly at her sister as she spoke, was saying they were expected to have all donated supplies brought to the station in time for an early morning train. Clara forced her mind to practical matters. It seemed to her that if food were wanted, bread and cakes would keep best during the trip north, so she set the girls to baking, and sorted through the family's clothing, packing all they could spare into boxes.

When she finished, she suddenly remembered Aunt Flossie. Had Aunt Flossie heard the news and stayed at home herself? Or was she ill? Clara, with the second possibility in mind, wrapped up one of the new warm loaves of bread and, leaving her daughters hard at work in the kitchen, set out.

The older woman lived on the far side of the park in a rambling house far too large for a single occupant. One of the first houses built of wood some fifty or sixty years earlier, when other structures in southern California were still simple one-story adobes, it had been the proud possession of a German immigrant, Kurt Mendenhall, who made a modest fortune prospecting for silver then sent back to Europe for his family. His daughter, from the age of fifteen on, had lived in this same house, and as she remarked cheerfully, "I'll die in my own room. That's the way I want it."

Flossie was fairly reticent about herself. But gradually, over the years, Clara had come to know the bleak facts of her friend's life. An only child, Flossie had taken care of both her mother, who retreated from this strange foreign land by becoming a chronic invalid, and her mother's spinster sister, who coped by keeping a bottle of brandy hidden in her room and in a gentle drunken haze sipped the years away. Flossie's father, robust himself and evidently repelled by the sickroom atmosphere of his home, seldom entered it, electing to play checkers elsewhere with his cronies and only presenting himself for an occasional meal.

Flossie was forty when her mother finally died, followed

to the grave almost at once by the vague, glassy-eyed sister. Kurt Mendenhall then came home to stay, but by this time he had a problem with his breathing and needed a strong shoulder to lean on going up and down the stairs. Flossie was happy to do all she could for him. Even if she hadn't been such a homely woman, her age pretty much precluded any hope of finding a husband. *Vater* was company, during all the lonely evenings.

For several years, she busied herself with such customary pursuits as sewing for the poor and working at an orphanage, until the family money ran out. About that time, Chutes Park was being planned, and she happened to hear that the man who had been promised the ferris wheel concession had died from the kick of a horse. She went to call on the man's widow and the upshot was that Flossie owned and operated a ferris wheel. She had found something she really wanted to do with her life.

Clara heard the heavy tread coming across the planks of the hall floor and then the door, with its finely etched and beveled glass, was thrown wide in Flossie's hearty manner.

"Clara, you just caught me," she said. "I've been down at Arcade Station all day, helping organize the relief committee. You can't think how folks shilly-shally, even with the best will in the world. Is your donation ready?"

Clara was thankful that it was.

"I thought you might be sick, Aunt Flossie, when you didn't come to work this morning. So I brought you a loaf of Dell's bread."

"Never been sick a day in my life. You know that. But I thank you. I'll put it in with my things because there will be plenty of poor souls needing bread. Sam will be taking you over in the morning?"

"Taking me where?"

"To the station. We're all to meet there and help load."

"I don't know. He and Captain Baldwin are testing a new kind of big dirigible today and tomorrow. They're out in the country, far from everything, so I don't suppose they've even heard. Anyway, the girls and I can ride the streetcar."

"You'll never get on it. Not with the crowds I saw today. No, Clara, I'll pick you up in my wagon. If its big enough for a ferris wheel seat, it'll hold everything you and I will be bringing."

"Thank you." Clara was thinking again what else she could give. She didn't want to be put to shame by Aunt Flossie.

However, when she and her daughters stacked their boxes

into the big lumbering wagon the following morning, she felt
satisfied she'd been generous. Aunt Flossie, up on the driver's
seat, viewed the load with approval.

"Seems we can hold our heads up. *Sehr gut*. But that's no
more than I'd expect from you." Then as she started up the
horses, Clara sitting beside her and the three girls perched on
boxes in the back, she added, "Something fine happened last
night. The Jobbers Association passed one of their resolutions,
aimed at any greedy sons-of-guns planning to take advantage
of a business in trouble up in San Francisco. Doesn't it restore
your faith in human nature?"

Clara, who had only the vaguest notion of what the Jobbers
Association might be, nodded agreement, and her friend went
on, "The local merchants have been stripping their shelves to
send help, just as we've been doing in our homes." She glanced
back at the load. "My, Clara, you have been generous! Those
nice warm coats! Certain you can spare them?"

Clara was uneasy, expecting some anguished protest from
Dell, whose extra coat was on top of the pile. But the girl
remained silent, her face preoccupied.

"Well, as *lieber Vater* used to say," Flossie continued, "'a
good deed will keep you warm.' That was when I'd be shivering
in the early morning, fixing his breakfast. Far better the cold
than the fires those poor folks are fighting up north. I've seen
a fire or two in my time and there's no hardship to compare."

She continued to discourse until the wagon rumbled up to
the station. There being no porters in sight, she began to unload,
saying, "Might as well get started." Each of them took one of
the heavy boxes and staggered through the press of people,
emerging finally on a platform by a half-filled freight car.

"We'll drop everything here, Clara. Dell, you and Lillian
bring along the rest. Your Ma, Joanna, and me, we'll wait for
you."

Even as the two girls dutifully disappeared, a train was
pulling in on the other track and then even Aunt Flossie, watching the people who emerged from the cars, fell silent.

These passengers could never have been mistaken for anything but what they were—refugees from a disaster. Their
clothing torn, dirty, sometimes charred, and their faces set with
shock, they stood forlornly on the platform. But at once from
an onlooker there was a joyful cry of recognition, then another
and another, and the reunions began. More often than not,
those being embraced, man or woman, broke into tears.

"These are the lucky ones," Aunt Flossie observed. "Having someone to come to."

Gradually the small group of refugees thinned, until only eight or nine were left. These despondently began to straggle toward the station.

"Look at that child!" Aunt Flossie exclaimed, pointing to a thin figure enveloped in a large reefer jacket, a boy of about ten who limped slowly and stiffly behind the rest. "He's a brave little man. See, Clara, his legs are burned!"

Clara gasped. It was true. From well above the boy's knees his legs were bare, and the skin was striped a bright cherry red except in spots where an ugly discharge oozed.

As they all stared he turned and looked back. He was not crying now, but his face was caked with gray dust and on his cheeks could be seen the clean furrows made by tears. His eyes were wide and blank, as if he still saw only horror.

"Poor child," Clara breathed, thinking, *Suppose one of mine was so hurt? And so alone?*

"Somebody is bound to be meeting him, but what a shame they're late," Aunt Flossie muttered angrily. She strode along, keeping the pitiful group in sight, and Clara, clutching Joanna's hand more tightly, followed.

At the station door a smiling, well-dressed woman appeared and took a position before the refugees. "Welcome to Los Angeles," she said. "Please don't worry if your relatives haven't yet found you, because it's bedlam here this morning, as you can see. Now, if you'll all step to the counter inside, we'll get your names and the names of those you intend to visit. . . ."

The little band moved forward again, this time with more purpose. The boy, however, edged away. Then, spinning awkwardly around, he limped as fast as he could in the opposite direction.

He was stopped by Aunt Flossie's widespread arms.

"Sorry, ma'am—" He tried to free himself but Flossie's strong grasp tightened.

"Hold on here, young man," she said. "You've got to wait for your kinfolks. You don't want to get lost."

"I do! I got to! Lady, don't tell on me, will you? I sneaked onto that train. I sat on the floor. There wasn't no places for them without relations, but I couldn't go home. There wasn't no— I couldn't!"

He struggled wildly. The tears had started again.

"Please, Aunt Flossie, let him go," Clara begged.

"Go where? He's got no place to go, he just said as much. Do you, boy?"

"No'm." He stared down at the ground. Or perhaps it was at his legs, because he gave a convulsive shuddering sob.

"Where are your parents?" Flossie's booming voice was unusually gentle.

"They was kilt. Our house burned and the roof fell in. They was both kilt."

"You're certain of that, child?"

"Course I'm certain! I saw 'em . . . afterward." The brief sobbing stopped, to be replaced by anger. Anger at the memory and anger at her for reviving it.

"What's your name?"

"Tony," he answered shortly.

"Well then, Tony, there's only one thing to be done with you. For tonight at least, you'll come home with me. Can't have you wandering the streets."

Clara said, "You must be hungry, Tony. Miss Mendenhall is a wonderful cook, you'll find. And she has a nice clean bed for you."

The boy said nothing, but he stopped trying to pull away.

Joanna dropped her mother's hand and edged closer. She reached out and touched the grimy sleeve of his voluminous reefer.

"Do your legs hurt dreadfully?"

He nodded, embarrassed.

"Oh." Joanna's eyes filled with tears. "I burned my hand once. I know. Poor boy."

He felt a sweet strong flood of relief. Until now, in San Francisco and through the long hours on the train, all the people, even the ones who'd been kind, had been too full of some terrible agony of their own to worry about his. The old man who had cut his stockings away from the burns had been as careful and easy as he could, but all the time, it was clear, he was thinking of something else, something that made his jaws clamp and his hands tremble. Even the woman who'd brought him water on the train—she'd done it because he reminded her of her son who had died in the earthquake. She said as much. She kept looking at Tony but not seeing him, murmuring the other boy's name over and over. Tony Bonnard hadn't mattered.

No one had asked about *his* pain. Or cried for *him*.
Only this girl.

Chapter 8

Ralph Wilson came striding along the promenade encircling
the lake, easily outdistancing any Sunday strollers and oblivious
of them. *So he was back!*

Clara, catching sight of his tall, lean figure, caught her
breath, then wondered at her own strong and conflicting emo-
tions. There was, first of all, simple relief that he had lived
through that nightmarish disaster in San Francisco, a relief she
would naturally have felt for any acquaintance. And that was
all he was—an acquaintance. She barely knew him. They had
exchanged only a few words, nothing more than common courtesy required.

Then why was she filled with such a surge of excitement,
as though this day which had begun just as any other were a
brighter gold and reaching toward a farther horizon? Why too
did she feel a tinge of apprehension? There was a strong physical attraction between the two of them that she could no longer
deny, but she was quite safe here in the confines of the ice
cream stand, and even if she weren't, she was a good woman.
Married.

While still at a distance, Ralph's gaze caught hers, and she
watched him come, unable to look away. She saw on his face
both his pleasure at the sight of her and his familiar frown of
puzzlement. There was something about her, so he'd insisted
more than once, that he remembered from some other time and
place. But she dismissed his claims as only his imagination.
If she had ever encountered Ralph Wilson anywhere before,
she was certain she would not, could not, have forgotten.

He had almost reached her stand when Aunt Flossie, sitting
beside the ferris wheel and overflowing the small hard seat of
her chair, shouted, "*Gott sei Dank*, Ralph Wilson, you're back

safe and sound and you got my message. Don't know anybody
else can get this cranky thing going again."

Ralph didn't seem to hear. His steps were slowing at the
counter where Clara stood. Then, oddly, Clara became conscious of Adeline nearby in the ticket booth, and she turned to
glance at her daughter. Dell had been busy counting money,
but now her sturdy fingers, still holding a few coins, were
motionless. Her widened eyes were on Ralph and her face had
paled. Because Clara had also experienced relief, she recognized Dell's.

Ralph said, speaking to Clara, "Well, I'm back."

Forced to comment, Clara said, "I'm sure we're all pleased
that you are."

"What a terrible time you must have had!" Dell called across,
her voice overloud. "What with the fire and all. Were you in
danger?"

He turned to look at the girl as though for a moment he
didn't know who she was.

"Not much. No, miss."

"I'm so glad! That is . . . we all are. . . ."

"Thank you, miss," he answered, and Dell sat back in her
booth, smiling. "I'd like so much to hear all about it," she
said. "Men do have such exciting adventures."

Clara said quickly, because his gaze had already moved
back to her, "Mr. Wilson, I hate to hurry you, but Aunt Flossie
needs you right away. Already this morning she's taken a big
loss."

He grimaced but nodded, and moved away toward the ferris
wheel.

Clara, deeply disturbed, did not stop to make certain there
were no customers approaching for ice cream. She left her
booth and hurried to her daughter's.

"Adeline," she admonished, "I see no reason for being so
forward with Mr. Wilson."

"I was forward? Someone had to be pleasant and welcome
him back. You are always so rude to him yourself."

"That's as may be. But there's a difference between being
pleasant and pestering a strange young man, making a nuisance
of yourself—"

The words were badly chosen, and Clara realized her mistake at once. Dell had sprung to her feet, red blotches staining
her white face. Yet what else could her mother have said,
emphatic enough to impress the girl? For Dell to be setting her

cap for a man who cared nothing about her would be a shame; Clara had good reason to know the futility of this particular infatuation.

Dell, her fists clenched but controlling her anger, answered with surprising dignity. "He's not a stranger, you know. The rest of us around here like him! Excuse me, Mama, I have work to do, even if you don't."

Clara walked unhappily back to her stand.

Ralph, meanwhile, had begun probing the mechanism of the ferris wheel with his knowing, skillful hands. Aunt Flossie was full of questions about the earthquake, and Ralph, replying in brief monosyllables, was even more taciturn than usual.

Aunt Flossie gave a good-natured snort. "I've a boy from San Francisco staying with me, and you'd think by this time I'd have heard all there was to hear about the earthquake. But no, he's as close mouthed about it all as you. Only difference is, he's got reason, poor child. His pa and ma were killed."

Ralph only grunted again, and Aunt Flossie, finally giving up, left him to his work. She plodded across the grass to Clara.

"Where is Tony today?" Clara asked, welcoming the escape from her thoughts.

"I sent him to school."

"School?"

"Why not? His legs have healed. They're badly scarred, always will be, but he's getting restless. Ought to be kept busy, aside from helping me. As I used to be told whenever I got lazy, 'Satan has work for idle hands.'"

"But before very long, he'll be going back to San Francisco."

"Will he? What has he got to go back to? He's got no family left, and the city's a wasteland of broken buildings, thieves, and vandals, so the newspapers say. Soon, I guess, they're fixing to rebuild everything, but for now it's no place for a young boy alone."

"No," Clara agreed. "Not alone. But I thought—wasn't providing for homeless children one of the first things the rescue committee planned to do?"

"So I heard. They should be grateful to me for taking one boy off their hands." Aunt Flossie sounded as though she didn't want to discuss the matter any further. "Anyhow, I've got to get back to Ralph . . . won't we all be glad, though, when Ralph is here in the park all the time? We won't have to send for him and wait around whenever things need fixing."

"Here—all the time? What do you mean?" Clara wondered if she sounded as disturbed as she felt. An occasional word in passing, his eyes searching hers, that was one thing. But to be near Ralph every day, aware continually of that queer spark of excitement—

"Didn't you know?" Aunt Flossie had noticed nothing out of the ordinary and clearly assumed Clara to be as pleased by the news as she was. "He's the one putting up the roller coaster. Seems his Pa died, back in the Midwest somewhere, and he's come into an inheritance. That's why he went up to San Francisco, to arrange for the cars and machinery and all the lumber. Lucky for him most of it was shipped before the quake. Don't know what would have happened, if he'd been . . ."

Clara had stopped listening. So he did have the money! He'd be in the park all the time, from now on. Every single day.

Olive said, "Who is the skinny little boy who came to school with you? I saw you get off the streetcar together."

Lillian rolled her eyes in exasperation. "He's an orphan. From San Francisco. Staying with a friend of my family's so I had to show him the way." Lillian, at twelve, had developed little round knobs of breasts and her waist was narrowing very satisfactorily. She took a lively and curious interest in young men, but Tony Bonnard, a year younger and still not even as tall as she, did not qualify for consideration.

"It's a nuisance," she added, "because they'll know at home that we leave school at the same time, and when he comes home and I don't they're bound to wonder."

"You're studying at my house, not at school. That's easy," Olive said. "And if your father is as keen as you say about you going to Normal School after we graduate, he'll be happy to hear it."

Normal School. Reminded, Lillian groaned. She hadn't the slightest desire to become a teacher. The prospect seemed almost as dismal as working in Chutes Park.

Still, Olive was right. Papa would believe her because he wanted to, and she wasn't really lying. She and Olive did study together now and then, and Lillian enjoyed those times, sitting with her books at the shining mahogany table in the Sengstacken's second parlor. She felt so very much at home.

Usually though, there was nothing pressing in their homework and the stolen hours could be wasted in any number of pleasurable ways. Often, like today, she and Olive, daring and wicked, would drift about the city, riding streetcars wherever they wished and ending up in some restaurant for buns and tea.

Again, on the occasional afternoon when Mr. Sengstacken was at home, he might take his daughter and her bosom friend for a drive in his big White Steamer touring car. There were quite a few automobiles on the streets now, but none as magnificent as his. Lillian loved to sit with Olive on the seat beside portly Mr. Sengstacken while the motor roared and the wind blew her hair and the car jounced along the rough street, the horn continually going *Ooga! Ooga!* at some bewildered dog.

To her deep chagrin, her own family still used a horse. Papa's old carriage had worn out, and though Lillian had hoped he'd buy a White too, he'd said he couldn't afford any kind of motorcar yet. He bought another surrey. It was only a very ordinary two-seater with a fringed canopy, but Mama and Dell and Joanna had all made a fuss over the bright black enamel and the green leather upholstery. Her family was so old-fashioned—all except for Papa's dirigibles. Papa being an aeronaut was the one thing, Lillian thought, that saved her from total humiliation.

That and being close friends with Olive, whose father was one of the richest men in town.

Walking toward the car stop, she gave Olive an affectionate glance. Olive wasn't pretty, but if one of them had to outshine the other and get all the admiring glances from the boys, Lillian was very glad it was herself.

"Here it comes—race you!" she shouted, and the two girls, hand in hand, skirts caught up out of the way, ran for the corner. When Olive's big cartwheel hat blew off, they burst into gales of laughter, as though watching the fine straw get crushed under streetcar wheels was the funniest thing in the world.

A block away from the stop, Tony was resolutely headed in the opposite direction. Even though his legs hurt him still, he was determined to walk all the way back to the house without limping. Also, he had to think what to say to Miss Mendenhall whom everybody, himself now, too, called Aunt Flossie, though as far as he could tell, she really wasn't anybody's aunt.

She'd surprised him the evening before by suggesting he

stay on with her for good. She'd been rather gruff, and at first he wasn't sure she meant it. But then he caught her looking at him anxiously, and he knew she did.

The house was much grander than he was used to. His father had been a fisherman, and a good one, but there never was much money. It was a treat to have such a nice big room, and the food was really good. Miss Mendenhall—Aunt Flossie—cooked him anything he ever said he liked. But he was lonesome. The boys at school had their friends already. They ran in packs like dogs, and he didn't blame them. He'd had his own special gang of boys up in San Francisco, so he knew how that was.

He'd wondered several times lately why he was down here in Los Angeles at all. It was hard now to remember what he'd been thinking that terrible night after he found Ma and Pa lying twisted and broken in the smoking rubble. His legs hadn't been burned yet. Why hadn't he gone to look for Nick? Stayed with his best friend's family?

But he had gone! The recalling came gradually, still very hazy and unclear. He had run to the diRosa's and found their house still burning, and he hadn't called out for Nick or asked anyone, he'd just stood there. His stomach had churned and he couldn't look away. He'd known, as surely as if he could see through the scorching sheet of flames, who was inside, dead. Nick.

After a while someone, he thought now it was a policeman, had said, "Go on home, boy. The streets aren't safe." It was an order, but Tony hadn't answered or moved. The man must have seen something in his face then, because he said in a quieter voice, "I'm sorry, son. If you're alone, try the train station. I think there's some kind of shelter set up. At least I was told there was. Homeless people will be able to take a train to Los Angeles if they've relatives or friends to go to."

Tony, not even realizing he'd heard, finally drifted away.

Then, on Market Street, as he passed some burning buildings, the one just ahead, giving a strange thundering crack, exploded, the side walls falling outward and a great red ball of flame bursting and growing from the center. Before he'd thought to run backward, a wrought-iron railing, glowing red-hot, fell from the sky and bounced against him, pinning him to the cobblestones. He heard his flesh sizzle, but he felt nothing, not then or for a little while afterward. He finally worked his legs free, and although he was shaky, stood up and went on, ducking through the crowds and staying as far from the sides of buildings as he could, terrified the same thing might happen again.

Without consciously meaning to go there, he found himself at last in the jam-packed Southern Pacific station. He was told, after he was able to work his way up to an official in a blue uniform, that the next train wouldn't be until morning, so he collapsed in a corner on the floor. Now his legs began to come horribly alive. They hurt him so much he thrashed and moaned, even whimpering like a small dog. He was ashamed. He heard Pa's voice in his ears, saying, "Big boys never cry," and he wanted to stop. He tried, especially because he hated for Pa, looking down from heaven, to see him being such a baby. But he could not make himself stop.

An old man, squatting nearby and hearing his sobbing, had tried to be kind. He'd peeled away the burned pants and stockings and gone to get wet cloths, which hurt terribly at first then helped for a little while. But the old man wandered off and never came back.

Tony faced the rest of the night alone. He never slept. He remembered how clammy his hands had been when he clenched them together, and how, after they turned off the station lights, he kept his eyes on the little high windows, waiting for the grayness of morning, telling himself the pain would be gone in the morning. There was only one good thing about such pain. It filled him. It filled every inch of him, so that he couldn't think about Ma and Pa and Nick.

In the morning when they called the train, his throbbing legs were so stiff he could hardly stand. But he somehow hobbled to the platform and pulled himself aboard.

There wasn't an empty seat—even the aisle was crowded with people—so he huddled close to the door. The wind blew in the crack, and although his legs seemed still on fire he was desperately cold. Some valises were piled in a corner, a man's reefer jacket thrown on top, and Tony, far beyond fear of punishment, openly reached for the jacket and pulled it on. Then, his jaws clenched, he set himself to be a man, the kind of man Pa would have been. The only time he cried out was when a lady's rough woolen skirt brushed against the hot tenderness of his legs.

So here he was. He knew now he'd only come because he was running away from his pain and his grief. San Francisco was where he lived. Even if there was nobody to go back to, he wanted to be in the place he was raised, a place where he felt at home. He'd tell Miss Mendenhall so this very afternoon.

"Hello there, Tony."

A shiny new surrey was reined to a stop at the curb, and a small man was peering at him from around the blades of a big propeller which took up most of the front seat. For a moment Tony didn't know who the man was, then the name came to him. Mr. Fritsch. Lillian and Joanna's father.

"How was school today?" Mr. Fritsch was asking the usual difficult grownup's question.

"All right, I guess."

Sam studied him. Sam had never been a new boy in class himself. He'd lived all his boyhood in one place. But he could imagine how it would be.

"I wonder now. Will Aunt Flossie need you, or could you be spared for the afternoon? I'm going to take this new propellor out to the field and I ought to check on one of the dirigibles. There's an exhibition tomorrow, and I want everything ready. Like to come along?"

"Yes . . . yes, sir, I would!"

"Hop in, then. You'll have to ride in back with Joanna."

Tony swung himself in. Joanna smiled happily and said, "Papa's going to take me up with him soon. In the dirigible. He promised. Maybe he'll take you, too."

Tony caught his breath. Ride up in the sky in a dirigible? But of course she didn't mean it. Her father would never—

Sam looked back at him. "Why not—if you'd like to. We'll do it one day soon."

The vision Tony had had of himself boarding the train, bravely returning alone to San Francisco, faded at that precise moment and was forgotten.

He sat back, contented, beside Joanna.

Chapter 9

White gulls dip their wide wings
Across the azure sky,
It looks so very easy,
I wish that I could fly!

Their beady eyes aglitter
They laugh out loud to see
Running on the beach below,
A wingless girl like me.

For Joanna, who lacked Lillian's pretensions, the school days were halcyon, and should have continued so. She liked studying, she wrote short happy poems which the teacher sometimes praised and read aloud to the class, and best of all, she had her own bosom friends, Bonnie and Mollie Lowe.

The three girls were together so constantly that the occasions when Joanna rode out to the dirigible field alone with Papa and Tony became rare. Usually the Lowe twins accompanied her to the park in the afternoons, and if Lillian had failed to take over from Mr. Brundage—as was usually the case—they helped with the deer pen. Afterward Clara would treat them all to ice cream.

Other days, the girls went to the big house belonging to Mr. and Mrs. Matt Conrad, who were the twins' aunt and uncle, and with whom they lived during the wintertime because there was no schoolhouse up on top of Mt. Lowe. On one unforgettable occasion Joanna had been invited to accompany her friends up the mountain for a weekend, to stay at one of the grand, luxurious hotels the Lowes owned and operated there. For a long time afterward, Joanna could talk of little else, reciting for her family interminable details about the interurban ride through Pasadena to Rubio Station, then the cable

63

car, clanking up and up and up, and finally the last wild and
scary passage on a small open trolley, crossing dozens of high
trestles and swinging around horseshoe curves. She was not
sorry, she stated, to have arrived safely at the graceful Swiss-
style building at the peak, perched amid fir trees and *real snow*,
and so high up that from the veranda—imagine!—one could
see all the way across the valley to the ocean. As for the hotel
guests—Joanna wished Mama had been there just to watch
them and listen. They were so elegantly dressed and spoke so
many foreign languages, because of course the Alpine Tavern
resort was famous all over the world.

At home, too, Joanna's contentment seemed destined to
remain undisturbed. There had been no more talk of selling
the carousel. Indeed, from the careful way Papa studied the
park receipts at the end of each week, it was clear this source
of income was still very important to them all. Dell continued
to smile proudly when she handed him the record of so much
money put in the bank—as proud, Joanna thought, as if the
carousel were Dell's alone, as if Dell were the only one who
worked hard in Papa's absences. But who could mind? Not
Joanna, whose days were crammed so full of companionship
and dreaming and laughter.

It was Clara who first noticed a change in her youngest
daughter. All of a sudden Joanna's afternoon work with the
deer became a steady, regular occurrence. No more did she go
elsewhere after school or bring the twins to the park with her.
She was quiet and subdued and it seemed to Clara that when
Joanna was unaware of being observed, there was an expression
of such bewildered pain in her small face that her mother's
heart was wrenched. The explanation—that the twins had gone
away, perhaps never to return—hardly seemed sufficient.

Sam, busy as he was, also became worried. "What kind of
childhood is she having?" he asked Clara. "She's only ten. She
should be playing, not working hard all the time."

Clara caught the bitterness in his voice and understood it.
Whatever rosy visions of the future had been in Sam's mind
when he spoke of a dirigible sightseeing business had not as
yet come to pass, even though many months had gone by. He'd
made plenty of practice ascensions and was fully qualified; the
large airship had been built and flown. But still there was no
excursion service and consequently little money.

The major setback had been Captain Baldwin's unexpected

lack of enthusiasm. For months the owner dragged his feet, still insisting that the dirigible hadn't been tested enough and that the public lacked confidence in airships. Then on the very day when he finally gave his consent, Roy and Sam had a piece of bad luck. The rudder cable of the large airship snapped in midflight and the two men were set down many miles from their starting point. It was a mishap Baldwin was quick to seize on. He pointed out that had the dirigible been in service at the time, he would have had the prohibitive costs of transporting all the passengers back to their homes, and perhaps paying for their inconvenience as well.

The upshot of the ensuing heated argument was Roy Knabenshue's resignation from Baldwin's employ.

Sam tried in vain to persuade his friend to stay. "We both know Captain Baldwin has strong opinions, Roy. But he recognizes what a fine aeronaut you are, and surely, in time—"

"He recognizes only himself. He's a hard man to get along with, Sam. Don't you know it was his arrogant rudeness that cost me the prize money in St. Louis? Anyway, my friend, I've decided. I'll take the smaller ship, which is my own property, and I'll do exhibitions back in Ohio. With my reputation, it's time I worked alone anyway. Without Baldwin, that is. I'd be mighty pleased, Sam, if you'd come with me."

Sam shook his head. His home was here. His steady income—at the park—was here. And he'd learned by now that the airship business was chancy. If he were to continue with dirigibles—and he couldn't imagine not doing so—he must remain with Baldwin, who had a strong financial stake.

He made one last appeal. "But what about the big airshow, Roy? It's less than a year away. You and the *Arrow* have been touted as the main attraction, even more than the balloons or those pesky little aeroplanes we hear so much about. Everyone who flies anything at all will be here."

"And I will be here, too, you may be sure. Meanwhile, you'll be Baldwin's only pilot, getting valuable experience. What's wrong with that?"

So Roy went. From then on, the calls on Sam came far more frequently, so that his absences from the park were continual and he missed Roy sorely. The excursion service would be started some day, he could not doubt that, but in the meantime, the thought of Clara still selling ice cream and Dell never able to take a day off (though, to be honest, she had never asked for one) made him feel guilty and ashamed.

As for his little Joanna...

"I've been worried about her, too," Clara answered, "but when I ask, she says nothing's wrong. And we must remember that taking care of animals may not seem hard work to her. She loves animals—horses, dogs. Deer, too."

"What about her friends? I haven't seen those twins here lately. I liked them." Sam had to smile. "Particularly the one who always used *we* instead of *I*."

Clara smiled, too. The twins, although much alike, had not been identical, and the one named Bonnie, the leader, always spoke out firmly for both. "You won't see them anymore, I'm afraid. It's too bad. Their parents were asked to manage a grand new hotel in New York—they're very well-known, because of the success of their Alpine Tavern—and I gather they accepted the offer at once. There are plenty of schools back East, of course, so the twins went with them. The move was very sudden, and I suppose at Joanna's age such a parting seems a tragedy."

Sam, with so much else on his mind, let the matter drop. But Clara, idle and a little bored during a slow hour of the afternoon, said to her youngest daughter when she appeared, "Wouldn't you like to invite some of the girls from school for a party?"

"No!" Seeing Clara's astonishment, Joanna added lamely, "Most of them...say such silly things. I'd rather be alone."

Clara had always supposed, never having been to a real school herself, that being with other girls one's own age must be heaven. She was bewildered.

Joanna said, "Mama, none of them are half as nice as the twins. Oh, I do miss them so!"

"Then why not write them a letter? I'm sure they'd love to hear from you. You could make up a special poem to send, too. One about friendship."

Joanna clearly was tempted by this idea. Animation briefly lit her face. But it faded and she said, "No, not just now."

So she wasn't just missing the twins. Clara wanted to throw her arms around her daughter, comfort her for whatever else was amiss. But Joanna had turned away, murmuring, "I've got to hurry, Mama. Mr. Brundage is waiting and I'm already very late." There was something forbidding in the straight spine and the even tone of voice and Clara remained unhappily behind her counter.

Joanna ran along the lake, but once away from the ice cream

stand her steps slowed and her shoulders drooped.

"Oh, Bonnie. Mollie. Why did you have to move away?" she whispered. "If you'd been here, nothing like this would have happened to me. You would have believed me, wouldn't you? *Wouldn't* you? I'm almost sure. But not sure enough..."

She neared the pen. The familiar musky, rather sweet, and not unpleasant aroma of deer reached her nose, and the sight of the little animals crowding forward was comforting. But Mr. Brundage had shrugged his narrow bony shoulders into the coat of his black serge suit, shiny with age and wear, and he was grumbling. This was the third Wednesday in a row that Joanna had kept him late.

"I've told your father, missy, if you girls can't be on time I'm quitting. That Lillian was always late, and now you're starting the same shenanigans."

Joanna was chagrined to feel the prickling of tears. It was too much, Mr. Brundage scolding her, too!

"Hello, Joanna."

Tony had come sprinting up. He said, "It isn't her fault, Mr. Brundage. You know she'd have come if she could. I wouldn't be surprised but what she had to stay after school again. In her grade they make them take turns cleaning the erasers."

Mr. Brundage gave a snort and departed.

"How did you know I had to stay after?" Joanna asked. In a dejected way, she began to set out more water in the pails.

"Wasn't hard to guess. I heard—" He stopped.

"You heard—what?" she asked, frightened.

"Nothing," he said quickly. "Just that...you've been kept in every Wednesday. You aren't cleaning erasers?"

"No."

"Thought not. I'm surprised at you, Joanna. Girls don't usually get in trouble."

His voice was lighthearted, inviting her to smile, but she only nodded glumly. "I wouldn't be either, if the twins were still here. Nobody would have dared to say I—"

"You what?"

Joanna shook her head mutely. Stricken eyes gazed off at the scaffolding of the roller coaster, on which the gaily patterned cars carried their loads of screaming, laughing passengers. *They* didn't have a care in the world, she thought with envy.

None of them had been treated so unfairly! And the worst

of it, she was coming to realize, was that she didn't dare confide her trouble to anyone, not even to Tony. What would he think if she repeated for him the ugly accusation that echoed in her head, day and night—

Miss Johnson, I don't want to tattle, but I did see Joanna take it. Joanna's a thief, Miss Johnson!

She'd thought and thought about those lying words, astonished that a plain ordinary girl like Nadine Seymour would have said them, and astonished most of all that Nadine hated her so much.

Nadine, she'd finally decided, was paying her back. Nadine had supposed, when the Lowe twins first came to school, that they would be best friends with her. Her family was rich and important; the Lowes were rich and important. So Nadine was always following after them, wanting to be with them. But they hadn't cared who Nadine was. They liked Joanna better.

For a while, being good-natured as well as kind, the twins had included Nadine in their plans. But then quiet little Mollie mentioned to her sister that she'd seen Nadine copying answers out of a book when the teacher's back was turned.

Bonnie had said in her sturdy, matter-of-fact way, "Nadine is a sneak and we don't like sneaks. We won't invite her home with us anymore." And Bonnie's word was law. The twins and Joanna went off together, laughing and having a good time, and Nadine was left behind.

Nadine hadn't given up, though. She tried hard to separate the threesome.

One day in class, when Joanna gave the right answer to an arithmetic problem after Nadine had gotten it wrong, Nadine put up her hand. She said, "Miss Johnson, I don't think it's fair."

"What isn't fair, Nadine?"

"That problem. Of course Joanna would get it right because it's about money."

"Just what do you mean?" the teacher said sharply.

"I mean, Joanna gets lots of practice adding up money at home. Her mother is *in trade*. Mrs. Fritsch sells ice cream— at a park stand." Nadine shot a triumphant glance at Bonnie which implied, *You see? Joanna's a common nobody*.

"Really, Nadine, I fail to appreciate—"

"Miss Johnson—" Bonnie was already on her feet. "What she says is just plain silly. We're not as good at arithmetic as Joanna, and our mother's in trade, too. Our mother"—she turned to stare with cool brown eyes at Nadine—"our mother runs a hotel. Sometimes she's even had to make the beds."

And Mollie chimed in, "That's right, she has."

Joanna smiled gratefully and with love at her two staunch friends.

Suddenly, though, they were gone and then Nadine, to Joanna's surprise, seemed to want to patch things up. She said to Joanna, "I know it wasn't your fault that snooty Bonnie talked about me behind my back. Just because she's from one of the oldest families in town, she needn't think she's better than anyone else."

Joanna, listening, told herself that never, never would she be friends with Nadine.

"Bonnie isn't snooty! She and Mollie are the nicest girls in the world. Nicer than you'll ever be."

After that the trouble began. At first there were only little incidents. As Joanna passed Nadine's desk, Nadine might thrust her foot out into the aisle, and Joanna would trip, catching herself against the chair ahead and bruising her side. The next time she could not resist retaliating by giving a kick at Nadine's white-clad legs, but Nadine cried out in exaggerated pain and caught the teacher's attention.

"We try to be little ladies and gentlemen in this school, Joanna," Miss Johnson said severely. "You will come and stand at the front of the room until lunchtime."

So Joanna, rigid with embarrassment, stood facing the others for forty minutes, staring unseeing at a paperweight holding down a stack of graded papers.

The paperweight, a small glass prism, was known to be Miss Johnson's treasure. Rumor held that a lover, now long dead, had once given it to her as a token of his devotion. True or not, the bauble always graced a corner of her desk, and many a chastized student had contemplated his sins while gazing into its sparkling crystal depths.

Every child in the class, therefore, felt a thrill of excitement when, on a rainy afternoon some days later, as they milled in the crowded cloakroom getting their coats and boots together, their teacher's voice rose in an anguished cry: "My paperweight! It's gone!"

Miss Johnson had not been too unnerved to rush to the classroom door and throw it shut, preventing any of them from leaving. Her face was white, her lips pinched.

"It was right here only a minute ago, before all of you went to put on your coats. Some boy or girl in this room has taken my paperweight, and I suggest he or she return it at once!"

They gazed back at her in fascinated silence.

"Very well. All of you take off your coats again, hang them up, and open every one of your satchels. I'm going to get to the bottom of this!"

The search began. Every coat, every overshoe, every satchel was turned out. Like the others watching, Joanna felt only a horrid curiosity. One of her classmates had actually tried to steal. Who?

Then it was her turn to endure the inspection and in all her life she would never forget the sudden sharp resentment that gripped her. These were her things, her clothing. Mama had made that cape with such care. Miss Johnson had no right . . .

But right or not, Miss Johnson had snatched Joanna's cape from the hook and was thrusting her hand deeply into the pockets.

Miss Johnson gasped and her eyes widened. Her hand came forth slowly, then opened.

Resting on her palm was the sparkling paperweight.

Now the crowded cloakroom was so still it seemed no one breathed. And Joanna, even in the tight press of boys and girls, was suddenly all alone.

But she wasn't guilty! She'd taken nothing!

"No! No, it wasn't me!" she stammered, her throat tight.

Why was her face so flaming hot and her hands so clammy? Why, when all this was some terrible mistake, did she feel so sick and frightened she could hardly speak?

Miss Johnson said grimly, "The rest of you—all except Joanna—put on your coats."

There was a shuffling noise. No one seemed to have heard Joanna, no one answered her, although she imagined she could feel any number of furtive glances.

Oh, Bonnie, why aren't you here to tell them I wouldn't steal? They'd believe you.

The only one who spoke at last was Nadine. Sidling out, she said, "Miss Johnson, I don't want to tattle, but I did see Joanna take it. Joanna's a thief, Miss Johnson!"

"Your helpfulness comes a little late," Miss Johnson told her dryly. "Shut the door behind you, please."

The latch clicked as Joanna, fortified by outrage, burst out, "That was a lie! She didn't! Because I didn't—oh, don't you believe me?"

Miss Johnson said wearily, "Joanna, I'm so disappointed in you, so appalled. I really must talk this over with your parents."

For one brief moment, Joanna felt a surge of relief. Mama, Papa—they'd be able to convince Miss Johnson. They'd never allow anyone to think she had stolen anything!

But how could they be sure, when it was her cape? How could anyone? She could not bear it if Papa, Papa particularly, had the least doubt. . . .

"Oh, no, Miss Johnson! Oh, please not!"

Her distress was so palpable that Miss Johnson's expression softened.

"I can certainly understand your not wanting them to know. Yes, deeply shocked as I am, I can understand that. And perhaps, being found out had been enough of a lesson for you. I do hope so."

"But I didn't do it, Miss Johnson. I did not!"

"Really, Joanna. You were caught red-handed, so you may as well admit it. Now, will you promise me never to steal again?"

"No! Because I never have, not even once, I never would—"

She was shaking as if she had a chill and suddenly tears were streaming down her face.

Miss Johnson said unhappily, "Come, Joanna, you'll find that once you admit your guilt—"

"No!"

"Well, then, you leave me no choice. Unless you confess at once and promise me you will never steal again, I must take this up with your father."

Miss Johnson was striding toward the door, and Joanna, panicking, ran to stand in her way to stop her. She heard herself shouting, her voice broken by sobs, "I promise, yes, I promise. I won't steal. I won't! I won't! I won't!"

"Child! There's no reason to get hysterical. That's enough! All right now. For the rest of the term, once a week, you'll stay after school and write one hundred times, 'I will not steal.' A very light punishment indeed, I would say." Eyeing Joanna's shaking figure uneasily, she added, "The other children, your friends, they will soon forget. You'll see."

Will they? Joanna wondered. I don't think so. And something inside her hardened. Not one of them had spoken up for her. Not one had said, "We know Joanna. This isn't true."

Her friends? She had no friends now. Only Tony.

She realized she still stood in the deer pen, a bucket in her hand, and that Tony had been telling her something. He was waiting for her to answer.

"Aren't you excited, Joanna? I guess you haven't been listening. Your Pa wants to know if you'd like to go up with us again. We'll be using the big dirigible and you can pretend to be our first paying passenger. Want to?"

Tony, whenever he spoke of making ascensions, sounded rather self-important, but she didn't mind. She was aware that right now he was trying his best to cheer her up.

Yes, she was very glad she still had Tony for a friend.

Chapter 10

The hours Joanna had to spend at school were long and wretched, and her new raw loneliness did not ease. In part, the latter was by her own choosing. There were, as Miss Johnson had predicted, classmates who quickly forgot she was in disgrace. There were even some who were openly admiring of such a daring exploit as stealing the paperweight. But Joanna told herself fiercely that she'd never forgive anyone who had slunk away from that room in silence, abandoning her to her undeserved fate. Nadine she ignored, as though the girl did not exist; to Miss Johnson, who was responsible for the hateful chore of writing "I will not steal," she was polite and remote. Miss Johnson was shown no more poems.

Once the schoolday was gotten through, however, there was much to look forward to. Joanna was enjoying herself, as she'd never imagined she would again, just being with Papa and Tony.

When she told Papa that yes, she would like to be going again with him and Tony to the dirigible field, he'd been pleased. Right away, having long ago given up counting on Lillian at the park, he'd arranged to have Mr. Brundage stay overtime.

He'd said never mind the expense, his little girl deserved to have a bit of fun, too.

Mama agreed wholeheartedly. Dell had pursed her lips but surprisingly said nothing. Dell was strange these days, anyway. She kept arranging her pale blond hair in different ways and rubbing her cheeks to make them rosy. There was an air of secret excitement about her. Papa told Joanna it must be that Dell had her eye on some young man, although who it could be was anybody's guess. Only time would tell.

Shortly after three o'clock one April day, Joanna and Papa were on their way to Aunt Flossie's to pick up Tony. When Papa reined in the horse beside the steps of the wide wooden porch, Joanna, in a great hurry, jumped down from the carriage seat, ran across, and, calling Tony's name threw open the heavy house door without knocking.

She saw at once that she'd burst in on one of the German lessons Aunt Flossie sometimes gave on her free afternoons.

Aunt Flossie frowned at her, but the tall, gray-eyed young man standing at the fireplace, a book in his hand, didn't seem to mind the interruption, and when Aunt Flossie said, "Charles, this heedless child is Joanna Fritsch," his smile broadened.

"It isn't hard to guess," he said, "she has to be Lillian's sister."

"You know Lillian?" Joanna was surprised. He was even older than Dell, she was sure.

"In a way, yes. You might tell her Charles Gold says hello. A very pretty girl."

"Yes, she is," Joanna agreed cheerfully. She said to Aunt Flossie, "Isn't Tony ready? Papa's waiting."

"I'm sorry, no. Sam didn't say he was coming so soon, and I sent the boy on an errand. He'll be right back, though. You can take that chair and wait, quietly."

Aunt Flossie looked at the tall clock ticking loudly in the corner, then at her pupil. "*Jetzt. Sollen wir fortsetzen, mein Herr?* We should be getting on, you know. If you're to leave for Switzerland in only a few months—"

"Oh, my! Are you really—" Joanna clamped shut her mouth guiltily.

"We must not be interrupted," reminded Aunt Flossie.

"A moment, Miss Mendenhall," Charles said. "I'm afraid the young lady may burst if we don't let her speak."

Aunt Flossie sighed. "Yes, Joanna?"

"That's why you're learning German, Mr. Gold? To go to Switzerland?"

Joanna's daydreams in recent weeks had centered on just such a faraway place. She could envisage herself now as another Heidi, tending goats on the lush green Alpine meadows, never having to see either Nadine Seymour or Miss Johnson again.

Charles said, "Yes, I expect to be in Switzerland and Germany, too. I'm to be a foreign correspondent for the *Los Angeles Times*."

The touch of boyish pride with which this was said made him approachable all of a sudden, and Joanna declared, "I think that's grand! How terribly exciting to be sent so far away to get the news. Would they ever let a girl do that?"

He answered gravely, "I don't see why not, if she was qualified. She'd first have to start as a cub reporter here at home, though. I've been working for the *Times* for more than a year."

"She'd also have to be a great deal older than you are, Joanna," Aunt Flossie said tartly. "And know many more languages. Mr. Gold speaks French already."

"Aunt Flossie, will you teach me German, too? I could just sit and listen next week. I wouldn't be in the way."

"Mr. Gold is paying good money for these lessons. He shouldn't have to—"

"I don't mind. Not at all," the young man said.

"Joanna, come on." Tony burst into the room. "Can't keep your Pa waiting, we're late enough as it is." He threw Aunt Flossie a glance of reproach and added, "Potatoes are on the sink."

"Then run along, both of you."

Charles said, "*Auf Wiedersehen, Fräulein Fritsch.*"

"*Auf Wiedersehen!*" Joanna, repeating the words, found herself wishing she could stay on this very day to listen to the lessons, and then afterward to hear more about his newspaper work from Mr. Charles Gold, who was so courteous and kind.

Still, for soaring in a dirigible, the April afternoon was as beautiful as could be. It was delightful to look down from the gondola on all the tiny trees and houses, the hills stained orange and yellow and purple by spring wildflowers, and finally the sea, stretching away to meet the sky. The sea was like a peacock's tail, she decided, and the sky cerulean. Or should the word be *perse*? What kind of blue was perse?

"Nice, isn't it?" Papa said to her. "But nothing like the view we had a year ago. You were along that day. Remember?"

"You mean when the great white fleet was in?"

"Lord, yes. Don't imagine there'll ever be such a sight again."

He was referring to the show of might President Teddy Roosevelt had provided the other nations, mustering the United States battleships and taking them on a tour of the world. Those great white ships, sixteen of them, plus all the innumerable smaller vessels attending like stout ladies-in-waiting, had made a stop in San Pedro, anchoring in a long row inside the breakwater. They'd drawn tremendous crowds of spectators to the bluffs and shoreline every day of their stay.

Papa was right, the sight had been breathtaking from the air, but Joanna had secretly been more impressed by what she had seen at night from their own carriage driving along the cliff top. Every vessel had seemed to be outlined in fire. Thousands of incandescent bulbs were strung along the deck lines, up military masts, out the yards, down the sides of the funnels—from stem to stern, from top to water's edge. This was the naval fleet of America, and it had been Tony that night, his deepening boy's voice solemn and proud, who said what many others must have been thinking: "With all that power, nobody would dare go to war against us! Not ever!"

At this moment though, there were only a few small merchant ships in the wide harbor below, and Tony clearly wasn't thinking about war or a great white fleet. Joanna could see that he was totally absorbed in trimming the balance of the dirigible. Tony had learned all about an airship instantly, it seemed. His body was able to sense when some little adjustment needed to be made, and his hands knew just how to make it. As Papa said, Tony was ready to make ascensions alone, and if the dirigibles had been his, Papa would have let him. Papa had gotten himself a son, after all. One after his own heart.

Joanna, slightly bored by the endless maneuvering, was watching both their faces, and she was struck, suddenly, by their similarity of expression. Contentment, that's what it was. And *love*. Love of just soaring along about the earth. Looking at Papa then, and remembering how much of his time was spent up here in the sky, Joanna began to wonder some things that had never occurred to her before—adult things, about Mama. Was Mama lonely, left out as she was? What did Mama dream about?

Was Mama happy?

Oddly enough, elsewhere, Clara was being asked that same question.

With very few people would she have let a conversation progress to such an intimate point, but this was Uncle Paul. His arrival, at long last and without warning, besides filling her with joy had made her feel not a grown woman of almost thirty-four but a mere girl, as she'd been when she saw him last. Paul Perkins was old now, and she'd been shocked and saddened by his frailty, but to her he was like a father still.

He'd appeared only that morning, just as she was leaving the house. She'd taken his crooked body, shrunken and much smaller than hers, in a long, close, wordless embrace while silent tears fell on his bent shoulder.

Then when he gently freed himself, she'd blown her nose and smiled.

"You've come, finally."

"Yes. My carney days are over."

"And you'll stay? I've written you so often, but I couldn't seem to find just where the carnival was. Sam and I both want you. Please say you'll stay!"

"For a time anyway. But here we stand on your front steps and I see you were just going out somewhere. Shall I rest here a little and wait for you?"

"I was on my way to work. In the park. I sell ice cream."

"Then go. After a while I'll come and find you. Clara . . ." He studied her. "You are a beautiful woman. Your mother would be proud. Do you remember the day when she paid that quickie artist to sketch you? Money was scarce, but—"

Clara was busy ushering him inside, and while listening absently, she was trying to figure where in the house he would be most comfortable. Joanna's room was tiny, but it was closest to the bathroom. Joanna could move in with Dell and Lillian, share Lillian's double bed. . . .

She heard Uncle Paul say, "Things were never the same for us, were they, Clara, after my sister died?" and she agreed. But later that afternoon, after he'd hobbled over to join her at the park, the words surfaced in her mind and troubled her into cautioning him.

"Uncle Paul, I have to ask you, don't talk about Ma to Sam."

They were sitting at the tiny table behind the counter of her booth. Business was slow and she could offer him a dish of ice cream. He occupied the chair where Joanna's doll, Mrs. Merriweather, used to sit, and Clara had the feeling still that the inside of this small shack was a kind of refuge, where nothing real and unpleasant happened. Only make-believe. Little parties. Good times.

"Why not?" Uncle Paul asked.

"Because Sam . . . he's a bit, well, you might say, old-fashioned. He doesn't approve of Ma, the way she lived."

Uncle Paul stopped eating. "I'm sorry to hear that. And surprised. He never met her, so I suppose you mean he's ashamed of the carnival. I expected better of Sam."

"Not just the carnival. There were certain things—my dancing, mainly. Dancing so naked. I can't really blame him for that, but at the time it was the natural thing for me to be doing, wasn't it? As Ma said, I wasn't any good at the trapeze. Anyway, Sam doesn't want the children to know about it—although I wouldn't mind if they did. Well, all but Dell." Clara gave a little laugh. "Adeline was named for Sam's mother and must be something like her. It wouldn't surprise me.

"The point is, Uncle Paul, Sam is so good to me, I don't mind letting him have his way in this."

"But feeling as he does, won't he object to my being here?"

"Good gracious, no! He has a lot of respect for you. He's been hoping you'd come. Just, as I say, remember not to talk about the past with him or the girls."

"I'll remember. Now Clara, tell me about Sam's work. Surely you didn't say he goes up in dirigibles?"

"Yes, dirigibles. He loves flying—this same 'old-fashioned' Sam we've been talking about, Uncle Paul!"

Clara was glad to let the conversation move into a safer channel, and she told him in a rush all about the ascensions that took Sam away from her so much of the time.

"And you, Clara—are you happy?" Uncle Paul asked. She realized he was looking at her hands, no doubt wondering why, as she talked with such enthusiasm, she was pleating the edge of her apron with her fingers.

She wished passionately that just for an hour she could be the child she'd once been with him, and tell him what troubled her. She'd tell him how strange it felt to watch her daughters grow up—why, the youngest was already ten, and Adeline was sixteen, a year older than Clara herself had been when she married! The girls were growing up, facing all the exciting experiences of life, and she, it seemed, was standing still. It

was as if she were marooned on an island in a river while the
current carried all the rest past and away, and she could only
watch them go. She was trapped—no, that wasn't fair—she
was being kept safe in a quiet, peaceful place. But inside her
flowed more strongly than ever her own current, one of curiosity and energy and passion. Of what value were peace and
safety? She was bursting with longing for something more.

"Happy? Yes, of course I am," she said.

"I'm so glad. You were a happy little girl, and I hoped—
ah, Clara. I see a customer coming."

"Oh?" She rose, then knew even before she looked out who
the customer was. Always she knew—by the way her breasts
rose and tightened, by the warmth that ran through her body
in a flood.

"Good afternoon, Mr. Wilson." She hesitated. "Uncle Paul,
this is Mr. Wilson, who owns the roller coaster. My uncle,
Paul Perkins."

Uncle Paul, with his good manners, so unlike a carney in
this as in all other ways, had pulled himself awkwardly to his
feet. His deformed back rose above the level of the counter,
and Ralph, Clara realized with a surge of anger, was staring
at it with apparent astonishment. But then Ralph's gaze shifted
to herself, and she recognized that something had changed.
The question that had been in his eyes for so long was gone.
He wore a grim little smile.

He said to Uncle Paul, "Glad to meet you. Yes, sir, very,
very glad! You come from Missouri, don't you? I recognized
your—your Missouri way of talking, although I ain't been
there myself in quite a while."

Clara, puzzled by this spate of words from the usually taciturn Ralph and made uneasy by his smile, said quickly, "My
uncle has had an exhausting journey and I don't want to tire
him out. I was just going to walk back to the house with him,
so if you'll excuse us—"

"Clara, I am exhausted and that's a fact," her uncle said.
"But you needn't—"

"That's right," Ralph put in, "She needn't and she oughtn't.
Mrs. Fritsch should stay to look after her customers. But I've
a boy running the roller coaster, so I'm free. I'll walk along
with you myself."

Clara, alarmed, could think of no excuse for refusing. Her
uncle, no doubt resenting the suggestion from this strong young
man that he needed help, but too courteous to protest, said,

"Well, then, we'll be going along. Clara, is there anything you'd like me to do to help with supper?"

"No, there isn't, Uncle Paul. One of the girls might be home after a while. Just tell her who you are."

He nodded and hitched himself away on his crutches. Ralph was striding along beside him, and she could tell by the way he leaned over the frail old man, talking then waiting for an answer, that he had urgent questions to ask. She gazed after them, puzzled, and as always lately with Ralph, feeling in her acute awareness of him a touch of fear.

Chapter 11

The December weather was unusually beautiful, even for California. Sunny and clear, with the snow on the mountains visible from almost every vantage point in Los Angeles. Tourists came to stay in Pasadena and the coastal resort towns, and thinking with pleasurable shivers of the snowstorms bedeviling their homes back East, they sunned on the beaches and strolled beside the lake in Chutes Park.

Native Californians, having accustomed themselves to such winters, were less appreciative, and two of the Fritsch daughters, upon being released from school in the afternoons, managed to experience precious little of nature's beneficence.

The youngest, thrice weekly, was to be found in Aunt Flossie's large, gloomy parlor. When Papa inquired as to Joanna's progress in the German language, he was assured by her pleased instructress she was doing well.

"She applies herself," Miss Mendenhall said. "But I must say she has a good example set before her. Young Mr. Gold is a natural with languages and he is kind enough to help."

It was true that Joanna worked hard, absorbing grammatical peculiarities and getting her tongue around the pronunciation fairly quickly. But her secret enjoyment, during these sessions, lay in now and then hearing about Charles's experiences in foreign places. Charles, it appeared, had spent two summers by himself in France. Over the weeks, he told Joanna bits and pieces about the *pension* he lived in, the endless bookstalls along the Seine, even his bread and cheese picnics by bicycle into the countryside.

Answering all questions as seriously as if she were an adult like himself, he seemed to enjoy reminiscing, opening windows for her she might never have looked out otherwise. Soon gathering that she enjoyed putting words together on paper, he told her about the small band of American writers and artists who were beginning to group themselves in Paris.

"Are some of them women?"

"Well, I have heard of one, Miss Gertrude Stein, who is said to be a promising poet. A very odd way of expressing herself, she has—with no punctuation and lots of repetition. The idea is to use words for their sound rather than their meaning, if I've understood, and I probably haven't. . . ."

Joanna listened intently. One could, it seemed, write any way one wished, just so long as it was *art*.

She sighed. *Someday. Someday.*

Meanwhile, to be practical, couldn't she work for a newspaper as Charles did? Surely that wasn't an impossible dream!

Lillian, on those same glorious afternoons, had discovered, with her friend Olive Sengstacken, a novel and entrancing form of entertainment. They spent every nickel they could lay their hands on attending Talley's Electric Theatre. The nickelodeon was still considered slightly disreputable, and therefore, to sit in a darkened room watching a film gave the girls a delicious sensation of wickedness.

After a time, these two regular customers, very young high school girls from the looks of them, attracted the attention of the manager of Talley's, Bert Lange, a good family man but an ambitious fellow. He admitted to himself that if these were his daughters, he'd want to be told where they were spending their time. However, while his first impulse was to learn who they were and inform their families, another possibility came to mind and his good intentions were forgotten.

Olive he had no interest in. It was Lillian he found so remarkably pretty—and not only pretty but possessed of an unusual, impish appeal, heightened by her obvious efforts to appear sophisticated. He shrewdly guessed it was only after she left home in the morning that the long blond braids were swept up on top of her head and some little spitcurls hastily twisted in place before her ears. The rouge on her cheeks would have had to be applied even later, after school. Yet in spite of these incongruous embellishments, or perhaps because of them, there was a charm about her which Lange's knowledge of the film industry told him should not be wasted.

Lillian and Olive were just leaving their seats as the lights came on, when Lange approached them.

"Excuse me, young ladies."

The girls blanched. Could this heavyset man, wearing elastic suspenders over a sweat-stained shirt, be someone sent by Olive's father to find them?

"I'm the manager here. Mr. Lange."

"We haven't done anything we oughtn't," protested Olive. Lillian said nothing, only gave him a faint, appealing smile.

"Of course not," Lange said heartily while his eyes appraised Lillian from head to toe. "But will you both step into my office? I have some good news."

The girls, reassured, looked at each other. Talley's, to encourage business, had a ticket lottery each day, and they supposed they must have won something, maybe a pair of china cups. Free tickets for another performance would be even better.

They followed him eagerly into his tiny, dingy office, Lillian gazing with awed curiosity at the big projector as they passed the booth. Lange motioned them into the two straight chairs before his desk and got down to business at once.

"I've been asked, you see, to keep a sharp lookout for promising young actresses. You young ladies, it seems to me, might fill the bill. Of course the decision would be up to the studio."

"You mean—act in the flickers? Us?" Olive found her voice first.

"That's the idea. Either of you ever acted before?" The question was merely a gambit. He knew very well they hadn't.

"No. Do we have to of?" Olive's face had fallen comically.

Lillian, however, with a bravado that pleased but scarcely deceived him, said, "I was in a school play once."

"You were?" Olive looked at her, surprised, then added hastily, "Oh, yes, I remember. I was in it, too!"

"Splendid," Mr. Lange said gravely, "Experience helps although it isn't always necessary. You saw Mae Marsh in the film today. Wasn't she good? The fact is, Miss Marsh never acted in her life until she went to work for Biograph."

"Is that so?" Lillian could not help betraying her excitement now. For the first time all of this began to seem real. Perhaps it *was* possible that she could become a film actress like lovely Mae Marsh. She, Lillian Fritsch!

Lange had been watching her. He said, "It sounds as though you young ladies are interested. I will set up a meeting with your parents, as they'll need to give their permission, then the studio can—"

"They'd never!" Olive cried. "My mother won't even let me see a flick! She'd simply die at the idea of me being in one."

"Is that so?" Lange restrained himself from pointing out that only minutes before she had been sitting in his nickelodeon—seeing a flick, as she put it. "What about your parents?" he asked Lillian.

She had been thinking hard. She was not nearly as certain of her family's reaction as Olive was. After all, Papa had twice brought them all here as a treat on one of the rare days when Chutes Park was closed, and he and Mama had thoroughly enjoyed themselves. But watching a film and acting in one were two different things, she suspected.

"I think I'd better talk to them first." She was realizing that when the subject was raised, unless she was very careful, they'd discover how deceitful she had been all this time. She'd go to Mama first. Mama hadn't a suspicious bone in her body, and if either parent could be persuaded, Mama could.

At this point Mr. Lange was letting a thoughtful silence prevail. He was tempted, having been provided a good excuse, to exclude Olive. But a disgruntled girl could make trouble. Furthermore, although he didn't think so, Lillian might need to believe that she and her friend were having the adventure together. He said finally, "Parental permission can be got round, sometimes. Are you both at least sixteen?"

"Oh, yes!" was said in unison.

Not sixteen then, Lange thought, but he hadn't expected better.

"Let's do this. Suppose you come back in . . . shall we say three days? In the afternoon at four. I will have a producer here to speak to you. If he thinks either or both of you are suitable, it will be time enough then to worry about meeting with your parents."

Olive exclaimed loudly, "I don't care whether mine will let me or not, I'll run away. I want to be an actress!"

"And you?" Lange asked Lillian.

"I want to, too. Oh, yes!" She was smiling, her lips full and soft, her sapphire eyes round, half innocent, half knowing. He nodded, well satisfied. Being the agent for this girl, assured of a part of her earnings, might some day be important indeed.

"Mama," Lillian said, "I have to talk to you." In the dusk, Clara was leaning on the counter. The park was closing, but a few stragglers were still in view on the path around the lake.

Adeline suddenly popped up from the depths of the darkened shack behind Clara, startling Lillian. "Finished, Mama," Dell announced. "The walls are scrubbed down." She frowned at Lillian. "Haven't you taken over yet from Mr. Brundage? Joanna went off to another German lesson again today! Really, I think I'm the only one who does any work around here."

"What about Mama?" retorted Lillian, hiding her impatience.

"Well, yes, Mama," Dell said grudgingly. "But you? Have you fed the deer or haven't you?"

"No. And I won't, I promise you, until I've had a chance to talk to Mama alone."

"Oh? Secrets?" Dell wrung out her wet rags with a strong snap of her wrists, expressing her opinion of such foolishness. "I haven't time to waste like the rest of you."

"That will do, Dell," her mother said. "Did I ask you to wash the walls for me?"

"No, but they needed it. Oh, very well, I'll go take care of the deer myself."

"Is that really why you're going in that direction—or do you need an excuse to pass the roller coaster?" Lillian threw out the taunt carelessly, and was startled by the glare she received before Dell stalked away.

"What is it, Lillian?" Clara asked uneasily. She had no intention of discussing her oldest daughter's unfortunate infatuation. It was too bad Lillian had such sharp eyes.

But Lillian had already dismissed Dell from her mind. She drew a deep breath and said, speaking rapidly, "I've decided what I'd like to be, Mama. I don't want to get married—or teach school as Papa's been suggesting. I want to be an actress."

"Go on the stage?" Clara gasped.

"No, Mama. Be in the moving pictures."

"Oh, I see." Clara, relieved, berated herself for having taken Lillian's pronouncement seriously. Young girls did sometimes dream of going on the stage, but even Lillian, with her vivid imagination, couldn't in her heart believe it was possible to *be* one of those shadowy creatures cavorting in a jerky fashion on the screen. Clara herself wasn't entirely certain they were real people!

She smiled, thinking she understood. It was delightful to remember the two afternoons the family had spent at Talley's first entranced by the film—in which, now that Clara thought about it, the heroine did have a fresh provocative prettiness like Lillian's—and then by the fun of singing along with the piano accompaniment while a beautiful slide was shown illustrating the words. For weeks afterward, Clara had gone about her work humming, "Hello, Central, give me heaven."

She said gently, "It's a lovely idea, isn't it?"

Lillian looked startled. "I'm so glad—but what about Papa? Would he mind my thinking about it?"

"Papa would understand. He's been young himself."

After all, girls faced real life soon enough. What harm was there, for a little while, in imagining the impossible? Clara had built a few castles in the air, too, at that age.

It was a shock therefore to hear Sam bluntly approached on the subject that very evening. Lillian, it seemed, did believe there was a decision to be made, and at once.

Not surprisingly, Sam spoke his mind. "Absolutely not! Put such a ridiculous ambition completely out of your mind."

Lillian shot her mother an anguished glance of reproach. She cried, "But Papa, why not? I'd make lots of money, and I'd only have to go to New York once in a while. Most of the studios have a location here now—"

"Go to New York? My daughter?" He turned to Clara and shouted, "Is she completely insane? By the Lord Harry, I should have stayed in St. Louis, running a good, respectable business. My wife would be at home, my girls would have the sense to look for husbands—"

Adeline, who was sewing and at the same time listening with the rest of the family, broke her thread with her teeth and interrupted. "May I ask, Lil, how you know so much about the flickers?"

"I've been told. By the producer himself. I—"

"Really! How did you meet this so-called producer?"

"At the—I was introduced. By someone who asked him to speak to me. You stay out of this, Dell Fritsch!"

"Well, Lillian," her father said, "whatever you were told, be good enough to forget it. A girl of fifteen does not go off alone, unprotected, working with men who will take advantage of her."

"Fifteen isn't so young," Lillian said sullenly. "Mama was married when she was fifteen."

"That she was," said Uncle Paul, looking slightly amused. No doubt he, like Clara, thought Sam was sharpening steel on a foeman who didn't exist. How could a simple schoolgirl become a film actress?

"Lillian, not another word!" Sam shouted. "Fifteen, sixteen, twenty-five—the answer would still be no! The very idea of you parading yourself before strangers sickens me!"

No one answered him. Lillian, in a theatrical flood of tears, ran away upstairs. Sam looked around—at Dell, plying her needle vigorously; at Joanna, who stared down with unseeing eyes at the German grammar book in her hands; at Uncle Paul, whose face wore a pinched look. Finally at Clara . . .

"Come for a walk with me, Clara."

She rose woodenly, and together they walked out across the porch and down the steps.

Once away from the house, Sam said in a low voice, "Where on earth did she get such an idea? Was there really some producer who talked to her? The man should be shot!"

"I don't know or care. I don't see—did she ask to do something so terrible?" Clara was angrily defiant.

"Clara, she was serious! She'd had some kind of an offer!"

"Even so."

He stopped walking. "You surely would not want—"

"You spoke as though she'd be ruined just by being in one of those films. They didn't seem immoral to me. I enjoyed watching them and so did you."

"A young girl's reputation is precious, easily ruined—"

"Is it?" Clara's low voice was strident. "I seem to remember you didn't—when I was parading myself as you say—you didn't think I was ruined. Or did you?"

"Clara! Good God! I wasn't thinking of you when I spoke. Those days are long past, forgotten. . . ."

"Things aren't forgotten just because they're past. No, I think you remember very clearly, Sam. Always have and always will. You're deeply ashamed of what I did."

"No, Clara, no!"

He put his arms around her, pulled her close. But for the first time, in his embrace, she was still and silent.

Chapter 12

Uncle Paul had formed the habit of coming to the park with Clara to spend most of the day, sitting in the back of the shack napping, or perhaps reading or quietly talking to her, often in a reminiscent vein, a pleasure he had to forego at home in the evenings because of Sam. Clara worked as she listened, and after a while much of what he said went in one ear and out the other. She was too busy to give him her full attention.

Thus she missed it when he said, "Funny thing, that young fellow remembering me from so far back. Still, I guess having a humpback makes a man easy to recognize."

And again, later, "Small world, isn't it? California's such a distant place, you wouldn't expect to be recognized by anyone. I reckon the whole country's funneling into the West."

These days—and she would look back bitterly at their false promise—she felt safe and secure. Sam might be away every day now from dawn until late at night, preparing for the big air show scheduled to commence January tenth at Dominguez Hill. But with Uncle Paul almost always at her side, Ralph was keeping his distance. Indeed, he hadn't come near the stand in weeks, and the uneasy apprehension she'd felt for so long had ebbed away to nothingness. When she thought of Ralph she did so complacently, deciding she had nothing to fear from him—or from herself.

It was on a chill, rainy afternoon late in December, that she learned otherwise.

Uncle Paul, feeling the wet weather in his bones, took himself home well before his usual time, and no sooner had he gone than a familiar voice spoke her name, not calling her *Mrs. Fritsch* as he'd always done before, but simply *Clara*. Approaching swiftly, silently, he had given her no chance to sense that he was near, to rally her defenses.

She cast one wild desperate glance into the park. Most customers had hurried home when the gloomy downpour began, and she was one of the last concessionaires open. Even Dell, wanting to take the receipts to the bank, had left, and crotchety Mr. Brundage, miffed no doubt at Joanna being absent so often that week, had closed the deer pen early. Ralph, if he intended to be alone with Clara, had chosen his time well.

"Clara," he said again, and she could no longer look away. Rain had drenched his hair, made his shirt sodden on his lean, muscular shoulders, and unbidden came the desire to pull him close, make him warm again. Clara gave a small convulsive shudder.

"Yes, Mr. Wilson?"

"Why *Mr. Wilson?*" He spoke savagely. "The rest of the people here—even your own husband—they all call me Ralph. Why can't you?"

Her husband. The words hurt, yet unhappily, invoking Sam did not strengthen her. She could only think sadly that Sam had been right. He had known her better than she knew herself.

She said in a low voice, "Very well . . . Ralph."

"Clara, did your uncle tell you how I remembered him?"

"Remembered him? I don't know what you mean."

"The minute I saw him, it all came back, the thing that's been bothering me all this time. I used to be crazy about that baseball throwing game at carnivals. I spent hours and hours and a lot of money at your uncle's booth. I bet I won more prizes there than any other boy in the state of Missouri. Understand what I'm getting at, Clara? I was *there*—at the carnival—at the sideshow. . . .

"Clara, don't look so scared. Lord, Clara, I love you so much. It's just that I'm not holding back anymore, because I remembered you, too, everything about you, once I saw him— the hunchback—again. What threw me off, I guess, was the way you—well, the way you always wear such prim and proper dresses and look so respectable. Because in those days, you weren't—prim."

Thank you, Ralph, for at least not saying what you're thinking—that I was a hussy, if not worse. And why not—a girl who danced nude! That's what Sam thinks, too, though he won't admit it even to himself. He doesn't trust me, after all our years together . . . and I guess now he shouldn't. Otherwise, why do I feel so strange, so excited, knowing you watched me dance like that?

He was leaning in across the counter, his breath warm and clean on her face. She wanted to back away, but she couldn't. A lassitude possessed her. Her body was too heavy to move, her arms hung at her sides.

She stared into his eyes, seeing even in the dimness the gold flecks lighting the rich brown iris. Then, as she'd known it would, his mouth came down against hers. Urgently, hungrily, he kissed her, his lips seeming to search hers. And his hands that cupped her breasts were moving in little circles, the caressing urgent, and hungry too.

Until suddenly life flowed into her with such painful intensity that she cried out, and he stopped the cries with his tongue.

Finally, he drew back.

Still pressing her breast with the palm of one hand, as if the spell might be broken if they were separated, he reached quickly with the other and lifted the hinged part of the counter. She walked through and stood before him, head bowed, filled with black despairing shame yet unable to stop herself.

Ralph said huskily, "I've got an extra key to the boathouse— it's unlocked now—but we don't want to be seen there together. You go first and I'll wait a little."

Clara raised her head. Her eyes were glazed. "No, I must not!" she protested. But as she was speaking she moved closer, so that the length of her body was against his and she was feeling even through their clothing his hardness, her own terrible desire.

"Not here, Clara! The boathouse. Go. Oh, please go!"

She turned and walked slowly away, a forlorn unhappy figure in the rain. Ralph's eyes did not leave her until she had circled the lake and at length reached the small wooden boathouse, usually a center of activity but today deserted, its high windows uninviting black squares. She entered and disappeared.

Ralph padlocked the ice cream stand. He looked quickly around once more, making certain they had been unobserved. Then, in the empty park, he set off running to Clara, a man possessed by passion.

Chapter 13

For the historic Los Angeles Aviation Meet, which took place Monday, January 10, in the year 1910, the weather cooperated fully, presenting a clear and sunny sky. Twenty thousand spectators crowded into a big wooden grandstand for the opening events, and even more came daily thereafter.

Balloons, dirigibles, and flying machines suddenly dominated conversation on the West Coast. The newspapers wrote of nothing else. To describe a biplane's takeoff through the eyes of a spectator witnessing manned flight for the first time, one journalist rhapsodized:

"Over the grass—before your startled gaze—while your eyes are popping out—why, man alive, look at that!—the airship picks up astonishing speed! Like an express train she's flying, and hurrah! she leaves the ground, glides upward— higher! and higher! at one hundred miles an hour, off into the blue—hip, hip, hooray!"

Roy Knabenshue, back in California for the meet, steered his own dirigible around a captive balloon tethered to the grandstand, while just above him Sam maneuvered the *Arrow* in the same tight circle. A number of the noisy monoplanes and biplanes buzzed restlessly about them both like, Sam thought, pesky bluebottle flies.

The daredevil pilots of the flying machines were immensely popular with the spectators, especially a dashing Frenchman named Louis Paulhan who was wont to swoop his flimsy craft directly at the jammed grandstand, spinning away at the last possible moment, the engine sputtering in protest. Paulhan would then casually land in the center of the field, amid a roar of acclaim.

Sam regarded such recklessness with lofty tolerance. He had every respect for the skill of the pilots, but in his opinion the flying machines were a novelty, nothing more. The future of aviation, he often stated, lay with the dependable dirigible.

Consequently, he was deeply disappointed when he came to realize that Tony viewed the matter differently. Tony stood beside him watching the famous Glenn Curtiss whip a biplane around the pylons of an octagonal course, completing the mile and a half in just over two minutes and setting an international record. Tony turned to Sam and said, his eyes shining, "How I'd like to fly one of those!"

Ordinary boy words, but Sam knew Tony's heart was in them.

So Sam was not surprised, an hour or so later, to see Tony edge up to Monsieur Paulhan, not yet so famous as Curtiss and thus more approachable, and burst out with questions.

Fortunately the Frenchman spoke fluent English, and fortunately he had very few cronies of his own at the meet. He settled back and proceeded for some time to talk aeronautics with the eager boy.

On the following morning, early, well before the day's activities were to begin, Tony was there, watching with avid eyes while Paulhan put his monoplane through its paces, shouting down comments to his young admirer.

At a distance, Sam was busy working, filling the *California Arrow*'s ballonet with gas. He could have used Tony's help, had counted on it. But he hadn't the heart to interfere when, as they'd driven out to the field, all Tony talked about was monoplanes and biplanes and wishing he could learn how they were flown. Plainly, this was his opportunity.

"How are you, Sam?" It was Roy Knabenshue, who had come to squat comfortably on the ground nearby. Roy wore a disappointed frown.

"Fine, fine," Sam said. "But why aren't you getting ready for the dirigible race?"

"Had a bad tear in the silk. I've men working on it, but the mending's going slowly. I'm going to have to miss the morning race."

"Too bad," Sam sympathized. "That's the big one. But can't you be ready for the afternoon event?"

"Maybe. Don't know. Every newspaper man here has asked me that question. That, and—don't I wish now I'd stayed with Baldwin?"

Sam nodded. "If you had, you'd be flying the old *Arrow* instead of me. She's still the fastest we have."

"She's still a beauty. But I'll tell you now, Sam, I expected to beat you anyway. My *Missouri Star* would give anybody a run for his money. Well, that's the way luck goes. You'll earn some prize money today."

"Hope so. I can use it."

"Look—that crazy Paulhan! He'll try anything in that little crate of his."

Both men turned to watch for a moment as the monoplane landed, skidding along the turf and turning nose to tail where the turf ended.

Roy said in disgust, "He is crazy, I tell you. Think of the Wright flying team, having all kinds of records for altitude and distance, and yet two of their best pilots died in crashes in the space of a month recently. This Louis Paulhan acts as if falling from a hundred yards up is no worse than falling out of bed."

"He's just self-confident." Sam smiled. "Like anyone who flies. Besides, he's rich as cream, owns a chateau and a big estate at home, so I've heard. He brought three of those little machines all the way from France with him, so he probably wouldn't care much if he lost one."

"Unless he lost his life at the same time." Roy, still morose, regarded the cocky little Frenchman, now climbing from his aeroplane, without favor.

Sam returned to his work, but Roy remained nearby, surveying all the activity. At length he remarked, "By golly, Paulhan's going too far. You'll agree this time, when you see who he's letting take up his aeroplane."

Sam barely heard. He was thinking about Clara. Worrying. There was something different about Clara lately.

He might have thought she was still resentful because of that small quarrel they'd had a while back, but Clara wasn't one to hold a grudge. Yet it seemed to him that she'd developed a kind of reserve. That she wasn't welcoming him the way she used to. And there was the odd expression he'd been surprised to see on her face more than once when she hadn't known he was watching. It was a look of misery. No, worse than misery. Stark unhappiness! But when he spoke to her, the look quickly vanished.

He wished so much she had come with him today. He'd have been so proud having her here, especially if he won, and it seemed strange that she had begged off. Still, she'd never made any secret of her dislike for the sport and often had seized on some flimsy excuse to avoid the long hours of watching. Today's excuse had been that with the park closed, this was her chance to clean the house from top to bottom. So he and Tony had gone off without her—

Tony! Someone flying Paulhan's aeroplane?

Sam leapt to his feet. Oh, no, it must not be Tony! What did Tony know about flying one of those infernal machines?

But yes, it was Tony, and the aeroplane was already in the air. Paulhan was yelling directions from the ground but Sam doubted if Tony could hear. He was flying higher and higher all the time, and with the sputter of the engine right behind him, the loudest shout wouldn't reach his ears.

Roy said grimly, "Well, Sam, either Tony can fly and land that contraption by himself, or he can't."

The chances were, Sam thought, that he couldn't.

Sam continued to stare up, hardly blinking, as if by the power of concentration he could will the plane down safely. And he and Roy weren't the only absorbed spectators. Already word had spread. Everyone on the field gazed silently upward.

The little monoplane was still flying but erratically, sometimes high, sometimes low, dipping and ducking as though breasting heavy seas. Once it barely avoided slamming into the ground after coming within ten feet of the top of Paulhan's head.

The bantam Frenchman was apparently unperturbed. He continued his shouts of advice, waving his arms expressively. At last Sam heard the words he'd been waiting for, and dreading too: "All right, young man, bring her down! The way I told you!"

Tony, it appeared, must have been able to hear some of the instructions, because he gestured a brief acknowledgment. Sam got a glimpse of the boy's face, pale and stiff with concentration, and was somewhat cheered to see him take a quick glance at the rippling flag on the official's tent, making sure of the wind direction. So Tony was still in control of himself, if not of his machine.

Now he had started his descent, rocking awkwardly from side to side.

"Level out!" called Paulhan, sounding alarmed for the first time. "Get those wings level . . . No! No! Too *slow*—take her up again—quickly, before she stalls!"

"Jesus!" exclaimed someone behind Sam, "now he's going to loop over backwards."

But the aeroplane continued to climb steadily, and then, suddenly, it was apparent even to Sam that the youthful pilot's feel of the craft was improving. Paulhan, perhaps overcome by relief, had fallen silent, but even without his help Tony reached a safe altitude, and after leveling out began to fly in a wide steady circle. A triumphant circle...one didn't need the sight of the boy's gleeful grin to know that Paulhan's faith had been justified. At fourteen, Tony was flying solo. He was a pilot.

The Frenchman, also smiling and swaggering about, gestured with a wide sweep of his arm for another descent. Tony again waved back, this time with exuberance. This time he'd land perfectly, the grin seemed to promise, and at last Sam's fright was easing.

But Tony was already tasting the elixir of the limelight. For today, no matter what aviation records were broken, he would be the one talked about, written about by every newspaper covering the meet. And as the aeroplane touched lightly down and rolled forward, as he heard men shouting their friendly approval, his attention strayed. He was looking out the open side of the cockpit instead of at the stretch of turf ahead, and only became aware of something wrong when he heard Paulhan's yell of warning.

Too late. One wheel bumped up a small rounded knoll, the wing rose sharply, and then the plane turned over.

Sam, watching the slow-motion flip, wasn't overly concerned. Although the engine exuded a black smoke, there was no fire, and the light framework appeared to be undamaged. It seemed unlikely that the young pilot could be injured.

Yet, as Sam went running across the field, Paulhan and his assistant were already there, and they were pulling Tony out with peculiar gentleness. He gave a thin scream of agony as they placed him on the ground.

Sam pushed up close and sank to one knee beside the boy, whose face was twisted by pain, all the happy triumph erased.

"Easy, son," Sam said in a comforting voice.

"There's no fire? I'm so scared of fire—"

"No. Where are you hurt?"

"My arm!" The muttered words came from between clenched teeth, and then Sam saw for himself. Fighting back the impulse to lash out at Paulhan for risking the boy's life—what was done was done—he asked, tight lipped, "Where's the doctor? Supposed to be one here."

Roy said, "I'll get him, Sam," and disappeared.

The doctor came. Undeterred by Tony's groans, he probed

the peculiarly bent arm, and said in an aggrieved tone, "Broken. It has to be set, of course. I've no anesthesia here, wasn't provided with half the equipment the committee promised. Just wait until there are some real injuries—there'll be hell to pay. How can I possibly be responsible when—"

"Your responsibility be damned!" Sam interrupted. "Do something! Can't you see the boy is in pain?"

"A moment, sir! The boy is not a competitor, is he? Can't be at his age. Anyway, as I say, I've no anesthetic—"

The doctor stopped, suddenly aware of the expressions on the faces of Sam, Paulhan, and a crowd of others grouped around.

"Very well. As I say, here I can do nothing. Someone must take him to my office where my partner is looking after our patients today."

Sam thought, Roy will take him. Roy isn't making an ascension, but I've got one in half an hour.

Then he heard Tony's whisper, "Hurry, please, Mr. Fritsch. Please hurry!" and he saw the ashamed tears running down Tony's face. Although the boy brushed furiously at them with his uninjured hand, they continued to flow. This was no longer a day of triumph for Tony—or even for Sam in the coming race. All that remained in the boy's mind was the pain.

Sam glanced around quickly for Roy, but his friend was not in sight. Nor was Adeline—all his daughters had assured him they would be in attendance this morning to watch him try for the trophy, but it was still too early. Not even Joanna had come yet.

There was no time. And Tony, immersed in his agony, was only a boy. He shouldn't be turned over to strangers.

Sam said, "Will someone help carry him to my buggy? Easy now." He paused, and said to Paulhan, "You know Roy Knabenshue, don't you? Then do me a favor. When he gets back, ask him if he'll pilot the *Arrow* in this morning's race."

"From what I've heard, he won't refuse," Paulhan said dryly.

"No. But you can also tell him I should be back in time for the afternoon event. It'll be up to him to have the dirigible ready again."

Sam helped carry the boy he loved as much as a son, then drove the carriage, trying to avoid jolts from the bumpy street. The sight of Tony, hunched in the seat, the crooked arm cradled across his chest and his face dewed with perspiration, banished any lingering disappointment he might have felt.

Although there was an occasional suppressed moan when a wheel rolled in a pothole, the tears had stopped. The boy's teeth were gritted as he fought for dignity before Sam. Neither of them spoke until Sam, just before they reached the doctor's office, broke the silence.

"Tony, I have to admit I'm proud of you. But what a stupid, reckless stunt! How Paulhan could let you, knowing as little as you did—"

Tony managed a contorted grin. "He said I was a born flyer. Anyway, did you know much more before you made your first ascension?"

Sam started to retort, "No, but dirigibles are a great deal safer," and realized he'd been bested. Safer or not, between himself and Tony, he, Sam, had been the more foolhardy. He had Clara—and the children!

He said gruffly, "At least I didn't crack myself up. Well, let's go in. Afraid this won't be pleasant, but it may keep you out of those infernal flying machines."

If he hoped for some agreement from Tony, he was disappointed. Tony avoided his eye and silently followed him into the office.

Setting the arm turned out to be not nearly the ordeal Sam had feared. This doctor, the young partner of the hard-bitten man at the field, was compassionate as well as up to date on anesthesia.

Sam, of necessity, was pressed into service, holding the saturated sponge over Tony's nose and mouth. After the boy's eyes closed, the doctor competently stretched the arm and maneuvered the ends of bone back into place. By the time Tony woke, the arm was neatly encased in hardened plaster and strapped securely across his chest.

Groggy, he stared up from the table and then, no doubt feeling the pain recommence, fright darkened his eyes. But when he focused on Sam's face, the fright faded, replaced by a look of abject misery.

"Everything's fine," Sam said.

"No." The boy shook his head. "I was dreaming, I guess. I dreamt you won the race and all the prize money. You're too late now, aren't you?"

"Yes. Roy is taking my place. It doesn't matter."

"It does matter! I don't know how I could have done such

a thing, letting you bring me. I just didn't think!"

"Water under the bridge," Sam said firmly, "and I'll have another chance this afternoon. Right now, I'm going to drive you home. Is Aunt Flossie there, do you know?"

"No, she never is when the park's closed. She says it's her chance to get away, do all the things she hasn't time for. But if you're thinking I need—" Tony, more lucid by the minute, looked ruffled.

"I do, and don't argue. Mrs. Fritsch will be glad to come over, fix you a little soup, and just see that you're comfortable."

Now that the crisis was past, Sam was eager to get back to the field, find out how the *Arrow* was doing. Even though he'd missed out himself, he badly wanted Roy and the *Arrow* to win. It would be a sight to see, and if he left the buggy and rode out on horseback, he'd make it. Then there'd be the afternoon's event. . . .

At Aunt Flossie's house, he insisted Tony take another of the pills the doctor had given him for pain. When the boy was in bed, drifting off into a drugged drowsiness, Sam hurried home seeking Clara.

It was annoying to be met at the door by Paul Perkins and be told, "Clara's not here. Say, what's the matter? Was your race postponed?"

"Where is she?" Sam asked testily. "I need her help." He told Paul briefly what had happened. "Tony's all right, but he shouldn't be left alone, not with all the pain he's having."

"I can go," offered Uncle Paul.

Sam hesitated. But then, he thought, it *should* be Clara, and he made a decision more momentous than he realized.

He said, "A woman's touch would be best. Where is she?"

"Gone to the park, of course."

"The park? It's closed."

"Is it?" The old man was surprised and puzzled. "Could I have heard wrong? No, I expect she had things to do there anyway. Don't the deer have to be fed?"

Sam was becoming more and more disgruntled. Really, this was too bad. More time! He'd miss every one of the morning events.

"Never mind," he said. "I'll find her."

He strode away, down the several blocks, and passed into the silent park.

At her padlocked ice cream stand, he paused irresolutely.

There seemed to be no one about at all. Ordinarily, on days when the concessions were shut down, a few couples strolled beside the water, a few children played hide and seek around the enclosures, the merry-go-round, or the wooden scaffolding of the roller coaster. Today, because of the widely heralded aviation meet, an empty silence reigned.

He walked on, coming to the deer pen, and was pleased to see the dainty animals nuzzling at fresh piles of hay. She had been here and fed them.

But where was she now? If she'd gone back home, he would have met her on the way.

It occurred to him that she might simply be wandering about the park. Clara, when she had a little leisure time, liked to do that. Ramble along the lake, think her own thoughts, and watch the people enjoying themselves. Today, of course, there were no people.

He then noticed an odd thing. The window of the boathouse was open. The owner of the rental boats, a very meticulous man, would never have left it like that. He had quite an absurd fear of theft, although there was little of value that could easily be carried away.

As a matter of course, intending to shut the window, Sam turned his steps toward the small building, his footfalls noiseless on the grass. And then, reaching up, he chanced to look inside.

He stiffened. Froze.

If Clara had been facing that direction, she must have seen the shadow of his head and shoulders darkening the aperture. But as she lay, supine and lax, sprawled on boat cushions placed on the floor, her head was turned aside.

And Ralph, the man who was pressed close beside her, whose body was as naked as hers, had buried his face in her soft, full breasts. And with his hands . . . with his hands, he was . . .

Clara. His Clara!

With Ralph.

Clara stirred, as if even through her rapture she felt his gaze, and Sam spun away. He went running, running madly on and on, until he slammed hard against the fence at the far end of the park and came to his senses.

Then, falling to his knees, he retched into the desolate dry weeds of this neglected spot. When the waves of nausea finally diminished, he dragged himself to a nearby bench, still feeling sick and empty. There he sat for some time with this face in his hands, a small, defeated man, mourning for what he had lost.

Chapter 14

"*Glad you made* it back, Sam. Just in time," Roy said. "But I figured you would. You wouldn't miss both races. We'll have that contest between us, after all." When Sam didn't answer, Roy, binding the end of his frayed anchor line, glanced over. "Say, that boy of yours is all right, isn't he? You look so—"

"He's all right." Sam quickly busied himself, giving the *Arrow* a last-minute check. "Thanks for having everything ready for me."

"Had to." Roy's voice was matter-of-fact, although he continued to study Sam's face, puzzled by the gray hue but saying nothing more about it. "Wasn't sure until an hour ago that the *Missouri Star* would be mended in time, and if you weren't here . . ." He pulled out his watch. "Well, it's time to go, I see. Good luck, Sam."

"You too, Roy." Sam started to climb into the heaving framework of his gondola, then turned around. "You've been a good friend, Roy. I'd like to say thank you."

"It was nothing."

"I don't mean just this morning." He thrust out his hand. "Goodbye, Roy."

Roy smiled. "We'll meet, I imagine, on the platform to take our prizes. Winner and runner-up. There's nobody else in the same class with us, you know. We're the best."

The best? Sam thought bleakly. *How much did being the best matter now?* He listened for the gun, then signaled his crew to release the ropes.

The reliable old *Arrow* nosed up straight and fast, and although Sam felt none of his habitual lifting of the heart, he patted the taut sleek silk above his head in a brief gesture of affection.

He stared down, belatedly seeking his daughters in the crowd behind the roped-off area around the field. There they were, Dell and Joanna, waving at him and smiling.

God, he should have taken the time to speak to them, hug them both before he went up! He loved them so much! But there'd been too many chores to do to get ready, and he might have missed out. This was one ascension he couldn't miss.

He waved back until a shudder under his feet reminded him that he must attend to what he was doing. Automatically he began trimming the little ship, bringing it horizontal and steady. He didn't want it crashing before his daughters' very eyes, frightening them and leaving a grim memory forever. But then, as all the dirigibles began sweeping around the pylon in as tight circles as they could manage, he surreptitiously pinched shut the fuel line.

The engine coughed several times before it was finally silent. Powerless, the *Arrow* began to drift, moving out of the prescribed orbit and taking a path over the heads of the crowd. He heard Roy shout, "Too bad, Sam!" and he gave an absent wave of acknowledgment.

He looked again to where his daughters stood. Dell was making a show of disgust with her hands and Joanna looked disappointed. They were sorry he was out, of course, but they wouldn't be worrying. Both of them knew he'd landed a dirigible without an engine scores of times. Any greenhorn aeronaut could do it, and Sam, as Roy had said, was one of the very best.

The boastful but true words rang unpleasantly in his ears. If he could claim to be the best, he'd certainly paid dearly for the privilege. *Why* hadn't he stayed home with Clara instead of pursuing this childish passion? If he'd stayed home, the ugly thing that had grown up between Clara and Ralph couldn't have gotten started. Oh, why hadn't he stayed home?

But wasn't he fooling himself—thinking that just his being there would have made a difference? Remembering the tall good looks of the man who had stolen his wife, Sam admitted humbly that he must certainly have lost her anyway. What woman, choosing between Ralph and himself, wouldn't choose Ralph!

Oh, Clara, Clara, Clara . . .

The airship bumped roughly in a gust of wind and Sam roused himself to study the topography below. He was in the foothills now, just over what appeared to be a small ranch. A very steep slope of bare mountain rose not far away.

He worked at the rudder, and with the help of the wind the *Arrow* responded, gliding in the direction of the dry brown cliff.

As though the little ship had a mind of her own, however, she was slowly ascending and soon would clear the top. Sam let her rise until she was almost free of the formidable obstacle ahead, then he carefully began to release air. The dirigible leveled and was wafted again toward the rocky wall.

Pushed by the gusts, headed directly for the ominous jagged cliff of shale, the dirigible moved more swiftly. Sam didn't look away, only kept his hand steady, gripping the rudder tight so as to guide the hapless little ship to just where he wanted to go.

A moment more, then she struck. Even with all his skill, he'd come in a little high, and the balloon slammed across the narrow ledge, lodging against the inner wall. But the gondola, hitting the mountain's side with great force, was upended.

Sam, had he tried, might possibly have held on and saved himself. Instead he slid in an instant from the open framework, and hurtled down onto the rocks below.

Chapter 15

"Uncle Paul, isn't Sam home yet? The meet wasn't scheduled to last so late—here it is well after sundown! Where is he?"

"I don't know, Clara. Is something wrong?" Paul Perkins asked.

She had stormed into the house, confronting him with no other greeting. He was taken aback by her agitation and by the high, strained voice that seemed stretched so thin it might break, particularly surprising when of late Clara had struck him as far too quiet and subdued.

"I found this note, placed under a stone on the porch steps. Oh, Uncle Paul, it's from Lillian. . . ."

He said nothing, and his air of patient waiting calmed her a little. Her voice steadied as she asked him, "You didn't see her leave this?"

"No. I was resting in my room most of the day."

Clara shook her head. She said bluntly, "It's too bad. You might have been able to stop her. She's run away from home."

"Lillian?" He stared in amazement. "Why on earth—"

"Surely you can guess! To be an actress in motion pictures!"

"I see. Sam is going to be very angry."

This was so evident that no answer was forthcoming and Paul continued reflectively, "In a way, it's bad luck he feels so strongly. I know nothing about this new industry, but I'd think Lillian might do very well in films. But Sam has expressed his opinion in no uncertain terms—"

"And why shouldn't he feel strongly, when he's right? His own wife once danced nude in a sideshow. A girl who would display herself before men as I did is indecent, weak, a tramp!"

Paul, listening, realized there was more behind this outburst of bitterness than mere wounded feelings. Whatever Clara was brooding about, she had his sympathy, but at the same time he felt an old resentment. It had always seemed to him that the strong and healthy of this world, if they had no real troubles, went out of their way to find some.

He said, being practical, "Perhaps before Sam returns, we should try to bring Lillian back. When Sam came here looking for you, he left the buggy in the stable. If you'll help me with the harnessing . . ."

But Clara didn't move. She said slowly, "Sam was looking for me? When?"

"Around noon, I think it was."

"Where . . . did he look?"

"He must have tried the park. If he didn't find you there, I don't know . . . Clara, my dear, what is the matter?" Now he was genuinely alarmed.

"The window! Oh, God, the window—"

"What are you talking about? What window?"

"Never mind. It's nothing—" Her stricken expression gave the lie to the words. "So Sam came? I just didn't expect . . . I thought he was to be in an important flying event, something he couldn't miss...."

"He had to miss it. The Bonnard boy had an accident and broke his arm, so Sam dropped out of the race and took him to have it tended to. Afterward, he wanted you to go over to Miss Mendenhall's. I take it he didn't find you?"

Walking away, Clara stared outside, seeming to watch the tall palm trees sway in the wind. "No. I'm sorry I wasn't here at home. You don't know how very sorry!" She suddenly hugged herself, shivering. "The house is chilly tonight. Why hasn't Dell built a fire?"

"She isn't back yet. Neither she nor Joanna. I'll help you build one if you wish. But first, Clara, do you want me to go after Lillian? Where is she?"

"Oh, yes, Lillian. Here, you'd better read her note yourself. The problem is, I don't think we can find her."

Almost with indifference now, Clara turned and thrust the paper into his hands. He gave her a puzzled look before unfolding it and reading the few words aloud:

> Mama, I'm going away to New York to become a film actress. I did the only thing I could when Papa wouldn't listen—I told the producer I had Papa's permission. I even signed his name. Please forgive me for lying and being disobedient, but I can't help it. I want so terribly to do this, and how many chances will I get? Tell Papa he needn't worry about me, though, because I won't be alone. Olive is going, too.
>
> > Your affectionate daughter,
> > Lillian

"New York!" Paul exclaimed. "What can we do? We don't even know the name of the film company." He pondered, then snapped his fingers. "Of course! There is one obvious thing. Call the parents of her friend Olive, see if they have any more information. What is the family name, Clara?... Clara!"

Clara started. Still in a daze, she said, "Their name is Sengstacken. Please, Uncle Paul, will you call?"

It would be far more suitable, Paul thought, for Lillian's mother to be conferring with the Sengstackens, but he didn't argue. Clara had again turned away, presenting her back to him—and to the problem of Lillian as well, it seemed.

He hobbled out to the telephone. After he'd placed his call with the operator, and a male voice at length answered, he cautiously introduced himself. "Good evening, sir, my name is Paul Perkins. Lillian Fritsch is my grandniece."

Under the circumstances, the mention of Lillian's name might have been expected to provoke an immediate, perhaps violent response. However Mr. Sengstacken, and from the resonant assured voice Paul was certain it was he, merely answered pleasantly, "Yes, Mr. Perkins?"

Paul was bewildered. He could only proceed, feeling his way. "I wonder, sir, if you or Mrs. Sengstacken happen to know the whereabouts of my niece? She has not come home, and needless to say, her mother is worried."

"Lillian isn't here with us. However, Olive might know something of her plans. Would you care to speak with my daughter?"

"Indeed I would. Thank you."

A lengthy pause ensued—apparently even the wealthy Sengstackens kept their telephone in some remote back hall— during which Clara, evidently concerned once again for her daughter, appeared at his side. "What is taking so long?" she whispered. "Don't they know yet the girls have run away?"

"The girls haven't run away, Clara. Only Lillian. Olive is at home."

"Well! Lying certainly has become a habit with Lillian, hasn't it! Is Olive coming on the line? I'd better speak with her myself."

"Yes, here she is now." He backed away, handing Clara the receiver.

"Olive?" Clara said. "Olive, we must find Lillian! She left us a note, saying that you and she were going somewhere—"

"We *were* going, yes! We were going *together*."

"Then why didn't you?"

"Why? Because they were only fooling me! To get Lillian!" Olive, who until then had been furtively keeping her voice down, could not restrain herself further. "We were supposed to meet at the train station, but when I got there, they told me I wasn't needed. I said, 'You'll see, Lil won't go without me'— but she did. Some best friend she is! I won't ever forgive her. Never! Why, if she'd been the one they didn't want, I'd have—

"Yes, Papa, everything is quite all right! Of course I know

where Lil's gone. It's Dorff Pictures she went with, Mrs. Fritsch—

"Yes, Papa, I do know what I'm saying!" Olive broke off again, apparently in response to another incredulous interruption by her father. She said loudly, "But that's exactly what Lil did, Papa! She went off with those two men. With Mr. Dorff and Mr. Lange."

Clara, listening to this exchange, exclaimed in an aside to her uncle, "Sam was right! I should never have encouraged Lillian. Heaven only knows what will happen to her, what already has. . . . Yes, Olive?"

"Mrs. Fritsch, I guess I should tell you—although it was to be a secret—they're in Santa Monica right now, at the Arcadia Hotel, because Mr. Dorff is shooting on the beach tomorrow. After that, they go on to New York. And there's something else. Lil . . . well, Lil will be chaperoned." Olive parted with this information reluctantly. Her anger and disappointment were again evident. "They promised us—her— that she'd live in a boarding house with other girls. It was all to be such *fun!*"

Even with her father listening, Olive could not suppress this final wail of envy.

"Dear Olive, thank you for telling me. I'm very grateful. However," Clara added, suddenly mindful of the elder Sengstackens with whom Lillian's good name now rested, "we shan't rely on this Mr. Dorff's word, I assure you. Lillian's uncle will be fetching her home right away. This very evening. Good night, Olive."

Clara replaced the receiver on its hook.

"Well done," Perkins said. "And if you'll tell me where I'm fetching her from, I'll be off."

"Uncle Paul, I'll go with you. It will be best to take the train to get to Santa Monica. I only wish Sam and the girls were home. Sam . . . Sam would know what to . . ."

At her husband's name her voice trailed away, then Paul said, "They are home, I believe. Don't I hear steps on the porch?" As he spoke, Adeline pushed open the door.

But behind her was only Joanna. Clara stiffened.

"Why are you so late?" she scolded quickly. "Where is your father, girls? Your supper will be—" But staring at their stricken faces, she broke off. "Sam! Something has happened to Sam, hasn't it?"

Joanna ran and threw her arms tight about her. "Mama, oh,

Mama! We waited so long without knowing, and then when his dirigible was found—"

She couldn't continue, and Adeline, dully at first, took up the story. "The engine quit. Just above the field. But he's had that happen several times before, so we weren't worried, not then—a great dirigible pilot like Papa." She took a deep shuddering breath. "He drifted away. The hours went by and there wasn't any word, and after everyone else was back, all the men went off to hunt for him in cars and in the little aeroplanes. . . .

"Finally, a farmer called in. He didn't have a telephone so he'd had to ride into town before he could tell anyone. But then he said . . . he said . . ."

Dell, too, could not speak the final fatal words. As they hung in the air, her composure cracked. She cried loudly, "Papa, Papa!" and burst into keening sobs.

"He'd hit against the side of a cliff," Joanna explained. "He was thrown out and he . . . fell. There were rocks . . . Papa's dead, Mama."

Sam—dead? Dear, good, kind Sam—dead? Clara wondered that her own heart didn't stop beating, it felt so cold and still inside her.

"I thought dirigibles were safe! Didn't he always tell us they were safe?" This was Dell, crying out the disbelief, the shock they all felt.

Clara shut her eyes, saying to herself, *When I open them, he'll have walked in the door.* In the darkness behind her eyelids she could see his face so clearly, his eyes softening at the sight of her, his smile that was always ready for her even when he was tired, or discouraged, or unhappy—

Unhappy—dear God, he'd known! She was certain he had. Almost certain.

Sam! Come home, Sam! Don't do this to me. Don't make me wonder—always—

She opened her eyes and her uncle, watching, saw that they were bright with anguish. But she freed herself from Joanna's embrace and said quietly, "They'll be bringing him home tonight?"

"Yes, Mama, very soon," Joanna said.

"Then I shall wait here. Will one of you go with Uncle Paul to Santa Monica? Lillian must be told. She must come back at once."

Dell, always so jealous of Lillian, did not ask a question or even seem to hear. Her pain at losing her beloved father had obliterated all else.

It was Joanna who answered. "If you want me to, Mama, I'll go. But don't you need us all here with you?"

There was hurt in the young voice, and Paul said, "Your mother will be better for a little while alone, I think." He glanced again at Clara. Clara, standing stiff and tormented, was already alone.

Joanna, still in her bonnet and cape from the afternoon, walked to the door. As Paul hobbled past her, the girl looked back at her mother and said with passion, "I will hate flying for all the rest of my life. Flying killed Papa!"

Clara could not meet her eyes.

Part Two

1915–1918

Footfalls echo in the memory
Down the passage which we did not take
Towards the door we never opened
Into the rose garden.
                                        —T. S. ELIOT

Chapter 16

The ice cream concession had been sold, the deer had been sold. With her other new responsibilities, it was all Dell could do just to keep the carousel going.

Joanna had wept when the deer with their large limpid eyes were loaded into a wagon and taken away. Some were destined to spend the rest of their lives in a small park in San Diego, but what would happen to the rest she didn't dare think. She'd been so unhappy about them, in fact, she'd offered to give up her hard-won employment at the newspaper and go on working at Chutes Park. But Mama had said *no*, firmly. She'd said Papa had considered Joanna the brightest of his children, and had expected more for her than that.

Secretly, Joanna was relieved. She did so want to go on being a copygirl at the *Times* newspaper, every day after school sniffing printer's ink and nurturing her dreams of one day becoming a bona fide reporter. Come summer, she would have finished two years of high school, and that was enough. Then she'd begin working for the newspaper full time.

This June afternoon was so beautiful that even though she was all of sixteen years old, she swung her hat by the ribbons and skipped along the sidewalk. Then she remembered the terrible news she'd learned at the *Times* today, and guiltily slowed to a sedate walk.

How could she be so unfeeling? All those people—more than a thousand—drowned! A German submarine, which must have been manned by monsters, without a word of warning had fired two torpedoes into the steel side of the British passenger ship *Luisitania*, and most of those aboard her, men, women, and little children, had met their fate in the rough and icy waters off Queenstown.

The first brief stories to come in by wire were heartrending. An Irish trawler reached port with a cargo of bodies. Two drowned children were found clasped together in death, terror written on their small faces. Then a survivor was interviewed, a stunned and almost incoherent man who had been at luncheon with friends in the dining saloon, the dining saloon of first class, he repeated, as though still unable to believe that such an elegant, luxurious room shouldn't have been safe. The orchestra had been playing the "Blue Danube Waltz," and if anyone had mentioned danger, he'd have laughed. Yes, laughed! After all, the captain had assured them all that their swift Cunard liner could elude and outdistance any U-boat in the sea. Yet, almost in an instant, the dishes were swept away in a tremendous rush of water, the table was submerged, and his companions died. The *Luisitania* sank within fifteen minutes of being hit.

It was when word finally came that more than a hundred of the victims were Americans that Joanna had the full horror brought home to her. Charles Gold, her friend from the days of language lessons at Aunt Flossie's, the young man who had so kindly spoken for her at the *Times*, had only recently gone to Europe to cover the war. Could he have been aboard the *Luisitania*?

She experienced a few hours of wretched fear, her concern surprising her in its intensity. But late the same day a dispatch from the French front was delivered, bearing his byline, and she breathed again. Only to reflect that he was now in the trenches.

Everyone in America who could read knew about those trenches and what happened at the dreaded order, "Over the top!" News reporters, taking their own lives in their hands, had described how the soldiers carrying fixed bayonets must scramble out and dash across *no-man's land*, flinging grenades, struggling through barbed wire, and trying to evade gaping shell holes and land mines, only to die, so very many of them, under a withering barrage of machine gun fire. Those who lived to fight again did so back in their muddy holes, along with swarms of rats and other vermin. They were sick and exhausted men, profoundly grateful for a brief respite when it came—when the battle communiques reported, "All quiet along the Western Front."

A terrible thing, this war in Europe, and Joanna was exposed every day to the harrowing news.

Yet, when a girl was sixteen, when a May sun shone and a balmy breeze caressed her face and arms, it was impossible to agonize constantly over battles in a foreign land. This war had been going on for almost a year now, ever since Archduke Francis Ferdinand of Austria and Hungary was assassinated. His murder had touched off the tinderbox, and the truth was, it was all so far away!

Once again, she couldn't help herself—she forgot. There was an orange poppy bravely rearing its head among the weeds of a vacant lot and after she picked it and quickened her pace again, she was humming a dance tune, the new "Castle Rag."

Next week, when he returned from the Air Circus in San Diego, Tony would be taking her to Castles-by-the-Sea again. Such fun! The dance pavilion run by Vernon and Irene Castle at Long Beach was so popular that one needed reservations weeks in advance. Tony and she had already learned to rumba and tango, but Joanna loved best the old Toddle, now known as the Castle Walk. In fact, she loved dancing so much, more than almost anything, she could have done it day and night. The only real worry she had, except for her nagging apprehensions about Charles Gold involved over there in Europe's war, was Tony. Tony continued to fly aeroplanes.

They argued about this passion of his endlessly. Their most recent evening at the dance pavilion had almost been spoiled because as usual he insisted on treating her aversion to flying as a passing feminine prejudice, best dealt with by pretending it didn't exist.

They'd been sitting at a choice table at the edge of the shining wooden floor, and both were silent for a moment, admiring the graceful sweeping steps of the two Castles, Vernon and Irene, as they demonstrated the tango.

But then Tony, looking handsome himself and so respectable in his starched collar and cuffs, not at all like a daredevil flyer, had said as though his mind were faraway, "Say, I forgot to tell you. I heard the most amazing thing! A Curtiss exhibition pilot has looped the loop more than a thousand times. Can you believe that?"

Joanna pressed her lips together and kept her eyes on the Castles. Really, it was too much! Even here, in this enchanted pavilion! Ever since some crazy pilot had demonstrated that a plane could be flown upside down, Tony had been obsessed with doing acrobatics in the air himself. And what was almost worse, he insisted on telling her every bit of his progress, as though one day she'd reply, "Oh, Tony, how wonderful!"

"It's the same man, Beachey—the one I told you about

said, was Joanna, who'd been left in his care. They both, of course, knew the unspoken truth—that he'd been left in hers. She was sensible and capable, and took pains to make certain he didn't overstrain his back.

In return, he was a good companion. He did as much work as he could. Like many men who had long lived alone, he was an excellent cook, so tonight her tardiness wouldn't matter at all. A savory lamb stew simmered on top of the big cast-iron range, and lamb stew was one of Clara's favorites.

Joanna was setting the table when she heard the popping exhaust noise of an automobile out in the street, and she ran to the door. Yes, it was Lillian's car. Most people were content to drive a Model T Ford, plain, black, reliable. But this was a Hudson, a bright, cheerful yellow and chrome monster, but low-slung, containing only one seat barely wide enough for two.

The ladies removing themselves from its embrace did the car and its stylish appearance full justice. Once they had entered the house and divested themselves of their duster coats, protective hats, veils, and scarves, Joanna exclaimed with all sincerity about the clothes revealed beneath. Mama, though not so high fashion as Lillian, was more elegant than Joanna had ever seen her. Her gown was of watered silk with a short overtunic of lace, both fabrics being the same deep cornflower blue as her eyes. At her throat was a large chiffon rose that exactly matched the wide sash around her narrow waist.

"Mama, how lovely!" Joanna exclaimed.

"I still sew," was Mama's reply.

Uncle Paul chuckled, "You could hardly dish out ice cream in that outfit, though," and Mama laughed, but a little ruefully. Did she regret that those days of hard labor at the park were long over?

It was difficult not to gasp at Lillian's appearance, Joanna and her uncle were finding. Not for Lillian the restricting hobble or the high tight ruching around the neck. Her dress was cut in a U at the throat, and it was possible at times, when she leaned forward, to get an accidental glimpse of round, full, perfect breasts. Even the length of the skirt was different, with the result that the eye was drawn to a few inches of slim shapely legs, revealed between the hem and her high-heeled satin shoes, set with glittering buckles on the front. A deceptively simple, free-falling gown, which somehow combined youthful innocence with more than a hint of sophistication. Mama, one might suspect, no longer sewed for Miss Lily French.

Both mother and daughter wore their hair according to the dictates of fashion—Clara's neatly coiffed; Lillian's cut into short curls around her face, with three long gleaming tresses pulled forward across one shoulder. Joanna, whose own fair hair was piled loosely with pins atop her head, the pins having badly failed in their duty during a long day, permitting stray tendrils to escape about her face and neck, wished too late she had come home earlier, with time to tidy herself.

Her sister meanwhile was giving the room a casual scrutiny, as she had not been home in some time. She did work very hard, long hours, Joanna knew, and she wondered if Lillian, who must be earning a good salary now, and associating with others who did, was finding her old home small and tawdry.

Mama, having hugged Joanna and smiled fondly at Uncle Paul, said, "My, you two are a welcome sight. Even though you aren't very far away, we don't see you nearly often enough."

Paul said, "How is the weaving coming? Have you had an exhibit yet?"

Joanna glanced over at the fireplace, before which on the floor there lay a splash of green and yellow. Mama, surprising them, had brought it for Christmas last year, explaining that she'd purchased a loom—and, well, she thought this little rug would brighten the house. Joanna loved it. The colors were clear and clean. Like trees in sunlight.

But Clara gave her uncle a puzzled frown. "Why do you keep suggesting an exhibit? I'm not nearly good enough, and anyway, I only made a few rugs to keep myself busy. Just now I am more interested in painting miniatures. But let's talk about something important—Joanna, you wrote me that you did get work with the newspaper. That's splendid!"

"I was terribly pleased." Joanna flushed with pleasure at Mama's interest. Mama, these last few years, had given the lion's share of her attention to Lillian. Joanna had once overheard Uncle Paul chide Mama for her partiality, and Mama had said, "Hardly partiality. Duty. My duty to the one who needs me most." Which was puzzling. Dell, surely, poor unhappy Dell, needed Mama most. Yet when Uncle Paul himself suggested that might be so, Mama had answered sharply, "Dell I can do nothing for!"

"I was lucky that the paper would hire someone so inexperienced," Joanna told Mama.

Mama nodded, but Lillian spoke first. "And why did they?"

"I was introduced by an acquaintance, a Mr. Charles Gold,

who used to take German lessons with Aunt Flossie. I didn't ask him to help me—I wouldn't have had the courage! But when I went in to apply, he was there. . . ."

She had, like a coward, procrastinated for a matter of weeks, knowing full well how young she was and fearing the embarrassment of a summary refusal. But finally, driven by her conviction that this was the kind of work she wanted to do, she took the streetcar down to First and Broadway to the *Times* building. Though quailing inwardly, she forced herself to walk through the door.

There was a small reception desk but no one in attendance, and beyond, in the crowded, noisy, smoke-filled room, the frenetic activity was intimidating. She stood watching the newspaper staff, listening to the typewriters clack, and smelling for the first time the characteristic odor she would later always associate with this place—a smell compounded of tobacco, ink, and newsprint.

"Copyboy!" someone yelled, and when there was no answer to this imperious command the speaker jumped to his feet and stormed away into a room beyond, one hand clutching the mop of his hair in exaggerated desperation, the other holding with care a sheaf of manuscript.

To break into this very busy atmosphere required a brashness Joanna was far from possessing. She began to retreat, and it was then that Charles Gold issued from what appeared to be a small office, still carrying on a conversation with some invisible person inside.

"All right, Ed. New York first. But I'm next in line to cover the war. I want to get over to France as soon as . . . hello, miss. Can I—Joanna!" He stared at her, a broad smile breaking. "You've grown up a little, haven't you? How old are you now? Oh, I'm sorry. One doesn't ask a young lady such a question, does one?"

"It's all right." She was so glad to be talking to someone at last, especially glad it was Charles. "I'm sixteen."

"You were going on eleven, I think, when we took those lessons together."

"That's right."

"And I suppose you've come here today to be a reporter, just as you decided at that early age?"

He was teasing her, she knew. He really thought she must have come to inform the society editor about some party or other. People did that.

She said earnestly, "Yes, I have. Mr. Gold, please don't laugh—"

"I'm not laughing." And he wasn't.

"You see, I want to, very very much!"

"Then let's talk about it. Here, you can sit at Monica's desk till she gets back. It's private enough out here, and quieter."

She sat on the edge of the hard little chair, her confidence rekindled. He was being so very kind!

But he said, "Joanna, I'll be honest with you. Even with my recommending you, Ed McGowan, he's the city editor, won't take you on. Not as a reporter, when you've had no experience at all. I doubt if you can even typewrite."

"No. Do I have to?"

"I'm afraid so, these days. But you'd learn quickly, I'm sure. It's just—sixteen is years too young, I'm afraid."

She tried hard to hide her disappointment. "Well, then, I suppose I may as well go home. I was silly to think—but thank you—"

"Wait, you didn't let me finish. If you'd like, though, I can get you on as copyboy—I mean copygirl. You see, one of the boys didn't work out. Too lazy to come to work today and they need someone right now. Want to try it?"

"Oh yes, yes! Thank you! Oh, yes—"

"Fine. Ah, here's Monica." He looked over at a young woman who had just entered the building. "Our receptionist. Monica, meet Joanna. She's going to be working here."

Joanna, realizing she occupied the other's seat, jumped up quickly, and Monica took her place. She was petite, pretty, and very self-assured, Joanna noticed.

"Good," the receptionist said. "Another female around this place will be welcome. Charles, can you call for me about six tonight? I'm going to be getting home late."

"Sure can. Six it is . . . Come on, Joanna, let's go talk to our city editor."

Lucky Monica, Joanna thought fleetingly, and then was led away to meet Edwin McGowan.

"Charles Gold," Lillian said. "I remember him."

"Yes, he mentioned to me that he'd met you."

"You must tell me all about him and what he's doing. I saw one of his articles on the Kaiser. Clever. And he's quite handsome, isn't he, in a strong quiet way? A good deal older than you—he must be all of twenty-seven. . . . Oh, but of course, I forgot. For you there's always Tony."

"Always Tony? I don't understand what you mean."

Uncle Paul, at repose in his favorite armchair, rescued Joanna. He said, "So you're doing well, are you, Miss Lily French, out there in Hollywood? It seems only yesterday that Sam took me for a drive over that way and all I saw was farms—vegetables, flowers, livestock. I recall that the peas and strawberries were magnificent. There were a few houses, but on the whole I'd say there were more sheep than people. Things must have changed."

"Oh, they have, Uncle Paul! Changed greatly! Hollywood now is an exciting, busy place. It's become the true center for motion pictures, instead of New York.

"And all because of chance, did you know that? A man named Al Christie tossed a coin with his partner, who wanted to move their little studio from New York to Florida. Christie won the toss so they came to California instead. They needed very cheap property, and the best they could find was some acreage near a saloon out on a dusty country lane. They began making one-reel westerns behind the saloon, doing a good job, too, using real scenery, real Indians. Well, then, you see, other producers were quick to remark how few delays Christie had from the weather, and more and more came out here, gathering in the same area.

"Of course, it's really several communities now; my own company, for instance, is in Edendale. But to the public everything's Hollywood."

Paul, while amused by Lillian's proprietary air, was much interested in these glimpses into the new, burgeoning film industry. He noticed, however, that Clara no longer listened. She gazed out the window in the direction of the park, lost in her own thoughts. She must have heard all this scores of times, he supposed, and be tired to death of it, especially with the discouraging setbacks Lillian had had. So much time had passed since Bert Lange first set Lillian's feet on this enticing path.

She'd initially been hired by an obscure company with a shady reputation for the recruiting of underage girls, although to do her agent justice, with his strong faith in her potential, he had believed she wouldn't remain there long. And she hadn't. On the basis of this experience in minor parts, he'd wangled her a contract with a more savory outfit. Here she had just progressed to being the second lead in some serial cliffhangers, when disaster struck and through no fault of her own.

Some years before, Thomas Edison had begun suing independent producers for patent infringements, only allowing certain favored companies known as *The Trust* the use of the Edison camera. Naturally, the independents continued to import or construct their own bootleg equipment, and one of the common reasons for moving out of New York was to escape the eagle eye of *The Trust*. Lillian's second employer was caught, however, hauled into court, and bankrupted. Her toehold on the ladder thus was lost, and she was reduced to the ignominy of being an extra.

Of late though, she was on her way again. A real opportunity had come her way, and she was, she told her family with only slight exaggeration, on the verge of becoming a *star*!

She sounded to Paul's ear, although happy, surprisingly composed. He was disturbed by this air of complete confidence. Had she never considered failure? Bert Lange was right—she had the necessary attributes. But so did others. The competition was growing daily. The newspapers ran pictures of crowds of hopeful girls arriving every day on the trains, pretty girls, piquant girls, all appealing and young. So very young!

He sighed. No, Lillian would fight with everything she had, so failure to her was unthinkable. He only hoped she wasn't too inflexible, too brittle. Brittle things were so easily broken.

How different this girl was from her sisters! From Dell, who endured with stoic strength. Who was enduring now. Or from Joanna. Joanna with her sensible path stretching straight ahead—the work at the newspaper, and Tony. Her future, it seemed to him, he could easily predict.

But never Lillian's.

Chapter 17

It was true, Lillian had not failed to keep her eyes open to opportunity. Thus when a slim chance of working for Mack Sennett at the Keystone Company came along, she hadn't needed any of Bert's urging. She'd climbed on the streetcar and presented herself at the Edendale lot the next morning.

Early as she was, the studio had been hard at work for many hours, which didn't surprise her. She had long ago learned that because the light was poorest at noon when the sun was directly overhead, shooting usually began at sunup, stopped at ten, and might not resume until after two. So on sets that she passed, the unwieldy cameras were busily grinding, and the directors, shouting directions at the actors through their megaphones, already sounded hoarse.

With the jaunty yet very feminine gait that she'd practiced until it became habit, Lillian made her way toward the high, narrow, wooden structure towering above the various stages and backdrops surrounding it. A major Keystone actress, Mabel Normand, whose unassuming friendliness the night before had surprised and baffled Lillian, had suggested she try there first, and had added that if dearest Mack (so she referred to the studio head) hadn't come charging down to the lot because of some crisis or other, he could usually be discovered at the top, keeping his kingdom under close surveillance.

Mabel had smiled as she said this, and Lillian wondered uneasily if she herself wasn't being made the butt of some joke. Everyone knew the Sennett people were all great practical jokers. Even the boss himself had had his sense of humor tested when a full pail of water fell off the top of a door and dented his head. But Lillian, being practical, decided she had no choice but to assume Miss Normand's good intentions.

Used as she was to seeing screen personalities in person and finding many of them quite unremarkable—perhaps because who flew straight through a building—and that took some nerve all right! He's wild! Even I wouldn't try it. But I'm awfully pleased to say I've learned the tailspin. Just this week. Now if I can only master the Immelmann turn—"

He paused, but as she did not respond, he explained, "It's a combination half loop and half roll—"

"Tony!" She was stung into reproach. "The *Immelmann* turn? But that's German! I'd think you'd be ashamed to copy the enemy."

Tony retorted, "The enemy? I wasn't aware that *we* were at war." He looked at Joanna and his dark eyes lit with sudden excitement. "But that's just it, don't you see? If we do join in, I want to be ready. I may be only a barnstorming pilot, but I want to be as good with a plane as I can be, learn every trick the Germans know. Because I think war can be fought in the air and that's the way I want to fight it."

Joanna shuddered, envisioning the crude, open framework of Tony's little plane, but she only shook her head. No use protesting, borrowing trouble. America wasn't in it, most likely wouldn't be.

"Oh, look," she said, "the exhibition's over. Come on, Tony."

Then they were up and in each other's arms, the strands of electric lightbulbs bathing the floor in a flickering, many-colored glow. Joanna and Tony swayed and stepped in harmony, and Tony also seemed content to let the music wash away their disagreement.

Reliving the joy of their dancing together, Joanna smiled and walked in an unhurried pace along the sidewalk. Unfair as it might be, she thought, in America these were good times.

Reaching her house, she ran lightly up the steps. Only then did she recall that Mama and Lillian were coming all the way from Hollywood to have dinner tonight with her and Uncle Paul. Oh, my, they'd be here soon—she had nothing prepared! And with that, Tony and the war went out of her mind entirely.

Uncle Paul, as she might have known, had kept the date in mind. He was busily at work in the kitchen, whistling that low tuneless whistle Joanna had heard more and more often in the five years since Papa had died and Mama went off to be with Lillian and look after her. For Uncle Paul, Joanna knew, this very quiet life was good. His days were long and restful; he could sleep as late as he wished and he could read to his heart's content. The only responsibility he had, as he himself solemnly their charm only manifested itself when a camera crank was turning—Lillian still felt a stir of laughter bubble inside of her at sight of Charlie Chaplin, baggy pants, flip-flop shoes, black mustache, and all, shuffling his way onto a set. Then along came a tall, cadaverous man with bobbing Adam's apple, big soulful eyes, and a black-and-white-checked suit, the trousers of which rode high up his ankles. Slim Summerville who, as he passed, tipped her a wink. She was pleased, for she was incurably superstitious and felt that his friendly gesture might be a good omen.

She hurried on, dodging a lion being led on a chain as if it were a dog, hardly seeing the oddity, in fact, and soon found herself at the foot of the wooden tower.

With no hesitation, she opened the door and began to climb the staircase spiraling upward inside. It was a steep climb, up and up, toward the top story that soared a good thirty feet in the air, but she came at length to a platform on which a number of folding chairs were stacked drearily against the walls. Above the last few steps there was only a closed trapdoor, through which could now be heard a resonant bass, loudly, soulfully rendering "Asleep in the Deep."

Lillian rapped on the door overhead, and the singing broke off.

"Who is it?" Impossible to tell if the singer was annoyed by the interruption. The deep voice sounded sleepy, indolent.

"Lily French."

"Don't know any Lily French. Go away."

"You don't know me yet, but you will! Mr. Sennett, I must talk to you."

"See Joe Cavanaugh. Or Del Lord. Extras are hired in the north building . . . Abdullah, get ready to pound. In five minutes, I'm coming out." There was a noise of vigorous splashing, as if a large fish had stranded itself in shallow water.

"I'm not an extra," Lillian shouted. "I've had good parts in some very successful pictures."

She hoped she wouldn't have to be specific. At her old studio, now defunct, while she'd gotten some much-needed experience, she'd never had a starring role. But after a moment Sennett said, "Very well. I'll ask. Whose pictures?"

"I was with Sunshine."

She braced herself for probing questions, but Sennett, probably reluctant even to think about his late competitor whose unhappy fate could so easily be his own, merely said, "Young woman, Sunshine did serials. Melodrama. Cliffhangers. Never comedy. Surely you are aware that what we produce here is comedy? Be good enough to leave me in peace."

There was still her ace to play. She said calmly, "Miss Normand sent me."

"Indeed." A longer silence followed, punctuated by another heavy splash that might have been one of protest. Then the deep voice growled, "All right. Miss Normand doesn't do the hiring here, but I'll give you exactly two minutes. Abdullah, open the door."

The trap was thrown back and a moon-shaped ebony face, topped by a red-and-yellow-striped fez, gazed down.

Lillian stared back into the sorrowful agate eyes with lively interest. Along with the rest of Hollywood, she had heard about the gigantic ex-wrestler who was Sennett's masseur.

Abdullah gave her a nod of permission and she climbed past his gleaming bare shoulders. Then, although she'd been prepared by hearsay for what she would find at the top of the tower, her mouth pursed in a small whistle.

Most of the floor area was taken up by a black marble bathtub with silver fixtures. The tub was eight feet in length by five wide, and stood on ornate legs which were high enough to enable Sennett, soaking himself in comfort, to keep a constant lookout through the windows on all four sides.

"Well?" growled the bass voice, and Lillian's bemusement vanished. She concentrated on the owner of the room, Mr. Sennett, thinking as he ran a beefy hand through his thatch of thick black hair that he would be almost too perfect, cast in the part of a prosperous Irishman.

He was waiting, his florid face expressionless.

Guessing that his nudity, largely concealed by the frothy water, was expected to disconcert her, Lillian did not look away.

"Mabel—Miss Normand—said to tell you she thought I might be exactly what you're looking for. A comedienne, that is."

"Indeed. How well do you know Mabel? Don't bother lying."

Lillian was not tempted to lie. That this man and his highly successful female star had had an off-again, on-again romance for years was no secret. Even during their frequent quarrels they worked together. He'd know who his mistress's good friends were.

However the truth could always be stretched slightly.

"I know her to speak to."

"So you spoke to her. When did this conversation take place?"

"Last night. At a party of Fatty Arbuckle's."

"Who was Mabel with?"

Lillian shrugged. "I don't know. I think she must have been alone." The conversation was drifting far afield, and she tried to bring it back. "Anyway, we got to talking, and Mabel said she was sure I'd fit in here. She thinks so highly of the Keystone Kops and the comedies—"

"You needn't tell me what Mabel thinks of her own work," he said dryly. "Very well, if she sent you—let's see your knees."

This was far from the first time Lillian had complied with the same preemptory request. Pretty knees, she'd gathered, and the flashing glimpses of them that audiences received were crucial. Without fuss, she hoisted her skirt, revealing a little more perhaps than was needed. Lillian's legs were one of her best features and she knew it.

Sennett studied her, the shapely legs, the slender figure, the charming oval face. Then, looking, she thought, like a sleepy bear, he leaned back and shut his eyes. She was to learn that even in very minor matters, he never made a hasty decision. At length the eyes opened again, and he said, "All right. Report to Joe and he'll get you a costume. We're filming a Bathing Beauty sequence this morning. I suppose you can dance a little?"

"Yes, of course, but Mr. Sennett, I want to act in the comedies! Miss Normand said—"

"I make the decisions here, not Miss Normand." This, stated in his low but firm way, cut off any argument. "You'll start at twelve dollars a week. Good pay, too, considering that your lunch will be free. . . . Ready, Abdullah?"

That was all. Lillian was dismissed. He began to climb ponderously from the marble tub and she retreated, but not before giving him her smile, the one Bert Lange, her agent, told her to use often.

"Goodbye, Mr. Sennett. Thank you! I'll make good, you'll see."

"I'm sure you will, Miss French, or I wouldn't have hired you." He was on his feet. She turned and stepped away, wondering if she only imagined that she could feel his eyes watching that provocative walk of hers. She climbed down the steps, and the trapdoor slammed shut behind her.

She passed a bakery set on which the Keystone Kops were assembled for action, but she didn't linger, much as she would have enjoyed watching one of the famous pie-throwing scenes, all those zanies in police helmets and uniforms running about pelting each other with coconut custard. It seemed to her most important that she quickly locate Joe Cavanaugh and get herself officially hired. In all likelihood Mr. Sennett had put her out of his mind, but there was also the off-chance he just might bother to check with Miss Normand: "Mabel, just what *did* you say to that French girl?"

In actual fact, Lillian's recommendation from the actress had been briefer and far more casual than she'd indicated, although the conversation had taken place where and when she'd said. Lillian, through the earnest efforts of Bert Lange, had been one of the few aspiring young women invited to the Fatty Arbuckle party, otherwise attended only by established stars.

There had been the usual futile discussion with Clara ahead of time.

"Where is this party? The Hollywood Hotel? You know your father wouldn't approve of your going there so late at night. Anyway, respectable girls don't go to parties alone."

"I won't be alone," Lillian explained with what patience she could muster. There had been so many of these scenes, and they always ended with her doing exactly as she wished. Lillian suspected that Mama understood her through and through, knew these arguments were useless, and was only trying to please Papa who resided somewhere up in the sky and was still keeping an eye on Mama. "Bert's taking me. I told you that."

"I've never considered Bert Lange your ideal escort," Clara snapped. "A middle-aged man, and married."

This was so patently absurd that Lillian didn't bother answering. Bert had never made her an improper advance, and was quite frank about his objectives. He expected, through Lillian, to make money—a lot of it—to provide for his three children. Lillian's success hadn't come as fast as he'd hoped; after all, Hollywood was full of appealing young women and their numbers were growing daily. Even so, he firmly believed it was only a question of time.

Clara also abandoned the point. She said, "Very well, go!

I can't stop you. Sometimes I think I should give up and move back home, be of some use to Joanna. . . ."

Joanna, no mention of Dell, Lillian noted. Why had Dell's marriage so offended Mama that she'd even found an excuse to stay away from the wedding?

Her own interests crowded the question out of her mind, and she said in a conciliatory way, "No, Mama, please don't do that. I need you here. Living with one's mother gives a girl an air of respectability. The studios don't want actresses they think might cause trouble—there are too many others, and too much trouble already."

"Merely an *air* of respectability?" Clara's expression made Lillian uncomfortable and then mildly angry.

She said, "I don't let men take me to bed, if that's what you think," and watched her mother wince at her coarseness. But it was true, she didn't. Not for moral reasons particularly, but because she didn't want any distractions. There was room in her life now for only one ruling passion—her advancement in motion pictures.

"I don't drink, either," she added, which was true as well. She disliked the feeling of not being in control of herself, of not having her wits at their sharpest. One mild experiment had been enough. "So what are you worried about, Mama?"

"Drugs," Clara answered reluctantly, for to her even the dire word cast a shadow. Cocaine. Morphine. Heroin. The rumors that had reached her ears were numerous and frightening. Those young people, thinking themselves so worldly when actually they were innocents—foolish, trusting innocents, certain no evil could touch them!

Lillian said, "I suppose some of the actors may take drugs now and then. I don't really know. But they do say cocaine gives you pep."

"Lillian! You haven't . . . you aren't—"

"No, Mama, certainly not. I don't need that kind of help and I wouldn't like it, I'm sure."

"I'm very glad." To hide her relief, Clara picked up her shuttle and studied the half-completed work on her loom.

Lillian went to the party, as it had been a foregone conclusion she would. And Bert was proven right. The evening turned out to be of utmost importance for her, although there was no hint of this happy outcome during the early hours.

She'd felt such an outsider, standing about sipping her usual glass of selzer water (deceptive, and at the same time thirst quenching). All of the established actors knew each other and they congregated in tight little circles which shut out the merely hopeful. One man, well-known as a lover on the screen, did issue a whispered invitation to Lillian to view the art work on the walls of the adjoining bedroom—for this was a hotel suite, not a large ballroom as she'd allowed Clara to believe—but Lillian smilingly refused. She hoped he would remain at her side anyway, but he moved away, seeking out another of the neophytes.

Where was Bert? she wondered resentfully. He shouldn't leave her alone like this. But then her searching eyes discovered him on the far side of the room, deep in conversation with, of all people, the best-known actress present, the exquisite Mabel Normand.

Bert beckoned to Lillian and she hurried across to join them.

"This is Lily French, Miss Normand," he said proudly. "The one I've been telling you about . . . and Lily, this is—"

"Yes, I know!" No need to introduce Miss Normand! Tiny, slender yet curvaceous Mabel Normand was as beautiful in person as on the screen. Her dark hair lay in soft, natural-looking curls around her heart-shaped face, and her soulful nut brown eyes were the largest Lillian had ever seen. This actress already was acclaimed as one of the great comediennes. Every motion, every expression on her face moved an audience to smiles. But while most comics traded on awkwardness or stupidity, Mabel evoked an admiring and affectionate kind of laughter.

"Lily French," Mabel mused now. "What a good name for the screen." She was openly assessing Lillian. "Bert tells me you've had some experience."

"Oh, yes, Miss Normand, I have." Lillian was careful to hide her resentment. Surely Miss Normand must have noticed her in one of those serials, even if she wasn't the star! She considered explaining why she hadn't been, but held her tongue. No one wanted to hear any tales of hard luck. Whiners got nowhere. She said instead, brightly, "And I have confidence that I'll get a real break soon."

It was the right note. Bert was smiling.

Mabel nodded. She said to Bert, "I've owed you a favor or two for a long time, and I agree, Miss French is certainly as pretty as any of the Sennett Bathing Beauties. She should speak to Mack—and you can say I sent her."

"We'll do that, Miss Normand," Bert said, "and thank you!"

"Yes, indeed, thank you!" Lillian chimed in. Her mind was churning over the possibilities.

"Isn't Mabel something?" Bert exclaimed when he and Lillian were outside the hotel again, walking to his auto. His step was springier than it had been in months. "A great actress and a fine woman, too. Couldn't be finer! She's always ready to help someone."

In spite of the vistas unfolding in Lillian's imagination, this uncritical admiration annoyed her.

"After all, little Miss Normand was only paying off a debt to you, wasn't she?"

"Yes, but believe me, sister, most motion picture people have mighty short memories."

"Well, let's hope her help does me some good."

Lillian sounded composed, as always. But she barely slept during what was left of the night. She lay tense, her mind racing, as she waited for dawn and an hour late enough to call at Mr. Mack Sennett's famous tower.

Chapter 18

For Lillian, the following two years were filled with the excitement of being certain, quite certain, that although still a Bathing Beauty, she was on her way up. Finally, proving her right, one unseasonably warm June day found her dining in an intimate threesome with Mabel Normand and Zelda Thomas. Miss Thomas, an ethereal young actress from Universal, being groomed, it was said, as a rival for Mary Pickford, was a frequent visitor on the Keystone lot.

The hot, airless commissary was crowded, but only with actors under contract. The extras ate outside in the shade of some pepper trees, their lunch issued to them in brown paper bags; and very good lunches they were, too. But Lillian felt nothing but satisfaction as she observed the recumbent, still-costumed crowd through a dusty window. Never again would she be one of them, outside, looking in. She was not only the highest-paid member of the Bathing Beauty line, she'd had small acting parts in several pictures with Mabel, filling in for someone else, and after lunch today she was to have her chance in a leading role. It was difficult to simulate calm, but she watched the extras and ate her overdone steak and wilting fruit salad with every appearance of appetite.

There was good cause for her complacency. As a Bathing Beauty she had made good money. Currently she received $40 a week, and was getting what Bert called *good exposure* as well. Heavens, exposure was right! The bathing dresses were travesties of the usual bathing costume. The skirt came to above the knees, sometimes with a stiff wire laced through the hem which made it swing saucily like a bell. The girls wore white stockings up to the knees, with toe-dance-type shoes laced with ribbons around the ankles. The knees were exposed, and of course, whatever the low-cut neck of the blouse revealed. However, perky hats lent the costume a comic air of propriety, and the studio publicist made certain the public was told all about Blanche Payson, the six-foot policewoman who guarded the entrance to the girls' dressing room, and was quoted as saying grimly that if any actor on the lot thought he'd help a young lady get ahead and then reap his reward, he was very much mistaken.

But what Bert meant by exposure was that hardly a week went by without a picture being made with her in it. The Bathing Beauties quickly became familiar figures to the moviegoers, even though the girls provided only a small part of the famous Keystone humor that rocked audiences off their chairs. Even more important, the directors at Keystone, who attended showings of all the films, had their favorites and often cast them in small parts.

So Lillian had forced herself to be patient. And only today, her patience had been rewarded.

Mabel, hard at work herself for endless hours a day, had surprised Lillian by never forgetting she existed and always speaking pleasantly whenever they met. Yesterday, Mabel had stopped, as usual, and by chance one of the Kops, in full costume, had passed by. He'd rolled his eyes at Lillian, simpering a silly, admiring grin, and she'd given him a big wink right back, fluttering her eyelashes as if she were about to swoon in his arms. Her silliness had made both the Kop and Mabel laugh, and the next morning Mabel had said to her,

"Mack thinks you ought to have a try at being a comedienne."

Lillian refrained from retorting, "So I've thought all this time," and answered, "Oh, I'd love to!"

"I hope you're strong enough."

Little Mabel, who tipped the scale at less than a hundred pounds, worked hour after hour without seeming to tire. But mere endurance wasn't what she meant and Lillian, familiar with movie making on this lot, understood. Although times were changing, Keystone still used no stand-ins. As much was faked as possible, but if someone was required to leap from a burning building, he leaped. Into a net perhaps, but he leaped. If he was dragged by a runaway horse, he was dragged. Many of the actors were stuntmen by profession, but others weren't.

"You can ride a horse?"

"Of course." In fact, Lillian had never ridden a real "riding" horse in her life, and only once in a while had she straddled the back of Papa's mild old Ned. But wait, what about all the carousel horses? She almost laughed aloud.

"You've got to know how to do a *108*," Mabel continued.

"I do." Lillian spoke this time with genuine assurance. Anyone wanting to do comedy who hadn't mastered the pratfall was a fool.

"Well, then, there's no time like the present. The writers have come up with an idea for the Shriners' Parade this afternoon. I'm tied up on something else, so . . ."

Again Lillian needed no explanation. Just as they freely used the streets and local stores for background, directors always tried to take advantage of actual crowds in order to avoid the expense of hiring extras. There would be one quick runthrough on the lot, in order to time the action to fit the reels, then when the parade came past the cameras were ready to shoot.

So that morning they'd had the run-through, and afterward Lillian ate with Mabel and Zelda Thomas. It was easier than she expected, to conceal her excitement at the challenging prospect just ahead, because Miss Thomas was evidently unwell.

After a few polite and desultory remarks, the pretty Universal star fell silent, and sat staring at her untouched plate while her fingers played tremulously with a spoon. She was very pale, with a film of perspiration on her forehead.

Mabel, tiny as she was, as usual was paying full attention to her food, but at length she became aware of her friend's preoccupation and said, "Zelda dear, are you all right?"

"Oh, yes, Mabel. Isn't the Count here today?" The normally soft voice was taut as a stretched wire. "Surely—he's always at Keystone, isn't he?"

"I'm certain he's here someplace," Mabel answered, and Lillian turned as well to scan the crowded room for the tall, pleasant-spoken actor known as the Count. She'd noticed herself how constantly he was present on the lot, and wondered a little—the parts assigned to him were not only small and unimportant but infrequent. However his lack of advancement must not have disturbed him greatly because he was invariably smiling and in good humor. Even more remarkable, he was on a first-name basis with everyone, stars as well as other bit players.

At the moment he was not in sight, and Mabel reached across the table and patted Miss Thomas's hand reassuringly. "I promise you he's here. Let's go find him."

Miss Thomas sighed gratefully. "I do have a frightful hangover. Thanks for bothering." Already she was on her feet. She seemed to have forgotten Lillian altogether.

But Mabel, before hurrying off, took time to say, "Good luck, Lily," and in such a warm tone there was no doubt she meant it.

Lillian, dressed as a woman prison warden, yet looking, she was well aware, all the prettier for the severe uniform and stiff mannish hat, found herself in the studio "patrol car," a monstrosity capable of carrying, sardine fashion, fourteen Keystone Kops. Packed in as they all were, the humor naturally evolved from the jostling, and the lady warden found herself riding first on one lap then another, bouncing high with every swerve as the huge car wove its precarious way among the marching Shriners. Each time, she landed with her face pressed against that of a Kop, dead white, bristling with black mustache and eyebrows, and beaming with ecstacy at her sudden proximity. Each time, she walloped her partner before being bounced away.

As usual, most of the miming was impromptu. The writers never had time to map out details of their wild plots, and actors were expected to draw on their own talent for laughs. But timing was important, and the director, balancing himself on the seat of the camera car alongside, megaphone at his lips, constantly shouted orders.

"Anton, fall over the side!"

"Lily, not so stern! You like it. You *like* it!"

"Faster, driver—you're due at the corner now!"

Lillian never failed to respond to direction instantly. She first looked as prudish and annoyed as she possibly could, yet snuggled into each lap in turn with a perceptible wiggle. She could actually feel the cool regard of the camera, and it stimulated her to ham and gesticulate with abandon. She was totally absorbed, even forgetting while the scene lasted that her career was in the balance.

Up ahead in the crowd, under the eye of another camera, the pickpocket, who was Slim Summerville, had gone to work. The car full of Kops, with their arms flailing, their mouths open in shouts, sped up and was in full pursuit, leaving the marchers behind. But at the corner, the thief had overturned a barrel of liquid soap. The car slammed on its brakes too late, and swerved madly from one side to the other. Spectators scattered in all directions while Kops flew through the air like popcorn from a hot pan.

Lillian, still inside, spotted Summerville and leaped out, doing a 108 on the slippery paving. Jumping to her feet, she pursued him into the nearby bakery. Slim threw a pie that splattered on Lillian's face, the Kops arrived, and the usual comic fight ensued.

One take only. After all, the studio could hardly wait until there was another Shriners Parade to correct mistakes. For better or for worse, *The Pickpocket* was in the can.

Mack Sennett, after watching the screening, growled, "Not too bad, Lily," and Mabel, who had just returned from a filming at Catalina Island, for once looking exhausted herself, still took the time to say that she'd heard Lily French did very, very well.

But Mabel's friendship soon ceased to be quite so important. Four more quick two-reelers in as many weeks, and suddenly a few people were pointing out Lily French on the street. Bert Lange, one day, wearing a new tweed suit and a fine brown derby hat, suggested she buy a Russian wolfhound, outfit him with a fake jewel collar, and, dressing herself as stylishly as possible, be observed walking her aristocratic pet on Hollywood Boulevard.

Lillian's star was on the rise.

Chapter 19

"Wasn't that an absurd idea? But I did as Bert told me, and bought a dog. His name is Ivan."

"Why absurd?" Joanna was genuinely puzzled. "If you wanted a pet—"

"Oh, don't be so silly," Lillian said, but in high good humor. Dinner was over, Uncle Paul's stew had been delicious, and the family was displaying a gratifying interest in her experiences. "A Russian wolfhound is hardly just a pet, Joanna. Bert's idea is that Ivan, with his fancy collar and those long graceful legs, will give me a different image—put me more in the public eye."

"Your sister, Joanna, is nothing if not ambitious," Clara commented. Her smile took the slight sting from the words, but Paul turned to regard his niece. She sounded and looked tired. Although thinness became her, to his mind she was far too slender and he wondered with sadness if the violet shadows beneath her eyes would ever be erased, He'd noticed them first at the time of Sam's death and saw them deepen with Adeline's sudden marriage. Clara, for some reason, had been appalled by that news, and intuitively so, as it turned out.

As if she read his thoughts, Clara surprised him by saying, "I hoped Dell might be here tonight."

"I suspect she wanted to be. I invited her. But—" He grimaced. "It would have been difficult."

Clara nodded, acknowledging that the fault was hers—her refusal to allow Dell's husband to be included in any family gathering. Nor would he have come, she was sure, but none of them realized that. "How is Dell?"

"Healthy enough," he answered promptly. So much was true. Adeline's sturdy body never seemed to reflect any adversity or unhappiness she might encounter.

He was hesitating because there was more to tell, and he

wondered how forthright he should be. Had Dell confided in him in expectation that he would pass along the news to her family?

He decided she had. "In fact, although I'm certain it isn't common knowledge, she is going to have a child."

Clara said, "Is she indeed!" Her tone was tart.

Joanna exchanged a glance with Paul and both were silent, but Lillian remarked lightly, "Well, Mama, we all know Dell hasn't been very happy, so perhaps a baby will be good for her. I do believe she's cut out for motherhood—"

Clara interrupted, her voice cold. "I hardly think, Lillian, that you have any notion what Adeline is cut out for."

"And you do?" her daughter retorted. "You who haven't set foot in her house since she married? The rest of us at least visit her now and then."

Again Joanna looked uncomfortably at Paul. They found this exchange, indicative of long-standing friction, disturbing. Worse, Lillian was heedlessly treading on dangerous ground. Clara had made it very clear to them that her feelings on Adeline's marriage were a private matter.

After a short silence, Clara spoke to Paul, ignoring Lillian's outburst so pointedly that color flamed in the girl's face.

"So Adeline is to be saddled with a family, is she? That means she can never escape from him. Never! Uncle Paul, you could not have given me worse news."

Paul hesitated, then he said quietly, "Becoming a father can change a man."

"Nonsense. Forgive me, all of you, but you don't understand. Anyway, I don't care to discuss the matter further. Sam would be shocked to hear us talking about Dell's condition in the hearing of his two unmarried daughters."

"Heavens above, Mama!" Lillian exclaimed, and Joanna stared at her mother open-mouthed. Such a Victorian taboo had long since passed from fashion. And even if it hadn't, the Clara they knew had never been noted for primness.

But just how well did they know Clara? Paul reminded himself that the Clara of yesterday was not the Clara of today. He had been aware for some time that the blows she had sustained had changed her, perhaps irrevocably. The girl of the carnival, rather fey and dreamy yet possessed of a surprising fund of common sense, that Clara, dear to him, was gone forever.

In her place was this lovely remote stranger, the mother of

an aspiring motion picture actress, and herself an artist of sorts. For a year or two, weaving rugs had occupied her time. Of late, it seemed, it was the painting of miniatures. She would take a snapshot, study the two-dimensional sepia face, and then paint a portrait on the small ivory surface of a brooch. He had seen a sample of this recent work, too—she had given him a likeness of Lillian—and he found it good, just as the weaving was good. Yet soon, he was sure, her interest in this pursuit also would wane, and she would cast about for something else. She was an unhappy woman, frittering away her talents. A dabbler in the arts, and in life.

Clara wasn't the only one who had changed in the years since Sam's death. Joanna was no longer the dutiful daughter obeying without argument, and she said now, stiffly, "I do assure you, Mama, that I know where babies come from. Also how they are made. Anyhow, one woman's pregnancy isn't awfully important these days, is it? I mean, not with all the men dying in that dreadful war in Europe?"

Clara's eyes softened. For a moment she was the old warm and loving Clara as she said, "My little one has grown up, it seems. And she is quite right, isn't she, Uncle Paul? The values have changed, and if I'm not careful, I'll lose touch with both my girls."

Lillian said nothing. She was gazing at the floor. And Paul, catching a glimpse of her solemn expression, was convinced that until that moment the young actress, absorbed in her own affairs, had been unaware there even was a war.

Joanna, however, encouraged by this evidence of understanding, found herself returning to the forbidden subject. She spoke in a rush, as if wanting to voice her concern before resolution failed.

"You haven't lost touch with me, Mama, nor with Lillian, and you won't. Even if we don't always agree with you. But have you forgotten, Mama, that Dell is your daughter? Why do you continue to avoid her husband and never visit her house, as Lillian said? I know she married too soon after Papa died, but surely, if you care about her . . ."

The smile had vanished from Clara's face, and Joanna's words trailed away. "Care about her?" Clara said. "Certainly I do." She turned to Lillian. "I think we must go. Didn't you tell me you needed to be at work very early tomorrow?"

"Yes, Mama, that's right." Lillian began swathing herself in her driving apparel. The mention of the morning had been sufficient reminder, and her thoughts already were miles away from this house on Los Angeles Street.

Paul, however, decided that enough damage had been done and the evening sufficiently ruined that a little more discord wouldn't matter. He said, "Dell is going to need you, Clara, when her time comes. Flossie has no experience in such matters, and otherwise your daughter will be attended by strangers. Remember that, won't you?"

To his relief, she put her arms about him and kissed him. "I'll remember, never fear. Good night, dear Uncle Paul, Joanna . . ."

Chapter 20

Adeline raked the ashes from beneath the oven of her towering, black iron stove, and then stood leaning against the edge of the kitchen table, regarding with satisfaction the warm loaves of bread, set in a neat row.

She'd always loved baking, and although she felt nauseated almost all the time these days, a condition which for some reason wasn't improving as quickly as she'd been led by Aunt Flossie to expect, the yeasty aroma didn't disturb her to the extent that most food smells did.

She'd been up since four, because the dough had been rising overnight and she didn't want to leave it longer while she worked at the park. Now the day still stretched ahead, the long hours of running the carousel, and she marveled that she had once looked forward to that grueling work with such pleasure.

But even Adeline, unimaginative as she was, understood why her pleasure had soured. After Papa died, no one cared how efficient she was. No one said, "Dell, what would this family do without you!"

Oh, Papa, Papa, I loved you so. How I miss you!

"Breakfast ready?" The words, as usual, were grunted at

her. Lost in thought, she hadn't heard his footsteps on the stairs.

"Yes. Sit down."

He took a chair beside the oilcoth-covered table, and wordlessly she slid three fried eggs from the skillet onto his plate. Slices of ham followed, and bread, and a steaming mug of coffee.

As always, in his presence, conscious of the scorn he no longer took pains to hide, she felt herself shrivel a little. She said, breaking the silence and despising herself for sounding so eager, so placating, "Are the eggs all right?" There was no help for it. She would still give anything, do anything to please him, could she only guess what he wanted.

She never had understood why he married her. His proposal and her acceptance had been so brief, so lacking in feeling on his part. Yet he had asked her. She clung to this irrefutable fact as her shield against his indifference. He *had* asked her.

She'd been so shocked and devastated by Papa's sudden death that for a brief time she had actually forgotten her passion for Ralph Wilson. Then, a few days after the funeral, listless and for the first time dreading her work, she went to the park. In her consuming sorrow, she found it desperately hard to answer questions, to be patient with the children, to do simple things like timing the carousel, starting and stopping the mechanism. She barely noticed whether the customers even had tickets or not. Nothing mattered without Papa.

When evening finally came, she started home and had almost reached the front porch when she saw Ralph coming down the steps, away from the closed front door.

It was old habit to gaze at him surreptitiously, admiring the lean jaw, the deep-set eyes, the agile muscular body; today, in the midst of her grief, she could not prevent herself from doing so again, wistfully.

"Have you been calling on Mama?" she asked. There had been a steady stream of somberly dressed visitors. Papa had had a wider acquaintance than anyone guessed. That steady, quiet, generous little man had been well liked.

She thought Ralph would walk on past her, but he stopped.

"She won't speak to me," he said angrily. "I've been here every day, and she won't let me in her house."

"Why, I can't understand that! You were Papa's friend."

Ralph did not reply, but she saw his mouth tighten.

"Well!" Dell told him indignantly, "I'll just have a talk with Mama. She shouldn't be rude to anyone who is kind enough to call. Especially you."

For the first time, he looked directly at her. For the first time, as she was well aware, he was actually seeing her.

"Why me? What's so special about me?" He seemed uneasy.

Dell was not a bold girl. But at last he was listening. Her chance might not come again.

"Everything! You're the handsomest man in Los Angeles. Or I guess the whole country. The world!"

"You think so, do you?" He studied her face, seeing the heightened color, the quick rise and fall of her breathing, the eagerness.

He turned away and for a moment gazed intently at the front windows of the house as if he thought someone behind the white lace curtains might be looking out. Then suddenly he took Dell's hand and, tucking it into the crook of his arm, said, "Adeline, you and I should become better friends. Come along, I'll buy you supper."

That was the beginning, and his attentions were enough to push her grief into the back of her mind. They were together every evening.

To her mystification, he insisted on their meeting well away from the house. It was as if he imagined Mama wouldn't approve his courting her. No doubt going about in public with a suitor so soon after a tragic death in the family was almost scandalous, but Dell couldn't believe that Mama, so unconventional herself in many ways, would object on that account. As for Papa, he would want Dell's happiness, she was certain. When she was in bed at night, she could almost see his dear kind face smiling at her from heaven, and hear his voice telling her he was pleased she'd found a man she loved.

But when she remonstrated with Ralph, urging him once again to come and call for her properly, he said flatly, "No. And that's all I have to say, Adeline."

He had made it clear more than once that he didn't like for her to argue or insist after he'd stated his wishes, so she who had been so outspoken all her life held her tongue.

There were other small disappointments. She would have liked to go some evening to Castles-by-the-Sea. She'd heard Joanna talk about how pretty the place was, and she was suddenly longing, after all the years of working hard with very little pleasure, to be one of those flighty girls in flowing pastel dresses, escorted by a handsome young man in flannels and a straw boater. She and Ralph would have a choice table by a window, and sit sipping soda water (he, perhaps, might want something stronger, although she'd noticed he didn't seem to care for strong drink). They'd be listening to the strains of "Meet Me Tonight in Dreamland"—

Sitting? Listening? Why, they might be dancing! But she'd never learned to dance, while Ralph no doubt was an expert. Maybe he'd be willing to teach her.

She ventured to suggest the dance hall. But to her deep regret, he displayed no interest, and he never did take her there.

Instead he would escort her to a modest restaurant, where the food was served quickly, leaving little need for conversation. Ralph, so far as Dell was concerned, had always been a silent and reserved man, and she refused to let his taciturn nature diminish her exhilaration. Just being with him, that in itself so unbelievable, was enough.

Although the evening usually ended immediately afterward—he was, she told herself stoutly, only doing the proper thing, protecting her good name—on one occasion he surprised her.

"How about going to the flicks tonight, Adeline? I like them."

She agreed, of course, although the idea was distasteful. She had so strongly disapproved of Lillian's headstrong determination, even in the face of Papa's death, to continue her work in those disreputable motion pictures. When Lillian went back to Santa Monica three days after the funeral and Mama, grim-faced and looking quite unlike herself, also left in order to chaperone her, Dell had felt nothing but scorn for such callousness.

Indeed, watching the dew-fresh young heroine smile and cast her falsely innocent, provocative glances at the hero, Dell would have walked out of the theater were it not that Ralph, who sat with eyes fixed, clearly had no intention of leaving until the film ended.

Although why he stayed, Dell afterward could not decide. When she asked him, "How did you like it?" he'd said with a shrug, "The films are all the same."

"She was pretty though, wasn't she? A bit like Lillian."

"Was she? Afraid she reminded me of someone else."

Dell didn't dare hope he'd been thinking of her. She knew he hadn't when he added curtly, "Someone from years back."

In truth, Dell's doubts were growing, and she was beginning to despair, her only real encouragement being that he continued to spend so much time with her.

She was totally surprised, therefore, when, as they walked one evening through Chutes Park toward the silent house where only Uncle Paul and Joanna now waited for her, he stopped abruptly beside the lake, and, with face averted, gazing out across the black water, said, "Do you want to marry me?"

She swallowed, unable to speak.

"Well, Adeline?"

"You're—you're asking me to marry you?"

"I said so, didn't I?"

At the note of impatience, she said quickly, "Yes, but I didn't really think you . . . you never seemed to care that much about me—"

What she was groping for was some small sign of the affection that she had understood usually existed between a husband and wife.

He said, "We've been keeping company for several weeks."

"We have, haven't we. And I've had such a good time, too, Ralph!"

"Good. Then I take it you accept my proposal?"

"Yes, oh, yes! I can't think of anything more wonderful than to be your wife." Bewilderment still gripped her, but she tried to infuse into the banal words all the joy she had dreamed she might feel.

If her voice was a little flat, he paid no attention. He seemed to be staring blankly at the dark shape of the old boathouse. Then he gave himself a small shake, and turned back to Dell. "We have a bargain then, do we?"

He stooped and kissed her. It was a strange hard kiss that bruised her lips.

Three days later, in the afternoon, they were married at city hall by a justice of the peace.

Dell had assumed her family would be present, and feeling that now was no time for estrangements, had intended to summon home her sister as well as her mother.

But Ralph, queerly, had been adamantly opposed. No one, not her family, not even Aunt Flossie, was to be present or even informed of their intentions until afterward. "My wedding is not to be one of those circuses," was all the explanation he would give.

Sick at heart, she pleaded with him, and tried in her indignation to insist. But when it became clear that the marriage itself was becoming endangered, she could only give in. Two strangers who happened to work in the building were the sole witnesses.

She wore her best dress—however, it was one she'd had for the last five years, and it hurt her to think of Mama once sewing the fine meticulous seams, gathering the lace at neck and sleeves, and never dreaming as she fitted it on Dell that this daughter would be married in it and her not even invited to be present.

Ralph did buy Dell a bouquet of red roses, so afterward, when they reached his house, now to be her house, too, she took one of the buds and put it between the leaves of a large heavy book to press and keep. She recalled seeing just such a dried flower among Mama's keepsakes.

Ralph had said they had better postpone their honeymoon. The park was doing a very good business; summer was a poor time to be away, letting the roller coaster and carousel stand idle. Also, and this explanation he gave with a grim smile, in light of how quickly they had married after her father's death, the less fuss the better. People would be critical enough as it was.

She was deeply disturbed, and hurt, too. Could he possibly believe she had given that aspect no consideration whatever? That she would be hard and unconcerned about Papa? She, who had loved Papa most of anyone!

Still, she was learning to make no retort but simply to accept his decisions, so with the ceremony over, here they were, already ensconcing themselves in the small house where she would spend so much of her life from now on. It was the first time she'd seen the interior, and she looked around her with curiosity. As she might have expected in a bachelor's home, things were a bit shabby and not very clean. She'd have her work cut out for her, for some time!

Ralph moved about restlessly. He went through the rooms turning on all the electric lights, although dusk had barely fallen. Then his eyes fell on the trunk in which she'd brought her clothes, and he carried it off up the stairs as if he were glad for something to do.

"Shall I fix us some supper?" she called after him.

Over his shoulder he said, "I laid in a few things to cook for tonight." Then, after a pause, he added, "You can call your mother now and tell her, if you like."

"Oh, yes, I will!"

He disappeared from view upstairs, evincing his disinterest in whether she called or not. But Adeline had happily run to the telephone.

Clara listened in absolute silence to her daughter's news.

"Mama, are you there?" Dell asked anxiously.

"Adeline, I can't—I simply cannot believe this. You and Ralph?"

"Yes, Mama. And I'm so happy!"

Another long silence. Then came the words, spoken in a cold voice quite unlike Mama's, "Splendid. I hope you will continue to be, though I doubt it."

"Are you angry, Mama? I'm sorry, I just couldn't help— Ralph—and I, of course, felt that we shouldn't—"

"I quite understand, Adeline. Thank you for calling. Now you'd better get back to your bridegroom."

The connection had been broken, whether by chance or by her mother, Dell couldn't be sure. But what she did know beyond a shadow of a doubt was that in marrying so hastily and secretively she had deeply wounded Mama.

She remained standing uncertainly in the center of the dusty parlor. Finally, she moved into the kitchen and set herself to cooking the best dinner she could with the meager provisions Ralph had provided.

Later, after they'd eaten and her washing up was done, she returned once again to the parlor where they sat side by side in the only two upholstered chairs. There were a few awkward remarks by Adeline, which Ralph answered brusquely before he inquired, "Well? What did she say?"

"I'm afraid she wasn't pleased."

"No?"

"We should have told her before," Dell burst out. "Gotten her blessing!"

"Blessing?" He gave a savage little laugh. Anything but a blessing . . . from her. . . .

"Adeline, I'm going out for a while and you might just as well go to bed. Take a candle with you. There's no electricity on the second floor."

"But, when will you be back?"

"I don't know. For God's sake, don't ask me questions like

that! I ain't never liked anyone checking up on me."

She gazed at him numbly. He took his jacket from the coat rack and, saying nothing more, went out.

Would he want her to be awake when he returned? she wondered. Yes, of course, he would. How foolish she was. A bridegroom on his wedding night expected his new wife to be arrayed in her finest nightgown. . . .

She went upstairs, found the trunk placed in the largest of the two bedrooms, and took out a neatly folded cotton gown, white with sprigged pink flowers, which she had seen and admired in a shop window. It had been very expensive, but for once she hadn't counted the cost.

In only a moment she had undressed and pulled the smooth soft fabric over her head. She removed the pins from the heavy mass of her hair, letting it fall free in ripples to her waist, and then began to brush, counting the strokes carefully as she always had done, every night of remembered life.

Afterward, she studied herself in the small glass above the chest of drawers, not complacently but anxiously, telling herself that she might not be the prettiest of the three sisters, but she was not homely. The new gown she gave wholehearted approval. It was as becoming as could be.

Climbing into bed, she noted that the sheets were none too fresh but stifled the impulse to go and search the hall cupboards for others. She had no idea when her new husband would return, and she shrank from seeming overcritical of his bachelor housekeeping. Better to wait, she thought, and blew out the candle.

For a time, she lay wide awake, tense and anxious. The question hovering in her mind could no longer be ignored. When he did return, just what was it she would be expected to do?

The truth was, she hadn't a notion. She was eighteen years old, but all she knew was that when a man and woman did something together in bed, a baby might result. How that miracle came to pass, she had never been told. Mama hadn't volunteered the information and Dell, hating to admit any ignorance to her mother, hadn't asked.

But faced now with enlightenment, she suspected there was more than just kissing and hugging, and she shivered while stoutly reminding herself of how much she loved Ralph, and how she had always in some indescribable way longed for his touch. As the night wore on, and she was left to lie in the darkness alone with her uncertainty, she began to think with a certain envy of the old house across the park, where Joanna now slept peacefully and where Dell's bed had always been her own.

It would all be all right, she told herself, if he would only *come*. If he would come *soon*. Put her silly fears to rest.

In the end she dozed fitfully, through sheer exhaustion.

When she awoke in the early dawn and found herself still alone, she snatched up her dressing gown and ran in alarm through the upper hall, and then discovered that at some late hour he had returned. In the close little cubbyhole that passed for a second bedroom, he lay sprawled, heavily asleep, on the rumpled coverlet of the narrow cot. He was still dressed in the suit he'd worn to his wedding, and the room fairly reeked of whiskey.

Chapter 21

Ralph, early in their married life, made it clear that Adeline was to continue managing the carousel on behalf of herself and her family, and for his part he wished no interference in running his roller coaster.

Dell therefore saw little of her husband during the day, and as he chose to spend most of his evenings out someplace, she was thrown on her own company as she never had been before. Too proud to seek out Joanna and Uncle Paul, thus admitting her loneliness, she became instead a frequent visitor at Aunt Flossie's.

Florence Mendenhall was once again the sole occupant of her cavernous house. Tony's first employment had been with a barnstorming group of flyers, traveling from county fair to county fair, and once he'd left home, he continued to find it more convenient, even though the air shows began to take place mostly around Los Angeles, to live with other pilots in a boarding house. He frequently came for the day, spaded up Aunt

Flossie's garden, painted the wrought-iron fence, and let her cook him large meals. But there was a void in Aunt Flossie's life. Secretly she missed him very much.

She therefore welcomed Dell all the more warmly, and the young wife found it good to have a woman confidante, even one so much older. Although of course she wouldn't dream of talking about Ralph or her marriage—her sense of loyalty forbade it—there could be consultations on the refurbishing of the house, or an exchange of recipes, or simply a companionable hour of mending.

Ralph, to give him his due, did not stint her on money. Usually, if she wanted some new rugs, or a pair of parlor chairs, she was free to buy them. The park had become exceedingly popular, and both their concessions were profitable. Any such purchases had to be made outside of work hours, but in the winter months the day ended early, and there was time for a hurried excursion down to Spring Street, on which Aunt Flossie frequently accompanied Dell and tendered advice, both women enjoying themselves. For Dell life was settling once again into a routine, she had come to accept Ralph's dour expression and lengthy silences as just his way, and the pain of Papa's death became less acute with the passage of time. She might even have convinced herself that she was happy were it not for the anguish and humiliation of her nights.

For the first week, Ralph had kept to the small back room. However, just as Dell was accustoming herself to this arrangement of separate sleeping quarters, one which even in her ignorance she realized was odd, the situation changed abruptly.

She was in the process of undressing one evening when he walked past her door, paused, then pushed it open. Caught unaware, she turned toward him, having no time to snatch up a robe and cover herself. She was naked in the soft, old-fashioned candlelight, and hot blood suffused her face and neck, but for a long moment, mesmerized by his gaze which slowly traveled the length of her stocky, well-developed body, she couldn't move.

When finally she reached for her nightgown, he said, "Never mind that. Get into bed."

Thankfully, she obeyed, pulling the cold sheet up to her chin. Then, unable to look away, she watched while he undressed. She had never before seen a man without his clothes, and her eyes were fixed in amazement on the strange appendage erecting itself from between his thighs.

Ralph pinched out the flame of the candle with his fingers and climbed into bed beside her.

What he did then, she tried afterward never to think about.

The violating act he performed on her resisting body not only seemed to her nasty and indecent, but was wretchedly painful. Its only redeeming feature was its brevity. When he was finished, Ralph simply rolled himself off and left the room.

So this was the marriage act!

She was utterly astonished. Mama and Papa could not have done this brutish thing. Not in the same way, surely!

From her bed at home, Adeline had had a view of the doorway of her parent's room, and more than once, she had seen the two of them entering together. Thinking themselves unobserved, Papa's arm was tight around his wife's waist and her head rested on his shoulder. There'd been an air of loving intimacy in the attitude of both people, as though something pleasurable was about to happen. Pleasurable to Mama as well as to Papa. Although Dell had never been able to imagine just what they intended, she'd felt left out and jealous. She realized this now—she'd been intensely jealous of Mama.

Remembering, she gave a short laugh. No girl in her right mind would be jealous of *her* with Ralph. All modesty gone, crushed under his weight, her legs pushed roughly apart while he—

It was his right, she admitted, and she'd never try to deny him. But she sometimes thought, if only he'd be a little gentler, go a little slower . . . because there were moments still, during the day, when if he accidentally brushed against her, she felt a hotness that wasn't repugnance at all and reminded her of the intense yearning she'd felt for him before they were married. But all little tendrils of desire died when bedtime came. Then she was conscious of only one hope—that when he came home he'd walk on past her room.

This hope, more often than not, was granted, and now, after more than four years, she believed she understood why. Other women were cleverer than she at hiding what they felt. Too, they were better able to find interesting things to say to their husbands. Who could blame Ralph if he was bored with her? She just wasn't an interesting person.

Her tongue-tied dullness would explain his long silences, his routine of spending his evenings at the saloon and elsewhere. Elsewhere, she gathered from a remark he dropped, being one of the notorious gambling halls clustered in the small town of Vernon, and her suspicion was confirmed by periodic spurts of parsimoniousness on his part.

Feeling at fault, because she was convinced he hadn't been a drinking man before their marriage, perhaps not a gambler either, she accepted these excesses. But what she could not comprehend nor find an excuse for was his outspoken contempt for her family. This was one subject on which he frequently expressed himself, and his cutting remarks left her bewildered and resentful.

"That youngest sister of yours," he'd say, "not very ladylike is it, to work at a newspaper? Hearing about sordid crimes of passion and talking over anything and everything with men? But your mother is the sort who'd encourage such loose behavior."

Dell, who had discovered that while thinking critical thoughts about her own family was one thing, listening to insults from an outsider was quite another, began an indignant denial, her voice rising, but Ralph cut her off.

"If you cannot control your temper when you hear some plain truths, I've no more to say."

However, on another occasion soon afterward, he remarked, "Lillian is certainly no better than she should be either. Surely you don't believe she became a Mack Sennett Bathing Beauty because of her talent."

"Oh?" Dell glared. She couldn't help herself. "Then what was the reason?"

"Some young director was smitten, I'd guess, or it might have been a cameraman, or even her agent, even though that Bert Lange is old enough to be her father. Somebody pushed her along in exchange for favors received, you can be sure."

"That's a lie!"

"Now, now. Is that any way to speak to me? Adeline, you might at least *try* to be a good wife."

Dell shriveled inside.

Ralph continued, "Let's not discuss that lot any more. I must be off. Just one other thing before I go—I've never cared for fat women. Aren't you eating too much lately?"

She'd been on the verge then of telling him she was with child. She was tempted to say, "Yes, I am bigger around the waist, and there's a reason." But apprehension held her back. Would he be pleased, or wouldn't he? If he wasn't . . .

She couldn't forget the one time she'd mentioned to him the idea of starting a family. It was after one of those wretched encounters in her bed. About to go out of the room, he'd paused, looked back, and said, for once with a touch of sympathy, "Adeline, you don't like this much, do you?"

Then he'd added in a different tone as she stared up at him, "Why in God's name did you have to throw yourself at my head—just at the wrong time?"

Pretending not to have heard the second question, she answered, "I guess I like it about as much as other wives."

"Think so?"

Encouraged by this lingering to talk, she said, "After all, going to bed together is necessary in order to have a baby."

"True, and that's the risk, isn't it? But the nights around here needed a little spicing up. I'll tell you, my girl, if you've got some notion about a baby, get it out of your head. Just suppose you had a boy?" He grinned at her, a grimace without humor. "Boys and men are beasts. Ain't I right? Selfish beasts. And all women angels! That's what we're taught at Mama's knee. Little girls are made of *sugar and spice and all things nice*. But young men, ah! *Thorns and briers and they're all liars*. As for old men, it's *whisky and brandy*...God, just whisky and brandy. Am I old already?"

She listened in amazement. She hadn't smelled liquor on his breath; he never drank at home, yet he must be drunk. What else would account for such bitter rambling? She didn't raise the subject of children again.

Nevertheless, here she was, pregnant. As the weeks passed, although bone tired—in all her life she couldn't remember being so tired before—she couldn't readily fall asleep at night. She would stare into the darkness, worrying, wondering if Ralph would be angry, and feeling a nagging guilt because others were privy to the secret she hadn't yet dared share with him. Because she'd succumbed to the temptation of telling Uncle Paul so that Mama might hear of it. And there was Aunt Flossie.

Aunt Flossie had been the first to know, unavoidably. While working at the carousel one morning, Dell had become so nauseated she couldn't continue, and had to call across to her friend, who fortunately hadn't yet started her ferris wheel, and beg her to take her place. Quickly! Then she'd run behind the bushes and been sick. On her return, Aunt Flossie naturally had inquired, "Not feeling so good?"

"No. I don't know what's the matter with me," she answered and then, the two of them happening for the moment to be alone, Dell had mentioned another symptom, the one that puzzled her most.

"How long has it been now?" Aunt Flossie asked.

"More than two months. I'm not usually late. Do you think something is terribly wrong?"

But the older woman was smiling. "Don't look so worried, *Liebchen*. I'm no expert, but I do know that morning sickness is very common in your condition."

"My condition?"

"I'd say you're going to have a baby."

Adeline had felt her heart jump so for joy it almost leapt from her breast. A baby!

She asked softly, "How long will it be before I show?" She was remembering Mama before Joanna came. Dell had been seven then, plenty old enough to notice how very round Mama grew—as though she'd swallowed a watermelon. And then, one night, there'd been a great commotion in the house, and Dell and Lillian were hurriedly bundled over to Aunt Flossie's and put to bed there. And the next morning when they were allowed to go home, Mama was still in bed, late as it was, and the sheet pulled up over her form revealed that the watermelon was gone, or almost so. Beside Mama's bed was the same cradle Dell and Lillian had once occupied, now freshly painted once again, and in it, snugly wrapped, was a sleeping baby. All that could be seen was a tiny, red, wizened face and a tuft of soft blond hair.

"Her name's Joanna, girls," Mama said. Her smile at them was radiant. "Did you ever see such a darling?"

"Where did she come from?" Lillian demanded, her five-year-old voice aggrieved.

Mama opened her mouth to answer, but Papa, who had been standing at the foot of the bed beaming, looking proud, cut in quickly. "God brought your little sister. We must all be grateful to him."

Lillian gaped. "God did?"

Dell had also been trying to imagine a visit from God, this small bundle in his arms, but she turned on Lillian and said sharply, "You heard Papa say so. Now hush!"

The two girls lingered in the room for a time, taking turns dutifully at rocking the cradle. Soon though, the tiny face puckered and there was a wailing cry. Papa scooped the funny little thing up, to place it in Mama's arms, while Lillian and Dell were shooed out.

"Go and play, darlings, Mama's tired."

Lillian took herself off at once, but Dell sidled slowly out, her eyes on Papa.

Behind her, she heard Mama say, laughing but with a slight touch of severity, "At least you didn't tell them it was the stork. Oh, do shut the door, Sam, and sit on the bed beside me. She can't be hungry yet; maybe she'll be quiet if she's held by her father!"

The crying did stop. Papa must be hugging the baby, patting it. Dell had not felt much affection for her newest sister at first sight and she felt less then.

But looking back after all these years, she remembered most clearly of all Mama's air of unquenchable happiness. Now it was to be her own turn to have this wonderful experience. She would grow fat around the middle, too, and one night her baby would come—somehow. Certainly God wouldn't walk into the house carrying him or her; it must be some kind of mysterious process even Papa couldn't explain, because Papa didn't lie. One way or another, the baby would come, and Mama would be there to help. Dell and Mama hadn't ever been close, but Dell had hated their long estrangement since the wedding. It would be such a relief to hear her say, "Dell, I'm proud of you! You and Ralph have a beautiful child—"

Ralph.

Her smile faded, and Aunt Flossie, noticing, said, "What's wrong? You were looking so pleased, but now—"

"I am pleased," Dell answered. "I'm very pleased."

She couldn't tell even kind Aunt Flossie that she had no idea what Ralph would say to the news. That even after years of marriage, she knew Ralph not at all, because they were like strangers living in the same house.

Chapter 22

As it happened, the initiative was taken out of Dell's hands. Ralph Wilson learned he was to become a father only a short time after Paul Perkins gave Dell's sister and mother the same news. The disclosure came as a result of a rank injustice suffered by Florence Mendenhall.

"Aunt Flossie?" Dell had rapped several times and, receiving no response, pushed open the heavy front door, which was never locked, and entered the house. "Aunt Flossie? Are you ready?"

The two had planned to go marketing, primarily for meat, as vegetables galore grew in neat rows in the large Mendenhall backyard.

To Dell's consternation, she discovered the older woman sitting motionless at her kitchen table, her ungainly body slumped and slack. Aunt Flossie did not look up, but merely said in a low, tired voice, "You go, *Liebchen*. I'll give you the money and you can buy me a loin of pork."

"Are you ill?" Dell asked in alarm. In all the years she'd know this staunch friend, first her mother's then her own, such an eventuality had never occurred before. Aunt Flossie was as robust as Dell was herself.

"No. Not ill. Not in body anyway."

"Then what is it? Please tell me!"

"I'd sooner not." At last, however, she raised her head, the usually shrewd but kind eyes dulled by misery. "But there, perhaps I should. Perhaps you too will not want to come here anymore."

"Not come here? What are you talking about? Please, please—"

"This terrible thing—this sinking of the steamship *Luisitania* by Germans! All those people lost. The newspaper this morning said more than a thousand dead."

149

"Yes, but what—" Dell had meant to ask, "What does that have to do with you?" but she stopped, a vague understanding forming in her mind.

"Adeline, I was running the ferris wheel this afternoon, just as always, when a woman began shrieking to her husband, 'Listen to her! Listen to this foreigner—she's a German! Our neighbors, the Burlingtons, were on that ship—the whole family! All of them may be dead, even the baby, such a sweet baby, and here we are—paying good money to a German. . . . Oh, God, what are we doing?'

"The woman was weeping. She was beside herself, and her husband, glaring at me, led her away. Then others who were waiting left too, muttering about *Huns*. Someone called me a Hun—*a Hun*, Adeline!

"I had to shut down my wheel. I don't know whether . . . whether I can reopen after this. . . ."

Until the last, when her deep voice broke with emotion, she spoke dully, giving a simple, factual account of what had happened. Aunt Flossie was a realist, Dell knew. She was indeed contemplating closing the business she had made for herself and so much enjoyed.

"How could they be so unfair?" Dell exclaimed angrily. "You've lived in America since you were a child!"

"Then you—you, yourself—don't feel any different toward me? It's my accent, of course. I was fifteen when I came here, too late to lose this terrible accent—"

"I certainly don't feel any different! Why, you're the best friend I have."

"Thank you." This humility from a woman so capable and strong and ordinarily so independent further illuminated for Dell how devastating the afternoon's experience had been.

She said thoughtfully, "I think you're right, though. It might be best if you don't run the ferris wheel—just for a time, until all the outrage dies down, and until the final reports are in— after all, there may not have been so many lives lost as they are saying now. . . . Is Tony in town?"

"No. There's an air show in San Diego."

"Then let me take your place at the park. And if someone asks about you or says anything, I'll tell them just how wrong they are. I'm sure I can make them see that there are plenty of people with accents, good people, who wouldn't want to blow up a ship. Aunt Flossie—don't shake your head—you must let me!"

"It's kind of you to offer, Dell. I knew I could count on your support." But she hadn't really counted on it, Dell thought sadly, recalling the questioning glances. "But who would do your work at the carousel? No, dear child, I can't accept."

"There's no problem. I'll hire a boy for the time being."

"You would do that, wouldn't you!" Aunt Flossie's face brightened a little. "Your father told me once that he could depend on you, above all others."

"Did he, Aunt Flossie? Did he really?"

"Yes, and he was right. My dear, if I let you help me, and I'm not at all certain I should, I, of course, will pay for the boy. That is the only way I would even consider such an arrangement. . . ."

Ralph said irritably, "I don't understand. Why not let the hired boy run the ferris wheel? Why should you trust him with the carousel money?"

"Because I'd like to win back Aunt Flossie's customers if I could. Only someone who is well acquainted with her can explain to them, make them realize that what goes on over there in Europe has nothing to do with a good woman who just happened to be born in Germany long ago. Gracious, Ralph, you like Aunt Flossie!"

"Do I? I've never thought about her much. I worked for her now and then, but I am not—like you—a friend." He eyed his wife and remarked, "Don't know as I want to be either. She *is* a German, remember. Sinking that ship was nasty business."

"I suppose she fired the torpedoes? Ralph, how can you—"Dell began heatedly, but then she saw his expression. "I do believe you are only saying such foolish things to upset me. Well? Do you agree that I do her a good turn? After all, she's helped us out more than once."

She realized to her chagrin that she was feeling strong resentment at having to ask his permission. The carousel was not his, it was her family's. Besides, she'd already promised Aunt Flossie and couldn't back out now. But if he refused? A good wife, an obedient wife would agree cheerfully, as he no doubt would point out.

To her relief, he only shrugged and said, "It isn't me you have to answer to, if you're robbed blind. Suit yourself."

* * *

So Dell took over the ferris wheel operation, and enjoyed the change, especially as she was able quite easily to keep a watch on the hired boy at the nearby carousel. As she had hoped, the old customers, many of them recognizing her, began queuing up once more, and she was able to respond calmly to their remarks about Aunt Flossie.

"You've bought this ride?" someone might ask, adding, "I hope so! We don't want to do business with any Germans."

"No, I haven't bought it. Miss Mendenhall is away just now and I'm pleased to be able to do her a favor. She's such a fine woman! Strange, isn't it, how hard it is to lose an accent. She's been in this country, you know, for almost half a century. Hardly remembers anyplace else, and is as good an American as you'll find anywhere."

"I suppose she might be at that," more than one listener conceded, perhaps recalling belatedly that there was a foreign accent or two in his own family. After a few weeks, the hostile questions, like the public indignation over the sinking, began to die away. Dell was pleased.

However she was finding the work surprisingly taxing. She still felt tired and unwell, and she hadn't reckoned on a blistering sun. The ferris wheel stood unprotected in the glare, and although she wore a large straw hat, by afternoon she felt lightheaded and frequently looked with longing at the shade provided by the wide top of the carousel.

Then, one day, when she had worked for a number of hours without resting, for the bright hot weather brought long lines of customers, with no warning at all she fainted.

When she came to her senses, she was lying on the grass, a ring of strange faces gaping down at her. Ralph was pushing his way through the crowd, saying, "Never mind. I'm her husband, I'll take care of her. The ferris wheel will be closed for the day."

His cool firmness quickly dispersed even those wishing to be helpful.

"Adeline, are you able to stand?"

"I think so. Give me your hand. But I'll have to sit on the bench there for a bit."

He helped her to the bench. "Now then," he asked grimly, "what happened?"

"I must have fainted. That's all."

"Fainted? You?" He stood looking at her with a puzzled

expression. "Adeline, that's hard to believe. You're as strong as a horse."

Still a little dizzy, she answered before she thought. "What a charming way you have of putting things."

So seldom had she spoken sharply to him that he looked surprised and wary. He said, "All right, then, you fainted. There must have been a reason, woman. Aren't you well?"

Aware of his impatience with her, and annoyed with herself for presenting difficulties, suddenly she was weary of dissembling. She said quietly, "Well enough. I'm going to have a baby."

She'd guessed he wouldn't be pleased in the way the ordinary husband would, but her disappointment was sharper than she'd imagined when she saw how shaken he was.

"It's wrong!" he exclaimed.

"What is?" She stared at him.

"For us to have a child. You and I."

"Wrong? Oh, Ralph, why?" The cry was torn from her.

"Because—a baby should be born from love."

He could not have said a more hurtful thing. But through her pain and humiliation, she recognized that they were talking to each other as they never had before in the years of marriage. He was speaking to her directly, as though at last he wanted to be honest, wanted her to understand.

What a strange place for this to happen, Dell thought, with her half lying on a bench in Chutes Park! With people passing, perhaps overhearing. But other people had never been real to Ralph. She doubted if, most of the time, he even knew they were there. Take their money, show them where they should sit in the roller coaster car, perhaps answer pleasantly if he were spoken to, but their faces were a blank to him.

Love. A word she'd never heard him speak before. It was sad that he should use it now and in such a way.

"I'm quite aware that you don't . . . love me," she said stiffly, although she hadn't really, consciously, known until then. She'd told herself she was a disappointment to him, a poor wife unworthy of the kind of respect Papa had shown Mama, but it had been a consolation to suppose that Ralph's affection for her was equal to that of most husbands. Now she was looking into his face and reading what he truly felt. In his deep-set eyes, she found pity. And remorse. But no love.

"I couldn't. I never could," he told her, confirming her

thoughts and putting a final end to hope. "I shouldn't have married you, Adeline."

"Then why did you? *Why?*"

"Because I loved—another woman. One who couldn't say no when I took her, but didn't really care a damn about me, not in any way that mattered—and I would have died for her! You see, then I wanted to hurt her. Make her think of me always with you. Make her burn with jealousy as I burned. Oh, marrying anyone—you—was a mistake, a rotten thing to do. I've only made both of us miserable. I'm sorry."

Dell was marveling at herself. What he was confessing should have infuriated her. But his open unhappiness and his contrition—brief perhaps but undoubtedly sincere, as though he really did regret the pain he'd caused—these aroused her tenderness. She wanted, more than anything else, to comfort him. And who knew? After this, perhaps they would be a little closer.

She said in a low voice, "A child might make you more content."

"Why in the world should it? No, Adeline. I'll have to think what to do. Don't worry, I'll stay with you until the baby comes, at least. Whatever happens, I'll see that you don't want for anything."

A chill of foreboding ran through her. What did he mean— he would stay with her until the baby came?

"In the meantime," he said, brusque once more and sounding himself again, "use the sense God gave you and stay out of this hot sun. Let Miss Mendenhall solve her own problems."

Chapter 23

The last sweet notes of "Roses of Picardy" had just faded away. Joanna and Tony were strolling back to their table when the band swung into a poignant new song imported from England, "Keep the Home Fires Burning." A few couples started once again to dance, but Irene Castle's graceful, chiffon-clad figure, seeming to float with scarves, appeared at the podium, and she motioned them all to their seats.

Where was her partner and husband, Vernon Castle?

The sad strains continued, but softly, so that all those gathered at the pavilion could hear what Mrs. Castle, alone tonight at the top of the wide, empty floor, had to say to them.

"My dear friends," she began, and the last rustles of conversation ceased.

"I call you my friends, because we have all had so much pleasure here together, and Vernon and I have come to know many of you well. So now, I confide in you as friends.

"Although I am an American, Vernon, as perhaps you know, was born in Norwich, England. For some time, he has been very unhappy that his countrymen were engaged in fighting a terrible war while he remained with us in far-off, peaceful California. Yesterday, he asked my blessing, and said he believed his place was in England. He is a trained flyer, so he has gone to join the British Royal Flying Corps.

"I will try to carry on here without him. I hope . . . I hope you will help me. . . ."

Her voice broke, and she stood for a moment with her head bowed. Then, attempting to smile and failing, she turned and walked quickly from the podium.

Joanna gazed after her, trying to imagine what it must be like to watch a man you loved go off to war. To know that he was over there, trapped in the midst of carnage and killing, his own mutilation or death possible at any moment.

But the horror of what Irene Castle—or any wife—truly felt, Joanna told herself, could only be known through experience. Her own anguish at thought of the danger to Charles Gold was a nagging ache that never entirely went away, and he, of course, was not a lover. Just suppose he was a lover . . .

Tony, his voice solemn, was saying something, and tardily she listened.

"So fighting with planes has become important after all, Joanna. I told you it would."

"Yes, you did. And I guess that's a very good reason for me to be glad America is staying out of the war. Poor Mrs. Castle!"

"You'd worry about me? If I had to go over?"

"Indeed I would, silly! I'd worry myself sick."

"More than you worry when I'm only barnstorming and

giving some of the crowds at the fair a thrill?" he teased.

"A great deal more. It's dangerous enough, your stunt flying and showing off at the fairs, but nobody is trying to shoot you down."

"I guess that's right."

The band was now playing another tune, one which fitted his mood, and he pulled her to her feet and put his arm around her waist. While they danced, sweeping low as they'd learned from the Castles, he sang in her ear, "Let me call you sweetheart; I'm in love with you. Let me hear you whisper that you love me too—"

Her clear contralto soon was blending with his tenor, yet he realized that to her it was only a song, and he lacked the courage to stop singing and whisper the words in earnest. The chance passed, because the rhythm soon changed to that of the good old "Grizzly Bear," which meant a close embrace, she hugging him tightly as well, but the pair of them were rocking madly from side to side, their feet stomping and sliding in the fast steps they both loved and which made them laugh aloud from exhilaration.

Seated at the table again, sipping a Coca-Cola, she said, "Guess what, Tony. The newspaper has given me an assignment! I'm to write a feature on Hollywood."

"You?"

"Why not me?"

"You aren't a reporter. Copyboys—girls, I mean—don't write. You've said so."

"No, they don't, and of course I didn't expect to, not for a while—but the city editor, Mr. McGowan, is a rather unpredictable person. He called me into his office yesterday, and said I was to have my chance now to show him what I could do! It happened, undoubtedly, because of a letter Charles Gold wrote, which he showed me and which read something like, 'I was back in England for a time, and went to see an American film, one of those Keystone Kop things. Believe it or not, I recognized the girl in it—Lily French. That's what she calls herself now, but she's really Lillian Fritsch whose sister works for you. So if you need someone with a passport into a studio, you have her, Joanna Fritsch, right at hand.'"

Joanna fell silent. She was smiling, remembering what else Charles Gold had written and how pleased she'd been when her eyes fell on the postscript: "Joanna's a very bright girl, Ed, if you haven't discovered that already. Nice, too."

Tony said, rather meanly, "Then you got the assignment because Lillian's your sister?" He didn't want her feeling grateful to Charles Gold.

"Of course," Joanna agreed cheerfully, "and no doubt Mr. McGowan expects to have to rewrite everything I submit. But it is exciting all the same. I called Lillian right away, and she said I could come Monday afternoon, so tomorrow Mr. McGowan will tell me more about what he has in mind. . . . It will be awfully hard, Tony, to find an original angle. So much of Hollywood has been covered already—the actors' clothes, their cars and homes, even their offscreen personalities. Do you know, for example, that Charlie Chaplin is really a very shy, retiring man? He lives alone in a plain bachelor room at the Los Angeles Athletic Club."

"No, I didn't know and I honestly don't care. . . . Say, Joanna—"

"Yes, Tony? Oh, I'm sorry for running on so. It seems all I have on my mind these days is the newspaper—and the war."

"And me? Say you think about me a little!"

"But I do! I've told you often enough how I hate and fear aeroplanes, how I wish you'd give up flying, find some other work."

"Yes, I know," he said earnestly. "And if you asked anything else in the world of me, *anything*, I'd do it for you. Because Joanna—" He swallowed hard. "There's something I've never told you, but I think you must have guessed. . . ."

"What is it, Tony?" She gazed at him, smiling, puzzled, until at last he burst out, "Just—I love you! I always have."

"And I love you, Tony," she answered serenely. "You're my best friend."

"I don't mean love in that way. Good Lord, we're not children! I mean I *love* you. I want us to belong to each other. I want to marry you."

She stared at him, her smile fading. "Tony, you can't be serious. I'm only sixteen. I couldn't—I don't want to marry anybody."

"I don't mean we should marry now. No girl would want to tie herself up with a fellow who makes as little as I do. But later on, well, nothing would mean anything at all to me without you. I love you so terribly—and I think you care about me, too, don't you?"

She nodded, and said slowly, "I care very much. But I don't know whether it's in the way you mean. I've never really

thought about us in that way. We have such good times together
and all, but—"

"But what?"

"I don't know! I'm just not sure. What is it you want me
to say?"

"Nothing much now, I guess . . . just, 'Yes, Tony, we belong
together and later on I'll marry you.'"

"That's nothing much? My dearest Tony, that is a lot!"

Joanna jumped to her feet, hiding from him her troubled
face. She said gaily, "This is no place to be serious. Shall we
dance?"

He did not press her further and appeared willing simply to
enjoy the remainder of the evening. But when he took her
home, in the deep shadows of the porch, he ventured something
he'd never done before. Taking her by surprise, he put his arms
around her and kissed her. A soft kiss, asking nothing in return,
but his lips lingered on hers as though he could hardly bear to
let her go.

When they drew apart, he said triumphantly, "There! You
liked that, I could tell."

"Yes—yes, I did. But I wish I hadn't."

"Why not? What's the harm when I love you so much?"

"None, I suppose. But everything's different. We were so
happy and comfortable before. Now I have to look at you in
a different way."

"Good. I'm tired of being a best friend." He grinned in the
darkness. "Maybe this will help you decide how you feel. Good
night, Joanna. I'm going home and dream a little dream of my
Joanna." He went off jauntily, whistling.

"Well, Miss Fritsch, please sit down. Are you off for Hollywood this afternoon?"

The city editor settled his own lean, middle-aged body more
comfortably into the swivel chair, and before she had a chance
to answer he knocked out his pipe and filled it again from a
worn, leather pouch. He struck a match and made a series of
puffing noises while she waited.

"Well? I trust you're prepared?" From behind his wire-
rimmed glasses he was regarding her with the enigmatic gaze
his staff often found unnerving. Nevertheless, as usual in speaking to Joanna, who was the age of his own daughter, there was
a hint of avuncular tolerance, missing in his crisp orders to
others on his staff.

"Yes, sir, I'm leaving for the Keystone Studios now."

"Excellent. Although I must apologize for causing you to miss a day of high school. I must say, young lady, your expression reminds me of myself, many years ago back in Philadelphia, when I went after my first story. Excited but scared."

"That's it exactly!"

"Don't worry too much. I hardly expect you to give us anything of Joseph Pulitzer caliber. There, never mind my little joke. No doubt you'll do very well."

He paused to puff reflectively. "It's a fortunate coincidence that you have an entree to one of the studios. Very fortunate. This weird and wonderful vine mushrooming so suddenly from the sod of our city is becoming a cause for concern, and because the press hasn't been particularly kind to it in our reporting, we are less and less welcome, except of course for publicity purposes. My main source of information until recently has been a connection of Mr. Gold's—a friend of his family's, a Mrs. Gierek, part owner of the Selig Company. But with Mr. Gold in Europe . . .

"Miss Fritsch, I do not want just another glittery description of the fantastic excesses of this new industry. Do *not* bother to tell me about some monstrous set, such as the one D. W. Griffith is building for his extravaganza, *Tolerance*. We have all heard about that huge plaster replica of the ancient city of Babylon, featuring, if one can stomach the idea, Egyptian bas-reliefs and Hindu elephants mixed in with Babylonian bulls. As for filming, I doubt if there's a reader in this city who doesn't know that Griffith's cameraman, Billy Bitzer, is shooting the picture from the air, riding in a captive balloon pulled slowly back to earth. Bah!"

"Keystone hasn't any elaborate sets, and probably no balloons," Joanna assured him. "Lillian tells me Mr. Sennett never spends a nickel he doesn't have to. He even uses the city streets for background most of the time."

"That's a blessing. So you won't be tempted into hyperbole. But perhaps you'd like to hear what I do expect, or rather hope for, from you?"

"Yes, please!"

"We plan a series of articles—exposés, actually. Los Angeles, by and large, is still very provincial, a highly moral town and a prime temperance center. So the gambling dens of Vernon have offended many of our citizens for years. And now there's Hollywood. We hear rumors about liquor and drugs and wild fortunately on this day of all busy days was visiting the studio, that the Russian wolfhound, Ivan, at that moment being led onto the set by Mabel, had a bigger part than his owner.

The scene was a small, seedy hotel lobby, this time constructed on the lot. Joanna, perched on a folding chair before the stage, watched fascinated, then laughed until she cried as the little man in the baggy pants gallantly tipped his hat to pretty Mabel before getting one foot hopelessly entangled in the dog's leash and the other entrapped in a brass spittoon. Lillian, a lady haughtily wishing to avoid such riffraff, and therefore marching, nose in air, from the lobby, was caught as well. Finally, as Chaplin stumbled and clasped his arms around her, she slapped him for the unintentional liberty.

After she had stalked out the door, Lillian's part was ended, and for a time she was able to join her sister as audience.

"Lord, what a day! I've really been put through my paces. All morning out on Santa Monica pier, falling in and out of a damned rowboat. Then this."

"But you're finished now," Joanna said. She was secretly shocked by this easy coarseness of speech her sister had acquired.

"Ah, but she's not finished," said the fat man overflowing a chair on Lillian's left. He chuckled without sympathy, his cherubic face wreathed in the sly smile for which he was famous. "We're doing one of my films next."

Lillian said, "Joanna, this cruel man is Fatty Arbuckle. But I'm sure you recognized him without being told."

"Yes, I did." She started to add, "And I love your pictures," but stopped herself. How bored they all must be, hearing that stock phrase! Besides, in this case it really wasn't true. She'd never found Arbuckle amusing. Not like Chaplin, or Ford Sterling, or Slim Summerville.

But Arbuckle obviously didn't notice the omission. He had begun outlining the schedule for the afternoon, talking to Lillian; and Joanna, ignored, became aware that to him, anyone who wasn't important in the movie industry was as good as invisible. How strange it must be, she thought, and unpleasant, to be one of the unimportant people here. Someone like an extra.

An idea stirred and her mind drifted away from what Arbuckle was saying. There were extras in this picture, a number of them as she could see. They were now before the camera, because the scene had shifted to outside the hotel. Chaplin, attempting to exit through the revolving door, was being slapped back by each turning wing, although the dog ran through with no difficulty. On the street a crowd of people streamed past, paying no attention as the little man waved and gestured, miming the desperate words, "Catch the lady's dog, please!" Mabel, behind him, wept copious tears.

Although excited by her nebulous plan and impatient to be started, Joanna remained rooted in her chair, spellbound by Charlie in his difficulties. At last the dog was captured, Mabel gazed up at her hero in adoration, and he beamed back at her while trying surreptitiously to prevent Ivan from chewing on one of his enormous shoes.

"Cut!"

The set emptied. The extras hurried toward the big trestle table which held the sack lunches provided by the studio, and Joanna watched as they settled themselves on the sparse grass to eat, some in groups, others alone. Her attention was caught by an older man who went to sit well away from the others but awkwardly close against the ramshackle outer fence.

Curious about him, she turned to her sister who was still engaged in conversation with Arbuckle. Joanna heard him say, "Haven't you gotten to know the Count yet, Lily? Most of us do, sooner or later."

Lillian was looking a little puzzled, but then he added, "In this business, run out of steam and you're left behind," and Lillian's chin came up.

"I won't run out of steam. Not ever!"

She turned away from him, and said to Joanna, "I'm sorry, darling. You're so quiet I almost forgot you were here. Enjoying yourself?"

"Yes, indeed . . . Lillian, have you noticed that man?"

"The old character over by the fence? Everyone here knows about him. He's an extra, and a pretty good one, I guess. At least he's hired frequently—which is more than most can say. Just lately, in the last few months, it seems every hopeful in the United States has decided to come out West and try his luck in Hollywood. At a call for extras, it's a regular crowd scene, all of them pushing, scrambling, elbowing each other. And for nothing; in the end most are turned away—"

Lillian's complacency annoyed Joanna, and she interrupted. "I still don't understand why the man sits so close beside the fence."

Lillian shrugged. "It's rather a joke, you see. He has a very large family, and not much money. So he shares his lunch with his wife who waits for it every day on the other side."

The other side, Joanna mused. The other side of the fence was poverty. The other side of all the laughter and the fake glitter was—what? So many articles were being written about the successful actors and actresses—but weren't there also stories to be told of the failures, and their heartbreak?

She jumped to her feet. "Do you mind if I just wander around a little, Lillian? Everything's so new to me—and very exciting."

Lillian looked relieved. "I was about to suggest that very thing myself, as I've another shot to do before lunch. Suppose I find you when I've finished? We can eat in the commissary. Who knows what famous people you'll see!"

Joanna said, "I'd like that. Goodbye, Mr. Arbuckle."

Receiving an indifferent nod from the fat man, she took herself off and soon was wandering among the groups of extras, all of whom appeared more interested in food than in conversation.

She'd never interviewed anyone before. How did a reporter start a conversation with total strangers? "Pardon me, I'm from the *Los Angeles Times*—?"

Instinctively she shied away from such a blunt approach. Instead, she eased herself down on a narrow strip of grass beside a girl of about her own age, sitting alone and, like the others, quite evidently enjoying her lunch. She had large amber eyes, a generous mouth, and a small pert nose, all in a clear-skinned oval face—undoubtedly, Joanna decided, the beauty of her high school.

"May I join you?" Joanna asked.

A friendly smile reassured her. "Of course. But where's your lunch?"

"I don't have one. I—"

"Oh, you didn't make it on the call. Too bad. Maybe they'll need more extras later this afternoon, so don't you give up."

Before Joanna needed to answer this generous encouragement, the girl said, "If you're hungry, would you like to share mine?" The offer was real enough, but Joanna did not miss the relief her prompt refusal brought. The girl then folded over the top of the sack and stowed it carefully away in her large mesh bag. "The pay isn't much," she confided, "but it's a nice surprise to get so much food. I can take home what's left—there'll be enough for supper."

"Is this your first time as an extra?"

"Yes, and I'm so excited! Ever since I came to Hollywood, I've been trying to get in a movie any way I could, but it's dreadfully hard."

"You came out here on the train?"

"Yes, and golly, what a long trip!"

"Where from?" Joanna was trying to guess, listening to the twang in the pleasant voice. "The Midwest somewhere?"

The girl nodded, her face softening. "Indiana. Evansville, Indiana. Down on the Ohio River." She finished the apple she was eating, looked with regret at the nibbled core, then tossed it away. "I've been here four months. Four long months. Don't you get so homesick sometimes you could die?"

"I was born in Los Angeles."

"Really? Lucky you! Listen, you being a native, maybe you can help. I'm sharing a place with some other girls, three of them—and all from Ohio, but they weren't acquainted before they came—isn't that something? Anyway, we found this little apartment-hotel, they call it a *court*, not far from here. We like where it is, all right. We need to be close to the studios and not ride a streetcar a long way out every day. You know how it is: 'Be here by four in the morning or there isn't a chance!' But the rooms are dreadful—so filthy dirty and with cockroaches as big as mice!" She shuddered. "Have you heard of any nicer place close by? A really cheap one, I mean?"

"No. I'm sorry. But Miss—"

"My name's Polly. Polly Koontz, although I call myself Polly Kelly professionally. Pretty, isn't it? Polly Kelly . . .

"Well, maybe now that I've been an extra once, I can get more work. But golly, there are so many of us, such a crush always when there's a call for extras! How about yourself? Do you get work often?"

"Well, not the kind of work you mean. To be honest, Polly—and my name's Joanna Fritsch, by the way—I'm learning to be a reporter. For a newspaper. The *Times* sent me out here to get a story about movie people."

"Oh," Polly said flatly. "Then why waste your time talking to me? No one wants to read about extras."

"I think they might."

"We're just nobodies."

"So far, maybe." Joanna agreed, "but you might be the stars of tomorrow. Who knows? Polly, I've been thinking about you and your friends. You're all somebody's daughters, and the readers have children themselves. They'd be angry if they knew how you had to live. And when people are angry they help. At least, as a human interest story it would arouse sympathy for the young women—and men, too—who work as extras."

"There aren't so many men, so they do much better. Boys and men of all ages do better. Even that old fellow over there. He scrapes by. It's only we girls..."

Polly was silent for some time, her face troubled. Then she nodded. "You won't use my name? I don't know how my father could get to read your newspaper, way out in Indiana, but somehow he might. I'd never want him to know I live this way. He's so good to me, so proud of me, and so far I haven't had to do—what the others do, because he sends me money now and then."

"No, I promise I won't use your name. It's too bad about the hotel."

Polly nodded. "At first I thought I couldn't bear staying there, but you get used to dirt and smells. Those things really don't matter, not compared to— The trouble is, there are so many of us, all suddenly crowding out here, clawing tooth and nail to get ahead, and all full of our own crazy ideas and dreams. You don't know what it's like!

"Why, some of the girls get so hungry they'll do anything. And when they're picked up on the street making offers to a strange man, and not doing it very well because they're so scared, they get arrested. The police ask them, 'What's your occupation—aside from prostitute?' and they always say, 'Movie actress,' because that's what they are. They—we—we think of ourselves that way, don't you see? It's the same when a girl gives up and kills herself. Her friends tell the police, 'Movie actress.'"

Joanna gasped, and Polly gave a small, suddenly hard laugh. "I don't know how immoral the real Hollywood people are, but they do get blamed for a lot!"

"But why—if things are hopeless—why not just go home?" Joanna asked faintly.

"Go home? Admit to everyone, your family, all your friends, that you weren't good enough, pretty enough? Besides, tomorrow might be your lucky day. If you can only hang on—"

"Ah, Joanna, there you are!" It was Lillian, briskly approaching.

Joanna waved her hand, then turned back to Polly. "Oh, I'm so sorry! Here comes my sister, and you and I have just begun to talk. Could you possibly meet me later?"

But Polly had glanced in the direction of the lilting voice and jumped to her feet. "That's Lily French!" she exclaimed excitedly. "She's not really your sister?"

"Yes. How about meeting later on—"

"Oh, I will, sure. But first, how about introducing me to her? Lily French! Imagine that! Your sister!"

"I'll be glad to introduce you."

Joanna sighed. Just the thought of actually talking to one of the exalted personages on the lot had transformed Polly. Her eyes were wide and worshipful. She glowed with eagerness. No, Polly was not ready to go home a failure. Not she nor any of the other Polly Kellys.

From every train they alight, all these young girls, fresh from the farms of the Midwest, from cities like Tulsa, Indianapolis, Columbus. All were the prettiest in town, at home. All are convinced they can and should be motion picture stars.

Go to the Santa Fe Station as this reporter did, sit at the Fred Harvey counter, and watch them arrive, in droves, chattering, hopeful, excited.

Last night, a girl from Iowa named Sandra, starving and cheated by a pimp, took her own life. She shot herself. Sandra had never succeeded in being hired even as an extra, but on the police blotter, she was identified as "movie actress." No doubt she would have been pleased.

This dark, seamy side of the—

"Joanna," Uncle Paul called, "Didn't you hear me? The telephone is for you."

Reluctantly, she put down her pen and made her way into the hall.

"Hello, Joanna." It was Tony. "I just wondered—oh, Joanna, have you decided?"

"Decided? About what?"

A gloomy silence fell at the other end of the line but she didn't notice. In her mind, she was happily framing the next sentence of her article.

Chapter 25

"What a day! I'm ready to drop," Lillian said to Mabel Normand, who had been working alongside her now for twelve hours straight, and little Mabel was the one who should have wilted.

Mabel only said, "That's the way it goes sometimes. Whenever Mack has fifty extras hired, believe me, kiddo, we're going to finish."

How did Mabel do it? The slender Keystone star appeared so fragile, yet she was obviously whalebone and steel under those small feminine curves. Watching Mabel at work was a revelation, and trying to emulate her made Lillian bone tired and grudgingly envious.

Only last week they'd done a picture using a new technique, filming a train up in the Tehachapis by placing a cameraman on a truck racing alongside the tracks. The scene, an engine chugging up a steep grade just as the sun rose and the steam mingled with the pine trees, had been startlingly beautiful. But the director, Pathé Lehrmann, had no way of determining at once whether the result was good on film, so several times during the day, when another train happened along, the actors stopped whatever else they were doing and they shot the beginning again. As a result, the day was even longer than usual, yet at sundown Mabel showed no signs of flagging.

Today's picture, once again set in the mountains, was also an innovation. It was an experiment in casting. Mabel and Lillian were a striking contrast in appearance—one so dark and one so fair—yet both had a mischievous, often beguiling smile quite at odds with their sweet, virginal faces. Lehrmann had had an idea, one tremendously gratifying to Lillian. He'd suggested that the studio might try using the girls together, and just as Dorothy and Lillian Gish were becoming well-known, these two, as a pair, might be even more popular. Privately,

parties and—forgive the unvarnished word—sex. But rumors
aren't enough for a reputable newspaper. We need facts, and
any that you can bring back will be welcome. If the movie
people are truly becoming a blot on our landscape, I for one
am prepared to launch a crusade. Clear?"

It was indeed clear, and disheartening. As she had expected,
the newspaper was taking advantage of her relationship to a
film actress. Which was all right—but not to spy! And even
supposing she were enthusiastic, how did Mr. McGowan think
she could ferret out any secrets in only one day on the lot?

More rankling, he'd said nothing about the makeup of the
article she was to write. Its length, for example. The chances
were he really intended to pass on to a seasoned reporter whatever information she might obtain.

Although she'd told Tony she was prepared for this to happen, Joanna felt her back stiffen.

"I'll do my best," she said.

Her best, she was promising herself, would be different—
and much better—than he expected.

Chapter 24

Lillian was so tired she could hardly stand, and there were still
many hours of shooting left before sunset. Even then, if the
reel weren't finished, Mack had said they were to go into
artificial lighting. These Little Tramp pictures were so over-
whelmingly popular that each one grossed more than the last,
and Lillian could guess yet another reason for making them as
quickly as possible. Mack Sennett had not gotten where he was
without a shrewd knowledge of actors. He knew ambition when
he saw it, and recognized that Charlie Chaplin, shy and retiring
as he might be, wouldn't remain long with Keystone.

Meanwhile, Charlie and Mabel were starring together in this
film entitled *Mabel's Strange Predicament*, and for once Lillian
didn't resent being lower down on the billing. It was an achievement even to be in a picture with Chaplin, so after her exit she
could joke good-naturedly, telling her sister Joanna, who un-

Lillian was amazed that Mabel agreed. If she were Mabel and already a star, she'd never allow herself to be teamed with someone less prominent like Lily French!

But Mabel, tranquil and self-confident as ever, had voiced no objection. She was known as a trouper, loyal to the studio and willing to try anything a director asked her to.

Even with her cooperation, this filming went slowly. Pathé Lehrmann was a hard man to please. He'd been and still was an actor and stunt man himself, and in his own way legendary. Lillian had been told over and over about the day he first went to work for D. W. Griffith at Biograph.

The Biograph plot had called for some soldiers to scale a three-story building. Lehrmann appeared in costume on the roof with the other extras, but unlike them, when told to pretend to fall, he leaped out into space. He landed expertly on his backside, rolled for a distance, then bounced to his feet.

Griffith, dismayed at missing such exciting action on film, was said to have roared, "You were not on camera!" whereupon Lehrmann replied, "I was just rehearsing, sir. I'll do it again." And he did.

Such a man was not one to coddle his own actors. In the climax as planned, Lillian had been tied across a railroad track, while Mabel ran precariously across the tops of some approaching freight cars (this time rented for the purpose) pursued by the mustached villain. Lillian got free in the nick of time and swung up on the train; then the two girls tried to escape by jumping into the river as the cars passed over a bridge. They floundered ashore, dripping water, and after a long chase ran into the welcoming arms of the Kops.

The reel had to be shot that day. Working on location was expensive, because while the unused railroad tracks were free, trucking the extras to the site and the use of the old train were not. The costs mounted with each hour that passed, and in spite of being a perfectionist, Pathé, as daylight failed, was happy to be more or less on schedule. He gave his cameraman the OK sign with finger and thumb, and shouted through his megaphone, "I think we've got it, girls. Get back close to the train and we'll wrap it up."

The actresses were feeling the chill through their wet clothes, but both were once again artfully made up and looked prettier than ever. They ran along the track, past the groups of bit players and extras who were talking among themselves, yawning, or stretched out on the meadow grass.

Mabel stumbled, and Lillian for the first time sensed exhaustion in her partner. But then Mabel seemed to be scanning the nearby crowd. Suddenly she darted from the rails and paused to speak to a tall, smiling man. The Count. Lillian, from the corner of her eye, saw him slip something into Mabel's palm, then Mabel's fingers lightly brushed her small face, and almost as though she had not been gone she was back beside Lillian.

They reached the train, looked back, and Pathé shouted. No time to even catch a breath. They again began the long run which ended in the arms of the Kops.

"One last pose," Pathé said, looking pleased. "Miss Normand with Arbuckle, Miss French with Summerville . . ."

The filming finally was finished, and, much later, the routines of dispersal. The two female leads, the cameraman, and Pathé Lehrmann all rode back to Edendale in the director's pride and joy, his Crossley, a powerful, bright blue British sporting car. As Mabel and Lillian still were very damp, he managed to provide each of them with a thin blanket, which protected his red leather upholstery but still left them shivering in the wind as the evening temperature dropped to its usual December low.

Nevertheless, well recovered from her momentary weakness, Mabel seemed to feel no discomfort. She chattered in a bright, humorous vein all the way home, admiring Pathé's enormous car, congratulating the cameramen on some unusual shots, and reiterating her belief that Lily French was as good a comedienne as there was in Hollywood.

Lillian, listening warily to Mabel's compliments, failed to detect a note of insincerity and was as puzzled as always.

She had once asked Bert why Mabel put on such a show of liking everyone, and Bert had said, "I doubt if you can understand this, Lily, but it's not a show. There isn't a jealous bone in her body. She's a rare one, I'll tell you."

Lillian had looked her disbelief.

"See for yourself, Miss. *Fly catching* goes on in every film in every studio. They all do it—but not Mabel." *Fly catching* was scene stealing, and he was right, everyone did it who could. He'd added dryly, "As a matter of fact, in that fine art, some of those clowns could take a lesson from you."

Lillian was not at all displeased by his comment, but she was no closer to figuring out Mabel than she had been.

Once back at Keystone, and glad the long cold drive was over, she hurried with Mabel to their little cubbyhole dressing

rooms to change into dry clothes. Still required of them for
tonight was the usual conference with the writers about the
next day's shooting, and Mabel was skipping along, light as a
feather, whereas Lillian's feet felt so heavy she could hardly
pick them up.

She said, "Must you walk so fast? Lord! I don't know how
you stay so peppy."

Mabel stopped to wait for her. "I don't know either, except
that when I'm working I just don't think about getting tired.
Today, though, I must admit I was starting to drag. I hardly
ever go to the Count, because Mack's so down on drugs, but
once in a great while—"

"The Count? Why go to him?"

"Lily, dear—I thought you knew! He's the man who sells
the cocaine, not just here but all over Hollywood." She gave
her warm laugh. "Are you sad? Are you too tired to go on?
Or maybe you have a hangover from the party last night. The
Count will take care of everything, right away!"

"Oh." How, Lillian wondered, could she have been so blind?
"Then that friend of yours, Zelda Thomas—"

"Yes." Mabel's heart-shaped face suddenly clouded, and
she started walking again. "Zelda takes so much! I guess she
needs it, but the cost! I think the Count must be one of the
richest men in Hollywood. The first stuff he gives you is free,
but after that..."

Lillian had stopped listening. She was gazing down at Mabel's feet, those tiny feet that earlier had been stumbling and
now were stepping out so lightly and quickly. Mama had said
that drugs were something terrible. That a girl who took them
was ruined. But look at gay, lively Mabel. A little coke today
hadn't hurt her a bit!

Another party. This one in a beach cottage in Santa Monica,
remote from everywhere.

There had been the usual boring argument with Mama before
she left. Clara had begun by saying, "Lillian, haven't you ever
heard of resting? You've been up since long before dawn. Even
you can't go on forever, burning the candle at both ends."

This was so, Lillian recognized. But it irritated her to realize
that Clara's reservations about the party stemmed from different
fears entirely. Mama was absurdly dismayed by the accounts
she read in the newspapers lately, all exaggerated, of course,
and full of such words as *orgy, sex, drugs*.

"Just tonight—stay home," Clara pleaded, but she made the mistake of adding, "as your mother, I insist that you do."

Lillian's cool anger flared.

"You can't insist, Mama. I became twenty-one last month. I'm quite old enough to decide how to spend my evenings."

Clara's cheeks reddened as though her daughter had slapped her, and Lillian averted her eyes. She was feeling what she didn't want to feel: contrition and pity. Mama did lead such a boring life. First the weaving, and now those little miniatures.

She almost blurted out, "I'm sorry—" but Clara spoke first. "I'm not accomplishing much here anymore, am I? Never mind. I just want you to know that I'm going home to be with Dell when her baby comes."

"Why not? I think you should." Lillian, dressed in a shimmering green evening gown, with a white fur wrap around her shoulders, walked toward the door. "I must be on my way. Good night, Mama."

"Lillian," her mother said with deep urgency, "please, be careful. Your father would never forgive me, if you—"

But Lillian was gone.

The pounding of the surf on the pilings just below was audible in the big, pseudorustic living room with the wicker furniture pushed back against the walls, audible even above the shrill scratching of the Victrola. People were dancing and drinking; there was a table covered with liquor bottles and glasses, and Lillian noticed at once that an embossed silver box, the lid thrown back, occupied the place of honor on the mantel.

Even though the room was crowded, she was alone for the moment. She strolled across to look curiously inside the ornate box, and saw it was filled with a white, almost transparent powder.

As she lingered there, a well-known actor from another studio brushed past her and helped himself to a large pinch of the substance. He placed it in his nostrils, sniffed, and then turning to her with a smile of satisfaction asked her to dance.

The room seemed too hot and she wondered if she were feverish. Ill or not, she felt far too stiff and sober to enjoy herself. *Sober*. She was always sober. Just as Mama would wish.

Well, a drink might help, and for once Mama was going to be disappointed.

"I'd love to! But may I have some champagne first?"

"As much as you like, little girl. I'll get some for both of us," he said, his bold eyes approving her. When he returned with their two brimming glasses, she drank hers thirstily and asked for more. How cool and delicious champagne was—a pleasure she'd been missing all this time!

Glasses in hand, sipping and gazing into each other's eyes, they danced together, she and the famous actor. He was less good-looking off the screen than on, she decided, but she let him lead her out onto the narrow deserted balcony above the sea, and even managed to simulate a delicious shiver when he slipped his hand inside her dress. But when he tried to draw her into one of the bedrooms, she declined as graciously as she could, giving him a flutter of her eyelashes and a look which promised, "Another time—when it's just you and me."

Then all at once the pretense of being gay and lively and flirtatious became too difficult altogether. The room was warmer and closer than before, and she was dazed with an exhaustion which the drinking now only seemed to worsen. She had to push back the temptation to collapse on one of the soft tempting beds, and knew then that, early or not, it was time for her to leave. Hoping her ignominious retreat would go unnoticed, she slipped out of the house, started her shiny new Fiat, bought to replace the no-longer-chic Hudson, and headed off down the deserted beach road.

If she hadn't had a flat tire partway home and so had been able to sleep for even a few hours, the decision she made on the following day might have been different. But when the little car began to thump and swerve and she pulled over to the side, a long night stretched ahead.

No use waiting for help. The dark road showed no other headlights; indeed another car might not pass for hours. She had never changed a tire, had no idea how. To make her situation worse, a light rain had begun to fall, and already, huddled in the open seat, she was getting soaked. Her white fur wrap smelled unpleasantly of dead rabbit.

She stepped out on the gravel and began to walk.

"Hangover, Miss French?" asked the Count. Although his pale eyes lacked warmth, he had an understanding and reassuring manner.

She looked quickly toward the busy set. No one was listening.

"Yes, terrible!" Confession to him was easy. "I've heard you can help—and quickly. I've a scene to do soon, but my head is throbbing like a drum—"

"Certainly, my dear, I can help." He was reaching into his pocket and he handed her a tiny box.

"Do you know what to do? Just sniff it. Don't be afraid to use it all, and you'll feel better at once."

"Thank you. What is the charge? I don't want to be indebted."

"Quite all right, Miss French. Don't worry about it. I'm one of your admirers and always glad to be of service."

Chapter 26

"Joanna—"

She had just started down the steps of the *Times* building, and a tall, well-remembered figure from the past stood at the bottom, smiling up at her.

Seeing him there was so unexpected that for an instant she didn't respond.

Then she hurried, ran the rest of the way down, exclaiming, "Mr. Gold! You're back. . . ."

"Only for a few days. There happened to be a ship and I was able to come home. My father's heart gave us a scare."

"Oh, I'm sorry!"

"He's out of danger now. I've just been with him. Tell me, still enjoying your newspaper work?"

"Yes, Mr. Gold, I can't tell you how much!"

"Good. But when we were studying together at Miss Mendenhall's, I was Charles. If you don't mind, Joanna, from you I like Charles better."

"All right . . . Charles." She fell silent. Why did being with him make her feel shy and a little breathless? Of course he was older than she, a man of the world, but that hardly seemed enough of an explanation.

No, it wasn't shyness entirely. She wanted his good opinion,

and was being cautious, she supposed, so as not to appear
stupid or gauche. Whatever the reason, she was standing tongue-
tied when she wanted to ask all about France and the front and
those hazardous sailings back and forth—a thousand questions.

He said, "I often wondered whether you'd stuck it out with
the *Times*, and I'm glad to see you have. I should have known,
though. You were so very earnest, applying for the job."

Joanna flushed. "You make me sound like a schoolgirl."

"Isn't that what you were—and still are? Is innocence so
bad? Better enjoy it while you can." His voice was suddenly
harsh and his slate blue eyes were like deep wells of pain as
he stared away into the distance. Studying him, Joanna saw
how greatly he was changed, just by those months he'd been
in France. He was too thin now in his civilian clothing, and
there were lines etched into his face. He had gone blithely
away, and come back a different and older man. He had also
once had innocence, and lost it.

She tried to imagine what he had experienced, day after
day, living with soldiers at the front. Although she realized
humbly how futile any efforts of hers at understanding had to
be, she longed to offer comfort, to try to help him drive away
the demons that tortured him, whatever they were.

"Was it so bad?" she whispered.

"Yes. Before I went to France, I was like you, I too believed—" His words came slowly.

"Yes?"

But he gave himself a small shake, and the grim abstraction
faded. His listened as the nearby church bells tolled the hour,
and exclaimed in his normal tone, "How this day has flown!"

"Please, don't let me keep you. If you're here for such a
short time—you must be terribly busy. It's nice to have seen
you though, Charles."

"No—don't go yet! I'm only wondering if . . . you see, I'd
like very much to take you out to dinner. To celebrate."

"Celebrate what?"

"Oh, anything at all. Whatever's good, new, or wonderful
for you. Shall we say your job?"

"It's not new."

"No. But we didn't do anything about it before. The trouble
is, I promised tonight to make a call—"

Monica? Joanna wondered.

"I understand," she said, impatient with herself for being
so childishly disappointed, and added simply, "I'm sorry."

"Please wait—I guess I'm not being very clear. I'm only saying that if you wouldn't mind making a short stop with me afterward, we'd have time to dine together now. Are you free? Will you?"

"Yes, I'm free," Joanna said promptly. She was thinking that this was going to be quite a different evening from the one she'd anticipated tonight—the quiet supper with Uncle Paul and then a game or two of checkers. "I must call home first, but I'd like to go with you. Very much!"

"Good." He sounded inordinately pleased.

The evening *was* different, one she long remembered. Dinner was in the dining room of the elegant Alexandria, downtown at the corner of Fifth and Spring Streets, a hotel the *Times* had described in 1906 when it was opened as "a gem set in tile, steel, and marble" and which remained, ten years later, the most important social center in town. Charles told her, as they crossed the shimmering, richly hued carpet spanning the lobby, that this promenade was called "Peacock Alley" and was the most popular meeting place for movie talent and producers outside of Hollywood. The fact that there were no luminaries visible tonight made no difference to Joanna. It was exciting enough just to imagine her sister Lillian one day standing on this magic carpet and being offered a top star's contract.

Charles had Joanna's hand firmly tucked under his arm, for which she was glad. His tall figure, even in an ordinary suit, looked distinguished. She, on the other hand, what a drab little mouse she must seem in her plain gray skirt and white batiste bodice, both far more suitable for running about doing everyone's bidding at the *Times* than for entering this stylish hotel.

But Charles chose that moment to say, "The other men here are looking envious—do you notice? I'm escorting the prettiest young woman in the room." Her heart warmed to him for his tactfulness, and she resolutely put her qualms away.

However this precarious new assurance was put to the test almost at once. When she and Charles were seated at a table set with snowy white linen, a single red rose in a silver vase, and more varied knives, forks, and spoons than she had known existed, she was presented with a large menu. She opened the white leather cover, and saw that the listings were in French, and handwritten as well.

"I don't know—" she began, conscious of the hovering waiter.

"Would you mind very much if I order for both of us?" Charles said quickly. "There are some specially good things here and we don't want to miss any of them. This is, after all, a celebration."

"Please do!"

"Well, then." He spoke very rapidly, while she listened, unable to catch a single word in spite of two years of studying French in school. Charles and the waiter were conferring in what seemed to be a different language altogether. The first word she caught was *vin*, and then only because Charles hesitated after saying it, to glance at her then shake his head and add, in English, "No, no wine this evening."

After the waiter bowed and left them, she said, "I'm so envious! You can read that scrawl on the menu?"

He looked slightly taken aback, then the corners of his mouth twitched in amusement. "I've had a certain amount of practice, remember. Even in the smallest villages in France, the menus are written in French."

"Oh, of course." Briefly, she was hot with embarrassment.

But his low burst of laughter cajoled her into laughing, too, at herself, and after that she felt at ease. She could, it seemed, make a foolish remark without losing his respect. So when the raw oysters were brought, she didn't conceal her dismay at the prospect of eating one, was persuaded to try, and after swallowing the slippery thing admitted fairly that it was better than it looked.

Their eyes met, and again they both broke into laughter.

Joanna decided by the end of the meal that she had never enjoyed a dinner out quite so much before.

"Next, my great-uncle," Charles said, and by now she was prepared to be impressed. So the magnificent three-story house, as intricately decorated, curlicued, and gabled as any Victorian edifice of its generation, pleased but didn't overawe her. Even though they'd been riding in the very same unpretentious Chadwick automobile Charles had driven in the days when he went to Aunt Flossie's, it was clear by now that he came from a different social level than she, and equally clear that he didn't consider such distinctions in the least important.

Harper Johnson, a dapper elderly man, small and frail but with black unfaded eyes snapping with lively interest, was very much as Charles had described him.

"You'll like Uncle Harper," Charles had said as they drove out Grand Avenue. "He's a true patriarch of Los Angeles.

Hasn't been here quite as long as the city, but almost. In spite of a tendency to be a bit too frank at times, he has dozens of close friends, all part of the city's history, and he's hardly ever alone. A splendid old man."

Harper Johnson wasn't alone tonight. He already had two women visitors. One was in her late forties, with flaming red hair, whom Charles kissed and called "Aunt Barbara"; the other, of the same vintage as the old man but still remarkably beautiful, was introduced as Mrs. Phineas Bishop. The two older people had been playing chess, and Mrs. Bishop professed herself only too willing to be interrupted. "Harper is so good at the game," she explained, "while I—Harper actually said to me, the last time we played, 'Forgive me, Bets, but the object is to capture my king and defend yours, not the reverse.' . . . Charles, it's splendid to see you home again. Your parents are so delighted. Such a shame for them that you, their only child, are away so much—but of course they want you to be happy. Are you here for long?"

"No, I can stay only a few days more. But my father's obviously in good hands, between my devoted mother and you, Aunt Barbara. I want to thank you, and Uncle Jan, too, for all you've done."

The red-haired woman said brusquely, "The important thing is that he's really better, for which we are all so grateful. By the way, when we called there earlier this evening, we met Mr. McGowan of the *Times* just leaving. He is not one to hand out compliments wholesale, as you well know, but he told Jan that he wished you were twins, working on both sides of the Atlantic."

Charles smiled. "I shan't be missed here. They now have Miss Fritsch to take my place."

"Charles!" Joanna protested, and once again there was the secret laughter between them.

"Oh, by the way, Aunt Barbara," Charles said, "You may have run into Joanna's sister over there in Hollywood. She's Lily French. With Sennett."

"I've seen one or two of her pictures." Mrs. Gierek, studying Joanna, added, "Yes, there is indeed a resemblance—"

"I'm more interested in this young lady," Mr. Johnson declared. "So she works at the *Times*, does she? Intelligence as well as beauty. With that combination, you'll have no trouble securing your mother's approval, Charles."

His meaning was so obvious that Joanna turned scarlet with

embarrassment. Neither of the other women glanced in her direction, but elderly Mrs. Bishop began at once to talk about a dreadful episode of some five years back when the *Times* was dynamited, twenty people being killed in the blast and the building reduced to a smoking ruin.

"Unlike most of us, you never did believe the McNamara brothers were innocent of that crime, did you, Harper?" she concluded, and having launched her old friend into an impassioned discourse on the bombers, and on the reputed attempt of the famed lawyer, Clarence Darrow, to bribe the jury, Mrs. Bishop finally gave Joanna a quick reassuring smile before sitting back herself to listen.

"What charming ladies, both of them," Joanna exclaimed to Charles when they were outside again.

"More than merely charming. Did you know Barbara Gierek has made herself a power in the movie industry? As for Elizabeth Bishop, she was considered the loveliest, most spirited lady in all of southern California in her day.

"And I'll tell you something, Joanna." He reached across in the dark car and took her hand in his. "I've an idea that the girl I'm with tonight may well turn out to be the successor of one of them. Which will it be?"

He was joking, of course. But Joanna, only too conscious of the pressure of his fingers, was too flustered to laugh. She said earnestly, "If I have a choice, it's Mrs. Gierek. She's succeeded in what she wanted to do. Oh, I don't mean I'd like the film business; that isn't for me. But my dream is to write something good—as you do."

He nodded. "And why not?"

They drove the rest of the way in a companionable silence, Joanna not as tranquil as she pretended. Had he forgotten that he still held her hand?

He hadn't apparently, because once out of the car, he firmly took it again as they walked up the house steps. He said, "The last several days will have to be my family's, but I still have two evenings free. I'd like to spend them with you, Joanna."

"Oh, yes! But surely you have other things you should do."

"None I would enjoy nearly as much." A light kiss brushed her lips. "Goodnight then."

Chapter 27

On the following day, both Charles and Joanna worked late, and it had been dark for some time when they walked together down the steps of the *Times* building.

Charles said glumly, "Something has come up. Our city editor, a good friend but far too energetic, wants me to go to Vernon tonight. It seems there's a new gambling club just opened and nobody else is free to cover it."

His disappointment was obviously sincere, and she was pleased. Especially as she could see no reason for canceling their evening together. "That sounds interesting," she said. "If you don't want to write the story, I will."

"I almost think you mean it. But Joanna, Vernon isn't the place to take a young lady."

"This young lady would like to go, all the same."

He hesitated, then laughed. "Very well then—but please don't tell Uncle Harper the next time you meet him. Or he'll decide I don't deserve you after all."

Joanna grinned back at him. "He'll also decide I'm no lady." So they set off for his Chadwick automobile, and as they walked he was whistling softly. Joanna, matching his long stride with two of hers, thought happily that whatever demons he'd brought home from France were being kept at bay.

The small city of Vernon was, as she'd often heard, a nest of gambling houses. But lately it had become much more. The shrewd promoters had gradually developed the area into the major sporting center of the South Coast. There was a track for horse racing, one for dog racing, and a baseball stadium where the Vernon Tigers played. The Arena attracted the greatest boxers of the day, and pictures of James J. Corbett, James Jeffries, and Billy Papke adorned the walls of the palatial saloons.

Charles and Joanna had a surprisingly good and inexpensive

dinner at one of the restaurants, and then he set himself to complete his *Times* assignment. The new Hawaiian Village was open by now and in full swing. At the long mahogany bar, a crowd of sports and dudes jostled each other three-deep. Most of them were dressed to the blood, with a pleated silk shirt of the gaudiest color set off by armbands of another brilliant hue, and a gold watchchain, festooned with twenty-dollar gold pieces and a gold toothpick. A diamond stickpin, horseshoe shaped, a long, loose suitcoat, and a gold-headed cane completed the costume.

The owner of this establishment had claimed newspaper coverage because of the music provided, which was strangely at odds with the glittering patrons and the free-flowing liquor. A bevy of women with ukeleles played soft, lilting Hawaiian songs, heard here for the first time in America. While Charles walked about, talking to bartenders and croupiers, Joanna stood for a time just listening and admiring the grace with which the scantily clad, black-haired girls used their hands as well as their bodies to lend meaning to the words.

Gradually she became aware of the small definite sounds of gambling, the click of chips, the riffle of cards. Nearby was a second and larger room, and she looked curiously through the haze of cigar smoke over the poker tables. Beyond, she could see a large flat wheel being spun, and she was just promising herself that she'd ask Charles when he returned how the game was played when her attention was drawn again to the poker players. One of the patrons, a man somberly dressed in sharp contrast to the others, sprang up and threw his cards on the table. He shoved his small stack of chips forward to the dealer, then, rocking impatiently on his heels, stood staring at the women musicians.

His air of savage discontent was so marked that it held Joanna to the exclusion of everything else about him. Then came the shock of recognition.

Ralph Wilson. Adeline's husband was a gambler at Vernon, hunting his diversion alone and where he could. Nor was he a stranger here. She heard a croupier address him by name.

Joanna, supposing herself unobserved, turned away, but he said harshly, "Well, well. Little sister's come to Sin City. I'll bet anything Mama doesn't know."

"I'm here with one of the other reporters." She tried to sound unconcerned.

"Is that a fact now! Your family talks so high and mighty,

don't it? But one girl's an actress, and you turn up in Vernon. If I ever have a daughter, she sure as hell won't show her face in a place like this."

"Who is this man, Joanna?" Charles was at her side, his voice ominously quiet.

"My sister's husband."

"I'm finished now, so we're leaving."

The Chadwick roared away much faster than it had come. Joanna, glancing at Charles' profile and noting the grim set of his mouth, asked diffidently, "Did you really have enough time?"

"Yes . . . that fellow was right, of course. I should never have taken a girl your age to such a place."

"Aren't you forgetting? I invited myself."

"So you did, little Miss Independence." He gave her a brief smile, but her hand, lying on the seat between them, remained unclaimed.

At her door, he said, "Once again, for the record, I'm sorry."

"For what?" At last she let her indignation show. "I was having a wonderful time, until I met Ralph—and he, surely, wasn't your fault. Vernon is a part of life, Charles, and I wanted to see it. Goodness, I'm a reporter, too."

"You are, and a good one. Tomorrow then?"

"Yes."

So, even though there was no kiss, because she was too young and innocent and he'd been so rudely reminded of the fact, there was to be yet another evening.

"I thought we'd go to San Pedro tonight."

"Fine."

He shook his head in mock wonderment. "Most girls would say, 'Why San Pedro?' and look askance, at least."

"I'm not most girls. Anyway, I've an idea that if you suggest going to a place, there's something there worthwhile."

"Nothing newsworthy," he teased.

"Oh? Then I'm disappointed. I supposed you always put your work first."

"Make no mistake about it," he answered, suddenly serious. "I do. Always. But tonight I'm free, thank heaven, so we'll go visit my favorite restaurant."

"I thought San Pedro was a small town. And tough."

"Right on both counts. Very small and very tough, as waterfronts often are. Beacon Street runs the old Tenderloin in San

Francisco a close second—for drunken sailors, prostitutes, thieves, and murderers. But the town itself is really just a fishing village and, as such, a melting pot from Europe. Where we're going is a lot more respectable than that fancy palace of last night."

Half an hour later he brought his car to a stop on a quiet street well away from the water. What seemed to be a series of tiny stores in a single large building filled the block on one side, and one of these places, in contrast to the rest, had a brightly lighted window.

"Come along," Charles said. He opened the shop door, disclosing a diner, only large enough for six stools. Behind the counter was a stove on which pots simmered, and tending them as he chopped meat on a board was a very tall, solid man with a broad face.

"Hello, Peter," Charles said. "May I present to you Miss Joanna Fritsch. Peter Perkov. Peter's a very old friend, Joanna. We were boys together down here on the water, and in case you're wondering, he and his family came from Dalmatia, making him, by heredity, absolutely the finest cook around. I think you can see from his size why there's never any trouble in this place."

The huge cook flourished his cleaver then, grinning, tossed it aside, leaped over the counter, and gave Charles the embrace of a bear. "Sit, old friend! I'll cook for you and your beautiful woman. No, you eat first, then we talk."

They'd hungrily disposed of gigantic quantities of pot roast and *sarma*, cabbage leaves rolled around meat and rice, and *mostaccioli*, a pasta in a deep red sauce, all accompanied, for Joanna, with her first glass of wine, because Peter insisted that sweet red wine was a necessity with his food. Then, after the two other customers had gone, Peter stood leaning on the oil-cloth-covered counter, talking to Charles. They recalled old times with shouts of laughter. They sobered and discussed the war, and with his old friend Charles spoke freely. Joanna said nothing, only listened, sipping what was left of her wine.

Charles became aware of her, and took the glass from her hand. "That's enough for a beginner, I think, and a little fresh air is probably in order. Cabrillo Beach isn't far. Would you like to walk on the sand?"

"Yes. Barefoot," she said, and giggled for no reason.

Peter Perkov waved to them, and the car sped off, soon to stop again in the darkness next to a calm expanse of ocean beach. Overhead hung a full moon, so that the sand gleamed white with an illusion of utter cleanliness.

Forgetting to take off her shoes, Joanna ran down to the water, Charles close behind her. They began to walk along the edge.

"Oh, Charles, look!" she breathed.

Utterly quiet, together they gazed at the great blue heron standing majestically on one thin leg, against which small wavelets of black water rippled. Then Joanna inadventently moved, and with an unhurried flapping the great bird winged up and beat its way into the distant sky.

"Wasn't he beautiful?" she breathed, and in her excitement stepped backward—into a hole dug that day by children. She lost her balance and would have fallen, but Charles caught her.

For an instant, they stood teetering together, laughing. But his embrace tightened and the laughter stopped. They gazed into each other's faces for a long moment, then he began to kiss her. This was not the light easy caress of two nights before but a series of long lingering purposeful kisses that made her gasp. Her arms crept up and tightened about his neck.

But with that Charles stopped. He gently disengaged her arms.

"First I ply them with wine, then take them out on a deserted beach. Nice fellow."

"You didn't do anything—"

"Quite right, I didn't. But that's not to say I didn't want to. Come along, you're going home."

He strode ahead of her to the car, and she followed, feeling subdued and a little sad.

Once again, back on her own porch, and he was leaving. Returning to Europe. This magical interlude she'd enjoyed so much was over.

He said, "You've grown up quite a lot. So much, really, Joanna, that I almost forgot myself:.. if I write to you now and then, will you answer? I'd just like to know that a good friend is listening."

When she nodded, he said, "Thank you, Joanna," and she felt touched and honored. She was Charles Gold's friend. A good friend. What more did she want?

Chapter 28

"*Does it hurt* terribly?" Aunt Flossie asked, for the first time in her life feeling helpless. She was out of her element. Clean an entire house in record time, organize a drive for charity, go over a jumbled account book and spot the error at once—these things she could do without effort. But if one didn't count her years of waiting on her father, she was not much used to tending the sick. She had never watched a baby being born.

"Not too much," panted Adeline, lying. "Has Ralph—" She was forced to stop and clutch her abdomen while sweat popped out in beads on her forehead.

"He's gone for the doctor. They'll be here any minute." Although Aunt Flossie tried to sound confident, she was already wondering why Ralph wasn't back yet. Surely he'd been gone far longer than necessary. Or perhaps not. Time did go so slowly when one longed for it to pass. "There, there—it's bad, isn't it?" Agitated, she mopped Dell's face with a cool cloth. "Try to lie back. Please, *Liebchen*, you don't want to hurry things—not till the doctor comes."

She cast about for some diversion. "I called your mother several hours ago. You'll have her with you, very soon."

Dell's eyes snapped open. "Mama? She's coming? But she—"

"Didn't you think she would? Then you don't know Clara as well as I do."

"No, I didn't . . . she's never stepped foot in this house. Oh, I'm so—" The words were cut off by another hard spasm, but Aunt Flossie, in spite of her sympathy and apprehension, was smiling.

Good, she thought. It will be good to see mother and daughter together again. The cause of their estrangement had never been explained; even Dell herself didn't seem to understand it.

184

But all that would soon be in the past. Clara had replied, just as any other mother would, "Thank you, Aunt Flossie, I'll leave here at once. At once!"

Downstairs, the heavy door slammed open. It was too soon for Clara, but Flossie was even more pleased and relieved to hear mens' voices.

"They're here," she said gruffly, hiding her emotion. "Ralph and the doctor. Now you can rest easy."

Adeline, throwing herself about on the bed, did not answer, but her mouth twisted in a grimace of amusement. Rest easy, indeed!

The two men pounded up the stairs and ran into the room. The rotund, middle-aged doctor surveyed with a single experienced glance the condition of the mother-to-be, and said, "I'll take over now, Mr. Wilson. I'll ask you to wait, sir, down in the parlor. From the looks of things it shouldn't be too long . . . madam, I suppose you will assist me?"

Reassured by his presence, Aunt Flossie said, "I will do what I can. But I'm not much experienced in childbirth."

"Perhaps not, but I am. Just now, what I want from you is a basin of warm water and some soap to wash my hands."

Clara, approaching Adeline's house for the first time, slowed her steps then stopped before the plain, freshly swept porch.

How could she go inside—where he, Ralph Wilson, lived? Even now, so long afterward, just his name, Ralph Wilson, sickened her.

What she had done with him in the boathouse by the lake now seemed so utterly incomprehensible. It was true she'd been a bit lonely, and yes, a bit resentful of Sam's protectiveness. And worst of all, it had seemed to her that life was passing her by. Then Ralph came, and with his long lithe body had called to something inside of her and made her answer.

Was it because he'd offered a depth of feeling she'd never had and desperately wanted? Or was it simply because she needed somehow to feel free? Or again—oh ugly, degrading thought that she'd tortured herself with so many times, hadn't she simply proved that Sam's intuition was right—that she was too weak to be trusted? Night after night, lying alone in her bed, she'd mulled over the reasons for her fall, so certain that Sam's death lay at her door that she could scarcely bear to go on living herself. Yet the answer still eluded her. All she could ever be certain of was that for a brief time she'd been as entwined and bound by her desire for Ralph as a helpless rabbit in a snare.

But with Dell needing her today, she was determined that the past must be forgotten, her separation from her daughter ended. Turning her back on Dell as she'd been doing, just to avoid him, was another wrong, and this one—even so late— should be righted. Clara drew a deep ragged breath, stepped up to the door, and rapped.

She prayed there would be no answer and that he wasn't waiting just within, relegated as fathers were, to pacing the parlor floor. If he were away somewhere she could run upstairs, find her daughter's bedroom. . . .

But the door was pulled open.

Ralph said bitterly, "Well, Clara, you've come at last."

He stood back, and conquering her last reluctance she entered. To avoid facing him, she cast an absent eye around the parlor, at the dark, heavy draperies, at the solid but unimaginative furnishings, all good value for the money but cheerless. Flossie had advised Dell, Clara knew, but neither of them was in the least artistic, neither of them knew one color from another. Clara, who did, should have been here.

A rush of guilt for this minor neglect swept through her. Absurd, when she had so much larger sins to atone for!

She said, "I must go up to her at once."

"No hurry, the doctor's there. And Miss Mendenhall."

He stood between her and the stairs, clasping the back of a chair. She noticed that his knuckles were white.

"I'm her mother."

"So you are." His tone was sardonic. "Well, you've waited this long to see her, another minute or two won't matter."

"I wanted to come before. How I wanted to! I hated not seeing her!"

"Why didn't you then, I wonder?"

"Because it seemed . . . best. What if she should guess? Ralph—you didn't tell her?"

His face grew taut in anger. "I'm not a good husband, I grant you. But I'm not a monster, either."

"Then it's all right, I can face her—"

"Wait! All this time . . . Clara, wait!" She had tried to push past, but his hands had left the chair, were on her shoulders, turning her toward him.

Clara went rigid. "Not a monster? Prove it! Here in this

house, her house—while your child is being born—do you dare to think of me?"

"Don't *you* think of *me*? Don't you, Clara?"

"No! We don't matter to each other. We never will again."

"Because I married your daughter when I was beside myself with hurt and anger? Clara! Good God! You wouldn't see me or talk to me. I hardly knew what I did. I only wanted to punish you, but what a mistake—I did us all a wrong. If only I'd waited, if only I had!"

"No, Ralph, don't imagine time would have helped. After Sam died, there could never be anything more between you and me."

"But why? In God's name, why? I loved you! You are the only woman I ever loved, from the time I was a boy and first saw you dance at the carnival. Oh, sure, it was wrong for me to take you when you were still Sam's wife, but afterward, after he died, we could have married. So why wouldn't you see me, talk to me? Ever since I got turned away at your door, I've hated you, but I still love you, too. I can't help myself—"

He broke off. Clara was looking anxiously past him, wondering why there was only silence above. He understood, and said impatiently, "The door's shut. She'd never let me hear her scream. Too proud... Clara, answer me!"

"Very well. But take your hands away."

His grasp loosened, dropped from her.

"I wouldn't see you," she said flatly, "because I couldn't bear the sight of you. I had enough torment as it was. Anyway, for me, what was between us wasn't love. Why, I hardly knew you! I admired and respected Sam. I cared deeply for him. All of that put together is what love is, and for the terrible thing I did to him, for the pain I caused him, I'll be sorry to my dying day."

"But he didn't know—"

"Yes, I think he did. I'm certain he did, because for an instant there in the boathouse that last time I felt strangely uneasy, as if we were being watched, yet when I turned my head, there was no one at the window. Afterward though, when Sam crashed into the cliff, I was sure. I hated myself and you, and whatever I might have felt for you beyond mere lust curdled like cream struck by lightening. It was soured. Finished."

"You mean that."

"Yes."

They stared at each other.

Then there was the sound of a door opening upstairs and they heard a small, querulous cry.

"Oh, listen! Listen, Ralph, your baby's come."

She pushed past him, went running up the stairs, and he followed.

From behind the door just at the top of the stairs, Clara could hear low voices. And that little cry. She turned the knob and went in.

"I'm her mother," she said quickly into the doctor's brief, inquiring glance. He nodded, although he continued to give all his attention to the small creature he held in his hands.

"It's a girl, Mama. Isn't she beautiful?" Adeline, drained by exhaustion of every emotion except joy, greeted Clara as though they had parted only yesterday.

Clara said, "I'm so glad for you, dear Dell," and stooped to kiss her daughter's cheek, smiling at Aunt Flossie as she did so. She then went to look over the doctor's shoulder.

"You'll stay for a while? Help us care for her?" Dell was asking.

"Umm—not stay here, no, Uncle Paul's expecting me, but I'll help you all I can. . . ."

She spoke absently because she was studying the baby. Beautiful was the right word. The head wasn't misshapen as with most newborn infants, the features were small and delicate, the hair was a golden fuzz. This was one of Clara's own daughters, born again.

She heard Dell say, "Ralph, it's a girl, just what you wanted!" and Ralph, who was beside her gazing at his child, sucked in his breath. His fingers gently touched the tiny satiny cheek.

But Clara, past that first rapturous look, was thinking, *How blue she looks! And gasping for air—such a struggle—*

She glanced at the doctor's intent expression and a coldness settled in her heart.

Then Ralph asked the question she had not had the courage to voice. "Her breathing—she can hardly cry. Is that natural?"

The doctor gave him a sharp, admonishing look. He said reluctantly, "There is a problem, yes. The blueness means—"

He was interrupted by Dell's cry. "A problem? What kind of problem? Will she be all right?"

The answer when it came, stiff and without conviction,

silenced her. "I will certainly try to see that she is. I will try my best. Please, Mrs. Wilson, don't upset yourself."

Clara turned, looking into the wide terrified eyes of her daughter.

"He doesn't give up easily, I'll say that for him." Ralph was pacing the parlor floor again, in the same path he'd worn before the birth. "But it's useless, isn't it? She's far weaker now. I could see that for myself."

Aunt Flossie, seated on a tufted chair in one corner, continued to gaze at the floor. She felt such an intruder. It had seemed to her, many hours ago, that she should quietly go home, leave this stricken house to Dell's husband and mother. But Clara had stopped her. "No, Flossie, stay!" And she supposed she had been of help. At least she'd prepared a meal which no one ate.

Clara, standing at the window, said, "It seems so to me, too. I'm very much afraid."

"I wanted her too much! I didn't think I did, but as the time came . . . I wanted a girl, one who would look exactly like— her mother." He'd paused before those two final words, and Clara knew he hadn't meant to say them at all, that he'd hated the necessity of saying them.

Aunt Flossie ventured a comment. "Surely, if the worst should happen, and God grant it won't, you and Adeline can try again. Although I'm sure that's cold comfort now."

Ralph didn't answer. Only continued his steady, fast pacing.

Then there was a single wild scream from upstairs, and they were all aware of what it signified. An ominous silence followed.

"He asked us to wait," Clara said uncertainly. "But one of us—you, Ralph—should go up."

Ralph, who had stopped stock-still in the center of the room, gazed at her blankly. He didn't move.

A minute passed, then the doctor came walking woodenly down the stairs. He looked tired and defeated.

"Yes, I can see you all know. It's over. I'm deeply sorry, but there was nothing I could do. I've heard of cases like this, where there is a defect in the heart itself, a small hole perhaps, but they're rare. Someday, I suppose, we'll have the science to repair such a hole, but not now.

"And your wife, sir, is in a state of shock, which is wor-

risome. After the first outcry when I told her, she turned her
face to the wall, weeping silently. I've given her something to
make her sleep, which will take effect quickly, but if you care
now to go up, perhaps you can comfort her."

Ralph gave a short grunt of a laugh. "Perhaps. But who do
you think will comfort me?" As though he became aware then
that something more than a few harsh words was expected of
him, he added, speaking too quickly, "No, if she's going to
sleep at once, I won't disturb her. I think I must go—out—"

He walked heavily to the door. Clara had never before heard
his tread drag. Those dragging steps sounded on the wooden
porch. Then he was gone.

"I'll go up to her," Clara said. She started for the stairs,
then looked back. She said to the silent doctor, "You did all
you could, I'm sure."

"Her heart just wasn't strong! There was nothing more—"
He sounded anguished suddenly, as though he were young
again and hadn't yet lost an infant.

"I understand."

Clara ran up to the room where Dell lay. Entering, she
averted her eyes from the still little body, now wrapped in a
blanket, its face covered, and placed in the cradle meant for a
living child.

Clara pulled a chair close to the bed and took Dell's hand
in hers. "I'm so deeply sorry, Dell! But things do go wrong
with babies. Often, unhappily."

"Not with yours." Dell sounded not so much bitter as defeated. "I'm no good at anything, you see, Mama. Not anything. I can't even bear a healthy child."

"Hush, hush. That's not so. You'll try again, and next time
it will be perfect."

"No. I've lost Ralph. There will never be a next time."
Although her eyes were shut, tears seeped from between the
lids and coursed down her pale cheeks. "The baby might have
made a difference. Just lately I thought he was coming to want
one as much as I did . . . he's gone, hasn't he?"

"Not gone—just left the house for a little."

"You see? He would not even come up to speak to me! Oh,
Mama, I tried so hard . . . and I've lost him."

She was quiet for some time, the forced sleep almost upon
her. Then her eyes opened blearily one last time, but they no
longer sought her mother's. She withdrew her hand, withdraw-

ing herself, turning away as she always had from closeness with Clara.

"No, that's not so, is it?" she said flatly. "A woman can't lose a man she never had."

Clara did not answer, her own pain almost more then she could bear.

Chapter 29

It was Saturday night again. But the October evening dripped with fog and occasional rain, and Joanna said to Tony, "I think Castles-by-the-Sea might be damp and chilly tonight. Why don't we do something else?"

The truth was, for her it was no longer possible to dance the hours away in carefree enjoyment. The loss of Dell's baby, and her sister's dull misery, unchanged almost a year later, had shocked Joanna as no description of carnage in far-off Europe ever had. This was intense sorrow, seen and felt at home, reminding her of the time just after Papa's death.

Too, the sight of Irene Castle, still valiantly leading the dances, was depressing, because Joanna happened to know, perhaps better than Irene did, the extent of the dangers Vernon Castle was facing. He was flying mission after mission, and it was well-known at the newspaper office that the casualty rate among British pilots was high indeed.

Joanna worked full time now for the *Times*. She was regularly given small stories to write—a dog show in Anaheim, a wedding, the dedication of a new public building. This day she had just returned from Catalina Island, where she'd been sent to do a feature on the little resort town of Avalon and its recovery from a devastating fire the previous November. She'd reveled in the ocean crossing on the stylish *S. S. Cabrillo*, even though the voyage was little more than three hours each way.

Doubtless because she was so new to her task, she found all her small assignments of interest. Engrossed as she was, she tended to believe that her country's policy of neutrality was sensible and right. Indeed, most Americans, even though partisan for one side or the other because of ancestry, were of this opinion. The flurry of outrage over the sinking of the *Luisitania* had subsided, following German assurances that no United States shipping would be interfered with. Woodrow Wilson, after all, was running on a platform of "punishment not intervention." He would never, he promised, take his country into war.

But if Joanna were tempted to agree too easily, she'd been brought up short by Charles Gold. He'd written to her finally, not just sent a message through Mr. McGowan, but a long letter to her alone, and he told her how bewildered he was by the indifference of the United States.

It's as though the battles of the Somme are only tremendous spectacles, Joanna, creations of D. W. Griffith or Cecil B. deMille, to be shuddered at for an hour or so then forgotten, as people go on, immersed in their daily routines which for them are the only reality.

I cannot stand back! I cannot view what's happening coldly and dispassionately. I've watched too many men, some of whom had become close friends, give up their lives . . . I tell you, this war is nothing but slaughter, and it will go on and on and on, because without the intervention of our country, no end is in sight.

There had been more, a bitter outpouring of personal grief which only rarely had seeped into his public dispatches. Then his conviction:

The United States cannot remain aloof forever, try as it might. Vernon Castle, for example, is well-known everywhere, and surely there will be an uproar if he is killed. I fervently hope that may never happen, but Castle flies as many missions as any two other pilots, he is dedicated, fearless—and quite probably doomed.

Of course, he's an Englishman by birth, and there will be those who shake their heads and say, "It was his duty." But will they still turn aside after the American casualties begin? There will be some soon, as members of the new *Escadrille Américaine* are already beginning to dogfight in the skies over France.

Joanna, reading, had felt privileged to be Charles Gold's confidante. And to her pleasure, for they were after all friends as well, the letter concluded on a personal note:

> There's a song popular in England now that reminds me of you. "If you were the only girl in the world," so the words go, and the melody is beautiful. We've never danced together, have we? I hope so much that someday we can.

That was all. She'd stood pensively, with the letter in her hand, remembering how their last evening together had ended.

After he'd said, "Thank you, Joanna," he'd taken both her hands in his. But he made no move to kiss her again, and realizing that she had expected him to, she blushed in the darkness.

"Joanna—I'm going to be gone this time for at least a year, possibly much longer." He seemed to be speaking to himself rather than to her. "Even a year can be a very long time."

Abruptly he released her and stood back. "Goodbye, my dear, *auf Wiedersehen*. Do you know, the German we learned together has been a great help to me, but when I speak it to some prisoner, I'm always reminded of those studious and very pleasant afternoons in Miss Mendenhall's parlor. Do you remember them as clearly as I do?"

"Yes. Oh, please, Charles . . . be careful!"

"I will certainly try. I'm no hero."

He'd gone then. Yes, she was his friend, a good friend, one he trusted and was fond of. But that was all.

Tony was, as usual, agreeable. He said, "If you don't want to dance, why don't we go to the movies? There's a theater down on First Street that's showing a western with William S. Hart. Or, and probably you'd like this better, how about the new *Perils of Pauline* at the Bijou?"

Joanna laughed. "You're right, I dearly love Pauline and her wild adventures. But there's another film I'd rather see, Tony, if you wouldn't mind. Remember that article I wrote about movie extras? The one Mr. McGowan liked so much?"

"He liked it so much he chopped it in half and ran it on the last page," Tony growled. Secretly, he was less than enthusiastic about her working at the newspaper, a job which, with all the sordid news stories there were to be covered, didn't seem proper to him for any young woman, particularly his Joanna.

"That wasn't so bad," she said. "The series had been cancelled, and I was lucky to be printed at all. Anyway, the girl in the article, Polly Kelly, was an extra, just one among hundreds, trying to break into Hollywood. And she's making it! Not long ago she called to tell me she had a part in Virginia Pearson's latest film."

"She's a vamp? Like Virginia Pearson?"

"Hardly! Polly couldn't be. She's the wholesome type. The nice girl next door. It's just a small part, she said—but would you like to go?"

"Fine, let's," Tony said amiably. Anything Joanna suggested suited him. Anything she asked, in fact, he was willing to do. Except, of course, give up flying.

"How did you like it?" Joanna asked. The rain had eased up temporarily, and they were breaking the streetcar ride with a stop at a busy soda fountain. Joanna adored ice cream sodas.

"Umm, all right," Tony said between the last delicious spoonfuls of a three-scoop banana split. "But I didn't think much of the story. Or of Virginia Pearson, either. I didn't think she was so irresistible, and once she got a little down on her luck she turned into a bad woman. I prefer a different sort of girl. One with pluck. Like you."

"Like me?"

"Yes, you. The loyal kind, who'd stand by her husband no matter what happened."

"You believe I would?" Joanna was touched.

"Yes, I do. I'd never lose faith in you." He pushed away his empty dish and leaned back on the legs of the bent-iron chair. "Joanna, you're the one girl in the world."

"If you were the only girl in the world—"

Was Charles a good dancer? she wondered idly. He'd written that he wanted to dance with her. Yes, probably he was. He was so terribly capable in every way, and they got along so well. When they were together again, it would be like another line of that song, the one that went, "There would be such wonderful things to do. . . ."

"The only girl for me," Tony was saying firmly. Then he added, "I want to marry you."

"Tony, please—not now!"

"Why not now?"

"We can't talk about something so, well, so personal. Not here in this crowded place."

"I don't mind. I'd like the whole world to know that you're my girl."

"But I'm not! That is, I'm not anybody's girl. I told you before, Tony, I'm not ready to marry."

"Even if it means I go off to war without knowing where we stand, you and I? Without having your promise?"

"What do you mean—going off to war? Our country isn't at war."

"No, it isn't. Maybe it never will be, and I'm getting restless. I'm a very good pilot, and exhibition flying isn't enough—not when I believe America should be helping out over there. *I* should be . . . Listen, Joanna, in the battles of Verdun and the Somme, the air fighting has been important, and lately I heard the most wonderful piece of news. There's a squadron of American flyers in France right now, flying fighter planes. They call themselves *Escadrille Américaine* and it's a very special group. They use the kind of planes I'm used to—"

"You needn't go on. I've heard about it. Tony Bonnard, you're not thinking of going over there? You'd join up while we're still neutral? Tony, you might be killed, and it isn't even our fight!" Entirely forgetting the people around them, Joanna's voice had risen to a wail. "Tony, no!"

"From what I've heard you say lately, you think it should be our fight."

"No—no, I don't. Oh, I don't know what I think! We can send supplies, we can help, but—"

"Not risk our lives? Not really be in it? Sounds like stuffy old Woodrow Wilson talking. Oh, Joanna, I'm not going to get killed. I'm a good pilot. You know I am."

"I hate flying!" she replied with such passion that those sitting nearby fell into silence and listened with avid interest. "I hate it! I hate every kind of aircraft there is. Papa was a good pilot, too—and what happened to him?"

"I know, honey. I know how you feel. But a man has to do what he believes is right—"

"Nonsense! Not you. You'd be doing it for the thrills. Just as you do that Immelmann roll, and fly upside down, and try every other harebrained stunt. It will be even more exciting, I suppose, if someone is shooting at you?"

"Joanna, listen—Joanna, where are you going?"

"Out of here!"

Tony threw some money on the table and ran after her onto the street.

Matching his stride to her quick agitated one, he said, "That isn't true, you know—or not entirely. I do want to help beat the Huns, but why I go doesn't really matter, does it? The point is, I'm going—and I'm asking you to marry me first." He took her hand and held it as they walked. "Don't you see? Then I'd be certain to come back safely. I love you too much not to come back."

"Oh, don't be so melodramatic, Tony," she said angrily. But his devotion—which was real enough—troubled her. Suppose, after she refused him, he did go—and then didn't return?

Would she always have to live with her grief and guilt?

"No," she said, "I've told you. I don't want to marry anyone. Not for a long time."

But for once, refusing him, her voice lacked conviction.

Chapter 30

Joanna was having nightmares, she who had always slept dreamlessly except for one brief spell, after Papa's accident, when she'd been jolted awake by the hideous vision of a dirigible dipping and falling, the gondola swinging inexorably toward the trees.

But when Papa died, there'd been no fire. In her nightmare now, a matchbox of a plane, Tony uselessly fighting the controls, spiraled out of the sky with a trail of black smoke. The instant the little plane smashed into the ground, there was an explosion. Now flames enveloped the cockpit, trapping the man inside. . . .

She screamed aloud, her own body thrashing in agony.

"Joanna, what is it? Wake up!"

The electric light was switched on, and Uncle Paul, looking

frailer and more hunchbacked than usual in his dressing gown, stood beside her bed.

"Are you all right?" he asked anxiously.

"It's Tony! Tony was shot down...or I guess I dreamed he was. It was horrible! The plane burned, and he couldn't get out."

Paul ran a hand through his thin silver hair as he pulled his thoughts together. Ignoring her words *shot down*, he said, "It's true, my dear, he could crash. Flying is dangerous. But if you must imagine such a macabre event, I'd like to point out that he would most certainly be dead on impact. The flames wouldn't matter.

"Why dwell on the worst? Tony's been barnstorming for years now, and so far he's been lucky. Besides, his life is flying. I doubt if even for you he'll give it up."

"No, he won't. But it isn't just flying. Much as I hate those crazy stunts of his, I've grown used to them. Uncle Paul, did you know he's planning to go to France and fly against the Germans?"

"I'm not surprised. As soon as I read about that American air group, I thought of him."

"I thought he had more sense," Joanna said tartly.

"Then you don't understand him as well as you should, being so close to him. He's intensely patriotic, and worried about his country's honor. A man—"

"Please don't say 'A man has to do what he believes is right!' If that isn't the most sanctimonious and pretentious excuse for doing just what one pleases, I don't know what is."

"I wasn't about to say any such thing," Paul protested. "I only intended to point out that a man who thinks as Tony does and who loves aeroplanes would naturally leap at the chance."

"Then he loves them more than he does me."

"I doubt that. There is more than one kind of love. Take your father. Sam adored Clara, yet you know how he felt about dirigibles."

"Yes...please, Uncle Paul, sit down in that chair. Are you warm enough?" The terror had ebbed, yet she needed the comfort of his company a little longer. She pulled her blanket more closely about herself, and said, "I want to ask you something. About marriage."

"My dear child, I am hardly an authority. I've never been married."

"Perhaps not, but you are a very observant man. Now, this

is what I'm wondering. Mama and Papa were happy together. That much I'm sure of."

"Yes, I believe they were. A good, solid marriage."

"I imagine Papa loved her from the moment he saw her?"

"He certainly did. I was present at that first moment—well, almost the first moment." Paul smiled as if at some small joke, but he didn't elaborate.

"And Mama? Did she feel the same?"

"Now, how would I know that? You should ask Clara, not me."

"But I think you do know. She was even younger than I am now, and you were like a father to her, so she told us."

His lips set stubbornly, just as they always did whenever one of Clara's daughters probed into the past, but Joanna said, "Then I can guess the answer. She married him for other reasons, but grew to love him. Am I right?"

"Perhaps," Paul said reluctantly.

"So that can happen."

She was silent, reflecting. But when her uncle pulled himself awkwardly from his chair, she cried, "Please don't go just yet." She was gazing at him with the deep blue eyes so like Clara's, and he sank back.

There was so much more she wanted to know. Had her mother been attracted to any other man, a man like Charles, when she made her decision? Had she hesitated, torn, as Joanna was?

She, Joanna, had let herself imagine, after those three unforgettable magical evenings, that Charles cared for her. They'd gotten along so well, *fitted* so well, almost thinking the same thoughts, it seemed. She'd felt so at ease, yet so excited. Hadn't he felt the same?

But Charles had never really said. Never given her any reason to think he regarded her as any more than just a good friend. He'd kissed her, yes. Very tenderly, with passion even. But she'd seen enough of the world to know that with men this meant little. Men didn't love every girl they ever kissed!

She'd actually considered writing to him, telling him honestly about Tony, see then what his reaction would be. But there wasn't time. There simply wasn't time, not when letters had to follow Charles about, the way they did, sometimes for weeks.

Besides, what could she say? "I've had a proposal of marriage, Charles. Do you want to ask me yourself?" If he'd wanted to, he would have, surely. Age didn't make that much difference. A man going away for a long time must want someone waiting, someone to come home to. See how she was being beseiged by Tony! His most frequent argument was "Won't you give me some happiness before I go?" by which, bless his heart, he meant only marriage.

Uncle Paul was waiting. She could see that he'd started to shiver again, even huddled in his warm robe. Poor hunchbacked man, so wise in most respects, but so inexperienced in matters of love. What help could he really be to her?

She said, "I'm sorry, I shouldn't keep you any longer. And I'm all right now."

"Very well. Good night then, my dear. And please, no more nightmares."

There were no more nightmares, but Joanna still would have liked to seek advice. Unhappily, there was no one to confide in. Not since Bonnie and Mollie Lowe had she had any close friends of her own sex. Aunt Flossie presented the same drawback as Uncle Paul, never having been married. And Mama, the obvious person, the one Joanna would have chosen first, was temporarily in New York with Lillian, who had been loaned for two pictures to an eastern studio.

Only Dell was left, and to Joanna's mind her eldest sister was a living, breathing example of what not to do.

Here was a girl who had been so passionately in love she couldn't wait a decent interval after Papa's funeral, and been so ashamed, in consequence, that she couldn't even bring herself to ask Mama's permission. She'd been blinded by her infatuation!

Joanna had not been blinded by the attractions of Ralph Wilson, nor, she was sure, had Uncle Paul. They'd suspected from Ralph's dour behavior that Dell's love was not returned in kind. But as the wedding had taken place before they were informed of it, there was nothing to do but hope they were mistaken.

And now, what an unhappy change that marriage had wrought in Dell! Gone was all confidence in herself. Before she even spoke, she seemed to look to Ralph for approval. And since the death of their baby, she'd become as morose as he, listlessly doing the work she'd once so enjoyed, going through her day as though it too were merely a chore to be finished.

If such unhappy subservience could result from marrying for love, then liking a man, enjoying his company, remembering gratefully how he'd always stood by her and been her closest friend, and now, feeling respected by him as well as badly wanted, all that might be better. Might well be more than enough.

In early November, six weeks before he was to leave on a merchant ship from New York, Joanna accepted Tony. They were married in nearby St. Joseph's, Tony being a Catholic by birth and conviction. He had been able to persuade the young priest, who was sympathetic to his predicament, to shorten the banns as well as marry him to a non-Catholic, provided only that she promise, afterward, to finish taking instruction in the faith.

The audience, scattered in the huge brick church, may have been sparse, sparser than necessary because Joanna, for reasons she couldn't define, did not invite anyone from the newspaper, but the ceremony was solemn and impressive. As it should be for a wedding, she thought, further assuaging her doubts.

Her mother, with the help of Aunt Flossie, the two of them sewing almost continually for a week, had made her gown. The white satin, ribbed through the bodice with strands of fine imported lace, was embroidered with rosebuds at the hem, at the throat, and on the short train. Their pale yellow was a subdued echo of the color of her hair, which fell to her waist from beneath her wide-brimmed chiffon hat.

She came slowly down the aisle, very slowly because it was Uncle Paul's arm in which her hand rested, she in fact supporting him though he walked as straight and proud as he possibly could and she hoped no one would guess.

She looked ahead. Tony waited at the altar, looking so grand with a stiff wing collar, white bow tie, and swallow-tailed coat that she hardly recognized him. Then she caught his solemn, uncertain smile, and suddenly remembered a small boy with burned legs, all alone and in pain, running through a vast train station full of strangers. He'd needed her that night, young as he was. He needed her still.

She smiled back, and saw the uncertainty vanish in a wide grin of delight.

Chapter 31

Tony soon was gone. He boarded a train for New York, and from there he was scheduled to take a merchant ship for Europe.

Joanna, knowing how vulnerable those unarmed ships were to enemy attack, lived in dread during the days of the sailing. Granted, vessels not flying the flag of England or her allies were supposed to be left unmolested. However, the Germans had declared a *war zone* around Great Britain, in which vessels of any nation, if discovered there, would be sunk. And even outside this area, German submarines had recently attacked several neutral ships, excusing the action on the basis that they could hardly take the risk of stopping a suspicious appearing ship and asking to see her papers when a submarine lying on the surface made such an easy target.

After several weeks passed with no word of a sinking, Joanna breathed easier and tried to close her mind to what Tony would be doing next—dogfighting in the air, such a deadly and dangerous game—and *game*, she thought bitterly, was just what it would be to him.

At length a letter arrived, and enclosed with it was a snapshot. Tony, in aviator's uniform, grinning, his cap cocked rakishly, stood beside a small biplane, and his hand pointed to the flowing script which decorated the fusilage. Joanna could not make out what was enscribed, but this didn't matter as he informed her proudly at the end of his letter that the plane's name was *Joanna*.

She crumpled the thin sheets in her hand and burst into angry tears.

A short time later, she began to suspect she was pregnant, and when another month went by she knew it was so.

Fortunately, except for a poor appetite and a lack of energy, she felt fairly well and was able to do her work at the newspaper. In fact, to have her mind so thoroughly occupied, she decided, must be helping to stave off the usual feminine malaise of the early months.

In March, when she found herself unable to fasten the waistband of her skirt, she knew that discovery could no longer be postponed. Indeed, Uncle Paul had for some days been giving her mild looks of inquiry though he'd said nothing.

Heavy of heart, she asked if the city editor of the *Times*, Mr. McGowan, might see her for a few minutes, even then hoping he would be too busy that afternoon and her announcement needn't be made quite yet. But then he said, "Of course, come into my office, Miss Fritsch—pardon me, Mrs. Bonnard—please sit down," and she was committed.

It did not help that his first words were, "I intended to speak to you today anyway. You've been doing splendidly, and will shortly be getting a raise in your salary."

To her astonishment as well as deep chagrin, Joanna once again dissolved into tears, a feminine weakness she had always scorned.

"Here now," Mr. McGowan said, looking baffled. He awkwardly tendered his handkerchief. "Surely, a commendation isn't an occasion for grief?"

"I'm so sorry, I'm just not myself. It's . . ." She added more quietly, "I'm going to have a baby."

He digested the news for a moment, then asked, "And is that the cause of your distress? I confess to liking babies. My wife and I had several children ourselves."

"It isn't the baby!" she broke in. "I like babies, too. But I hate to leave here. I shall miss all this—my work—terribly!"

"I see. There is that to upset you. And also, no doubt, your husband, they tell me, is in the thick of it in France?"

"He's a pilot, flying with *Escadrille Américaine*."

"Brave fellow! Well, if it's of any consolation, many other Americans will be going over soon. I expect this country to be at war with Germany within a month. Did you read this morning's dispatch? Another American merchant ship sunk with no warning!"

Joanna shuddered.

"And then Germany's message to Mexico, intercepted last month, in which she suggested Mexico become her ally, and promising in return to help them recover the land ceded to us after the Mexican War. What an impertinence!"

Agreeing, all Joanna could think about was that no longer would she be a part of this world where the news was so current and exciting. Tragic no doubt, but exciting.

"Well," Mr. McGowan said, pulling a forward a pile of manuscript and indicating that the interview was at an end, "we will miss you, young lady."

She rose to her feet, feeling heavy and awkward for the first time.

Then Mr. McGowan peered up at her again over the wire rims of his glasses and said, "Did I ever tell you you remind me a little of my daughter?"

"No, sir."

"She married and moved to New York, to start a family. A bright girl, like you. Had to give up teaching ... I'll tell you what I'll do, Mrs. Bonnard. Later on, if it's possible for you to have your mother or someone care for the baby part of the time, perhaps we can arrange something—so that you can come back to work."

"Oh, Mr. McGowan, thank you!"

"Never mind thanking me," he said dryly. "If I'm right about the war, this office will be desperately short-handed."

Nevertheless, she knew his offer was magnanimous, and her gratitude was heartfelt.

Now, however, she was stranded at home, and had to read the newspaper like any ordinary citizen in order to learn that on April 6th, four days after President Wilson declaimed solemnly that "the world must be made safe for democracy," the United States officially declared war on Germany. The leisurely stream of life in America was transformed into a roaring flood of wartime activities. Liberty bonds were sold to support the draft, all men between the ages of twenty-one and thirty were required to register, and Uncle Sam appeared on recruiting posters everywhere, pointing a stern finger and mouthing the words, "I WANT *YOU*." George M. Cohan had not yet written the poignant "Over There," but as soon as he did, the words were sung all over America, sung with pride and tears because at last the Yanks were in it.

> *"We're going over, we're going over,*
> *And we won't come back till it's over,*
> *over there."*

Government agencies were striving to mobilize an almost totally unprepared economy. Weapons must be produced, food must be conserved. Most important of all, the public morale must be kept high, and spearheading this drive with gusto were the motion picture producers. As a very minor consequence of their efforts, Joanna, being Lillian's sister, heard from the editor of the *Times* again, far sooner than she ever expected.

The telephone rang, and it was he, suggesting with unusual diffidence that, if it wouldn't embarrass her too much and only if she were feeling up to it, he'd like her to take on another Hollywood assignment. Would she?

Would she! Standing in the hall of the quiet old house, her heart was drumming with pleasure.

What kind of story did he have in mind? she asked, and it was a measure of the progress she had made in her short time at the newspaper that he answered her seriously and promptly.

"Hollywood's gone to war. Already." He gave a grim laugh. "Did you happen to see a popular film last year called *Civilization*, in which women, in order to stop a battle, refused to bear any more children, or as they so chillingly put it, any more 'cannon fodder'?

"The pacifists and isolationists among us were pleased. But all that's changed. Now the filmmakers are going to the opposite extreme, their justification being that Wilson's committee on public information has created a Division of Films, aimed at selling the war to America. One picture's appeared already—*The Little American*, in which Mary Pickford is the innocent victim of a leering, sadistic Prussian officer, and I've been told that worse atrocity films are in the making. There'll be young French women raped by the merciless Hun, children in occupied zones abused, and, here at home, our new munition factories riddled with sinister spies who speak with German accents. All these story lines are presented as fact, yet our own Charles Gold, who knows the war intimately, has never even hinted at such horrors. Why? Because they are imaginary!

"I myself find this rigged propaganda very frightening. Can anything good come from sowing false seeds of outrage and revenge? Take the strong popular feeling already present in this country, find a few scapegoats—"

He paused, and she realized with surprise that this ordinarily self-contained man was fighting to control his emotion.

"On the day war was declared," he resumed, "the *Times* ran an official announcement at the bottom of page one, assuring any foreigners among us that if they only conducted themselves properly they'd suffer no loss of property or liberty.

Can such a fine promise be kept? Not if all the rest of us begin searching for spies beneath our beds!

"Mrs. Bonnard, I want you to visit your sister's studio, and then Mutual Films, where that young actress Polly Kelly works—as I remember, she's a friend of yours. Get in some other places, too. However you can manage it, get in. Find out if the motion pictures have sources of information that we haven't. And if not, as I believe you'll discover to be the case, please write a piece that will let in a little sanity and fresh air. . . ."

Joanna had been too excited by the prospect of working again to give much consideration to Mr. McGowan's final and, to her, rather farfetched point about the dangers of injustices at home in America. So it was a rude awakening, only one day before she was to meet Lillian, to learn that his apprehensions were well founded.

Dell, early in the morning, came to the house, and for once her dull lethargy had lifted.

"Joanna," she announced abruptly, "I'm worried about Aunt Flossie."

"Why? Is she ill?" Joanna was alone, Uncle Paul having had gone for one of his short painful strolls.

But Dell shook her head impatiently. "No, it's simply the problem of her being German. She never sounded so German before and it wouldn't have mattered if she did. But nowadays—"

Joanna's attention sharpened. "You're right. I was talking to her not long ago, and her accent seemed thicker, more pronounced. How could that be?"

"Who cares how? It just is. Much thicker, in public anyway. Now I don't pretend to know as much as you about Europe and the war, but even I can see that people don't like to hear her. They glare as soon as she opens her mouth. But does that make her be quiet? No! She just talks louder, even throws in German words when she knows the English perfectly well."

"She did seem upset that day," Joanna mused, "but she didn't say why. She only reminded me, quite sharply, that many foreigners came to this country long ago and are now good Americans—more patriotic than some of the native born. That may well be. . . ." She paused, remembering Peter Perkov, the giant Dalmation cook in San Pedro, and his cheerful "I won't mind fighting!"

"But when people are seeing their men off to war and at the same time being told what monsters the Germans are—" Joanna continued.

"That's exactly what Aunt Flossie can't bear," Dell interrupted. "She says she's for America right or wrong, but it maddens her to hear the Germans called Huns and monsters, as though they had no honor or decency. . . . Joanna, the worst was yesterday, when I rode with her on the streetcar and she began talking to me in German—just as though I could understand it! I tried to make her be quiet, I begged her, but the more I begged the louder she spoke, and heaven knows German is not a quiet language at best. People were muttering all around us. I heard a man say to his wife, 'Do you think that woman's a spy'?"

"A spy? Aunt Flossie? I cannot believe anyone would suggest such a silly idea!"

"Those were his words," Dell asserted. "And now I've got a problem. She has a toothache and should visit the dentist this morning. Ordinarily, I'd just shut down my park rides and go with her—I don't care at all anymore what happens to the business. But there's a big rally at Chutes Park today and they'll be selling Liberty bonds, and I promised I'd keep everything open. Joanna, Aunt Flossie must not go alone. Not as queer as she's been lately."

"No. You go on to work. I'll keep her company," Joanna said. Dell no doubt exaggerated, but if Aunt Flossie were attracting attention, even rudeness, she must somehow be persuaded to be careful. Joanna would add her own voice to Dell's.

Aunt Flossie, however, was clearly in no mood to receive advice. She issued from her house before Joanna even reached the door, saying loudly, *"Ich habe es eilig—Dieser Weisheitzahn tut mir weh."*

"I'm sorry I'm a little late. I don't hurry as well in my condition, somehow. But why are you speaking German?"

"Never mind," was the grumbled answer, after two women had passed by on the sidewalk. "You understood me, I think? I'd hate to miss the dentist's office hours, with this wisdom tooth giving me such trouble, so we really must hurry. That is, if you insist on coming. It's kind of you, but quite unnecessary. Do you expect me to faint from pain?"

As she was talking, she went sailing ahead, bulky Joanna in tow, and they arrived at the corner just as the streetcar came clanging to a stop. Flossie stumped aboard, paying for them both before Joanna could stop her, and dropping the coins in the box without any of her customary pleasant greeting to the driver.

Joanna followed meekly to a seat at the rear, only mildly reassured by her companion's sudden and glum silence. She stared out of the window. It seemed wisest not to try to start a conversation.

They were approaching Flower Street where the dentist's office was located when Aunt Flossie got to her feet and without warning began to speak.

"Jetzt, Joanna. Wir müssen aussteigen."

"It's our stop. Time to get off!" Joanna chimed in brightly, covering most of the German words with her clear English. Aunt Flossie shot her a sardonic look, but disembarked saying nothing more.

As they climbed the stairs to the dentist's office, Joanna, despite the inauspicious moment, attempted to remonstrate. "I really think you shouldn't do that. It's, well, it could even be dangerous."

"Do what?" Aunt Flossie innocently patted her sore jaw.

"You know very well! This speaking German so much. Right now—it is too bad, but there is such a lot of feeling—"

"You prefer my deplorable accent in English? I think one may as well be hanged for a wolf as a sheep, if you take my meaning. In any event," she added testily, "I've no intention of speaking anything but English to Doctor Herold. He might pull the wrong tooth."

The extraction in due time was finished, and she emerged. Now she was obviously in pain, and Joanna, stifling her uneasiness at thought of the return trip still ahead, commiserated with her.

"Thank you, dear." She who had always been so independent sounded briefly like her old self, saying, "No need to baby me. It's quite bearable, although I may be about as pleasant as a wounded bear for a while. Shall we go home? And Joanna, perhaps you are right. Perhaps I've been making too much of the . . . the other matter."

Relieved, Joanna accompanied her friend back on the street-car, which this time was crowded. They found places, however, on the long bench running lengthwise. The car rolled away, stopped, rolled away, stopped, took on more passengers, and Aunt Flossie, nursing her aching jaw, again said nothing.

Joanna, therefore, had no premonition of trouble when a polite young man, spotting a narrow empty space beyond Flossie said, "Pardon me, ma'am, might I sit there?"

Flossie's swelling face broke into a cordial smile and she at once hitched herself closer to Joanna. "Of course, of course!" she boomed. "There's plenty of room for us all."

Just opposite rode an elderly man and wife. He was continually muttering, evidently from an enfeebled mind, while to quiet him his wife patted his hand. But after Flossie had spoken, the dribbling words all of a sudden stopped. He said loudly and clearly, "Did you hear that, Irma? We got us a German spy, right here in the car!"

The wife, far more sensible than he, replied, "Now dear, those nice neighbors of ours back in Missouri talked that same way. They were lovely people."

"That's different, Irma! We knowed them—"

"A spy? Where?" cried a female voice some seats away. Then it seemed the entire car was silent, every passenger craning his neck in Flossie's direction.

She, her face whitening, stared across at her senile accuser, and said slowly, "A spy? A spy, you say? *Nein, nein. Sie lügen! Gott in Himmel, Sie lügen!*"

The gutteral words shattered the stillness.

"There—that's the one!" someone shrilled in triumph, and a thin woman, toward the front jumped to her feet, sobbing hysterically.

"Our George is in the army, he'll be risking his life, may even be killed—just because of terrible Germans like her. And look at her—she rides safely here with us!"

Everyone was on their feet. The aisle was filled. The conductor had stopped the car and was ringing his bell persistently, and over the loud clanging, he shouted, "Please, you must all sit down. Please!" But no one obeyed.

"Listening in on our conversation, are you?"

"Murderess! What about the Belgian children?"

"*Nein! Nein!*" denied Flossie, but only once more. Then she drew herself up, and through shaking lips scornfully defied them. "*Ach, Joanna, sie sind schwachköpfig!*"

Imbeciles all, she was declaring. That's what they were, too, Joanna thought bitterly, but as the clamor rose and the palpable hatred enveloped Flossie, and herself with her, all that came into Joanna's head was that they only had three more blocks to go. Three short blocks. Why didn't the streetcar move? They were trapped back here—

Then fear galvanized her. The woman whose son was serving in the army was forcing her way toward them down the aisle, and more than one male passenger shook his fist and shouted. But Joanna only had eyes for the old man across from her, as he raised his cane, jabbing with it, threatening Aunt Flossie and threatening her too.

Joanna shrank back in terror, knowing the pointed cane could so easily harm her unborn child. Could kill it.

They must get out, she and Aunt Flossie, at once!

She stood up, showed herself, so that no one could misunderstand the bulge at her waist, the indisputable evidence of pregnancy.

Keeping her attention fixed on the wild-eyed old man, she said sharply, "Nonsense! You should all be ashamed. This woman is my friend, and a fine, loyal American. Good heavens, don't any of you have relatives who were born in Germany? Are they all spies? I hope not!"

An unborn child still brought respect. The clamor died. And suddenly the soldier's mother backed away and let them through. As Joanna and Flossie made their way to the exit, they still ran a gauntlet of angry glares, but no one tried to stop them. The conductor, doubtless as glad to see the last of them as they were to leave, maneuvered the door open, and then they were safe outside. Still a little distance from home, but they were only too glad to walk.

"I was so frightened, I thought I'd be sick," Joanna told Uncle Paul. She sipped at a cup of tea and felt the warmth drive away a little of the cold terror she still felt, thinking of the wild-eyed old man.

"Thank God you both got away safely!"

"We're safe. With just a nasty taste left in our mouths. It was horrible, Uncle Paul, in a way I can't describe."

"Miss Mendenhall must be persuaded never to take such a risk again."

"I believe she's persuaded now. But in a way, I'm sorry. When I left her, she seemed so sad, so beaten, and not at all herself. She told me that from now on, until the war is over, she'll simply remain at home. She thanked me for my help, but when she said goodbye at the door I felt as though it really was—goodbye."

"Indeed." Paul ran an agitated hand through his thinning silver hair. "It's a shame. I've always considered her a brave and splendid woman."

"Which she is. Well, I'll tell you this—I wasn't at all convinced that Mr. McGowan wasn't exaggerating when he spoke of spy rumors, but I've learned. And if only one innocent person's rights are lost, we must be ashamed for all of us."

She added thoughtfully, "At least now, I can write my article with total conviction."

Chapter 32

Joanna had visited the Sennett lot for the better part of an afternoon, and finally departed. After escorting her to the gate, and advising her as to ways of gaining an entrance elsewhere, Lillian gave a sigh of relief. She was fond of Joanna and willing to help her when she could. Heaven knew she could sympathize with a girl's desire to get ahead, and if Joanna chose to enter the stodgy profession of journalism, good luck to her.

Unfortunately though, there were aspects of the film industry that no one involved in it would willingly see publicized. Joanna had presumably been sent to investigate the war pictures, and that was all right. Even though the atrocities being fed to the public as facts were dreamed up in some studio writer's head, every one of them was possible, and what was wrong with bolstering morale, anyway? The United States was at war and needed all those engines and munitions and such. Needed enthusiasm! Joanna might not agree—but whatever she wrote on the subject wouldn't matter much to Keystone. Comedy simply didn't lend itself very well to horror stories.

No, what was worrisome was the everpresent possibility of scandal. If Joanna, using the war films as an excuse, was looking into the use of hard drugs or perhaps just immorality in general, she'd find plenty to write about. Many of those who were most successful in this wildly growing, incredibly profitable business, were living high, wide, and handsome. People like Roscoe Arbuckle, who considered themselves far above ordinary standards of behavior, and free to try anything.

Take drugs. The only one sold openly was cocaine, because everyone knew it was absolutely harmless. There'd even been a very funny and well-liked film called *The Mystery of the Leaping Fish*, in which Douglas Fairbanks played a doped-up detective named Coke Ennyday. *Joy powder*, some called it, and it didn't hurt you, just pepped you up, kept you from feeling headaches. With coke you were flying. Doing your work well. Never feeling tired!

Still, as Joanna might have discovered just by chance, there were other kinds of drugs, taken for the thrill they gave and carelessly kept ready in a dressing-room drawer or in the pocket of a costume. Film actors weren't noted for prudence.

They weren't noted for morality either. In spite of dragons like Blanche Payson, the six-foot-tall ex-policewoman whose duty it was to protect the young actresses, not all those angelic faces on the screen were the mirrors of virtue they seemed. Fastidious Lillian found the wild drunken liaisons she heard about distasteful, and although she kept her opinions to herself, she often wondered, as today, how conventional Los Angeles would react to the truth. For that matter, why limit the shock to Los Angeles? Surely the people in Iowa or Minnesota or Massachusetts were as straitlaced as here!

Fortunately in her own studio, Mack Sennett, who set the example, more or less appeared to share her views. Perhaps less rather than more, although no one really knew. His lengthy love affair with Mabel Normand notwithstanding, he sometimes interviewed hopeful young girls in private rather than under the gimlet eye of Abdullah. Lending a little credence to the rumors was the fact that such interviews always appeared to take place immediately after he and Mabel quarreled.

Usually, when the two had one of their violent, emotional fracases, everyone at the studio was aware. Mabel, always so punctual, would fail to appear in the morning, and the King of Comedy would stalk around the lot, savagely critical and very far indeed from any appreciation of humor.

Today had been just such a day. Lillian had introduced Joanna, whereupon Mack, hardly his usual level-headed self, amiable, even flattering to representatives of the press, had snapped, "You've been told, Miss French, that the studios are all wary of sabotage, now that we're at war. I realize this young woman is your sister, but no visitors *means* no visitors."

This was so patiently absurd and Joanna was looking so upset that after he'd strode on, Lillian said to her soothingly, "Pay no attention. He's just angry because he and his—well, because of a personal problem of his own."

Just in time it had occurred to her that the Sennett–Normand love affair shouldn't be aired to Joanna, even though after so long a time it had almost achieved respectability.

Joanna, however, was displaying no interest in Mack Sennett's private life. "His remark about sabotage—do you think I can quote him?" she asked. "That's a real danger, you know, our getting to believe there are spies and enemy agents everywhere."

Lillian murmured some noncommittal answer and, having the secret reservations she did on her sister's visit, was careful not to prolong it with further discussion.

As she returned from the gate she came upon Sennett, pacing the street like an angry elephant.

"I'm sorry, Mack," she hurried to say. "You're right. Rules are rules. Even if Joanna is my sister."

"She's also a newspaper woman," he answered shortly. "We both know the threat of sabotage is pretty much nonsense, but there are other reasons for being discreet."

"I was discreet, I promise you."

"We all have skeletons in our closets," he continued dourly. "Which I, for one, would hate to see aired. Has she ever asked you why Mabel and I aren't married? Not that it's any of her damned business."

"No, never. I don't think she's even aware of your, ah, special friendship."

"I suppose *you'd* like to know the answer though? You and everyone else here?"

Lillian said calmly, "I can't speak for the others, but I'm not so stupid as to pry into the affairs of a man who can make or break me."

"Come on now—you're not even curious?" His prominent eyes had begun to study her.

"No." She added with deliberate primness, "Going to just one Hollywood party, seeing girls sell themselves for the smallest part, is enough to make me ill. And faithful as you and Mabel are to each other, well, I like that."

The big man snorted. "Faithful, is it? Well, Mabel has been, you're right, and she's far too good for me. But she's as hard to pin down as a moonbeam. And the rare times she does feel like marrying, it's I who's not in the mood, or I've other things on my mind. Or we fight. Like last night. . . . damn it, in the end I let her have her way, and then she laughed at me!"

Lillian had a feeling the conversation was straying onto shaky ground. Mack was not noted for freely given confidences, and she suspected that if he continued on in this vein, there would later be serious regrets on his part, regrets which would do her no good.

His bold scrutiny was also making her uneasy. She said, "Excuse me, Mack, but I've still got a scene to shoot. Pathé will be getting impatient."

The producer snorted. "We both know that Pathé is behind schedule as always. What's the matter? Am I so damned unattractive you can't talk to me?"

"No." She looked him over in her turn, as open about it as he'd been. His big strong body, his rugged face, the shock of unruly black hair. "You're very much a man, powerful, very male. But—I did promise Pathé. A director can be late if he likes. I can't."

"All right, go!" Suddenly smiling and cajoling, he added, "But I do think you might be able to help me straighten things out with Mabel. Come to dinner with me tonight and we'll talk."

Talk? She was certain she recognized the look in his eye, and instinct told her to say no. Mabel might be as hard to pin down as a moonbeam, but Mack was her man.

On the other hand, refusing him point-blank would be a mistake, too, especially when he put his invitation on the basis of a favor. Dinner in a restaurant sounded harmless, and it must seem so to Mabel, too, should she come to hear about it. After dinner, well, Lillian had good reason to go right home. Shooting the next day would be on a full schedule, starting early.

"Thank you, I'd like to," she answered, and remembering Mack's reputation for hating to part with a dollar, she said jokingly, "I warn you though, I'm a good eater. it will cost you a pretty penny."

"No it won't, my girl. This is my housekeeper's night out, but one of my many skills is cooking. I'll expect you at my house about seven."

He made his familiar low sound, halfway between a growl and a chuckle, turned on his heel, and left her.

Two hours later, arriving on the stoop of his palatial new bungalow up in the hills, her heart was hammering. What she had done to extricate herself from her dilemma had seemed clever, possibly even funny, when she'd thought of it. She was remembering now, too late, his flaming Irish temper.

He opened the door, a wolfish grin on his large face. The grin vanished, replaced by a frown of thunder when he saw she wasn't alone.

Lillian, with hard-won composure, said, "Good evening, Mack. I brought along an admirer of yours. Do you know Polly Kelly?"

She held her breath. She'd carefully chosen his uninvited guest, who was at present being billed by the great. D. W. Griffith as *America's Kid Sister*. Polly was instantly recognizable, her honest, wholesome face appearing on theater screens everywhere, and Lillian was banking on Sennett's business acumen. The possibility of stealing such a popular actress from Mutual Films would certainly spring into his mind.

But was this lure sufficient to distract him? She couldn't tell. He was no longer frowning, and he said heartily, "Come in, girls. Glad to meet you, Miss Kelly. As I told Lily here, an old bachelor like me learns to fix his own meals, and I've become mighty good at it, if I do say so—" But after all, Mack Sennett was an actor, too.

He was leading them into a large room lighted only by the flickering of gas flames in the fireplace, where orange logs, ceramic and indestructible, warded off the chill of the April night, and by the soft glow of the candles on a table set for two. The scene had been laid for a seduction, but Lillian was not tempted to smile. She said, avoiding his eye, "Where shall we put our coats?"

"In the bedroom." He was scowling again, no doubt reminded that he'd had other plans for his bedroom.

"I'll take your things," Polly said to Lillian. Then, "Where do I go, Mr. Sennett?"

"All the way down the hall, Miss Kelly."

Lillian surrendered her coat and the large driving hat with matching chiffon scarf. After Polly had gone, she said hastily, "It's strange, isn't it, what makes a film actress a success! Polly's looks are only ordinary, wouldn't you say?"

She expected him to argue, perhaps point out sarcastically how appealing Polly's open, *ordinary* face was to the ordinary man, but he only replied with steely emphasis, "My, you must have worked fast this afternoon."

He was right about that, Lillian agreed to herself. Although once she'd decided on a plan the pieces had fallen into place fairly easily. She'd needed a third person to be present at his house with her—then even Mabel could hardly object—and to avoid enraging him that person must be someone who would appeal to his acquisitive instincts as a film producer. She must also be willing to help, and Polly Kelly had at once come to mind. Polly had gotten her start as a result of Joanna's early article about her and might therefore feel some gratitude.

Lillian, knowing Joanna had gone directly to the Mutual lot after leaving her that afternoon, called Mutual and by a stroke of luck was able to locate her sister. She put forward her peculiar request. Joanna was reluctant even to ask Polly, but after Lillian several times assured her that no harm could possibly come to her friend's career as a result, Joanna finally agreed, and Polly good-naturedly said yes. She'd never been a chaperone in her life before, and she would try anything once. Besides, she'd heard that Mack Sennett was an excellent cook.

"Damn you, Lily!" Mack continued. "Mabel's going to laugh herself to death when she hears about this. The story will be all over town." His eyes were glinting with suppressed rage.

"I swear to you I won't!"

"But Mack—" She affected injured innocence. "I would think you'd be pleased. You'll have all evening to try to get her away from Mr. Griffith. I've heard you say more than once that you'd like to branch out into other things besides comedy, and then Polly Kelly would be a real feather in your cap."

She pushed firmly to the back of her mind the knowledge that what she was suggesting was impossible. Polly, only that morning, had signed a very substantial contract with Griffith, who was under the necessity of making a number of short, popular pictures for Mutual Films in order to finance his real love—the creation of tremendous spectacles, like *Birth of a*

Nation, which were so very costly. Polly had mentioned this news to Lillian because she wondered if they were being quite fair to Mack Sennett, but Lillian had shrugged and said, "I work for Mack. Suppose we let me worry about him."

Neither of them, it appeared, had needed to worry about Mack's possible disappointment. He was displaying not the slightest interest in acquring Polly, and his angry resentment was growing.

"Have I ever asked for your help in running my business, Miss French?" he hissed.

Lillian could hear Polly's light step at the far end of the tiled hall, and knew time was running out. There was only one appeal left to make.

"All right, Mack, I have to confess. I was trying to be funny. You're the man who's famous for practical jokes, but this one was on you. I admit it was a mean trick to play, but I hoped you'd be a sport and laugh."

"You did, did you?" he snapped, but she could see he was thinking it over. Some of the wildest, crudest, most elaborate spoofs ever had been perpetrated at the old Keystone, and he'd been as guilty as anyone. Always the victim was expected to be a sport.

As Polly entered the room, he broke at last into a slow, reluctant grin.

From then on, he was a pleasant and entertaining host, producing a tasty dinner, telling absurd stories about his early career in burlesque, and plying both his guests with champagne but not too much of it. Lillian ceased to worry, but her puzzlement remained. Why, as a motion picture producer, was he so totally uninterested in Polly?

It was only as he was escorting the two girls from his house, strolling through the crisp clear night to Lillian's car, that he deigned to give her the answer.

Polly was a short distance ahead, and Lillian could not resist whispering to him, "I must say I'm surprised. Even though you and Mr. Griffith are friends, I'd have sworn you'd try to take her away from Mutual."

"Then you aren't as observant as I thought." Mack pulled Lillian back, slowing their steps. "Although Griffith may not have noticed, either—after all, he's usually with her in sunlight or in bright artificial light. But as soon as she entered my house, I knew. The pupils of her eyes are like pinpoints. Your nice little friend, Lily—and she is nice, God, I feel sorry about it—she's taking hard drugs. Heroin, probably. She won't last."

"Are you coming, Lily?" called Polly, in her warm, lovely unaffected voice.

Lillian shivered, as though the night had suddenly grown colder.

Chapter 33

"*Miss Mendenhall—are* you at home?" Paul raised his voice, directing his inquiry toward the upstairs windows. He was certain she was. Across the sills blankets were airing in the old European way. Miss Mendenhall might leave her front door unlocked habitually, but she would never be away with the bedding so exposed to view.

"Ah, Mr. Perkins." Sure enough, her unruly, graying chestnut head appeared in the aperture above. "I didn't suppose it was anyone I knew. My friends always just walk in."

She retreated, and in a moment the front door opened and she stood before him. He saw at once that Joanna had been right. The stout figure was stooped, and in the broad fleshy face there was an unmistakable wariness despite a polite smile of welcome.

"May I come in?" he asked gently when she only gazed at him as if waiting for him to state his business.

"Why, of course. Forgive me. I only thought—"

She hastened to stand aside, and did not say what she had thought. But he could guess. He must have come with some explicit purpose. He'd never called before, and in her present predicament she wouldn't presume this to be a social visit.

But once he was settled in one of her comfortable parlor chairs, the old habits of hospitality asserted themselves.

"Did you walk all that way? Goodness! Just let me get you a cup of coffee. And I've some fresh-baked kuchen to go with it. Do you good." He was aware that her motherly concern had been aroused by his frailty, but for once he didn't mind. "Thank you, dear lady," he answered and leaned back, not troubling to hide a grimace of pain. "Coffee and your excellent kuchen would quite possibly save my life."

She hurried out into her large, high-ceilinged kitchen, and soon returned carrying a laden silver tray. She poured out a cup for him and he sipped slowly and with savor, feeling the hot strong drink warm his bones. Miss Mendenhall, after cutting him a large wedge of the cake, stood with arms akimbo, hands on her broad hips, watching him eat as though if his appetite flagged he would hear from her.

"Delicious," he said with sincerity.

A flush of pleasure crept into her face, obliterating a little of the wariness.

"No doubt you wonder why I've come." He paused, seemingly to remove any possible crumbs from his chin with the embroidered linen napkin she'd placed in his lap, but actually to bolster his courage. "Merely to say that I have every sympathy with you in what happened on the streetcar. The episode must have cut deeply. Further, the times being what they are, I would like, if I may, to offer my services as an escort."

He was well aware of the suggestion's absurdity. She was a big woman who could easily lift his frail body off its feet. As a physical defender, he would be worse than useless. Therefore, with even the hint of amusement on her part, he would have changed the subject and shortly, with thanks for the cake and coffee, have taken his leave.

But Aunt Flossie exclaimed, "How very kind of you!" Her mouth was working with sudden emotion, and she pressed it hard with her hand before saying brokenly, "You can't know what it means—for someone—someone besides my dear Adeline and Joanna—"

"Surely there are others, dear lady. You have so many friends, many of them the influential people who have lived longest in this city."

"Ah, but I'd be ashamed to tell them of my difficulties. Even though I count on their loyalty, to ask for it would be, well, begging for sympathy.

"You see, Mr. Perkins. I've always been able to look after myself, and others, too. It was I who was relied on to do the work, form committees, take up money for the poor. That is the Florence Mendenhall they all know and are friends with. I simply cannot let them see this other Flossie who must cower in her house."

"I understand," Paul said.

"Yes, I think you do. But I don't know how it is I'm speaking so frankly with someone I don't know well, whereas with those I do know well . . ."

"Has it occurred to you that your friends may feel hurt when they learn you have kept your problems to yourself?"

"They can hardly feel hurt if they never know," she replied with a certain tartness that was far more characteristic of the old Florence Mendenhall than humility.

He smiled. "One can only admire your pride. Although I might point out that pride is easily overdone. It was pride that led you to proclaim yourself unmistakably German on the streetcar, wasn't it?"

"I suppose so. All these lies I hear, about such good, kind people!"

"Yes." He did not point out that good and kind or not, the German people at present were the enemy. "May I assume then that you will permit me, as I am only an acquaintance, to be of help?" When she nodded, he continued, "We will put our heads together and figure out the best way to put your life back on an even keel. One thing I'm certain of, you must not remain sequestered in this house a single day longer. You must go to the stores again, do whatever else you wish, and I will accompany you."

"How kind!" Aunt Flossie said again. "It was worried me that I needed to take advantage of those two girls. I've had nightmares ever since about that dreadful day with Joanna. Just suppose someone had jabbed her, or tripped her up trying to get to me! As for Adeline, the *Liebchen* has more than enough to do with her work and keeping house."

It occurred to Paul that Adeline, now so lifeless and melancholy, might profit from the diversion of helping her old friend. But he remained silent, telling himself that this was not the time to argue the point. Later, perhaps.

Now it evidently occurred to his hostess that she might be imposing too much on him. She said, "You may be sure I welcome your offer, Mr. Perkins. I do indeed. But what about yourself? Surely you have more pressing things to do."

He said lightly, "I am neither in a family way nor overly busy. So it's a bargain?"

She gave a grim chuckle. "It is indeed. Now, sir, I have still another kind of cake in the kitchen. A fine old recipe that

I haven't used in years. Having so much time on my hands lately, I've taken to baking. Let me bring you a piece of that one, too, and you shall say which is best."

Without waiting for his answer she made for the kitchen, and he noticed she was carrying herself quite straight once again.

Paul sighed. She was not one to take all and give nothing. It was plain that already she was plotting to improve his health. And he who knew this couldn't be done mustered his defences against overindulgence in sweets.

Still, he was not at all displeased by the outcome of his call.

Chapter 34

To Tony from Joanna:

Yesterday morning your letter came, the one posted in Rouen, and at sight of the envelope, I thought you were safe again for a while. That was until I read all about your battle in the air against not *one* but *two* German pilots. I was completely terrified, yet from the way you described what happened, you could so easily have gotten away while their planes were still at a distance. Instead, all eager, reckless, exhilarated, you flew back to meet them! All right, you downed them both, but your own engine was in flames. Oh, Tony!

Begging you to take more care is probably useless, especially when the other fliers drink toasts to you afterward. I can only remind you, you are going to become a father, a man with responsibilities.

Things are much better here at home, particularly in regard to Aunt Flossie. She's stopped hiding in her house in lonely dignity, and is willing to go about again, escorted by Uncle Paul. He set himself to restore her spirits, and already she seems much the same as formerly, en-

ergetic and efficient, although not so outspoken. Indeed,
in that respect, she's gone to the opposite extreme. In
public, if you will credit it, she acts almost like a deaf-
mute, and makes Uncle Paul do all the talking to sales
people, etc., which is quite unnecessary as well as con-
fusing in places where she's well known. But Uncle Paul
doesn't object. He says they have a laugh or two together
when they get back to her house (while she's stuffing
him with food) and nothing is so beneficial for her as to
find something humorous in the situation. I've suggested
she write a letter to you herself, so you may be hearing
more about all this.

Thank you for asking about my article. The mails take
so long I'd almost forgotten. It was indeed published—
on the front page and with my byline! Not that my ringing
words did the least good. There are films showing right
now that are calculated to send American audiences into
howls of wrath. One of them, I understand, suggests that
German soldiers have cut off the hands of some innocent
little Belgian children. Uncle Paul, you may be sure, is
keeping Aunt Flossie well away from that one!

To Joanna from Charles Gold:
Heaven only knows when you will get this, and I can
only hope that soon mail will begin to trickle through
and find me again. Your letter is the one I've been waiting
for so eagerly. By one of those miserable mischances,
the only communication from home I've received in far
too long was from, of all people, Monica Zimmerly of
the *Times*, a brief ecstatic note about her new husband.
I was the one who introduced them, and of course I'm
pleased it worked out. She referred to some happy event
in your life but failed to elaborate. A promotion? A big
raise? Whatever it was, you deserved it!

I've been living, existing rather, in the trenches for
some time, an experience in horror and degradation I
won't dwell on. Suffice it to say, in addition to the
probabilities of getting killed or maimed, going crazy
from shell shock, or losing a foot from standing too long
in filthy water, the Tommies I'm with have been coping
lately with a very mundane but painful, bloody, and
worrisome problem—trenchmouth. The smell from it is
disgustingly bad, and with so many crowded together,

one almost wishes one didn't have to breathe. (An un-
lucky wish to make, as it can so easily be granted!)

To Joanna from Charles Gold:

This morning I am determined not to burden you with
tales of this hell on earth. But I can't seem to escape it,
even in my mind. Please, Joanna, let me think of you,
of the evenings we spent together, of home and the peaceful hills and roads of my beloved southern California.
Are the wildflowers blooming now? The purple-tinted
white mariposa are my favorites—

Oh, Joanna, what a great fool I was not to tell you
how I felt when I had the chance, but I thought, she is
so young, so very young, it wouldn't be fair. Now, when
I see or talk to any other girl, and there are still girls,
incredibly, living in this raped and devastated country,
all I can think of is you. I'm homesick for you, sick with
longing to be with you—

To Joanna from Charles Gold:

There must be something about being in the thick of
battle, where death is all about one, that makes any
pretense or silly convention the real sin. All I want to
think about, write about to you, my love, is truth. The
truth is—

I love you.

When did it start, this love? I ask myself. And what
did it feed on? We've been together so little. When that
funny little girl, so eager, so full of dreams, bounced
into Miss Mendenhall's parlor, did I suspect she'd be
someone to roam the world with? Certainly I was far too
pleased when that same lovely young person came so
ingenuously, innocently, seeking the start of a career just
like my own. So some notion of making her mine, sharing my strange lonely life with her, must have been
quietly growing, even then! You did feel some of that
magical attraction, didn't you? I couldn't be mistaken.
Not the way your lovely blue eyes have always lighted
as they looked into mine.

Absurd of me. I seem to have embarked on a courtship
by mail. And suddenly I couldn't be happier.

To Joanna from Charles Gold:

Please permit me to offer my belated felicitations on your marriage. I've only just received, all at once, four different letters from members of the *Times* staff, including yourself, acquainting me with the news. I can only wish you and your husband, who must be an incredibly lucky fellow, a most happy life.

To Joanna from Tony:

A fortnight has gone by without letters! Are you sick? Did they get lost? What happened? Remember, I hope for a letter from you written *every single day*. They may arrive here in bunches, like bananas, but I want desperately to know just what you're doing and how you are. I love you, and miss you so terribly!

We've had a very quiet week, then yesterday it all started up again. I'm getting pretty expert at combat flying, and yesterday I shot down my fifth enemy plane, which means I'm now an *ace*. So a group of us went into a village and celebrated. I don't think I was ever so drunk before. I know I wasn't, because at home I'm a pretty sober sort. After a while, some of the local girls came into the tavern, flirted a bit, and joined the men I was with. I just smiled and said, "No, thank you," in my bad French and left the others to it.

There's only one girl for me, and when I think how far away she is, I could bawl like a baby. So you see how much I need those letters?

Tell Aunt Flossie I miss her mincemeat pie. And tell yourself, keep telling yourself, how very much I love you.

To Joanna from Tony:

Thank you, dearest girl. Yes, I'm receiving your letters regularly again. Those you wrote during that one wretched fortnight simply got lost, I suppose.

Joanna, I do realize, only too well, that the baby will be coming one day soon and here I am so far away. But my dearest, I say it again, there is absolutely no way that I can come home. The Red Baron, (Manfred von Richtofen, a very great German ace) is still up there in the skies, and one day I intend to find him and prove that a Yank can fly as well—or better—than the best Jerry. Anyway, even if I did put in for compassionate leave as you suggested, I wouldn't stand a chance of getting it. How many of us, do you think, have become fathers since joining up?

You are feeling all right, aren't you? I shall be desperately worried until I hear that all is well, and that our fine little Antony has arrived safely. How do I know it's a boy? Only a feeling I have, that a crazy fellow like me would most likely father a boy. Do you know, I dreamed last night I was home, in our room, standing beside a cradle. Inside it was a child with your blue eyes and flaxen hair. The handsomest son a man ever had!

Oh, there is one bit of news coming from England, something I'm sure will please you. Vernon Castle, who has flown more than two hundred dangerous missions, all of them over enemy lines, is being sent to Fort Worth, Texas, where he will finish out the war as a flight instructor! I suspect I know how *he* feels about it, but no doubt his wife will be overjoyed. This probably means the end of Castles-by-the-Sea, as Irene will hurry down to Texas to be with Vernon, but never mind. We'll find another place to dance when I come home.

To Tony from Florence Mendenhall:

Joanna insisted I should write to you, although I'm not much for taking pen in hand.

I'm myself again. Mr. Paul Perkins has been kindness itself, and I don't know what I would have done without him. Unfortunately, the poor man is in very bad health. One reason may be that in recent years he's been getting along mostly on his own cooking. I don't mean to be critical of Joanna when I say this, because it takes a far older woman than she is to manage a man as stubborn and set in his ways as Mr. Perkins.

I hope you are taking care of yourself. Remember, keep your feet warm and your bowels open.

We will all be thankful to see you home again.

To Joanna from Tony:

You sound so worried, love, and you needn't be. Actually I've had hardly any fighting at all lately. We're being sent out on reconnaissance—searching out enemy gun emplacements, positions, and so on. Other times, we're ordered to strafe, and as to that I won't go into any details because I know how kind-hearted you are, but it is pretty awful. Both sides do the same, so there's no help for it, but don't think I enjoy killing men that way.

Until this assignment I didn't really know what war meant on the Western Front. God, I pity any poor devil down in the trenches, even a Jerry! Filth, lice, snipers, bombs—and the big guns in the background always booming, booming, booming. You've asked more than once if I'm ever frightened, well, I'd go out of my head with fright down there. Just as I would in a submarine. Those U-boat crews, prowling under the sea in a little cigar made of steel, with foul air and no room to move about and the strong likelihood of suffocating or being crushed, they are the enemy, and a terrible one, I grant you, but they are also very brave men.

I'm just grateful to be a pilot. If I die, it's a clean death and quickly over. We fliers have far the best of this war!

To Joanna from Tony:

Back to dogfighting, and I was never so glad! Just me and my sturdy little plane depending on each other, and when I get safely home to base, there's a bath and good food waiting and maybe a batch of letters from my wife.

Speaking of planes, sometimes we Americans in this outfit wonder what's being done about the war back in the U.S.A. Why aren't there any American-made planes? We hear rumors that the factories are tooling up with a new twelve-cylinder engine called the Liberty, but when it gets to Europe it's to be used in the British De-Havilland. My buddies and I find that downright embarrassing.

We don't really complain though, because these Spads are the best we've ever flown. Fast, quick turning, and with good visibility, they'll do just about anything. I don't understand how the machine gun mechanism works, but believe me, it's a beaut. It's timed to fire in between the revolving propellor blades, and those blades are turning fast! All a pilot has to do is sight and press the trigger.

Well, if I know you, you've heard enough about flying and fighting. But at least you can be sure I'm not riding around in an egg crate.

Lordy, Joanna, I keep waiting for a telegram! Isn't our baby ever coming?

Cablegram to Capt. Antony Bonnard US Div French Flying Corps Rec'd Rouen 5 Aug 17

MOTHER AND BABY ANTO*XYML* WELL CONGRATULATIONS PAUL PERKINS

Cablegram to Mrs. Joanna Bonnard WU Rec'd Los Angeles Aug 6, 1917

ANTONY OR ANTONIA QUESTION ADVISE AT ONCE EXCLAMATION I LOVE YOU TONY

Cablegram to Capt. Antony Bonnard US Div French Flying Corps Rec'd Rouen 7 Aug 17

ANTONIA REPEAT ANTONIA SHE IS BEAUTIFUL EXCLAMATION JOANNA

Chapter 35

"You're home finally" Ralph said in the surly tone long habitual with him. He was sitting stiffly erect in his chair by the fireplace, and although the hour had passed at which he usually ate supper, Dell could see that he'd made no effort to heat up the stew she'd prepared and left for him.

"Yes. Weren't you hungry?"

"I have a wife. It's her responsibility to cook my meal."

"Ralph, I did cook it. Joanna needed me! Mama and Lillian didn't get there until it was all over. I don't know what happened, but the pains suddenly started. The baby came very fast, and—"

"I don't care to hear the details! And I find your willingness to discuss them with me coarse, to say the least."

Dell flushed. "I didn't think—but yes, I suppose you're right." She sighed, castigating herself because it had just occurred to her that she should not have tried to tell him about the birth at all, for another reason entirely. He'd been struck too hard by the death of their own baby. He wouldn't want to hear about someone else's, and she could understand that. Ah, she could! Watching Joanna cradle in her arms the healthy, rosy little girl—another girl, too—had been agony. How then, in so blithely announcing the news, she could have ignored Ralph's grief—

"I'll get your supper right away," she said. "I'll only be a minute."

"Wait, Adeline, I got something to tell you. Something I been thinking about for a long time."

"Yes?" She gazed at him blankly.

"As I guess you know, I'm too old to have to register. For the draft. But—"

"Yes, you are, thank heaven."

"Must you always interrupt? It's a terrible habit, especially for a woman."

"I'm sorry."

"Well, I'm sick of sitting around here while other men are over there doing the fighting. So, couple of days ago, I went down and volunteered."

"You—volunteered?"

"I said that, didn't I? I'm to report to San Diego in a week's time. A troop train leaves there day after tomorrow."

Dell stared at him, her eyes wide with shock. He had taken this terrible step without even warning her, much less talking it over with her!

But why was she surprised—when he never did talk anything over with her? Papa had said she was a bright girl. With good judgment. Yet Ralph never had asked what she might think about anything, and if she tried to offer her opinion he didn't listen. He'd always gone and done exactly what he wanted to. And now this.

"You despise me, don't you, Ralph?"

"Oh, come on, Adeline, I never thought I'd hear you whine . . . but you aren't whining, are you?" He studied her briefly. "You sound almost cold—",

"I am cold." *I'm cold with pain.* "Answer me, Ralph. Have you always hated me?"

"So we're going to have another one of those damned truth talks, are we? No, I don't hate you!" He was speaking with an impatience that only pointed up his lack of interest. "But why do I have to say it again? I told you before, I never could care for you, not the way a man ought, for his woman."

She had then a devastating flash of insight. "I think I finally understand. You not only don't care, I don't even exist for you."

"You exist all right." He gave a grim laugh. "I am tied to you and to this house—and that's the trouble. I can't stand being tied. I suppose if the baby had lived, I might have been willing to settle into harness like a broken-down old horse, not caring who his owner was—"

"Now who's whining?" Dell said sharply, and felt a small rush of exhilaration. It felt good, she was finding, not to worry over each word, trying to please him when she couldn't. Good to talk back to him at last.

He gave a reluctant nod. "Yes, I guess I was. But be that as it may, I'm going."

"It's not the war, is it? You're leaving me," Dell hazarded, not needing his answer.

"Yes." He stood frowning in thought. "I'll tell you what I'll do. I have to admit, you ain't been treated fairly. And I won't be coming back to this part of the world. The house is yours; I already signed the papers at the bank. And, well, I figure I can't sell the roller coaster in such a short time, so that's yours, too. What with the coaster and the merry-go-round, you'll be the biggest concession owner in the park."

Briefly, she wanted to hurl his generosity back in his teeth, because through her black despair resentment was rising. But the surge of anger also held her from making the gesture. Why shouldn't he pay for what he'd done to her? Nothing was too much!

She said grudgingly, "You never were mean with money, I'll grant you that."

"No." He grinned. "Except when I had a bad streak at gambling. Well, that's all past." He held out his hand. "Let's call it quits with no hard feelings. What do you say?"

Her defiance faded. He was so handsome, tall, lean, with the features of a film star. That smile she so seldom saw was to her, even now, irresistible. She almost fell to pleading with him, could hardly resist the temptation. If only he'd stay with her, she'd try harder, she could make him happy. . . .

But she understood now, beyond any possibility of self-delusion, how hopeless her poor little dream was and always had been. She drew a deep breath, looked him full in the face, and willing her voice not to tremble, answered, "What do I say? I say, Ralph Wilson, get out of my house—and out of my life!"

"Aunt Flossie?" She pushed open the front door and blundered inside like a big moth blinded by light, only she was blinded by tears.

"Yes. . . *Liebchen—Mein Gott in Himmel!* What is wrong?"

Adeline stood, slumped, in the center of the floor. Her natural reserve still struggled to keep her silent. But she had come here to tell Aunt Flossie. She had to tell someone. She couldn't bear the knowledge alone.

"He's gone, Aunt Flossie. Ralph has. He's left me—and I'll never see him again!"

A rasping sound, the clearing of a throat, came from the corner of the room. Dell spun around and saw Paul Perkins struggling to his feet from a deep armchair. He said, "I should be leaving, Miss Mendenhall."

Dell gazed at him in utter consternation. It hadn't occurred to her that anyone else might be here. It was one thing to have betrayed her grief and shame to Aunt Flossie, quite another to have let a member of the family learn how weak and pathetic she was, what a failure as a wife, as a woman.

He cleared his throat again, and said, "Adeline, did you ever hear of Ralph Waldo Emerson?"

She shook her head, barely having heard the question.

"Too bad. I've always thought it a mistake letting you stay out of school. He wrote a few lines you might keep in mind.

> *Heartily know,*
> *When half-gods go,*
> *The gods arrive.*"

"What on earth does that mean?" she snapped.

"Merely that he, your Ralph, was flawed. Not good enough. You deserve better, my dear, and will one day find it. There. Having given my opinion without being invited to do so, I will leave you in the capable hands of Miss Mendenhall."

Although Aunt Flossie's eyes did not leave Dell's strained face, she said warmly, "Thank you, Mr. Perkins, for accompanying me again today. You are a true gentleman."

Paul gave a deprecatory wave of his hand and hobbled out the open door.

"Sit down and I'll get you some coffee. Have you had any supper?"

"No, but I couldn't swallow anything. I feel sick." Dell gave a convulsive shudder, and said bleakly, "Aunt Flossie, he told me once there was another woman. But it was long ago that he loved her. Surely, after all this time, these years of being married, he should have forgotten her, shouldn't he? He would have, if I were any kind of wife. But I'm so dull and stupid . . . dear God, even a dull woman feels! Why don't you ask me how it feels to be unwanted?"

Her voice was rising, and Aunt Flossie quickly said, "What exactly do you mean, he's left you? Where is he going?"

"To Europe. To the war. They didn't call him up, so he volunteered. No!" She raised her hand silencing her friend. "He didn't do it for any of the usual reasons. Not for patriotism. Not even because, like some men, he likes danger and excitement. He went because he couldn't stand living with me anymore. He made that very plain. He also said he is never coming back. He gave me the house and the roller coaster—and he's gone."

"The roller coaster, too?"

"Yes. Oh, how I wish I were a man! I'd love to just wander away myself, looking for some great exciting adventure."

"I doubt if being a soldier in this war is a great exciting adventure," Aunt Flossie said dryly.

"I didn't mean I'd want to go to war. I just meant—see the world. Go to the South Seas. Or China. Some place far off I've never been to and can't even imagine. Be footloose and fancy free, as they say. But I'm a woman. So I can't."

"No, but I think you're forgetting something," Aunt Flossie said thoughtfully. "The roller coaster."

"What about it? Lately, I've wished I didn't even have the carousel. That boy helping us has all he can do with just your ferris wheel, so now I'll have one more thing to work myself to the bone on."

"And that's good . . . listen to me, Adeline. After my father died, even though he was a hard man to live with, I was so lonesome I thought I'd never get over it. But I found there is a cure. Work. Hard work."

"I'm tired of work, I told you. Tired to death!"

"Wait. Let me finish. The carousel is partly owned by the rest of your family, but what Mr. Wilson left you is all yours. It can be what I've heard people call—what is the word? Oh yes, a nest egg. You know, the hen sits on an egg left on purpose to make her lay more in the same place. This is a nest egg for you, a beginning, this roller coaster, and if you are as smart as I think you are, money will accumulate and grow and soon you'll own something else, and then something else again. Making money grow is as exciting an adventure as any."

Adeline's damp, reddened eyes had lost their glazed look. "I couldn't. Not me. I'm not smart."

"Don't be humble with me, miss. I know better and so do you. Your papa used to leave you in charge of his business when you were too small to pull the carousel lever. You had a quick mind for making change and a shrewd eye for what the customers were doing as well.

"So I suggest you forget about Mr. Wilson for a moment. Come into the kitchen and let's sit down and talk about this. Are you certain you won't have some coffee, at least?"

"All right—just coffee. Aunt Flossie, I want to say, I'm sorry I haven't been around here lately to help you. I just had a feeling something dreadful was about to happen—with Ralph—and I was trying so hard. . . . Oh, Aunt Flossie!"

"That's enough weeping! No more! You aren't the weeping kind, *Liebchen*. Here, blow your nose. . . . You needn't blame yourself for not coming here so often. You've always done far too much for me. Besides, your uncle Paul seems to enjoy our outings, and I do believe, with my cooking, he seems a little stronger.

"Now then. That boy who works my wheel has a cousin. We might be able to get him to help out. . . ."

Chapter 36

Lillian was so full of energy she almost feared she might burst out of her skin. She was always like this, ready for anything they asked of her, just after a meeting with the Count. Those meetings were fearfully expensive, but she'd long since ceased to worry about the cost. There was no help for it. She needed cokey to get through her long day.

If she hadn't felt quite so exuberant, as though she were standing a little above the ground and invincible to any kind of difficulty or failure, she might not have let herself be so openly annoyed with Mabel Normand.

Mabel really was the limit. No human being could be as kind, generous, and eternally good-humored as Mabel gave the appearance of being, and Lillian wondered why she herself was the only one who wasn't fooled. Until lately, aware that her advancement largely depended on being chums with the star comedienne of the studio, Lillian had kept her scepticism well hidden. But today, when Pathé stopped the camera and said, "Lily, don't you think you're hamming it too much?" and then Mabel, quick to defend her as always, said—exactly as Lillian knew she would—"Oh, I do think Lily's funnier that way" Lillian cut her off.

"After all, Mabel, Pathé is the director here. He's the one being paid to decide what's funny."

Mabel, surprised, turned quickly to look at her, and although no one else could have noticed, just Lillian, because the two of them worked so closely together, Mabel's brilliant smile seemed to fade a little, lose its confidence. And Lillian thought, why, that's it! She needs to be admired by everybody. Including me. Any little doubt expressed, and she's not certain anymore how great she is.

Lillian said, "Let's take the scene again, Pathé, just from my entrance, and I'll tone it down. We can do it right now—unless Mabel objects?"

But Mabel's moment of weakness had passed. She exclaimed, "Goodness, I don't mind. My part can stand extra practice, too, I'm sure."

Pathé nodded, but his approval was directed at Mabel, not Lillian, who after all had been the one to agree with him. He said, "Good girl, Mabel. I can always count on you."

Lillian, hot with indignation, felt her irritation with her partner solidify into dislike—Mabel, who aroused such uncritical loyalty in everyone!

She hadn't realized Mack Sennett was present at the side of the stage, observing as he often did, until he growled, "Mabel, I want to talk to you. Give us five minutes, Pathé."

"Whatever you say." The director set his megaphone on a table and busied himself fishing a pipe and tobacco from his pocket.

However, Mabel stayed where she was. She said, "No, Mr. Sennett, sir. We'll do our scene now. If you don't care about wasting money while all these extras stand idle, I do."

It was plain, just from her tone and her not calling him Mack, that their quarrel, which had been continuing off and on for months and months, wasn't patched up yet. It was equally plain that she was making Sennett's temper flare. He set his jaw, then abruptly stalked away.

Later, when the scene was finally done and Lillian had changed out of her costume and was walking out through the gate, still feeling so energetic she bounced with each step, Mack Sennett rolled up alongside her in his one extravagance, his Simplex Speed Car, looking, muffled as he was in white driving coat, hat, and goggles, like a great polar bear.

"Where's your car today, Lily?" he inquired, almost having to shout above the throbbing of the big car's engine.

"It's in the garage for repairs again." She dimpled at him. "It always is. I'm not good at remembering all the mechanical things one has to do."

"I'll drive you home then. Get in."

She stepped onto the running board and sank low into the black leather bucket seat, her legs stretching away toward the mahogany dashboard which seemed at such an absurd distance she wondered how even Mack, tall as he was, could read the dials. Beyond loomed the great bowed-up hood, bright red, and a pair of gleaming brass headlights.

"Lovely!" she exclaimed as the automobile roared away.

"Yes, but I'm thinking now about getting a Mercer. Nothing

steers like a Mercer Raceabout I've heard. Best car in the world."

Lillian, although totally uninterested, gave him a saucy grin. "Then you don't agree with the saying: 'There never was a worser car than a Mercer'?"

"I know, I know. I've heard those Stutz-Bearcat owners, too. They're just jealous. The answer to that one is, 'You have to be nuts to drive a Stutz.'"

She was pleased that he'd offered her a ride, and also that he was being so pleasant and friendly. After the near-disaster of his previous invitation, he hadn't seemed to bear a grudge, yet he'd kept his distance and she'd wondered if she'd gotten off scot-free after all.

Then as they rolled up to the bungalow court where she and her mother lived, and his magnificent car purred to a stop just at the hibiscus-lined walkway, he said, "Lily, I'm more and more impressed with your work."

She'd been reaching for the handle of the door, but her hand checked, slid back into her lap.

"Yessiree, you've got talent—and good sense, too. I didn't miss your willingness to cooperate with Pathé. With a little extra coaching, you could be a star yourself, instead of just the straight-man partner for a top comedienne."

Lillian gazed at him in rapt silence. There was no need to pretend interest in this conversation.

"In fact, there's a very special starring role I have in mind, and after we go out to dinner tonight, we'll go up to the tower and talk about it. As I'm sure you're aware, I do my best thinking up there."

This was Mack Sennett, whose word was as good as any man's in Hollywood. If he said he had such a role available, he did have, and to play it meant a glorious opportunity for her.

For him though—what did he want in return?

"There's one thing, Lily," he went on bluntly. "You'd better be sure you understand. I'm not in the mood for tricks tonight. Abdullah goes home at sunset, and this time you come alone. Agreed?"

She looked over her shoulder toward the bungalow at the far end of the court. Furtively. Guiltily. As if Mama's eyes were on her from that distant window.

Then, although her heart was beating so loudly it seemed impossible Sennett didn't hear it, she shrugged with a fine show of indifference, and said, "Yes, I understand."

"Fine. I'll be back in an hour to pick you up."

"I'll be waiting right here." Another quick glance down the walkway and she added, "Alone."

They ate in the dining room of the Plaza Hotel on Vine Street, a popular place for the successful and well-to-do of Hollywood. Sennett took pains to introduce her to a dozen acquaintances as they progressed toward their reserved table, and Lillian could only surmise that he intended the fact of their being together here to come to Mabel's ears. The knowing leer of Roscoe Arbukle, present with one of his usual woman companions, an ambitious bit player, made this a certainty.

Lillian waved to him, forcing a gay smile. Her only consolation was that whatever lewd speculation Arbukle was engaging in was only that—speculation. He could hardly draw any definite conclusions from a dinner in a public restaurant. At least she fervently hoped not. She wanted to become independent of Mabel, not make an enemy of her.

The head waiter pushed in her chair, and she picked up the menu, but Sennett, looking beyond her, gave a grunt and rasped, "I thought I said *alone!*"

"I came alone." Lillian was bewildered.

"Then what, may I ask, is your friend doing here?"

"My—" She turned to follow his gaze, and understood. Polly Kelly was seated at a nearby banquette. With her were an older man and woman, conspicuous in the colorful, animated crowd around them because of their air of staid respectability. Polly, she noted absently, appeared ill. It could be seen that her eyes were inflamed and irritated, and she held a handkerchief to her reddened nose.

"Well?" Mack said. His voice was ominously cold.

"Mack, for heavens sake! Everyone in Hollywood eats here frequently. I'd have no reason to want Polly with us again, and even if I did, I hadn't the least idea where we would be dining. You didn't say."

"No, that's right, I didn't." He was mollified. They began to talk of other things, and Lillian tried to put out of her mind whatever else the evening would hold. Sennett was recognized as being a charming companion when he cared to make the effort, and he was extending himself now, telling droll stories about the early days of Keystone. But she could not help thinking that the image he was projecting to the other diners, that of a man enjoying himself hugely in the company of a pretty woman, would be reported in full back to Mabel. Mabel who intended to marry Mack.

Lillian was suddenly convinced she was making a serious mistake. She should stand up before it was too late and say distinctly enough to reach Mabel's ears, "Thank you, Mr. Sennett, but I must be going home." The temptation was so strong that she actually rose to her feet.

He looked at her inquiringly, and she couldn't utter the words. Anger him again? There was that role he'd mentioned. It was real, it must be, and it would be lost to her. Perhaps more would be lost, besides. Everything she'd worked for.

She had to get away from him though, at least for a minute or two, to regain her composure. She swallowed, tasting bitterness in her mouth, and said the only possible thing, the self-explanatory "Excuse me for a moment, please, Mack?"

"Oh. Certainly."

She made her way among the tables and out to the lounge for ladies. Here there were individual cubicles, far more luxurious than usual in their size and appointments. Ordinarily, a neat and courteous female attendant was present to be of assistance and to indicate which room was vacant, but she was away for the moment so Lillian pushed open the nearest door.

There stood Polly by the lavatory, a hypodermic needle in her hand. She was in the act of withdrawing its tip from her arm.

Polly started in alarm at the intrusion, then quickly dropped the needle in her bag and stood mopping her nose with a wet, balled handkerchief. Her expression, Lillian thought, was that of a trapped animal resigned to its fate.

"What is it? Heroin?"

"I thought the door was fastened," Polly answered dully. "I guess it wasn't. . . ." Then, "You won't tell anybody, will you, Miss French?" It was Miss French now, not Lillian or even Lily. Could this furtive creature with despair ravaging her face be the schoolgirl-fresh Polly Kelly, beloved by thousands? "I've tried to stop, honest I have. But I can't! Look at me—it's only been ten hours and I'm a wreck. What's really scary is, I need more and more. . . . Please, please—you won't tell?"

"No, but you'd better be more careful. Not shoot it so openly. You won't be working as an actress very long if Mr. Griffith finds out."

Polly was gazing at her with haunted eyes. "It isn't Mr.

Griffith I'm thinking about, it's my parents. They're with me tonight, visiting, and I just had to have a fix. I was starting to shake. I'll be all right now, I'll be fine right away, the stuff works so quickly. But I would just die if Papa guessed."

Lillian, uncomfortable, didn't answer, and Polly blew her nose once more, then turned to go. But she said one last thing before she went, speaking in a low hopeless voice and more to herself than to Lillian.

"I think, if I could go back home with them, be the sort of girl I was before, even just a nobody, it would be the happiest day of my life."

She couldn't go, of course. Polly could never go home. America's Kid Sister was a hopeless addict.

Lillian stood staring at the door for a time after she'd gone. Pity for Polly mingled with a superstitious foreboding for herself. An evening which began on such a somber note was almost certain to end badly.

However, she no longer had a choice. There was no turning back for her any more than for Polly. She primped her hair in the mirror, gave a perky little smile just for practice, and returned to the dining room. She avoided glancing at the Kelly table, and was slightly reassured that Sennett apparently found her as merry and animated as a man could wish.

Maintaining this brittle facade was more difficult later, when the Simplex throbbed its way through the studio gates and onto the main street of the deserted lot. As it rolled toward the tower, Mack's hand pressed her knee, and she faced the fact that time had run out. She was now in the kind of situation Mama had been warning her against all these years.

Silence lay between them as he parked just at the base of the tower. They left the car, and with deliberation he produced the key to the door. He flicked the light switch just inside, and in the cold glare of the naked bulb overhead she stole a glance at him. He wasn't homely, she reminded herself. If he made love to her, and she was certain he intended to, she shouldn't mind too much. She'd just shut her eyes, and pretend. Even if she'd never done this thing before, ever, she'd been an inadvertent witness often enough at wild parties to have a pretty shrewd idea what was required of a girl.

Mama, I'm sorry! Like Polly, I only hope you'll never know.

"I feel like having a bath," Sennett announced. "I'll go on ahead and get the tub started."

"Yes . . . all right."

He went off up the wooden stairs, his feet pounding loudly, for he was a heavy man. Lillian stared up after him. So it was going to be a romp in the tub first. Probably with the lights on. Almost certainly with the lights on. Was it as easy to pretend when he could see every expression on her face?

Although she climbed to the top very slowly and water had been pouring steadily out of the gold-plated spigots for some time, the huge black marble tub had only begun to fill. He sat in it, nude, and the water wasn't up to his hip bones. She averted her eyes.

"I don't mind sharing," he said jovially and predictably. "It's such a grand big tub. Take off your clothes, honey, and come on in."

All of a sudden, Lillian was blushing. She couldn't do what he asked! She couldn't possibly stand here and undress while he watched.

There was a brief silence, during which she felt his eyes on her crimson face, and then he slapped the water with one hand, making a big spray that sloshed onto the floor. He began to laugh, a great, booming belly laugh. Barely managing to get the words out, he was roaring so, he said, "By God, Lily, don't tell my you're a virgin? After all this time around movie studios? I just don't believe it!"

"It's true," she muttered.

"Then that's even better. . . . Oh, come on, girl, relax. You've nothing to fear from me, although you shouldn't lead men on the way you do. No, I think I've paid you back enough."

"What do you mean?" She was bewildered.

"One good practical joke deserves another, and by all that's holy, I like this one! Scaring you silly *and* making my Mabel jealous—because I'll be bound I got her this time. Good, eh?"

"Oh, yes, good."

"Glad you agree." Again he was convulsed. Finally he said, "No use wasting water, and since Abdullah's not here, I need someone to wash my back. You can do that at least, Lily the Lilywhite."

She knelt, feeling wetness seep through the skirt of her best silk evening dress, and began to splash water on his back.

"Here's soap. Rub it on."

Lathering her hands, she obeyed with as businesslike an air as she could assume. She had recovered her aplomb and was smiling as though she shared the joke, though she actually felt thoroughly disgruntled. She hadn't wished to be seduced, certainly not! But to be used in this way, and made fun of, when he hadn't really wanted her at all . . . Still, there was that part he'd mentioned. She opened her mouth to remind him, but he burst into deep, thunderous song, drowning her out.

"'For 'tis love and love alone the world is seeking!'—Rub harder, Lily," he interrupted himself to order. "Abdullah will have to give you some training in massage." The powerful baritone resumed. ". . . 'And 'tis love and love alone that will . . .'"

"Well, Mack. Rehearsing Lily to play a whore?"

It was Mabel's light, airy voice, and it was Mabel standing in the doorway.

Lillian leapt up and away from the tub. "He—he wanted his back washed—"

"I'd never have guessed." The snapped answer told Lillian that if there was humor anywhere in this ridiculous scene, Mabel for one didn't see it. Her eyes were as flinty as her tone.

"I'm just leaving. Good night, Mr. Sennett. Thank you for a pleasant evening," she babbled, and ran past Mabel and out onto the stairs.

She heard Mack roar, "Listen, Mabel, this isn't what you think. I only wanted to talk to her about her career—"

"I bet! Drooling over her all through dinner, too, weren't you?"

"Damn it, woman, what did you expect when you've been treating me so badly? Mabel—come back here!"

Lillian reached the bottom step and broke into a run, hearing Mabel descending like a whirlwind just behind her. She was barely out of the tower when Mabel caught her, grabbed her arm, and swung her around.

Lillian said, just as Mack had, "Mabel, it wasn't what you think!"

This didn't receive the dignity of an answer. Mabel's small fingers were like steel claws, biting in painfully. She said, "There's one kind of person I have a very low opinion of, Miss French! It's someone who only pretends to be a friend and is out for what she can get. I don't want to act with you again. Ever! Or see you around this lot!"

Badly frightened, Lily blustered, "Isn't that for Mack to decide? I do have a contract."

Mabel laughed, a harsh, unfeeling chuckle Lillian had never heard before. "Mack will do what I say. I'm sure you know that well enough. And contracts are easily broken. Don't make us find a way to break yours. You'll regret it."

The tiny comedienne released Lillian and pushed her away so hard she almost fell, spun and walked quickly back to the tower, Lillian gazing after her and knowing she'd spoken nothing less than the truth. Mack hated trouble. But if he were forced to choose, he'd certainly get rid of Lillian.

She was finished at Mack Sennett Studios.

Chapter 37

"*So you'll have* to find something else for me," Lillian was saying to Bert Lange. She had come very early in the morning to his office, but it seemed a telephone call had preceded her and he knew all about what had happened, which didn't give her much chance to soften the sordid little story. He'd listened without expression to Lillian's version, smoking a cigar and making no comment.

"Surely you're not shocked?" she exclaimed. "Nothing happened, and even if it had—"

"Lily, I won't pretend that this sort of nasty, self-seeking business doesn't go on all the time. You and a producer playing about naked in a bathtub—"

"I wasn't in the bathtub. I was fully dressed."

He continued as though she hadn't spoken. "That wouldn't have shocked me. Your private life is your own business. But when you try to stab Mabel Normand in the back—a girl who is so decent herself, who has done so much for you—"

"Please. Just one favor," Lillian interrupted. "Stop raving about Mabel. The one good thing in what's happened is that now I won't have to watch and listen to everybody fawning over little Miss Sunshine. I've been sick of her sweetness act for a long time."

"Is that so?" Confident of his support once he'd finished scolding her, she wasn't listening closely enough. If she had been, she would have been warned by his grimness.

"Yes!" she exclaimed. "Let's forget her, and talk about me. I've been practically a star for quite a while, so I shouldn't have too much trouble getting a really good contract somewhere else. Have you any ideas yet?"

"Plenty." He ground out his cigar in the heavy brass ashtray, and his gaze made a brief tour of the spacious office and its fine leather furnishings before returning to her. "Yes, plenty, but I won't be using them, and it wouldn't do you much good if I did. You see, Lily, I'm not dependent on your success anymore. Mabel has sent me a number of good clients and I've gotten others on my own.

"I'm not saying, if I was still trying to make my way I'd stand on my principles as firmly as I'm going to do. I have a family. I'm human. But I owe Mabel a lot, and since I don't really need you anymore—well, here's the way it is. I'm not your agent anymore."

"But Bert, you can't be serious!"

"Never more so. I will give you one last parting bit of information, though, absolutely free. Mabel is very angry, very hurt. I suspect she's going to warn off Paramount, Fox, Metro— all the others she makes pictures for now and then. If they hire you, they won't get her. See what I'm saying?"

"Yes." Lillian was silent a moment, appalled by the abyss that had opened under her feet. Then she asked, almost calmly, "What can I do?"

At last there was a glint of admiration in his cold regard. He said, "I expect you'll land on your feet somehow. Call around Hollywood—you won't be satisfied otherwise. And maybe you'll be lucky. Some smaller outfit maybe—"

"I don't want one of them! I haven't worked my way up this far to settle for some fly-by-night—"

"Well then, after you've given up here," he continued inexorably, "there's always New York. Since Mabel never would work in New York, it's wide open."

"Bert—are you sure you won't go on representing me? A bigger percentage maybe? Bert, after all these years—"

"Lily, I'm sorry. I wish you well, but no. This is goodbye."

Within three days, Lillian confirmed what she had known in her heart. If Mabel cared enough to use her influence, to put the matter on an "Either *she* works here, or *I*" basis, then every producer would, like Mack Sennett, choose Mabel. And Mabel, it seemed, had cared enough.

Little Miss Sunshine had a spiteful, nasty side after all, Lillian fumed. Couldn't they all see that? A really honest person, someone like Polly Kelly who admitted to a few human failings herself, would forgive and forget, might even find it all very funny afterward—Mack Sennett naked in that big bathtub and she on her knees, scrubbing away. . . .

Polly Kelly. Why, Polly had influence at Mutual! If Polly were asked to put in a good word . . .

She wouldn't have to tell Polly exactly what had happened, best not to tell her everything. Just get her sympathy and ask for a helping hand.

It was a matter of a moment to give the operator the Mutual number, and only another moment before she could hear it ringing.

"May I speak to Polly Kelly, please?"

"Miss Kelly isn't on the lot today." The cheerful voice dispensing this unwelcome information irritated Lillian profoundly, and she snapped, "Look here. I'm not one of her fans calling to bother her. This is Lily French."

The studio representative remained courteous even though she must have heard the Hollywood gossip. "Yes, Miss French. But what I told you is perfectly true. Miss Kelly is not here. She went on vacation this morning, quite suddenly."

"On vacation? Where?"

"She didn't say. Her picture finished yesterday, and she left right afterward." The voice suddenly became aggrieved and more human. "She does get so many calls, and I'll have to cope. The public is so inconsiderate. They have no idea how busy we are here—"

"I'm sorry for you." Lillian hung up.

"Is it necessary to be rude?" Clara, passing through the room and overhearing, rebuked her, but gently. Why her daughter was at odds with the Sennett Studio, and why she seemed to be having trouble locating elsewhere, she didn't understand. But with Lillian's tense misery she sympathized, and felt a fierce desire to help, no less strong because she realized how useless it was. "Bad news?" she ventured to ask.

"You might say so. My only hope, Polly Kelly, has gone away on a vacation. Even her studio doesn't know where she is."

Clara said thoughtfully, "That's the girl who's been friendly with Joanna, isn't it? Why don't you ask Joanna?"

"I may as well, I suppose," Lillian said grudgingly, but she went back at once to the telephone.

Joanna's number rang for some time, and Lillian was about to give up when her sister, sounding subdued, came on the line.

If Lillian hadn't been so immersed in her own troubles, curiosity would have prompted a question or two. As it was, she only felt a surge of relief. Perhaps her luck was turning.

However, Joanna, on being questioned, merely answered firmly that Polly was not available.

"What do you mean, she's not available? What an odd way to put it!"

"I mean—well, after all, her parents only left yesterday morning and Polly was tired out. So, as soon as the day's shooting was over, she went away."

"I learned that much from the studio," Lillian said with exaggerated patience. "She called you?"

"Yes. We've become good friends. She thought somebody should know."

"Know what?" Lillian pressed.

"Nothing! Just that she would be . . . on vacation."

"Then she also told you where she was going, didn't she? You would have asked and she would have told you."

"No! Listen, Lillian, I suppose you want another favor of some kind; you wouldn't call her otherwise. Well, she isn't to be bothered, do you hear? She can't—I mean, she won't— talk to you or anyone, so there's no use trying to track her down!"

"How secretive. Now I wonder why—" Lillian began, and then the answer clicked into place. She said sharply, "You can stop being so evasive, Joanna. I'm well aware that she's addicted to heroin."

She heard Joanna gasp before exclaiming in disbelief, "She confided in you?"

"No. I caught her shooting the stuff. She looked terrible, too, shaking and very ill until it took effect. I suppose she's off somewhere trying to rest up and get that bloom of health back. She'd better. It's her stock in trade."

Joanna sighed. "Since you know so much already, I may as well tell you the rest. She said there's a doctor who has helped other Hollywood people quit the drug habit. She's gone to stay at his clinic and try to get free of it herself."

"Quit heroin—*cold turkey*?"

"What? Yes, I believe so. It's the only way, isn't it?"

"God!" Lillian was contemplating what she'd heard about the tortures of withdrawal—the muscle spasms, the hideous pain deep in the bones.

"It's a private home," Joanna went on. "No one can visit. So whatever you want her for this time, you'll have to manage on your own. The doctor thought she'd be there at least six weeks—if his treatment succeeds."

"Let's just hope she can stand it." Lillian's mind, however, was already casting about for some other solution to her own problem, and the image of Polly Kelly, thrashing on her bed of agony, was fading.

Joanna said bitterly, "Yes, that's all we can do about anything these days—hope. Pray if we're religious. I do feel utterly useless!"

"Joanna—is something else the matter? You sound so— it's not just Polly troubling you, is it?"

Her sister, as if a pent-up dam had broken, cried, "Doesn't any sensible person hate and loathe this terrible war? I've been such a fool, living in my own little dream world. I never let myself believe that someone I care for could possibly be missing or . . . dead—"

"Is Tony—he's all right, isn't he?" Oh, no! Lillian thought. Please, not another tragic family crisis. Not right now. I haven't time to be decent and helpful.

But Joanna sounded surprised. "So far as I know. I had a letter from him only this morning."

"You did say . . . someone you care for—"

"Not *care for*, exactly." Joanna's tone became guarded. "I was referring to a friend. We all have friends to worry about and grieve over."

"Do we? Who is yours, for example?"

"Just a friend . . . oh, very well. Did you know Vernon Castle? I only heard this week that he's been killed. His dying was a particular shock because it was so useless. All the time he was flying missions in the thick of the war, risking his life again and again, he always got back to base safely. Then when he was sent to Texas as a flight instructor, he went up with a student and crashed. Poor Irene! I feel so dreadfully sorry for her."

"Yes, it's very sad."

Lillian, having problems of her own, didn't probe further. But she was virtually certain that while her sister was indeed feeling the deepest sympathy for Irene, it wasn't Vernon Castle who was the cause of her nervousness and despondency.

Joanna replaced the receiver on its hook and stood in the quiet hall, willing herself to walk away. She must not be bothering Mr. McGowan so soon again, asking for word. People would think it queer she was so concerned about Charles Gold—she, a married woman.

But ever since the newspaper editor had called her, she hadn't been able to get the awful nagging worry out of her mind. He'd first inquired if she might come back to work in another month or even earlier, his office being very short-handed now that so many reporters were in uniform. Then he'd asked the question that had stunned her.

"Has anyone told you Charles Gold appears to be missing? Several weeks have gone by with no word from him, not a single dispatch. So far we've put off telling his family, because what is there to say? After all, we really know nothing."

She had tried to respond normally, not sound as frightened as she was. "Is he reported missing? The casualty lists—"

Mr. McGowan had interrupted so impatiently that at any other time she would have been embarrassed. "Charles is a civilian! Don't you realize that even a soldier when wounded or killed may not be identified for days, perhaps weeks? Sometimes not then. War correspondents aren't kept track of at all—they pretty much go where they please, do what they please—unless some general objects, and most generals, I imagine, are too busy to bother. The Western Front is a blackened, smoking wasteland, with exhausted armies surging back and forth for grim possession. Of what importance is one man? No, Mrs. Bonnard, I'm afraid that if Charles is dead and his identfication lost, we'll never find out. It happens that way . . . Mrs. Bonnard, are you there?"

She'd said, fighting for composure, "I think you're quite right to wait a little longer before calling his family. But please, will you let me know as soon as you have any news? I'd be very grateful! I do consider Mr. Gold a friend, a good friend. . . ."

Chapter 38

During the remaining days before she would return to the newspaper, perhaps because Uncle Paul was spending so much of his time at the Mendenhall house, while Tony, thousands of miles away from her, seemed farther still because of the ocean which lay between them, Joanna sometimes felt that her only communication with the world was the homely black telephone hanging on the wall.

She would finish her housework, then for most of the morning keep busy with little Antonia, already, through the mysterious process by which babies acquire nicknames, known as Bunch. Bunch, as matter-of-fact as her name, had a decided mind of her own. She wanted to be sung to and amused, and when she was hungry there was little use trying to persuade her to wait. Afterward, it was a joy to Joanna to hold the contented child, rocking her, the warm, soft little cheek, redolent of milk, pressed against her own. Regretfully, at last she would place the sleeping baby in the cradle and go out to work in the neglected garden, but she was never too far away to be able to hear the child if she woke or the telephone if it rang.

From midday on was a lonely and dragging time. Yet when Aunt Flossie urged her to bring Bunch and stay the afternoon she made excuses. If Mr. McGowan should chance to call, and he only would if he had news of Charles Gold, she must be there.

Thus, about a week after her conversation with Lillian, she had sped to answer the telephone, and in her dread of bad news was relieved to hear only a strange female voice asking, "Miss Fritsch?"

"Yes—that is, I used to be Miss Fritsch, now I'm Mrs. Bonnard."

"Oh. I didn't realize—" The caller sounded disconcerted, and continued uncertainly, "This is Barbara Gierek. We met at the home of Harper Johnson—perhaps you remember? You came there one evening with young Charles Gold."

"I remember." Joanna's hand tightened around the receiver. Could this woman intend to tell her something about Charles? No, not if she mentioned him so calmly. She must not even be aware that he was missing.

"Forgive me for bothering you, Mrs. Bonnard, but I am trying to get in touch with Lily French. I believe Charles mentioned that evening that she is your sister."

"Yes, she is. She works at the Mack Sennett Studio. You can easily reach her there." Joanna was surprised that Mrs. Gierek, who was somehow, she recalled, connected with the motion picture industry herself, would need to be told this.

"So I thought, too," Mrs. Gierek said. "But no one at their office would give me any information about her. Oh, that's not unusual. Not with the rivalry that exists between the various motion picture companies. The Sennett people are also particularly sensitive right now, having just lost Fatty Arbuckle to Paramount. One can't really blame him for switching; I'm sure an offer of five thousand dollars a week would have been hard to turn down, but there's a banner flying right now above the Paramount gate—PARAMOUNT WELCOMES THE PRINCE OF WHALES—and even though he has a fine sense of humor, I daresay Mack Sennett isn't laughing.

"However, getting back to your sister, as I only wanted to borrow her for a picture, not steal her, and as Mack is what one might call a friendly enemy, I then called him direct. I learned that Miss French no longer works for him."

Barbara Gierek's clear voice paused. Perhaps she expected a comment, but Joanna only gasped, too surprised to speak.

"You didn't know? I rather hoped she had confided in you, or even better, come home to lick her wounds—in which case my search would be ended."

"Why do you assume she was let go?" Joanna asked a little stiffly. "If Fatty Arbuckle signed with someone else, perhaps Lillian did the same."

"I'm afraid not." Mrs. Gierek sounded genuinely regretful. "Mack is a blunt man. When he said to me, 'I couldn't have Lily around the place anymore. Not her fault, I suppose, but that's the way it is,' that booming voice of his had a ring of truth."

"Oh, dear!"

"I wish I hadn't had to give you bad news, but if you do

hear from Lily, would you be kind enough to ask her to call me?"

"She and my mother live in Hollywood. Have you tried there?"

"Several times. However, I shall again."

"Mrs. Fritsch? I'm Barbara Gierek." She stood before Clara on the stoop of the court bungalow, a small, straight-backed woman with a sprinkling of freckles on her middle-aged countenance and a mass of gleaming, strawberry red hair untidily confined beneath her hat. She was simply dressed, although far from inexpensively, as Clara was at once aware.

"Please come in. I'm sorry Lillian isn't back yet, but as I told you on the telephone, I expect her momentarily. . . . Won't you sit down?"

"Thank you." Barbara, for her part, was covertly studying Clara and with some surprise. Though I don't know why I'm surprised, she told herself. Those daughters, Joanna and Lillian, had to inherit beauty from somewhere.

She seated herself on the offered chair, her small, sensibly shod feet resting lightly on the floor, and while murmuring a pleasantry, something about a beautiful day for December, her eyes were taking note of the lack of knickknacks on the tables, the unfaded oblongs on the walls where pictures had recently hung, and the two humpback trunks standing strapped and ready near the door.

"I'm afraid I must have come at an inconvenient time," she said.

"It doesn't matter," Clara answered. "Things are in rather an upheaval, but I've done all I can for the time being. Lillian hasn't decided exactly when we're to leave for New York."

"New York? Indeed! I don't envy you the weather there this time of year."

Clara realized she may have been speaking too freely. She said, "May I offer you some refreshment while we wait? Coffee perhaps?"

Her visitor smiled, and Clara was struck by the extraordinary warmth suddenly illuminating what had seemed a rather plain face. "Thank you, no. I've just come from an enormous meal in our commissary. But tell me, I see a loom over there—are you the weaver? Surely your daughter doesn't have the time."

"Neither the time nor the interest. Yes, I used to do weaving."

"But you've lost interest, too? I'm sorry . . . if this rug is a sample of your work." She was gazing with admiration at the pattern of colors in the wool beneath her feet. "You are obviously quite artistic. May I ask, if it's not too personal a question, what you've turned to instead?"

Clara found herself answering without her usual reticence. "Lately I've been sketching costumes, that is, imagining what could have been worn in certain films. I do believe I enjoy this more than weaving, miniature painting, or anything else I've tried."

"Costumes? Oh, I see... may I?"

To Clara's distress, Barbara's sharp eyes had discovered a sheaf of stiff white papers, stacked untidily on a corner of the table. Before Clara could protest, she had risen briskly and the top drawing was already in her hands.

"Ah yes—here's Miss Normand. I don't recall a film in which she wore this gown, but the design is charming! Just whimsical enough... and easy for a studio seamstress to copy."

"Goodness, I've never shown any of these to the studio!"

"You haven't? I certainly wonder why not." Barbara turned to the next sketch in an unhurried manner.

"You don't understand," Clara said in desperation. "I only do this after the films are already made. I often go to the movies, and it's amusing to think about the different personalities of the actors and dream up other clothes to fit them. Amusing to me, that is. It's only an amusement!"

"But must you see the film first? Suppose you were given the story idea ahead of time, or perhaps you were asked to sit in on the conferences. Would you still have these original ideas?"

"I imagine so." Clara was tiring of the discussion. Lillian's studio, she knew, had more costumes than could ever be used. She'd been shown closets full of them one time when she visited the lot. It was a relief therefore to hear first her daughter's familiar step on the walk outside and then the rasp of the front door being thrown open.

Lillian, walking not quite as jauntily as usual, called as she entered, "I hope you have everything packed, Mama. New York, here we come! And be damned to Mabel Normand—"

Even before Clara's chiding, "Lillian!" she broke off, suddenly aware that a stranger was present.

"You have company, Mama?"

"No. This lady has come to see you."

"My name is Barbara Gierek, Miss French. I gather from

your remark that you have not yet signed with another studio?"

Lillian considered. Tempted by ill temper to retort, "And how does that concern you?" she refrained, not only to avoid her mother's censure but because the name had a tantalizingly familiar ring.

As she frowned, trying to place her visitor, the woman added, "I'm one of the owners of Selig Pictures," and Lillian was grateful she had held her tongue.

"I'll come right to the point, Miss French. I've seen several films of yours, and although they've been mostly comedies, the latest made me think you might be right for a major role in a more serious picture, one we're planning at Selig."

"A war film?"

Barbara laughed. "I think there are enough of those already, don't you? No, this is something rather different. It will be the story of Lilith, brought up to modern times." A glance at the young actress's expression, and she explained, "Lilith, in Jewish legend, was a devil in the form of a beautiful woman."

"Of course!" Lillian breathed. "My name, it's like an omen, isn't it? Lillian, Lily, Lilith—I am the one who should play the part!"

"My, no, I'm afraid not. A more mature, far more sophisticated type is needed for Lilith. Not an easy role to fill, but luckily we've someone in mind."

Lillian, trying hard to hide her disappointment and chagrin, asked, "Do I know her?"

"I doubt that you do. Sometimes I think Hollywood people pay no attention at all to the rest of the world. Actually, I'd prefer not to mention her name until we have her signature, but she is a famous stage actress."

"Oh, one of those!" Lillian said with scorn. "Usually they're such flops, and after being brought out here with a lot of fanfare and paid enormous salaries! They can't get used to not saying lines, and they haven't the least idea how to act before a camera!"

"This one has. She was one of the pioneers in our industry. Actually played in those very first, very crude movies."

"Then she must be terribly old," Lillian said sweetly, having forgotten the obvious fact that Mrs. Gierek too was on the far side of forty.

"Old but ageless," Barbara said, unperturbed. "As is Lilith."

"Then what part do you have for me?"

"That should be obvious. You being young and pretty would

play Eve. A present-day wife of Lilith's lover."

Lillian, for the time being, accepted the inevitable—that the starring role wasn't to be hers. At least, she reflected, she was saved from having to forage for herself in New York. All the same, one should not appear too eager, especially without Bert Lange to drive the bargain. Her mouth made a slight moue before she said, "Well, I don't know . . ."

"You must suit yourself, naturally." Barbara Gierek began drawing on her gloves. "Your acceptance—or refusal—isn't, I should tell you, very critical. Hollywood is filled to over-flowing with young, very pretty girls."

"Not with my experience!"

"A trifle less experience might in some ways be prefera-ble. . . . Well, I should be on my way. I'm sorry you aren't more interested, as I rather thought your—shall we say—armor of innocence, your brashness, would make a nice contrast to the sensuality of the lead."

"But I am interested!" Lillian said quickly. "I only wanted a moment to consider. Yes, I do believe—yes, I definitely want the part."

"A prudent decision." Barbara's glance rested briefly on the two packed and waiting trunks. "I'll work out the details with your agent then, shall I?"

"No, I no longer have an agent. He—he wasn't worth his commission."

"Dear me, you are an independent young woman!"

Lillian said nothing.

"Very well then, if you come to my office in the morning, you can talk terms with the gentleman who draws up the Selig contracts.

"Now, I really must go. It's been a pleasure to meet you, Miss French, and your mother, too. And I'm sure you'll find us easy to work with. Just one thing—you don't take drugs, I hope? Max Selig and I are adamantly opposed to any nar-cotics. Our lot is one place the Count, as he's called, is never permitted."

"No, I do not," Lillian said firmly, but thinking in disbelief, *Surely you don't believe what you're saying? There isn't a studio in Hollywood that can keep out cokey!* Quickly, she changed the subject. "I also want to ask a question—"

In these days of frustration, she hadn't bothered to check with Selig's because Mabel had made several pictures there.

If the studio hadn't yet been included in Mabel's angry vendetta, it surely would be soon, and Lillian might as well know the worst at once.

"Mrs. Gierek, Mabel Normand may come to you and say, 'If Lily French works for Selig Pictures, I won't!' Then what?"

Barbara frowned. "Are you asking if I would break your contract?"

"Yes."

"Well, as it happens, Miss Normand has approached us already. She was told that Gus and I make the decisions, not our actors. It's as well that you understand that, too."

Her warm smile reappeared and she resumed her energetic progress toward the door. Again, however, she paused, this time to speak to Clara. "I'd like to send our Mr. Bishop to call on you one day soon. Would you mind?"

Clara was bewildered. "Mr. Bishop?"

"Oh, didn't I mention him when we were talking? Mr. Bishop is something of an artist himself. He'll be much interested in seeing your sketches, and he may possibly bring an outline of the Lilith story to show you."

"But I couldn't possibly—" Clara began. Her protest was too late. Mrs. Gierek had hurried out.

Clara shrugged. Motion picture people! No doubt that was the last she'd ever hear about artistic Mr. Bishop, which was just as well. She could only too clearly picture him, a willowy little man with well-oiled mustache and too-tight clothing. The waspish sort.

She dismissed him from her mind, and said to Lillian, "Then we can unpack? I take it you are accepting her offer?"

"I hadn't much choice, had I? New York would be difficult, when I know no one there. Oh, what a stupid thing it was to offend Bert! But I did, what's done is done, and so far I haven't been able to get another agent. I'll have to manage tomorrow on my own."

"You'll manage." Clara was no longer listening. Her first thought had been, Thank heaven they could stay in Hollywood, close to Joanna and the baby—and to Adeline, who would surely, now that Ralph was gone, become a less hard and resentful woman.

Her second thought was to wonder just what the legendary Lilith looked like. A vamp, of course, a Theda Bara or Virginia Pearson, but much more. Ageless, as Mrs. Gierek had said.

Slim yet voluptuous, beautiful no doubt in a very seductive way, with long dark hair and black eyes that had seen everything and felt nothing.

And she'd wear...she'd wear...

Chapter 39

BATTLE RAGES ALONG THE SOMME
by Charles Gold
(Direct wire—exclusive dispatch)

WESTERN FRONT IN FRANCE, *April 20*—The mighty German assault led by Field Marshall Erich von Ludendorff along some fifty miles of the Somme River continues.

Launched in the desperate hope of driving a wedge between the British and French forces before the full might of America can be brought to bear, the struggle is bloody and costly for both sides. This correspondent, deafened by the unceasing boom of cannon, the ack-ack of machine gun fire, and the dreaded explosion of a shell, blinded and suffocated by a burning sour haze which never lifts, wonders how the brave Allied Armies can endure yet another hour, day after day.

Trucks full of gray uniforms roll past. The enemy has broken the line in many places, and came perilously close today to taking Amiens, the strategic rail center. But close was not good enough. The German troops were exhausted men, and the relatively fresh British reserves, rushed to the scene by train and truck, pushed them back. An important victory—as it signals, at least for now, the saving of Paris.

Joanna, reading these words penned somewhere in France by Charles Gold, felt an amazed gratitude. She had believed him dead. She folded the freshly printed newspaper and placed it carefully in a drawer to be read later, at leisure, at home.

"Seems to me there ought to be more in this story about our own boys!" grumbled a man in his sixties at the next desk, studying his own copy. He was one of those who had retired and then been brought back to work after younger reporters had left for war. "We've got thousands of men over there, must have by now, and Gold should have given them their due when he talked about winning that battle at the railroad center."

"Think so, Mr. Parker? Well, don't worry." Edwin Mc-Gowan on his way to his office, paused. "I believe you'll find stories aplenty about American bravery soon enough—though I don't suppose anything is soon enough for the parents of our fine young men. . . .

"Still," he continued, ruminating, "what I like about any report Charles sends is that it's accurate. He's there. And when America starts winning the war for the Allies, he'll tell us. We've done pretty well, just getting ourselves across the Atlantic.

"Do you know, Parker, I think we need another article to remind the public of what a momentous task it has been to create, almost overnight, an active duty army, train it, then transport it to Europe. Leaving out the enormous number of enlisted men to be put in uniform, I happen to know that when the United States declared war, there were only 9,000 officers in the entire federal service, and some 200,000 needed! Those selected for officer training camps could be sent for only three months, which isn't much, and some of them are already leading troops. The rest will be any day now, and by God, green as they all are, we'll be proud of their courage and heroism. We'll be proud. . . ."

He strode off into his office and shut the door.

Tom Parker said, "He's feeling the strain, and I can't blame him for that. So many of the men who worked for him are over there. But, by golly, he's wrong. We Yanks are in it now, aren't we? We're running the show. Don't know why the Frogs didn't make our General Pershing the supreme commander of the Allies instead of Marshal Foch because it's Pershing's boys will win the war. . . ."

Joanna, who had heard this sentiment expressed many times in stores, on trolleys, and on the street, had stopped paying attention.

Charles Gold had not explained to his readers where he'd

been during that long period of silence, or what had happened to him, but Mr. McGowan had once mentioned, as though Joanna knew, too, a hospital in Paris. It occurred to her now that the rejoicing of his friends at the *Times* over his reappearance in print and on the front might be shortsighted. One never knew in a war where safety lay—the shocking death of the British ace, Vernon Castle, had made that only too clear, but the odds were surely better away from the front lines.

She realized Tom Parker had been asking her a question. "Where is your husband now, Mrs. Bonnard?" he repeated.

Joanna broke into a smile. She said, "I've had good news, although he was cross and grumbling. He's being sent back to Pershing's headquarters to help merge into the U.S. Aero Squadron all the American flyers who've been with *Lafayette Escadrille*."

"But that's already been done, hasn't it?"

"Mostly. I guess there's a lot of confusion. He talked about paper work, files, records. He's inclined to be very impatient with routine work. But at least he's not flying!"

"Well! Look at this!" Parker interrupted excitedly, gesturing at the newspaper. "'Scuse me, Mrs. Bonnard—but right at the end, Gold does talk about our boys. A little anyway. Seems four U.S. pilots, dogfighting, stopped the Hun planes from strafing the trucks. How's that for saving the bacon of the British?

"But then—" Parker's exhilaration vanished. He said slowly, almost in a puzzled way, "They were shot down."

"Ready, Tony?"

"As I'll ever be. What a hell of a time to be sent back to headquarters!" He tossed his cap on top of his full kit bag and walked to the window again to survey the airfield outside. A plane had just landed, small and beautiful against the sunrise, and was taxiing toward the hanger. "I see Mark got back. Thank God."

"Yes. But Harrison is still out and overdue." John Hart, Tony's closest friend—the two of them the survivors of the outfit—tossed a cigarette out of its package and busied himself lighting it. "That was a bad night, Tony."

"I know. Damn it, I know! I'll never forgive the Old Man for not letting me go with them. He said orders were orders and I was to be on my way to Chaumont."

"Well? Why are you still here?"

"Staff car broke down." Tony grinned. "No other transportation."

"That Swede the infantry sent over couldn't fix it? I don't believe that."

"He's not a Swede. Just looks like one. He's a farm boy from Minnesota."

"I asked you—couldn't he fix the car?"

"He could have. Sure. If I'd have let him at it. But I thought his time was better spent working on the planes."

Hart laughed. "Tony, I think the Old Man is going to have one sweet time getting you out of here—oh, Jesus! Good morning, sir."

The two young men snapped a salute.

Colonel Harkias growled, "Harrison not back yet?"

"No, sir," Hart said.

"I've got orders to send at least four planes toward Amiens. The Huns are strafing the reinforcements and have to be stopped. It seems impossible, but unless I send Joe Terrill right back up, I haven't *got* four planes."

"I see four out there," Tony said from his place by the window.

"I'm not talking about planes, for God's sake! I'm talking about pilots."

"There's Hart, Bell, Sanderson, and me."

"You . . . *Bonnard*, are you still here? I told you to be on your way by midnight at the latest!"

"Broken fuel pump, sir."

"And the Swede couldn't—"

"No, sir. That is, I thought he should be repairing the planes instead. That's why you have four planes ready this morning. Sir."

"Damn you, Bonnard. When this American First Army ever gets itself organized, you're going to learn how to take orders. Well, all right! What are you two waiting for? Takeoff's in ten minutes."

He stalked out.

"Is he angry? Or not?" Hart asked.

"Hell, no, he's pleased. He'd have had mud on his face if he couldn't put up four of us as ordered. Let's go."

The Spads, because of the low morning fog, flew well apart. Occasionally, looking behind him, Tony could make out Hart and then Sanderson. Somewhere back out of sight was Bell.

They were on course—in the sky ahead was the haze of smoke shot through with dull streaks of red and yellow fire, and he could smell a familiar acrid reek. In the mudflats beneath him were the first trenches, those farthest to the rear and filled with artillery, and even as he looked down, the big guns backed on their haunches and shot forward, belching their shells and emitting hoarse metal screams of triumph.

Somewhere ahead was the river. And not far to the right must be the town of Amiens. Below him now ran a dusty potholed road on which a long row of ordinary produce trucks, open topped and jammed full—not of lettuce and carrots but of standing British soldiers—crept slowly but steadily.

Then he saw the planes. A Sopwith Camel was bravely facing up to two Fokkers, the three of them swooping, dropping away, circling one another, looking for the chance to train their guns. As one Fokker managed to engage the British plane, the other German suddenly detached himself, dived, and pulled out just above the line of trucks. His machine gun rattled, and the uniformed men in the first of the close-packed trucks seemed to bend at the waist and fall sideways, puppets with the strings gone slack. First one vehicle then the next zigzagged wildly from the road. One went careening away across the dry brown loam of an untilled field; the other crashed against a tree.

Tony had waved his arm in a signal to Hart, and not waiting for the others got the Fokker in his sights. He plummeted, his finger pressed hard on the trigger of his gun.

The German plane couldn't escape. Tony, in *Joanna*, was on his defenseless back, so close the little Spad was almost riding the flat red wings. The engine below spouted flames like a great opening flower, and the pilot, riddled by bullets, jerked briefly, then slumped and was still. Tony gave a salute of farewell as the stricken Fokker spiraled away, falling faster and faster, trailing black smoke in a banner.

Miraculously—there must have been a lull in the cannon fire—Tony heard a yell. Hart's voice, shrill with warning.

"Tony! Ten o'clock!"

He didn't have to look to know what was coming at him, high on the left. He threw his stick over, and began to roll away and down. Behind him he heard the firing, saw a pattern of holes stitched into his right wing, and felt a sharp splintered pain stab his right leg. His engine coughed, then coughed again.

He leveled out, glanced around. He was alone, and above him Hart had taken on his attacker.

Up, he must go up again! Join the fight. He and Hart backing each other as always.

But his engine coughed once more, and died.

At once he was gliding away, with no power and little control. He strained his eyes through the smoky haze, clutching the stick, and as he searched for a bit of empty flatland, the old familiar and calming words came, though he hardly knew he said them.

> "Hail, Mary full of grace,
> the Lord is with thee,
> Blessed art thou among women, and blessed
> is the fruit of thy womb, Jesus.
> Holy Mary, Mother of God, pray for us sinners,
> now and at the hour of our death—"

He found his flatland, and came down well behind the lines, hitting the rough barren furrows, bouncing up, then hitting again, running wildly forward to be stopped finally by a stone wall. The impact slammed his head against a strut just ahead of the cockpit, and with such force that he sat bleeding and half-conscious. He made a feeble effort to crawl out, but although his eyes were open, he couldn't see, and his leg felt as though it were caught in a vice. He thought he smelled a wisp of smoke, and went rigid, sweating with terror, imagining the plane catching fire with him inside, trapped and helpless. But as time passed, and the peaceful silence of this isolated farm remained unbroken except by the rumble of distant cannon, he knew it wasn't, after all, the hour of his death.

"Thank you, Lord," he said aloud. "Thank you."

The long period of time after that was never clear in his mind. He remembered only that someone, a farmer perhaps, pulled him out awkwardly and painfully, and carried him away over his shoulder. Later, he rode lying flat on a wooden truck bed while the black sky in his head swayed dizzily. The next thing he knew he was in bed, a lumpy cot in a hospital, he guessed, because occasionally someone called him Captain Bonnard and he was bathed and bandaged by skillful hands. Sometimes he was conscious, sometimes not; mostly he lay in a limbo between the two states, staring sightlessly.

Was he blind? The overwhelming fear never left him. He'd never imagined anything like this! Pilots lived or died. They didn't go blind. How could he return to Joanna—blind?

Joanna. Day and night, confused by the darkness that for him continued unbroken, he couldn't get her out of his mind. Not that he ever wanted to. Memories of Joanna were sweet and clean and free of fear.

Sometimes he even imagined her so vividly that he could believe she was there with him. Even in bed with him! But it was only when he was certain morning had arrived, with all the distractions of the ward swirling around him, that he let himself remember what being married to her had been like.

Their first night—in the elegant bridal bedroom at the Huntington Hotel. He had to laugh, really, realizing how ignorant they'd both been, because he, too, had never made love before. He'd never been tempted even. Joanna had been the only girl he had eyes for, all the time he was growing up. So he wasn't quite sure what to do, that first time in bed, though he tried not to let her know. He was awkward and fumbling, because he didn't want to hurt her and didn't know how not to.

Until she said, "Tony, let's just lie close together for a little—can't we?"

And he held her, her body cozily wrapped around by his, the two of them naked and warm together under the sheets. And gradually all the awkwardness went away. He discovered he knew how to kiss, where to touch and pet her, and finally when he couldn't possibly wait any longer, how to put himself inside of her.

After that he'd stopped thinking, caught up in the agony of his passion while it crested, then broke, and at last left him spent and satisfied and at peace. That final instant had been so splendid, far finer, because of her, than he'd imagined it could be, that he tried many times to remember how he'd felt. He couldn't quite, but he decided that for him, the closest thing was one of those fireworks on the Fourth of July, streaking up into the night and exploding in a great, silent shower of stars, red, blue, gold, and silver, that fell slowly in long caressing fingers of light. That was what happened inside of *him*, once he'd entered Joanna.

The best part was, after they'd done this wonderful thing a time or two, she began to want him just as much as he wanted her, and she experienced the delight for herself. She had a funny, warm little laugh she gave when it was over, while they were still lying quietly and happily. Then there was one more thing he liked to do. He liked to get up and turn on the light and take one last look at how beautiful she was.

Oh, God, would he ever hear that little laugh again—or would she only pity him if he were blind? And would he ever get to *see* her again, still lying on the bed, smooth skinned, shaped just as a girl should be, and with a tuft of hair at the top of her legs that was the soft yellow color of saltwater taffy?

"Tony—?" It was a male voice, breaking in.

Joanna fled, and Tony tried to identify who it could be, in this military place, using his first name.

"It's Jim Bell, Tony."

"Oh, sure! Glad to see you!" *See you.* I must be crazy as well as blind, he thought.

He put out his hand, and Bell grasped it.

"Tell me something, Jim," Tony said at once. "What's this room like? I know I'm sitting in a chair today, with a blanket over me like an old man, but I'd like to know what the room's like." Funny thing to want to know, but it bothered him to be in a totally unknown, unvisualized place. "I could have asked the doctors, I guess, or the nurses, but I didn't want to. Don't like to ask them such a dumb question when there's so much pain—and dying."

Bell said, "It's just a room. Eight men in it. It's—" He groped for something distinctive. "The walls are painted green. There's only one window, with a lot of trees outside, so the light isn't good."

"Or the smell either." Tony managed a grim smile. "They do their best, but someone in here's got gangrene. . . . Say, I figured Johnny Hart would come to see me before now."

Bell said, "Ah—maybe later he will. We've all been busy . . . no, that isn't so! Downstairs they said visitors should be cheerful, but damn if I'm going to lie to you. John's dead. So is Sanderson. They copped it that same day. I was the only one to get back. I was shot down, too, but I made it."

Although Tony said nothing, tears forced themselves from between his eyelids. He could feel them run down his cheeks. He said savagely, trying to control his grief and anger and failing altogether, "I wish it had been me! God, I wish it had been me!"

Bell said awkwardly, after a moment, "John and all the others—it's too bad. Still, I'm glad to be alive."

"You aren't blind! I'd rather be dead than blind."

"Well, I'm going to tell you something else I shouldn't. The Old Man asked me to talk to the doctors. They're not sure about your blindness, and your spells of unconsciousness, how bad they are. When the swelling inside your head goes down, your eyes could clear. They haven't told you yet, because they're not sure . . . does that help?"

"It helps. Oh, yes. You can't know."

They sat in silence then for a while. Although Bell had been with the unit only a short time, Tony felt closer to him by far than to any of the strangers by whom he was surrounded. The doctors and nurses were kind enough, but he and Bell were from one world, they from another. And the other patients in the ward, he'd gathered, were all infantry—doughboys. Good men, but they had their own hellish kind of memories, as he had his.

"Got to be getting back," Bell said finally.

"Come again, will you?"

"Yes, but I don't know just when I can. I'm being transferred tomorrow. The Old Man will drop by in a few days, though. Said to tell you. Oh yes, and there is somebody you know here in the hospital."

"Who?"

"The Swede. From Minnesota."

"What the hell's he doing here?"

"He was burned, but not too bad. It happened just after we took off that morning. Sabotage—somebody tried to wipe out the hanger. Threw fuel all over a plane, set it afire and ran. Olaf was right there. He tried to put out the flames and there was an explosion."

"Was—will he be all right?"

Bell nodded, forgetting Tony couldn't see him. "He was lucky, although his face isn't too good to look at. He's not crippled any. I met him walking down the hall when I came in."

Bell left, and Tony sat thinking. Usually, when a buddy died—and so many of them had—the best thing was to put him out of your mind. Forget he ever existed. But *Johnny Hart*!

He and Johnny, fighting the Jerry planes together, drinking afterward together, feeling cock-of-the-walk. Then, Johnny yelling, "Tony! Ten o'clock!" and saving his life, even if it turned out not to be worth saving. . . . If Tony ever got home, he'd go visit Johnny's mother. She lived in New York, some place called the Bronx. He'd take her Johnny's medals, tell

her Johnny was the best damn pilot in France, the best on the
Allied side anyway, and that Johnny had been the finest friend
a man could have.

Although slightly consoled by this idea, he felt suddenly,
unbearably lonely. When he heard the starchy swish of a nurse
passing his chair, he reached out and caught her arm.

"Miss?"

"Yes, Captain? Do you need something?"

"Will you do me a favor? There's a patient named Mickelson
somewhere in this hospital. Corporal Olaf Mickelson. I'd sure
appreciate it if you could ask him to stop in here."

Chapter 40

"Uncle Paul?"

"In here, Clara, in the parlor with our little Bunch. Thank
you for coming."

"Isn't Joanna at home?" Clara furled her umbrella, hung
her coat and hat on the hall tree, and hastened in to join her
uncle.

She paused at the side of the cradle, smiling at the sight of
the rosy-cheeked child who was trying, with an expression of
comic wonderment in her brown eyes—Tony's eyes—to catch
one of those waving, elusive little feet. Then after a glance
around the old familiar room, Clara went to stand before the
fireplace. There'd been a cold rain blowing as she walked from
the streetcar stop.

"But Uncle Paul," she exclaimed in sudden consternation,
having at last given him her full attention, "you don't look
well—not well at all!"

There was ample reason for her concern. He was thinner
than she'd ever seen him, and very pale, and though she was
certain it was impossible, his back appeared even more humped.
He was huddled in his chair inside a thick blanket, and as she

watched, he continually shifted his body in an effort to find a more tolerable position.

"Are you chilled?"

"No, only weak. And there's a little more pain than usual. But I've had such spells before."

"Where is Joanna?" Clara said angrily. "She should be here—not leave you alone. Does she expect you to tend her child?"

"Joanna started back to work last week," Paul said. "No, Clara—it's quite all right! Florence and I have promised to take care of Bunch for a few hours each morning, and Florence is enjoying the task so much she wishes Joanna would be gone a full day.... Ah—no. Florence is not here just now either, although she was distressed when I insisted she not come today quite so early. She worries absurdly about me, I assure you, even more than you do. However I wanted to talk to you alone." He added, placating his niece, "If you wish, stay until she gets here."

"I certainly intend to!"

Clara fell silent, waiting for him to broach whatever was troubling him, but he then asked, "How is Lillian? Is she settled again?"

"She is with Selig Company, yes. They've put off shooting *Lilith* for a month or two, until the lead actress finishes the run of her play in Chicago. Lillian is doing some other films for them in the meantime, but I'm not entirely happy about her. She seems so different somehow, changed. Well enough, I suppose, but—oh, perhaps it's only my imagination. Was it Lillian you wished to talk about?"

"No." He said then with reluctance, "Joanna."

"Good heavens—has something happened to Tony? Something worse than his being injured, I mean? Oh, Uncle Paul—surely he isn't going to be permanently blind?"

"No, Clara, calm yourself. Not so far as we know. The Red Cross reports that the doctors are optimistic. His leg's mending nicely, too, and he's stronger. He was able to write a long letter home, with the help of a friend who is also a patient at the hospital. His spirits aren't good, but that's to be expected. Did Joanna tell you John Hart, who flew with him so long, was killed in the same battle?"

"No. What a dreadful shock for him! And being hurt himself—" Clara said thoughtfully, "I really think Tony had come to believe he was just too good a pilot to be shot down. His friend also. To continue to go up like that in a flimsy airplane, taking his life in his hands every time, a man would have to feel invincible."

"That's very discerning, and I agree. But we've learned from his letter that a more tangible reason for his unhappiness exists. To him, flying was just about everything, except of course, Joanna. He wrote that he's been having brief spells of unconsciousness, blackouts one of the doctors called them. So even when his sight returns, he was told he must not try to fly again. Ever."

"Oh, poor boy, that is too bad! Although in the long run, I don't suppose Joanna would be too sorry about his having to find some other line of work. Uncle Paul, is that what's worrying you? Surely Tony will be sensible. He'll find a way to support his wife and baby."

"I think you underestimate the problem. But no, there's something else on my mind. Actually, I hesitate to tell you. Perhaps I've been reading too much into a slip of the tongue. And, as you know, I've always shrunk from prying into someone else's life. But after thinking the matter over for several weeks, I've decided that you, her mother, should be told. Then if you agree with me, the subject will be closed."

"Very well. I'm listening."

"As I say, it was only a small thing. It was what she said when I told her the cablegram had come—about Tony.

"You see, Clara, I was at home alone when the delivery boy appeared at the door with one of those ominous yellow envelopes which inevitably contain evil tidings. I signed for it and placed it unopened on the hall table to await her return. An hour or so passed, but she was still out, and I began to think I might be better prepared to help her bear a calamity if I knew exactly what it was. So I opened the envelope. I trust you would have done the same?"

"Yes, indeed!"

"The message, when I read it, was no surprise—short and very frightening, as it was sent before anyone could be certain that Tony's injuries weren't critical. At any event, when Joanna did at last come home, I greeted her with the announcement that some very unhappy news had come for her."

"She stared at me and said, 'It's Charles, isn't it? He's been killed, after all.'

"I was taken aback. I'm not acquainted with anyone named Charles and didn't know that she was. But I ignored her question and said as quietly as I could, 'Tony's been hurt. He was shot down, but he's in a hospital and still alive, so we can surely hope for the best.' She was overcome then with quite obvious and genuine concern for her husband, and the other man, this Charles, was not mentioned again, then or later. Who is he, Clara? Do you know?"

She shook her head. "No, Uncle Paul...thank you for mentioning this to me, but I think we had both better forget what must, as you said, have been a harmless slip of the tongue. Joanna is not the sort to—" Clara stopped and looked away.

"To be unfaithful to her husband?"

"Yes." Clara's voice was faint.

Paul said, "I'm glad you agree. After all, Tony did survive and will be coming home one day soon. For him the war is over, and we may thank God for that!

"Now, my dear, tell me about you. How are you keeping busy these days? According to the magazines, some of these Hollywood people are so colorful that good or bad they'd be interesting to meet. It's a shame you've stayed so aloof."

"I haven't entirely." Clara had recovered, and she gave Paul a teasing smile that reminded him, with a pang, of the light-hearted girl of their carnival days. "I had a caller just yesterday. About my costume designs. One of those things I do, as you say, to...keep busy."

Chapter 41

"*Mrs. Fritsch? I'm* Andrew Bishop. From Selig. I believe— Mrs. Gierek did call you about me?"

"Yes, forgive me. Won't you come in?"

Clara had been too astonished to speak. Where was the waspish little man in the tight suit, the supercilious artist she'd been imagining? Mild, well-mannered Mr. Bishop looked to her as though he belonged anywhere but in the motion picture business. Somewhere in his middle forties, he was beyond the age usual even for male actors, and as for being one of those excitable directors, cameramen, or film editors, his broad-shouldered solid figure, combined with a pleasant expression and an air of unhurried patience, made her think of other occupations altogether. A man who worked with both his mind and his hands—a ship builder, for example, she decided. Which was clever of her because ship building, she would later discover, had actually been his work as recently as three years before.

"Barbara Gierek was struck by your sketches," he began while being ushered into the parlor. The room had been put back in order, the brass candlesticks replaced on the mantel, the few pictures rehung on the walls. The sun was casting a golden spotlight on the many-hued wool carpet, and Mr. Bishop interrupted himself to say approvingly, "What a delightful room."

"Thank you. I don't like clutter, even though it is becoming all the rage now to have tasseled lampshades and a lot of aspidistra plants about."

"I fervently agree . . . are those the sketches?"

"Yes. I left them out for you. But I think I should apologize for taking your time. I'm not an artist. I really didn't want anyone to come, but Mrs. Gierek insisted."

He had picked up the small pile of drawings, and did not reply except to remark absently that he had a great deal of respect for Barbara Gierek's taste and ideas.

In a leisurely way, while Clara, feeling awkward, waited, he studied first one, then another, and another, asking an occasional question.

"This was how you visualized Francis X. Bushman and Beverly Bayne in *Romeo and Juliet*? or "Ah, yes, Mary Pickford in *The Little American* . . . and this must be Theda Bara. Was the film last year's *Gold and the Woman*?"

Clara was not much reassured by this evidence that the actors and actresses she'd chosen were recognizable, because she told herself that anyone with the slightest talent could make a likeness. It was far more significant that he was saying nothing about the costumes which were, after all, the reason for his visit. She began to feel somewhat annoyed with Mrs. Gierek, who was responsible for a busy man being forced to waste an hour or more in this fashion.

At length he had finished with the last sketch, and he turned to her, frowning in thought.

"I had the impression these were all going to be concerned with your daughter's films. Very few are."

"That's true. Actually, I'm less interested in the comedies. They are hard to improve on. Take Charlie Chaplin's baggy clothes. He wouldn't be Charlie Chaplin in a well-cut suit, would he? But the ones I did of Lillian were the top four or five in the pile and they were all Mrs. Gierek saw."

"Then let me understand exactly what you are doing. Is this correct? You view a film, any film, then go home and sketch the various characters as you think they should have been dressed."

"Yes." She added defiantly, "As I explained to Mrs. Gierek, it amuses me."

"I can see that. There's an element of your own keen enjoyment that enlivens what you design. Otherwise, I think they might not be nearly as remarkable."

"You mean—you like them?"

"Very much. In almost every case, I would say that your costumes are more suitable as well as more dramatic." He smiled, and in spite of her absorption in what he was saying she found herself smiling in return. "I don't want to overemphasize that point though. Costuming in general can stand a lot of improvement. It's pretty much slapdash, except for military uniforms, or perhaps for the characters in historical scenes where extensive research has been done."

Again Clara marveled at the incongruity of this man's involvement in a business she believed she had come to know well and dislike, and she said, "Mr. Bishop, if I may ask, just what work do you do at the studio? Mrs. Gierek didn't say. She just called you 'our Mr. Bishop.'"

"That's a probably as good a job description as any." His amused smile faded and he looked off into the distance. "When I came back to California several years ago—I was born here, you see, and when your life goes wrong, your first impulse, your need, is to go home—"

That's true, Clara thought. Except that for me, the only home I could remember was the house I'd lived in with Sam. Perhaps if I'd really lived somewhere else, not just a carnival tent, I'd have been able to go back there and forget a little.

"When I returned," Andrew Bishop was saying, "I wanted to work at something new, something completely different. My mother sent me to Barbara, an old friend of hers, and Barbara of course took me in, at Selig's. At first I moved from one skill to another, learning. But being so new, I could see mistakes that others didn't see, and when I turned out to be right more often than not, they began asking my advice, and here I am. A jack of all trades and master of none."

"It must be important not to get too involved—you wouldn't want to."

"No." His gray eyes approved her for comprehending. "If I look at the trees too closely, I no longer will see the forest. But so far I seem to know which way to cast my vote at Selig. What would best for the studio, that is."

Abruptly he changed the subject. "Tell me, Mrs. Fritsch, are you acquainted with the story of *Lilith*?"

"Just the bare outline. I asked my uncle, who is the well-read member of the family, and he said that according to Jewish legend, she was the first wife of Adam and was banished from Eden when Eve was created. Also, a poet, Dante Gabriel Rossetti, wrote about her:

> *It was Lilith, the wife of Adam*
> *Not a drop of her blood was human*
> *But she was made like a soft sweet woman....*

"And that's all I know."

"It's more than I was told at the studio. I must meet your Uncle Paul some time. Is he a schoolmaster?"

Remembering her own lessons that had been her only schooling, she said, "Yes, he is," and thought, Uncle Paul would be pleased. I must tell him.

"Getting back to Lilith," Mr. Bishop said, "Have you formed any ideas about her, what she might have worn?"

Clara had intended to deny this and so shorten a visit she had dreaded. But she'd never dreamed beforehand that the conversation would progress so favorably and so pleasantly.

"Only," she said, "that her dress, while contemporary, has to suggest a creature from another time and place, one who is in league with spirits and only masquerading as a human woman. I did sketch out something...."

She opened the table drawer and pulled out a drawing, then handed it to him.

A brief glance, and he nodded. "Mrs. Fritsch, we can use this."

"I'm glad. Then please take it."

"I couldn't do that. Not without paying you. I must confess

we were rather hoping that if your ideas were as good as Barbara thought you'd come to work for us. Design the costumes, see that they're made to your specifications, and so on. Do you think that might be possible? Or would your husband object?"

"My husband is no longer living."

"I am sorry." He was clearly distressed by his blunder.

"It's all right," she said, "you couldn't have guessed."

"Still it was a possibility, and I should have remembered how I felt when—after my wife died, someone made a careless remark."

"Please. It's a long time ago now."

"Very well. But as you are a widow, perhaps you will consider an offer? We're prepared to pay handsomely."

"I'm afraid not." The reminder of Sam had brought her to her senses. It was almost as if he were standing at her side, saying, "Come now, Clara, you aren't in Hollywood, this den of iniquity, for your own gratification. You're only here to watch over Lillian as best you can."

Still, she could not help feeling gratified by her caller's disappointed expression. He said, "If it's a matter of money, as I told you, we're prepared to pay very well. Tell me how much you—"

"The money doesn't matter." He must not think she was playing some hard, mercenary game. Not when he'd been so kind. "I just can't—not so quickly—"

"Clara, be firm! Tell him *no*!" Sam's voice again.

She said, "No. That's my answer. I'm sorry." And she *was* sorry. Very.

"If you should change your mind—"

"I won't." Sam was right, she had to be firm. Because she realized that in this short time, merely talking to Mr. Bishop, she was feeling—it was the first time in so many years—like a woman, an attractive woman. "But please do take the drawing," she said. "I'd enjoy seeing it put to use."

"Very well. But simply because I haven't given up. Good day to you, Mrs. Fritsch."

Part Three

1918–1919

*Dreams are true while they last,
and do we not live in dreams?*
—TENNYSON

Chapter 42

Tony was home. The engine was slowly inching along the last few feet of track, trying to settle with a final rasp inside the cavernous train shed. The platform was crowded, and he leaned out the open window of the car, searching the sea of waiting faces for a glimpse of fair hair piled high, a pair of wide-set blue eyes, and the sweetly curving mouth that for such a long time he'd dreamed of kissing.

And there she was, pressed in the throng. His Joanna, smiling at him from beneath the brim of a small, close-fitting hat, and waving gaily as she caught sight of him.

He waved back more slowly. He wanted in this moment just to gaze. To feast his eyes on his girl, his wife.

The train emitted a long hissing sigh and was still. Along its length, the dignified black porters threw open the doors, and jumping down themselves, set out the squat iron stools for the passengers' convenience in disembarking. Then the cars began to empty.

Tony and Olaf Mickelson, now that they'd finally arrived, were content to take their time—Tony because he was savoring in advance the exquisite pleasure of reunion, and Olaf because once again he was venturing into a new place and a new life, this time in unknown California.

In their worn uniforms, particularly Olaf's familiar khaki with the wrapped puttees of the infantry, they had been the object of friendly regard the entire trip. Passengers walking the aisle had stopped beside their seat to make conversation, easily and sometimes eagerly, as if the two men, the slender aviator and the massive, silent doughboy, were the sons of neighbors or friends.

"Come home early, boys?" No hint of criticism there. Tony's thinness and pallor, and the ugly scars, barely healed, that flamed on one side of Olaf's face, were guarantee enough that the two had done their duty.

Tony always answered for them. Olaf was a quiet, stoic young man who still, after months in the army, was unused to crowds of strangers and had no talent for small talk. His disfigurement hardly encouraged him to be more sociable.

"Yes, sir."

"Glad to be back, are you?"

"I can't say that exactly. Glad to get home all right, but I hated to leave before we'd beaten the Huns." *I hated to stop flying. Oh, God!*

"Well, you fellows are doing a fine job. We're mighty proud of you. Say, did you happen to get to Lorraine? Maybe you met my nephew, Jimmy Lester? He was in an infantry training camp around there somewhere. I heard that's what Pershing was trying to do—make sure young men had a little training at least, before they got sent into action. But the newspapers say the Yanks were mighty important in the recent battles along the Marne and it was our attack forces that took Belleau Wood and a couple of other villages. So I guess that isn't so, about holding them back?"

"We've been in the fighting all right. Yes, sir, a lot of us have. General Pershing could hardly refuse the use of his men when the German Army was so close to taking Paris. American troops fought all along the Hindenburg line, and they fought hard." *Died hard, too*, Tony added sourly to himself.

The passerby had kindly offered to buy his and Olaf's dinner in the train diner that night, and Tony had accepted. Olaf couldn't be persuaded and Tony made excuses for him, saying he hadn't been long out of hospital, which was true enough. Later, however, a waiter brought Olaf a tray of the best and most expensive food, lavishly paid for as well.

Now, disembarking, their benefactor said, "Good luck to you boys!" and was gone, and then Tony and Olaf were leaving the train.

Here she was, his Joanna! He had her in his arms, crushed tight against him, and he felt her tears wet his face.

"Hey, now! I'm back—this is a *happy* day!"

"Yes, so very happy, Tony. You're safe. Oh you crazy idiot . . . taking all those chances!"

"So I did, and I've paid for them." His happiness was dampened a bit by the reminder of the price paid and still to be paid. Paid for the rest of his life. But he pushed the dreary thought away, and noticing that Olaf had taken himself a few yards distant, he gave his wife a long and very satisfactory kiss, allowable under the circumstances even in such a public place. Then he said urgently, "I don't want to do a single sensible thing today! Nothing! Just be with you and get to know the baby. Where is she? I hoped you'd bring her!"

"I would have—I intended to! But as the train was running late, I couldn't come directly from home. You'll be with her though, in only a few minutes."

"I can hardly wait!" They smiled at each other, each envisioning that moment.

"Joanna, one thing I've been looking forward to for months— let's go dancing tonight, shall we? I don't suppose Castles-by-the-Sea is still open, not with Vernon down in Texas, but—"

"Oh, Tony! You don't know about Vernon?"

"Know what?"

She told him, and his euphoria at being back diminished still further. He even felt a tinge of resentment. Why did she have to pass on such depressing news today, when he'd just gotten home?

Evidently she sensed his edgy disappointment, because she asked, "Shouldn't I have said anything? I'm sorry."

"It doesn't matter."

"I only—well, I thought you'd want to know. You liked both of them so much."

"Joanna, I've liked a number of people lately, even loved a few of them. I've had friends, the closest friends a man can have, and almost every one is dead! Vernon Castle was only an acquaintance. Why should I care about Vernon?"

She was looking worried. "I'm sorry," she said helplessly.

"No, it's all right." He drew a deep breath. "But give me a little time!"

"Yes, of course."

He turned then and shouted to Olaf, who had been standing some distance away, his attention carefully elsewhere.

"Olaf—come meet Joanna! This is Olaf Mickelson, honey. We were in the hospital together. He knows all about engines, and we talked about airplanes to pass the time. I wrote you about him, remember?"

"I remember."

I'm bringing Olaf home with me, because he really doesn't

*have anyplace else to go. He was in love with a girl out in
Minnesota and she married someone else while he was gone.
Wrote him a letter and told him. Wasn't that rotten? I can't
understand a girl who'd take up with another man while a
fellow's back is turned. Especially when he's off fighting for
his country! Olaf's parents are dead, so he doesn't have any
reason to go back now.*

Joanna was smiling into Olaf's broad, badly scarred face,
with none of the furtive curiosity he had come to expect. His
big body visibly relaxed inside the ill-fitting uniform.

The three began walking through the tall doors which led
into the station and on out to the street. Tony was gratified to
see how Joanna was making Olaf feel easy. Walking between
the two men, she took both their arms, just as though she'd
known the Swedish farmer for a long time, and Olaf was re-
sponding to her inconsequential remarks, saying a word or two
himself, something he hadn't done with any of the strangers
on the long journey west.

"We go to the left," Joanna said, leading them along the
sidewalk to where a shiny black Model T was parked. "And
here we are!"

"This car is yours?"

"Isn't it grand? I told you, I came here directly from work.
You see, I decided to buy my own little Ford several weeks
ago, because I was having trouble getting about and finding
all the addresses the newspaper sent me to. I had to borrow
some money from Lillian, but I'll pay her back in no time from
my salary." She added proudly, "I've gotten another raise."

"This won't do, Joanna," Tony said heavily.

"What? My borrowing from Lillian? She didn't mind. Lillian's not at all stingy." There was a faint emphasis on Lillian's
name, as though Joanna might have asked someone else first,
her sister Dell possibly, and been refused. But Tony's mind
was on something else.

He said, "I meant—" and stopped with a glance at Olaf,
but his friend once again had turned his back and was gazing
with evident fascination at the lively traffic on the downtown
streets. "I meant," Tony continued, "that this isn't a good time
to be spending such a large sum. I haven't the least idea yet
how I'm going to earn us enough money to live on. Now that
I can't fly anymore, we'll have nothing coming in for a while."

"I don't understand! Why do you say—nothing coming in?

I just told you about the raise. I'm working full time at the newspaper. Aunt Flossie takes care of Bunch for me—she's at our house every day, has been ever since Uncle Paul became so ill—"

Tony, in a harsh voice, cut her off. "No, Joanna. No! I won't have it."

"The baby cheers her up—truly! Aunt Flossie used to believe that if she only tried harder Uncle Paul would get better. But he doesn't. He's failing. She says Bunch keeps her smiling—keeps her from letting him see how bad she feels."

"Aren't you listening to me, Joanna? It's not Aunt Flossie I'm talking about. It's us. I will not have my wife supporting me—and that's final."

"You'll find work right away, I know you will . . . wait. Are you saying you want me to—stop working?"

"I expect you to."

What was happening? Here he was on his first day home—no, not even the first day, more the first half-hour, and his joy had evaporated. All the lovely visions he'd had for so long were already showing themselves as nothing more than foolish daydreams . . . Joanna at the station, with little Antonia in her arms. The three of them, with Olaf, sitting on the sandy beach at Santa Monica, lazing away the afternoon. He and she going dancing tonight, being warm and cozy together afterward, then making love again at last. Was any of it to be?

Perhaps. Yet whatever else he was doing on this day of homecoming, he'd better bear in mind that if he didn't want to be labeled some kind of weakling, something less than a man, he was going to have to get out as soon as possible and hustle for work. Work that he knew in advance he was going to hate.

They were gazing at each other as if, he thought, there were a strong high fence between them. His absence had been too long. She wasn't a carefree girl anymore. She had changed.

He realized all of a sudden one small thing that was physically different about her, something he was amazed he hadn't noticed at once. Under the rim of her hat, he could see her slim neck and the tips of her ears! Her hair, her beautiful long mass of pale yellow hair, had been shorn off.

"You've cut your hair!"

"Every woman has short hair now. It's the style," she said dully. She was looking down, her face hidden. Perhaps grasping for something to say to him, her husband, she asked, "What's that little thing strapped on your wrist? It looks like a time-piece."

He shrugged. "It is. It's a new invention called the wrist-watch. I guess every man in uniform over there has bought one." He added bitterly, "It's all we have to show for the waste of a year or more."

Chapter 43

"How are you, Mr. Perkins? Joanna told me you've been ill." Tony was thinking that he wouldn't have needed any telling. The change in Paul's appearance shocked him.

"I had a bad spell, yes. But I've had them before and I am better today. Enough of that, now. Let me look at you."

Paul, from his bed, was gazing with affection at the young man he hadn't in his heart believed would ever return. His thoughts ran along the same lines as Tony's but were more optimistic. *Too thin. Pale. He'll need building up, but between Joanna and my dear nemesis, Florence, it will be done.*

He said, "I imagine you feel a little strange, being back. Things aren't quite the way you imagined?"

"Not quite." Tony grinned. With anyone else he would have smoothly denied any disappointment, but he admired Joanna's uncle and had always felt comfortable with him. "I guess I'm more prickly than Joanna expected, too. You've heard, I suppose, that I have spells of unconsciousness now and then. very short, less than a minute usually, but I've been told never to fly again. Or drive a car, which isn't nearly such a blow, but still a nuisance."

"I've heard."

Any hint of sympathy and Tony would have cut off the conversation. He was seeking advice, not a shoulder to cry on. He went on, "Somehow, I've got to support my family, and

I'm not qualified for much. I really don't know how to do anything except fly. Have you any ideas?"

Paul shifted slightly under the blanket, and absently suppressed a grimace. Pain was a companion he'd known intimately and learned to live with long ago. His attention was entirely on Tony's problem.

"You have assets which should stand you in good stead. You are honest and reliable, and even though you lack training, you're quick. Any merchant would welcome you as an assistant, I'd think."

Tony said evenly, "It may come to that. But to tell you the truth, just the thought of being indoors all the time working behind a counter, remembering prices, figuring change—well, it isn't what I want to do with my life . . . what else?"

"Outdoors, there's manual labor. But I hardly think you are up to it."

"No."

"A postman?"

Tony smiled. "I couldn't do all that walking. Not just yet."

"Well, let's see. Other outside jobs . . ." Paul considered and quickly rejected as unsafe for a man with Tony's disability such diverse occupations as directing traffic, or working for the telephone company, which would entail climbing poles to string wire. "Well, I'm sure something will come to us if we think about it."

"Funny how things work out," Tony mused. "My friend Olaf—Joanna's showing him the park right now, but as soon as they come back, you'll meet him—Olaf was a farmer before, and didn't go beyond eighth grade, but he's much better prepared than I am because he's a kind of jack-of-all-trades, a carpenter, a painter, and he knows a lot about machinery. He's a wizard with aircraft engines."

"You could learn. You could work around an airfield."

Tony's smile became so strained that Paul was stricken with remorse. "No, thanks," Tony said. "Just watching other fellows go up, I'd eat my heart out." Immediately though, his face cleared and his eyes lit. A baby's cry had been heard in the next room.

"Oh, oh! Joanna told me to pick her up if she woke. Excuse me—"

He went running to the small nursery that had once been Clara's sewing room. Just for this chance, he had stayed home while the others went off walking. He'd had one brief look at the child and Joanna had wanted to wake her then, but his Antonia (not Bunch to him!) had been sleeping so angelically he wouldn't have disturbed her for the world. He'd waited, and now here was his opportunity to be alone with his daughter, get acquainted at last.

He opened the door to the pink and white room. The little girl, not yet a year old, had pulled herself up by the bars of the crib and was standing on tiptoe, holding on. As he entered, her crying stopped. She looked at him doubtfully, then a tentative smile began to tilt up the corners of her mouth.

"Ah, after the rain, the sun comes out, does it?" He approached slowly, continuing to talk in a low, soothing tone. "Hello, Antonia. You won't know me, darling, but I'm your dad. I've been away, a long long time away from you and your mother, and how I missed you! That was the really bad part, missing you . . . sweetheart, you're just as I imagined you'd be. When Joanna told me you weren't fair like her, I knew you'd have beautiful dark eyes and brown hair—just as I remember my mother having. Like me, too. You're a Bonnard all right! Now then, do you want to get out of your bed?"

She raised her arms to him eagerly, but in letting go of the rail she promptly lost her balance and tumbled backward. There was an angry wail.

"Hey, you're all right! Just hurt your dignity a bit. All right, come to your dad."

He picked her up, without any of the uncertainty he might have felt had she not needed comforting. With instinctive skill he quieted her, holding her close and patting her plump, solid little back. He felt a surge of love that astonished him by its simple strength.

This was his daughter. His! To care for. To work for.

His solemnity vanished and he began to laugh aloud because wetness had soaked through the front of his shirt. "I've got a lot to learn about babies," he said, and laughed all the harder when he saw he'd elicited an answering chuckle.

His dilemma of how to dry the child was short-lived. He heard steps plodding heavily up the stairs and turned to find Aunt Flossie in the doorway, her square face beaming. "Well, Tony, so you've come home!" she said.

He held the baby aside in order to kiss Aunt Flossie's cheek, and her experienced eye caught the damp spot on his shirt. She took Antonia from him, moved to a table on which a soft padding had been placed, and proceeded to change the child and dress her while Tony watched.

"Do fathers ever do that?"

"I've never known one who did." She sounded surprised. "But come to think about it, there's no reason why not. Especially with Joanna gone so much, you would be a help. I'm here every day, but—"

"Joanna will be at home, too, from now on," he said, sounding grim even to his own ears.

"Is that so? She's quitting her work? Now that I wouldn't have expected. She loves it so. *Ach*, no—don't tell me she was dismissed?"

"Nothing like that. Aunt Flossie, what kind of a man would let his wife go out to work?"

"A sensible one, I'd think," she snapped. Making a visible effort, she then said, "Forgive me, I should know better than to interfere between husband and wife.

"But Dell is downstairs. She's come by to welcome you, too. Shall we go down?"

"I'll take Antonia," he said, and did so. He swung her to his shoulder, and held so high, the little girl crowed with delight. He bounded off with her down the stairs.

Flossie listened to his agile steps. Those spells of his—did they come on suddenly? She was relieved to hear him reach the bottom, hear him greeted by his sister-in-law. Then she went to knock at Paul's door.

As she did every day now, she braced herself to find Paul worse, but this morning she was agreeably surprised. He was exceedingly frail, that could not be denied, but there was more animation in his voice and manner than she'd seen in some time.

"Mr. Perkins, I do believe your health is improved!"

Paul said agreeably, "Being needed for something may keep me around a while yet. Right now, we've got to be clever and suggest some kind of work for Tony if he's to keep his self-respect."

"Seems to me there's far too much worry about that young man's self-respect. Did he happen to tell you his masculine pride forbids Joanna being a newspaper reporter any longer?"

"No, but I'm not surprised. Nor should you be," he added with wily diplomacy, "understanding men as you do."

He had coaxed a brief smile, but she said, "Your flattery

is all very well, but tell me this—what will his family live on
meanwhile?"

He meditated. "Doesn't Adeline need more help with her
park rides?"

"Adeline needs another workhorse. Someone strong. Besides, fond as I am of the *liebchen*, I've noticed that she pays
out as little money as she possibly can."

"In fact, you could say she's become a skinflint."

"And why not?" Flossie at once rose to Dell's defense.
"Making money is her new passion, and far better for her it is
too, than mooning over that good-for-nothing Ralph Wilson!"

"I agree," Paul said quickly. He was well aware that Flossie
had been having grave doubts lately about her advice to Adeline. The girl's singlemindedness of purpose was leaving little
room for any other thought or emotion. "A good solid bank
account is safer. Well, let's both think. Perhaps in the next day
or so we can come up with some other suggestion for Tony."

"Yes. Will you be all right? I must go down now. There's
work to be done with so many for dinner. Did you know Clara
and Lillian are coming, too? I'll send Clara up to visit with
you."

"Thank you. It's a nuisance, my being bed-ridden—"

"You would never be a nuisance," she said firmly. "And
it's not for long. I intend to have you up and about before you
know it."

"My dear Miss Mendenhall! No, it's not for long."

Fortunately his meaning escaped her. She tucked the covers
more neatly around his feet, plumped up the pillow, and departed. He lay staring thoughtfully at the doorway, long after
she'd gone through.

Clara and Lillian were the last to arrive at the old house.
They found Tony, Joanna, and the baby in the parlor with Dell,
as well as a large young man who had probably never been
handsome—his face was too broad and his nose was crooked
as though it had long ago been broken, and knit together badly.
As Clara approached, he leaped to his feet with a kind of
desperation. She gathered at once that he was ill at ease with
so many strangers, and that the shiny crimson scars across the
right side of his face further increased his discomfiture.

Lillian, after a glance, had hesitated. But Clara went to him
and said, "I'm Joanna's mother. Tony wrote us what a good

friend you'd become. You couldn't be more welcome in our family!"

"I thank you, missus. Seems to me, though, I ought to find someplace else to stay. There are so many in this house already." His voice was deep and strong, and Clara warmed to him for his diffidence.

"Only Uncle Paul, Joanna, and Tony now. And the baby, of course. There's a large room over the old stable that hasn't been used much since autos came in. It's a bit more private, and I think you'll be comfortable."

"More comfortable than I'm used to, for sure. But I want to say, just as soon as I find work I'll be paying my share."

"And that will be a help. I'm sure you and Tony will—"

She was interrupted by Dell, who had come up to them and been listening. Dell said. "Mr. Mickelson, Tony tells us you lived in Minnesota. Just what did you do there?"

"I was a farmer."

"Oh." She sounded disappointed. "I don't suppose you know anything about machinery?"

"I do. A little. Yes, miss."

"A little! He's got a real knack for it." Tony was momentarily distracted from the baby. She was using his swinging leg as a rocking horse, and squealing with delight. "Anyone who hires Olaf will be lucky."

"Really?" Dell said. "Well, I have a problem. The roller coaster started so slowly today I was afraid to keep it running. I don't imagine the trouble amounts to much, but if you could take a minute or two—"

Joanna said, "Dell, if I remember rightly, the last time this happened, even Ralph couldn't fix it. You had to call in someone from the company and it cost you quite a lot of money."

Tony grinned at Clara. There wasn't much doubt about Joanna's meaning. If Olaf fixed the roller coaster, he should be paid. Joanna would make certain he was.

"Oh, I hardly think this is the same, but of course we'll keep track of the time it takes." Dell gave her sister a sour look. "As I say, Mr. Mickelson, if you would just take a look at it—and before tomorrow morning so I don't lose any more business?"

"I'll be glad to try, miss," he said stolidly.

"Good." Dell had been giving his muscular arms and thick chest a businesslike appraisal. "Afterward, if you manage to fix the ride, we can talk about some other work that needs doing. I'm short-handed and can use a hired man." Another glance at Joanna, and she added grudgingly, "At the going rate."

Tony said lightly, "That was easy, Olaf. You're all set. I wish somebody needed a skill of mine."

Paul had fallen into a light doze as he so often did these days, and he woke to find Clara bending over him. When he opened his eyes, she bent and kissed his cheek.

"Clara, my child, how glad I am to see you!"

"I'm not a child, except to you, Uncle Paul." She laughed a little, the soft laugh he'd always loved and had heard little since Sam died.

"Tell me, how is Lillian?" he asked.

"A worry to me, as always. But I think this new studio she's with is a good one, good for her, I mean. Mr. Selig and Mrs. Gierek seem far more particular than most of them about their company's good name. Sometimes I've thought that Lillian—"

"Now Clara, she's a good girl."

"Yes, but too ambitious. It's a wild kind of business she's in. Oh, it is, Uncle Paul. I know. Sam was right. There are too many stories about drugs and the dissolute goings-on at Vernon Country Club and that notorious place in Santa Monica, the glittery, unsavory one the film people frequent—the Sunset Club. Nothing that happens is a secret anymore, and I can tell you this: While Los Angeles society doesn't mind being amused and entertained by motion pictures, the actors themselves are far from welcome at respectable gatherings. They've gotten too bad a reputation." She paused, then said, "It's all such a shame. The art of film making is so very exciting. And has such promise!"

"Clara, those costume designs of yours—aren't you tempted, even a little, to work at a studio yourself?"

"No, Uncle Paul. Sam would never permit it." Her face had closed.

He wanted to retort, "Sam is no longer here! It is you who have your life to live, and in your own way." But as always, since Sam's death, her remote implacability on the subject kept him silent.

So instead, he aired a personal matter of his own, and

startled her so much that Sam was again forgotten.

"Clara, I've been lying here thinking about an idea I've had for some time, and now I need to ask your help." He hesitated.

"Yes, of course! What is it?"

"I've grown very fond of Miss Mendenhall, who has been so kind to me, and I want to give her a gift—something that will please her. Nothing material comes to mind, because obviously she has far more worldly goods than I. Some little keepsake after I'm gone, perhaps, but that wouldn't really—"

"Uncle Paul, please don't talk about—being gone!"

"Are you, too, Clara, unable to face the truth? Never mind, let's not digress. I've learned, during the course of our friendship, Miss Mendenhall's and mine, that it is a deep grief to her that she was never married. Absurd as this may sound, I'm certain she feels that spinsterhood is a reflection on her as a woman.

"So, I intend to offer her my name as a parting gift. I will ask her to marry me, and I think she will accept. She's fond of me, and after all"—he gave a small wry laugh—"this husband will expect nothing more of her than she's been giving him already—loving care. Perhaps too much of it. What is important, she will no longer be a miss, but have the title she covets.

"Now, what I want to know is—will you help? Assuming she accepts, that is. Make the arrangements with a minister, and invite the family to a proper little supper party, following the ceremony here at the house? I want her to feel that my family welcomes her—"

"Oh, we do, we do! What a truly lovely plan, Uncle Paul!"

He had been tense, frowning, because in spite of his tone of assurance, he'd been fearful of what even Clara might say. His illness. Their age. And, viewed in almost any light, the absurdity of such a marriage.

He smiled with pleasure at her enthusiasm, and lay back, well content.

Chapter 44

"Joanna, I love you! I've missed you . . . so much. . . ."

The evening had ended at last. Then Tony and Joanna had gone for a long walk together in the balmy August night, encountering no one on the deserted sidewalk, and he'd tried to tell her, as she wanted, a bit of what the war had been like for him. He hadn't succeeded very well in the telling. He still couldn't talk about Johnny Hart dying, or anything about that last fatal mission. But he'd tried to describe how it felt to take off in the very early, cold gray dawn, and though he never mentioned it, she must have guessed at the fear, the terrible fear that toward the end made climbing into his cockpit one of the hardest things he'd ever forced himself to do. Still he'd gone out there, walking jauntily, waving to the ground crew. All of them had. He'd never forget Johnny Hart's cocky grin.

But now the talking was over. They were in bed in their old room. From his pillow, he could look out the window and see in the moonlight the roof of St. Joseph's Church where they'd been married—on its peak a cross, clear in the night sky. Funny, in all the times he'd imagined being back here with her, he'd actually forgotten this familiar sight.

He hadn't forgotten though, how, after he caressed her and kissed her and held her smooth satiny warm body close against him, she'd come alive, wanting him, and how her wanting him so much increased his own desire a thousandfold. Yes, she still gave that satisfied little laugh, too, when their passion had finally, finally ebbed.

He left her and turned on the light, just as he used to do and had dreamed of doing. "You are so beautiful," he said. "Please. Stay as you are. Just let me look. It's been so long, so very long. . . ."

What devil in her made her answer as she did? she wondered afterward. Breaking his mood. Spoiling everything.

She'd assured herself hours ago that she understood clearly why he'd said what he had at the train station. It was only because Bunch was so young. He thought Bunch needed her mother all of the time. Probably, too, he'd pictured his wife at home, waiting, looking exactly as she had when he left, being there to welcome him. When he came to realize how much working for the newspaper meant to her, he'd change his mind.

So she'd carefully put aside the shock of his unreasonable demand, deciding not to worry or borrow trouble. And as the festive evening progressed, with all the family making so much of Tony, she did forget. She found she was proud of him, fiercely so. He was undeniably handsome, and she was surprised to notice how much older and more mature he seemed. The boyish bravado, evidenced by the rakish pilot's cap he'd worn in the old snapshot, was now a debonair courtesy. His eyes were darker than she remembered, and whenever they met and held hers, she felt something flower and grow and press inside of her.

She'd wished then the guests would go home, so that Tony and she could make love. Shameless of her perhaps, but she'd welcomed that surge of desire. She was a married woman, after all. She didn't want to—should not—dream of any man but Tony.

And later, the climax of love, when it came, had been all any woman could ask. Why then did she answer as she did?

"Tony, is my body all of me you care about? Is this physical act all you wanted to come home for?"

She watched his face tighten, become wary.

He said, "Joanna, I've loved you all my life. Since I was a boy, too young to imagine sleeping with you. What on earth are you asking?"

Too late to stop.

"I only wondered, because I haven't noticed that you admire anything else about me now. You don't like my clothes, or my hairstyle, or—my job."

"So that's it."

"Yes."

He walked to the wardrobe and shrugged into one of his old robes. At the same time, she surreptitiously pulled up the bed sheet to cover herself. Neither of them now felt comfortable being nude.

"Then I'll explain again. I'm old-fashioned, I guess. I feel your working or not working is my decision to make. You did promise to love, honor, and obey, and—it's the normal way of things. My mother, your mother, every woman for thousands of years—"

"Oh, stop it! Good gracious—*obey*? It's only a word, Tony. Slavery's been abolished."

In the harsh light of the globe overhead, she could see a muscle jump, high in his cheek. But he held his anger in check. He said in an even voice, "Let me ask you something. If your father ever forbade your mother to work at that ice cream stand, because for good reasons of his own he didn't want her to, would she have defied him?"

"No." Which was undeniably true. Mama would not have argued as Joanna was doing, ending what had been sweet and good between her and Papa only moments before. "But she might have been very unhappy." Also the truth, now that Joanna thought about it. Her mother, always submissive and leading such a circumscribed life, must have badly wanted at times to rebel. "I think, though—I'm quite sure—that if Papa ever guessed she was unhappy—"

"So you're unhappy, are you? That's a fine thing to say to man on the very day he comes back. 'I'm miserable now that you're here, interfering in my nice, orderly life—'"

"Oh, Tony, stop! Don't twist my words. You know I'm glad you're safely home! So very glad!" But he had thrown off his robe, and with lithe quickness pulled on trousers, shirt, and shoes. He was striding toward the door as she asked in alarm, "Where are you going?"

"Out! I'll walk a bit alone, think about everything. Maybe I'll even understand your . . . oh . . ."

His voice trailing away, he crumpled to the floor. She was beside him instantly, crying urgently, though she knew he couldn't hear, "Tony, Tony, please speak to me!"

She'd been warned. The doctor in the faraway hospital had written to her, describing what might happen and urging her not to be frightened when it did. So she realized immediately that this was one of Tony's blackouts. In a minute or two he'd return to consciousness.

She knew, too, that even with her willfulness she couldn't have been the cause, but kneeling beside him, she was filled with remorse.

Chapter 45

Joanna eased the baby carriage down the porch steps, Bunch sitting at one end of it with such an air of regal disapproval that Joanna was reminded of pictures she'd seen of Queen Victoria. The child had to be wheedled into accepting this mode of transportation which, now that she could toddle on her own two feet, she considered an affront. But if she were to tire walking the five blocks to Chutes Park, she would be a heavy load to carry.

This September day, with the perversity of southern California weather, was balmy and cool, and Joanna's spirits rose. At moments like this, it would be easy to convince herself that it was a privilege to be able to enjoy Bunch's company in this leisurely way, not be saddled instead with the responsibility for her support.

Oh, it wasn't the responsibility she had been missing though! It was the work itself. She had so enjoyed being a reporter, taking any assignment given, then writing a good, solid article, knowing that it was solid and good!

Still, the idea she'd had just the other day could easily provide similar satisfaction. She'd always thought she would write a novel, so now she'd begin. It was disconcerting to discover that spinning a story out of one's head was different from writing about facts. So far the sheet of paper on her desk was still blank, but she'd think about the plot as she walked, try harder to assemble her ideas.

Tony, she supposed, would consider such unpaid labor a waste of time. Therefore it was reassuring to know, still keeping her own secret, that her paycheck from the newspaper really wasn't needed. Tony worked long and hard. He had followed Uncle Paul's recent suggestion and become a conductor on the Big Red Cars, as the Pacific Electric's interurbans were affectionately dubbed. There was no danger of anyone being hurt should he have one of his brief blackouts, as his job was simply to walk through and collect fares. The mild exercise seemed to be beneficial, and he enjoyed passing the time of day with an everchanging assortment of people.

He missed flying, of course. Nothing could take its place. But he seemed reasonably content, and had even told her he was. Uncle Paul, when she reported those words, would be pleased.

Pushing the carriage, she entered the park and soon spotted Adeline, herding customers into a roller coaster car. There was only a short queue waiting, but Joanna knew better than to interrupt her sister. Dell as usual was working steadily and efficiently, and only glanced up when the gondola was filled and on its way. Then she shouted over to Olaf, who was painting one of the cars that was out of service, "Don't dally with that now! I only hired an extra man for a day or two so you could be finished quicker."

"Yes, Miss Adeline," Olaf said. He continued his careful, skillful enameling, apparently unperturbed. But Joanna, embarrassed by her sister's bossiness, lifted Bunch out of the buggy, set her on the grass, and holding her by the hand made the slow walk to Olaf's side.

"Hello, Mr. Mickelson," she said. "Nice day, isn't it?"

He looked up, nodded to her, and said to Bunch, "Out to see the park, young lady?"

Bunch replied at some length in her own language.

"Tony tells me you like working here," Joanna said.

"I do. Don't reckon I'd be content, less I had a lot of work to keep me busy. Besides"—he gave her his distorted smile—"anything's better than war."

On impulse, Joanna exclaimed, "The time Tony spent over there is a part of his life I'll never be able to share, or understand! When he did those wild, reckless things, rushing up in the air to fight, even when the odds were all against him—"

"He was—is—a very brave man," Olaf answered. He frowned at his brush, edging the paint on in a fine, straight line.

He'd emphasized the word *brave* as if, she thought, to rebuke her for saying *reckless*, and she flushed. But she said in a low voice, "Please, tell me more. I want terribly to know! You see, from his letters, he seemed almost like, well, like a boy showing off, not really aware of the danger—"

"Guess it was that way at first. With a lot of the pilots. But when all your friends are dying, you soon come to realize it can happen to you and most likely will, the next time you go up or any of the times after that. You're scared, and scared bad, but you don't talk about it, you go on up anyway. That's bravery."

From his tone, she realized he had something else he wanted to say. She let him take his time.

"You see," he finally went on, "Tony's scared now. Maybe I shouldn't say this to you, he wouldn't like me doing it, but I couldn't help hearing that day at the station. He's trying his best, but he's scared of falling down at work, maybe losing his job, even losing you, because you might not think he's as much of a man as he was. It's not easy coming home, missus. Leave him be and let him heal up...excuse me for talking like this."

"Yes. All right—" Trying to cover her embarrassment, she abruptly changed the subject. "Bunch and I were on our way to visit my uncle and his wife, and I hoped I could say hello to Dell. But I see that as usual, she's busy."

Olaf shook his head. "Not as busy as she'd like. Business has dropped some the last few weeks. Too many other parks, I guess.... Missus—" The brushing stopped and his scarred face, turned to her, was troubled. "Don't know whether I ought to bother you about this, but something's happened, maybe you ought to know—if you're going to be talking to Mr. Perkins. Yesterday, when I was running the ferris wheel, a man come up to me and he seemed kinda crazy. Not crazy in the head exactly, but boiling mad. He shouted at me, 'Does that German woman still own this thing?' Before I thought, I said, 'Yes, sir, she does,' and I been wondering—was I wrong to tell him?"

"Did he ask you anything else?"

Olaf hesitated. He looked away. "Just...he said to me, 'You should be ashamed, doing for somebody like her. Why aren't you in the service anyway?' I didn't want to answer but I did, because I didn't want no trouble. I said, 'I just got back.' He stared at my face then and he must have seen I was telling the truth, because he said something like 'Well, my two boys was at Chateau Thierry, and if they was here, I wouldn't let 'em do what you're doing...but they ain't here—and never will be again! They was killed, both of them!'"

"Then I think he was starting to cry, because he rushed off. I was sorry for him. But I was sorry, too, I'd let him know about Mrs. Perkins and the ferris wheel."

"He'd have found out," Joanna answered. "He could have asked any number of people around the park. But I may suggest to Aunt Flossie that she stay away for a while—just in case he comes again."

As it turned out, however, she said nothing of the matter either to Aunt Flossie or to Uncle Paul. Her uncle had had a bad night and only an hour before had fallen asleep at last. His new wife was desperately worried.

"I was so sure I could help him, Joanna! But nothing does any good. He's getting thinner every day, and weaker. And the pain—the pain! He is such a good kind man. How can the Lord do this to him?"

Joanna crossed the room to the older woman and put her arms around her. She said, "Perhaps his health can't be mended, Aunt Flossie. But these few weeks, since you two were married—I've never seen him look so pleased, so content."

"Do you mean that? It would be a consolation to think so."

"I do indeed."

"He did seem to enjoy the wedding, didn't he? And I don't believe it was too tiring, even though he insisted on being on his feet for those few minutes—"

"The way he was beaming, he was enjoying himself. You and he made such a fine picture, too, standing before our fireplace, you in the beautiful white dress Mama made."

"Clara *would* make it for me, and she so busy with her costume pictures. There was no arguing with her. And then Adeline, too, insisting she'd close the concessions in order to stand up for me! Olaf and the other hired man were able to manage without her, but for Adeline that was a mighty generous thought. The *liebchen* has always been good to me. . . .

"Joanna, do you know what your uncle said, after the ceremony? He said, 'We may not have the long years together that other couples have, but we will be happier than most. That I promise you, Mrs. Perkins.'"

Flossie straightened, put away her handkerchief. "I try to be a good companion to him, the way I was to Papa. We play checkers every evening, and when he feels like reading, I tiptoe around like a little mouse."

Joanna carefully did not smile at the picture of the large, heavy-footed Flossie tiptoeing like a mouse. She gave Flossie's stout shoulder a final pat, then they no longer spoke of the invalid of whom they were both so fond but cheered themselves by playing with Bunch, building her a tower with wooden blocks and trying to teach her to talk. And having gotten Aunt Flossie to laugh again, Joanna hadn't the heart to sadden her with the story of the angry, grief-stricken man.

On the way home, she stopped by the carousel and bought tickets for herself and Bunch. Adeline accepted her money without protest, but Joanna, enjoying the child's delight, found she wouldn't have counted the cost if it were twice as much. Bunch, quiet with wonderment, sat beside her in the swan car, just as Joanna, when very little, had often sat beside Clara, one chubby hand resting featherlight on her mother's arm and her eyes wide and bright. When the ride was over, the little girl, still bemused, let herself be bundled into the baby carriage without protest.

Again, Adeline was very busy, so Joanna started home, the simple pleasure of the ride with Bunch fading as she walked.

The distraught father, mourning his two sons, returned to mind, frightening her. The horrible realities of war came so close, when people one knew were killed. Vernon Castle, who'd been so pleasant to her, danced so beautifully. Suppose it had been Tony who crashed instead of his friend, John Hart. But Tony was home, safe. Now if only Charles were!

It was a coincidence that she was thinking about Charles Gold at the moment she pushed the buggy around the corner into Los Angeles Street. Because, looking ahead, she spotted a man's familiar wiry figure on her porch. Edwin McGowan. She hastened her pace, and then seeing him begin to descend the steps, heading away, she called, "Mr. McGowan—wait!"

He heard, turned, and walked back to meet her.

"I almost missed you!" Joanna said, and asked anxiously, "Is there . . . news?"

"Good news," he answered quickly with a smile of reassurance. "The Hindenburg Line has been broken. I was on my way home and thought you might like to know before tomorrow's newspaper comes out. Charles is predicting that the war may even be over by the end of the year, so I've been thinking about what banner headline we'll use. Just the one word: *Peace*, I believe. But that's still in the future."

"Then there's been another dispatch from Charles?"

"Yes. This afternoon."

"Oh, what a relief! That the war is almost over, I mean."

How considerate Mr. McGowan was, to come out of his way to tell her! The events of the last year had greatly changed this aloof and cynical man. Finding the names of two of his reporters on the casualty lists had, according to other members of his staff, grieved him deeply. He was, they said, almost patient these days! As for his kindness to herself, he appeared to understand fully, even though she was a woman, what a wrench it had been for her to leave the newspaper.

She could not know that Charles Gold had long ago written to him, "I'm doing my best for you over here, Ed. So you do something for me in return. Keep an eye on young Joanna. She's quite a girl."

Joanna's marriage had not, in McGowan's view, altered this obligation. Nor did he wish it to. The fact was, from the beginning Joanna had reminded him strongly of his only daughter Martha, who was now married and living far away in New York. Being a widower and missing his Martha as much as he did, there was consolation in these brief visits with Joanna.

He said what he had really come to say. "Mrs. Bonnard, it's just as well you are staying away from the office for a while. The Spanish flu has reached Chicago."

She gazed at him blankly, her mind elsewhere. "The Spanish flu?"

He tried to speak lightly. "The *grippe*, if you prefer. Or, if you are English, the *Flanders grippe*, or German—the *Blitz Katarrh*. It's the *Wrestler's Fever* in Japan. The press hasn't been playing up the danger—we don't want panic—but surely you've heard that this ailment is sweeping around the world?"

"I know there's been an epidemic in the eastern states—"

"Not only the eastern states," he interrupted. "It's hit the Midwest now—as well as all of Europe and Asia before that. I'm sure we'll find when the toll is counted up that the armies in the trenches, both sides, have been losing more men to this plague than to the enemy. The only saving grace is that after a few weeks it moves on. *Epidemic* is the wrong word...." In his anxiety, he reverted to his former dry manner of speaking. "As a newspaperwoman, you should try to be more accurate. *Pandemic* means *of all the people*, and we here in California are naturally included."

"I see," Joanna said politely. Bunch, tired of this lengthy period of inactivity, had set up a howl, and Joanna had picked her up and stood trying to soothe her.

"It's best to stay out of crowds," Mr. McGowan said.

"Yes, of course," she agreed, but he could tell that inside she was growing impatient with him for being so fearful. A disease still as far away as Chicago! Besides, influenza might be a danger to the infirm, but someone as healthy as she, surely, had no reason to worry!

He was not surprised when she said abruptly, "Excuse me, Mr. McGowan, but I'd like to ask you a question. I'm trying to—have you ever written a novel?"

"No. That is, I did write one once but it was no good."

"I thought it would be so easy! Goodness, we live in such eventful times, so many things have happened lately, I thought a book would just write itself. But the story doesn't seem to work out."

"Don't rush it," he advised. "Fiction is different. Stories come from people, not events. And I've heard from other writers that their plots seem to creep up on them from the side and are elusive when they're sought head on. I think it's probably better to be very busy with other work and have to make time for your pen than to sit down with the whole day before you. Better for a beginner, anyway."

"Yes, well, thank you." For once he'd been no help at all.

Chapter 46

"Florence, my dear. Please. Don't cry."

Paul gazed at his wife, feeling as helpless as he ever had in his life. He cursed the infirmity which kept him chained to his bed when he longed to pat her shoulder and offer comfort. She sat over by the window, the one that offered the view of the park, but her face was covered by her hands, those large capable hands. Her back was bent, and her body shook.

"My dear, is it such a tragedy? You will buy another ferris wheel—"

He stopped because she had raised her head and turned to look at him. Her face was bloated and stained red from tears, but he didn't notice and wouldn't have cared if he had. She was becoming dearer to him every day that passed.

"It isn't the wheel," she said. "*Ach, Gott!* I would not weep for a thing made of wood and metal. It's the being hated. Hated so much! Paul—I am an American, I always have been since I was fifteen, so long ago, but this is no longer my country, is it?"

"Yes, it's your country! And he didn't hate *you*, he was simply deranged. They've caught him, you know. He made no effort to get away, but kept coming back, watching the fire, and watching the police question everyone. He was very agitated, Dell said. He seemed to want to be caught."

"But, if he didn't hate me, then why—"

"He hates Germans, and he thought you were one. He's not the first, is he, who has made that mistake?"

"No."

"My dear, it's over, and I'm sure nothing of that sort will ever happen again. The war is going well for the Allies, or so the newspapers tell us, and we can dare to hope that our young men will be coming home soon. People will be busy then, rebuilding their lives, and memories will fade. They always do.

"Besides, there were only a noisy few who imagined you were sympathetic with the enemy. Today, so Dell told me, when the man was arrested, several of those standing about expressed sympathy for you."

"Did they? Really?"

"One, a woman who evidently did not know you had married and therefore could not have been a personal friend, spoke up and said, 'Miss Mendenhall has been here in this park for many years. Why, I took my children on her ferris wheel when they were tiny tots. To blame her for what is going on in Europe is an outrage!'"

"What did the man say to that?" Flossie asked. "I suppose something like 'Nonsense, madam. She has a German accent and therefore must be a spy!'"

Paul was pleased to hear the note of sarcasm. His wife was recovering. "No, once they had him in custody, he seemed to lose interest in everything. Florence, let's forget him and look to the future. Let's talk about buying a new ferris wheel."

"No, I won't be buying one. That time of my life is finished. To tell you the truth, Paul, the park lately has been only a worry, and I don't seem to care much about it anymore. I'd even been toying with the idea of giving the wheel to Adeline—I owe her so much!"

At last Flossie came across the room and with a quick anxious glance at him seated herself in the chair beside the bed. "Will it be all right, if I never go back to the park? I want to be lazy for a while. Just be a housewife."

Translated, he knew this meant, "I'm needed right here to take care of you, because I must admit it now to myself, you aren't getting better." He didn't answer except to say lightly, "Housewives are far from lazy, if you are any example."

"You won't mind?" she insisted. "I know you get tired of my fussing."

He reached over and took her hand. "I won't mind. On the contrary, I shall like having my wife within call. But Florence, if you're giving up the ferris wheel, I do have a suggestion you might bear in mind. I seem to be developing a bit of a flair for fitting people to the right kind of work. Look at Tony. Wouldn't you say he's enjoying what I thought of for him to do?"

"Indeed I would! You were so clever. Being a conductor on a streetcar is healthful for him, too. Just enough walking."

"Strictly speaking, it's not a streetcar. The so-called Red Cars are trains, operating on regular railroad tracks, the only difference being that they're powered by electricity. But yes, your point is well taken. He does no driving, which would be dangerous, but merely walks the length of the train, collecting fares and giving information."

He smiled. "Joanna has told me how handsome he looks in his uniform. His slenderness, and the hint of pallor, give him an air of mystery that must attract some admiring glances and bolster his self-esteem. Best of all, the pay is good.

"Dear me, what was it I started out to say? Oh, yes, I've also thought of an occupation for you, should you want one, because I guessed some time ago that your interest in the ferris wheel has waned."

"What occupation? This is purely conversation, of course. I just told you I intend to stay home."

"Of course. But I thought, some day—if you should need to or want to—a tea room would be just the thing to keep you busy. You are such a marvelous pastry cook that people would flock to you. Well, it's an idea."

"And a very good one," she said warmly. "I think I would like that very much. If I ever . . . tire of staying home. Paul, you are a wonderful man."

"Thank you, my dear."

It was a fleeting moment, because they heard a knock at the door downstairs, and then Adeline's voice. Still, Paul's suggestion, and his kindness in proffering it, were never forgotten by Flossie.

Dell appeared in the doorway. "Would you mind very much if the officers come up? They want to talk to you, Aunt Flossie, and I thought Uncle Paul should hear what they have to say."

"By all means," Paul said genially. "Bring them up."

Shortly afterward, two policemen were standing at the foot of his bed, the taller one young and awkwardly silent, the other a short, grizzled man, cheerfully officious and at once recognized by Flossie.

"Good morning, Sergeant Grimes. How is your daughter feeling?"

"Much better, thank you, ma'am. . . . Mr. Perkins, you'll have no objections, I hope, to your wife signing a complaint? It's needed if we're to make a good case against the suspect. Which I'm very keen to do. I walked this beat for a great many years and I'm well acquainted with Miss Mendenhall—pardon me, Mrs. Perkins. What was done was a shame! I want to see this crazy man behind bars."

Paul said, "I have no objection to my wife signing whatever she wishes. But it must be her wish. What do you say, Florence?"

"Well, I certainly don't think anyone should be allowed to burn my property and walk away free, just because I was born in Berlin," she answered, her distress reviving.

"Nor do any of us," Paul said. "But the sergeant is asking whether you want to make a formal complaint."

"He should be made to pay for my ferris wheel, at least."

"I certainly agree!" Dell, who had been listening from the hall, leaned into the room to ask, "Sergeant Grimes, can't he be made to pay?"

"As to that, we'll have to wait and see what the judge says. Now then, Mrs. Perkins." He rearranged his sheaf of papers and presented her with the top one. "If you'll just sign this. Right on that line—"

"Missus, wait, please!" It was Olaf Mickelson, appearing behind Dell.

She looked over her shoulder at him in annoyed surprise. "I thought I told you to stay and take care of the customers."

"I left a boy in charge."

"What boy? Here, I can't have this. I'll be robbed blind!"

Olaf said to Flossie, "Missus, I did think you ought to know just why your wheel was burned. You see, the man talked to me, couple days ago. He didn't say nothing about it today, but his two sons, they was killed at Chateau Thierry. I guess he just had to hurt somebody, anybody, because he felt so bad himself. That's all I wanted to tell you. I'll be getting back to work now, Miss Adeline."

"About time, too," she answered, but the words were spoken out of habit. She was frowning thoughtfully at the carpet.

"Thank you, Olaf," Paul said, when no one else spoke.

Olaf nodded to him and went back down the stairs.

"Two of them," breathed the tall young policeman. "Both his boys. That's hard."

"Sorrow don't excuse what he did," Grimes said crisply. "Have you signed yet, Mrs. Perkins?"

"No. No, I haven't, sergeant, and I don't guess I will. I have German blood, it's the truth, and I do feel . . . nothing's going to ease that poor man's pain, but if it helps to have—"

"Aunt Flossie," Dell's moment of vacillation had passed. "You're forgetting. The ferris wheel was worth a lot of money and you should be paid back. That's only fair, so you have to sign."

"No, *Liebchen*. I really don't have to sign. Not if it means sending him to jail, a man who has trouble enough already. Let him go home, to whatever family he has left."

"Mrs. Perkins!" protested Sergeant Grimes. "He committed a crime. He destroyed your property."

"Did he? Who knows what really happened? Who saw it happen? Maybe the wheel caught fire of itself."

"But he confessed—before witnesses!"

"Pshaw! People say strange things when they're had too much grief to bear." She turned to Paul. "Am I doing the right thing?"

He smiled at her. "You're a fine woman, Mrs. Perkins. Exactly the right thing, I would say."

Chapter 47

Mr. Bishop called regularly every Monday at the bungalow court, and Clara, while steadfastly refusing to go near the Selig lot, had gradually fallen into the pleasant habit of providing him with costume ideas for whatever film the studio had in prospect.

He would accept a cup of coffee, and give her the gist of the latest story conference, then on the next visit pick up the sketches of her designs. He would also, from time to time, bring a discreet brown pay envelope, in which, after he'd left, she would find what seemed to her an exorbitant amount of money.

She justified keeping this money, even though it came from the disreputable motion picture industry, by telling herself that as she had never entered the gate of Selig Company, she was not really an employee. She was merely an artist whose work, happily, was being sold, and artists didn't demand credentials from their customers. Fortunately this distinction was clear to her, because the extra cash was very welcome. Joanna and Bunch were dependent now on Tony's modest earnings, and Clara was prudently determined to keep a reserve for them in her bank account, should it ever be needed. Tony, in a despondent mood, might decide that being a conductor on the Red Cars was not what he wanted to do with his life.

There was also Lillian to be considered, and this second daughter was far more of a worry. Lillian was apparently doing well at Selig. But the role of *Lilith*, still, although months had gone by, promised to some actress in Chicago, remained an obsession with her.

No matter what their conversation, she always reverted at last to her grievance. "Lilith, Lillian, Lily—it's the same name, Mama! Don't they see I was meant to be her? If I can't have that part, it will be an omen—my career will be over."

Clara, exasperated, would snap, "That's absurd," and try to tell her daughter the reasons why. In no way did Lillian even look like Lilith. She was too blond. Too young. A different personality altogether. She was being given roles that suited her, and her career depended on doing well in those. But Lillian refused to listen, and recently, having become aware of Andrew Bishop's visits, she'd begun pressing for Clara's aid.

"I'm only asking you to talk to him, Mama. You and he are friends—"

"Mr. Bishop's calls here are strictly business," Clara said, but Lillian ignored the interruption.

"He's a very important man at Selig, though it took me a while to understand why. I thought at first it was just because there's some old family tie with Mrs. Gierek, who is one of the partners and very important herself. But that isn't so. When he says something, they all listen—quite an achievement when you're dealing with motion picture people!

"I don't mean to say, though, that some others don't trade on their names, and maybe he ought to realize he's been used. This actress they're bringing out from Chicago to play Lilith— her name is Rose Bishop. Did you know she's his half-sister?"

"No," Clara said wearily. "But I can't see that it matters in the least."

"Can't you? That's the reason she was able to get the part instead of me. Because of nepotism."

"Because of what?"

"*Nepotism.* I was telling the Count what was going on, and he said that's what it's called."

"Who is the Count?" Clara asked.

"Oh, just a man.... somebody who's well-known in Hollywood.

"Well, let me tell you something, Lillian Fritsch. Even I have heard of Rose Bishop. She's a famous actress, one of the best. Hasn't it occurred to you that you've got the cart before the horse? Do you think she asked for the part of Lilith? Mr. Bishop told me that the studio had a lot of trouble getting her to take it. He had to call and persuade her himself."

"Oh." Lillian looked slightly abashed. But she rallied quickly as she always did. "Still, it never hurts to have a friend in high places. If you asked him, he'd make sure I get the part when she makes a hash of it."

"You're certain she will, as you put it so nicely, make a hash of it?"

"Mama, you should see some of the would-be movie stars welcomed every day to Hollywood. New York socialites, popular novelists, Lord This and Lady That—oh yes, European titles especially are fawned over, the fake ones as well as the real. No one ever remembers that U-boats have been sinking ships right and left, making it very sporting to get to America just now. After all, there is a war on . . . what did you say, Mama?"

"It wasn't important. Do go on."

"I forget what studio hired her. Not ours, because I have to admit Barbara isn't as gullible as most, but the latest bit of royalty to show up was Princess Beatriz de Ortega y Braganza, from Alhambra, Spain. Isn't that a mouthful? As everyone expected, on the set she was perfectly awful. And the funniest part was, she wasn't Spanish or a princess. She turned out to be a typist from San Francisco."

"I really don't see what point you're making," Clara protested.

"The point, Mama, is that very few of the outsiders they try to make pictures with are worth a cent."

"Are we talking about an imposter passing herself off as a Spanish princess, or about a stage actress with a fine reputation?"

"Either, Mama. They're both the same. Get them before a camera and they're hams."

Clara could only hope that the pictures Lillian was playing in weren't suffering from her daughter's constant brooding over the part of Lilith. If they were, she would be out of work shortly, and then Clara's earnings might be important indeed.

Monday morning therefore, as soon as Lillian had rushed away, found Clara straightening the house and with pleasurable anticipation getting ready for her visitor.

She set the latest sketches on the table. They were always placed in the same spot, and Andrew Bishop no longer needed to ask for them, which in an obscure way salved her conscience still further. It was as though his consideration of her work was beyond her volition. He would go immediately to the accustomed place and pick them up. Eagerly, too. There hadn't been one yet that he hadn't liked.

Today she stood for a moment studying what she had done. These were a set of gowns designed for the feminine lead opposite an obscure young actor named Rudolph Valentino, whom Barbara Gierek had arranged to borrow from some small company. Clara had liked one of the simpler dresses so much that she'd cut a pattern and sewed a duplicate for herself. Skirts were shorter now, the hem rising to midcalf, and she hadn't had the courage yet to wear what she'd made. Sam, she was certain, would disapprove of such a daring length.

Now it occurred to her that Mr. Bishop might find it advantageous to view an actual model rather than just a two-dimensional sketch, and not giving her doubts time to surface, she hurried to her bedroom and dressed in the new gown. She resisted the vain temptation to study the result in the long mirror in Lillian's room, but she knew that the low neckline, the softly gathered skirt slightly narrower at the hem, and best of all the lovely cornflower blue color, were flattering. They would be to any woman.

The doorbell sounded, and she quailed. *Should* she wear this revealing dress for Mr. Bishop?

The bell chimed again. It was too late now to change her mind. She went to open the door.

Mr. Bishop's raised eyebrows and brief hesitation convinced her she had made a mistake and for a reason which only now occurred to her. She was selling him the designs. Had she any right to use them?

"You caught me at the wrong moment," she stammered, the words sounding false in her ears. "I was trying this on . . . just to see if it really was what you needed—"

"Yes, it really is just what I needed," he said gravely.

"I shan't wear it in public, of course, until after the film's been shown."

"I wasn't worried." He smiled. "Please wear it any time you like. In fact, if I could persuade you—but may I come in?" The smile faded. "I've something, a problem, I need to talk to you about today, as well as see the sketches."

"Yes, indeed, please do." She hadn't felt so unsure of herself in a long time. Anxious to steer his attention away from her gown, she said, "I'm eager to hear what the next scenario will be."

"You should be able to guess." Mr. Bishop answered absently. He was thumbing through the sketches on the table. "With all the good news from France, our studio, like all the rest, intends to get a jump on reality. The war to end all wars will conclude with a display of fireworks, a stirring oration by President Wilson, abject groveling by the Kaiser, and, most important, the reunion of lovers. Our heroine goes to the station to welcome her soldier home. She is confident of his faithfulness, but there is growing suspense as the train empties and he does not appear, while all around her other young men are rushing into the arms of their wives and sweethearts—"

He paused to study a picture. Clara had never before offered an opinion of these preliminary plot lines, but this time she said, "I hope you won't forget the parents who will be waiting on the platform, too. The audience would feel such sympathy, watching fathers and mothers strain to catch sight of their sons who are coming home safe at last. Suppose you had a son coming home. . . .

"Mr. Bishop—why do you look like that? What is it? I've said something to disturb you. But what?"

He continued to hold the sketch before him but his gaze was unseeing. His face had set. "Nothing . . . there's nothing."

"Please. I think there is. Won't you tell me?"

He turned then to look at her. "The most innocent remark," he said. "One never knows what will touch a nerve, does one? In my case it was just your unexpected mention of a son coming home . . . I had one, you see, a son who did not come home. Oh, not from war—he was only twelve—but from the sea. He and my wife were lost together. I'm sorry, Clara, I certainly had no intention of burdening you with what is best left in the past—"

"Andrew, I'm sorry, so desperately sorry! All this time, and I simply never imagined—" It was not until later, after he'd gone, that she realized she had used his first name, as he had hers. She was only conscious of a desire to ease the pain she had uncovered. "Let me get coffee, and if you care to, if it might help, please tell me a little about them."

He said slowly, "I think for once I would like to. I've never been able to talk about Mercy and Jed before. To anyone."

"Then come into the kitchen. We can sit there—this time of day it's sunny and cheerful."

She led the way, and he followed. When they were seated at the table and the coffee served, she said quietly, "Your wife—"

"My wife's name was Mercy. It was a traditional name in her family and fitted her very well. She was a very kind and gentle woman, although as fierce as a lioness in her loyalty to me."

"I see." Clara looked away for a moment. "That's how a woman should be. No wonder you loved her."

I did, very much. We were a happy family. My occupation was building ships, just as my grandfather's had been there in Boston years before, and New Englanders have long memories. They came to me because of who I was, and stayed with me because I took pride in my work. I expected to live there, doing the same thing, for the rest of my life.

"But an accident changed that. Jed—he was twelve that day, his birthday—"

He stopped.

Clara said gently, "He was your only child?"

"Yes. He was one of those boys who is as at home in a boat as he was on shore. And like me he loved boats, and building them. He had just finished a sailboat, made in my yard with skill and loving care, and all his own labor. She was beautiful, about fifteen feet long, teak decked, and with a particularly high mast.

"On his birthday, we transported her down to the dock for him and dropped her in the water. I still had work to do that afternoon, but he invited Mercy to go for the first sail.

"There's no use dwelling on what happened. It wasn't the boat; she was sound as a bell. And it wasn't Jed being reckless; he respected the sea too much for that. But after they'd been gone for an hour or so, a sudden squall came up, and we could only guess he was carrying too much sail on that high mast, and capsized. . . .

"I'm certain they tried to stay with the boat—they both would know to do that. But perhaps Mercy got torn away, and he went after her. It was the next day before we found them, drowned, their arms locked around each other. . . .

"Afterward, I could no longer work within sight of that empty dock. And I'd lost my love for ships and the sea."

Clara nodded, finding nothing to say.

"So I came back to California. I decided I had to find work that was totally different. And I did."

They were both silent for some time, he remembering and she feeling a sympathy that was beyond words.

At length he shook himself, then reaching across, gave her hands that were clasped together on the table a brief squeeze. "Thank you, Clara. I feel better, just having spoken their names again. Perhaps I'm beginning to heal a little.

"And I want to say, I haven't felt so comfortable with a woman since Mercy died. Comfortable—not an exciting word, but a good one just the same."

"Comfortable is just fine," Clara declared.

And she told herself it was. It must be. She must ignore the undeniable attraction she felt for him and which, happily, he showed no sign of reciprocating. Otherwise she would have to forego these visits she enjoyed so much. She was Sam's widow, and she owed Sam fidelity now and for as long as she lived. She would not fail him again.

She wondered suddenly what it was Andrew Bishop had wanted to discuss with her when he arrived, and withdrawing her hands, she said, "You mentioned a problem. Is it something about my work—or Lillian's?"

Chapter 48

Lillian should have been enjoying her work. Barbara Gierek's judgment had been correct—Lillian did do well in roles other than comedy, and while this studio worked the same hard day as any other, there was not the added pressure of Sennett's constant penny-pinching that had driven the directors to finish a reel by sundown, thus keeping the same actors before the cameras, hour after hour. On the other hand, maintaining her appearance of cheerful enthusiasm and boundless energy was difficult now for Lillian, and becoming far more so as the weeks passed.

There were the queer spells of lethargy, worse than any fatigue she remembered. Yet in between, when the pendulum swung the other way, she was jittery, her heart beat so loud and fast she could hear it, and she was uncomfortably warm, perspiring even on a cool afternoon like this one. How could she feel so rotten when she was taking cocaine? The Count, who waited for her each day outside the Selig lot, said she needed to increase the dosage still further, and she did. But if she hadn't known how absolutely harmless cokey was, how good cokey was for your health, she would have been frightened.

More of a problem professionally, even than the dragging lethargy, was her smoldering resentment, which, if she didn't make the greatest effort, tended to interfere with her performance in the various short, frothy dramas Selig was churning out while waiting to begin its big ambitious picture of the year—*Lilith*. Oh, why didn't that stage actress arrive, try out in the part, and become a laughing stock for her efforts?

Hurry, Rose Bishop, hurry! Because when you've made a fool of yourself, I'll show them how a scene or two should be played. Then they'll see that Lily French should be Lilith. They must! They will!

"Miss French—I want to speak to you."

"Oh—yes, of course." She pulled her mouth into its accustomed provocative smile and turned to face Andrew Bishop.

"Perhaps we'd better walk a short distance away," he said. "We both want this to be confidential."

"Do we?" Lillian's tone was still light, but an alarm had sounded in her mind. He looked serious, and he was so very important at the studio. *Our Mr. Bishop* made a great many decisions.

In silence, she followed him to a deserted bench.

"This will do. Sit down, Miss French. Now, wasn't it your understanding that drugs are absolutely forbidden on this lot?"

"Yes." Her gaze never wavered. She was not an actress for nothing.

"Then you realize, if I am to do my duty, that you are dismissed forthwith?"

"But I . . . I don't take . . ."

"Don't lie to me, please. I should hate to think your mother's daughter is a liar as well as an addict. It's useless, anyway. I've seen you meeting the Count. But I can assure you that even without that bit of evidence, I'd have guessed. Your bouts of fatigue, alternating with jumpiness, your acting, which has grown progressively slipshod—no use listing other unmistakable signs—good God, girl, don't glare at me and say, 'What signs?' Just look at your hands!"

She had no need to look. She could feel them trembling, as they so often did these days. Protectively, she clasped them together, forced them to be still.

She said coldly, "You really must be torn, Mr. Bishop. I'm sure you want to get rid of me so that your overrated relative can keep the part of Lilith. A part that should be mine, and will be—if I'm still working for Selig when she gets here. But, there's also Mama to think about, isn't there? And I don't mean just because of the costume designs."

He had listened impassively until she mentioned Clara, and then his eyes narrowed.

"You're right that I'm trying to consider your mother," he said calmly. "I intended asking her advice before I spoke to you, but changed my mind. Why cause her the grief of knowing the truth unless I have to? As for Rose—if you can successfully compete with her when she gets here on Monday—yes, that's right, Monday. Her theater in Chicago has been closed because of the influenza outbreak there—I say, if you can manage to get the part you want so badly, you'll have my blessing.

"Right now, however, I am only interested in discussing something much more important to my studio. Your addiction."

"Don't use that word!" Lillian actually screeched, and hearing herself, flushed. She paused, then went on in a lowered voice that was no less angry and defiant. "I'm not an addict! Don't you even know what an addict is? It's someone like Polly Kelly—"

"Who tried to kill herself last month."

Lillian shivered.

He continued inexorably. "And who will succeed next time—or the time after. Who is already finished as an actress and as a human being. At age—what? Twenty-three, with all the world before her, lovely, bright—"

"You needn't go on telling me about Polly! That's just the point. She takes hard drugs—heroin. So it's no surprise she's ruined. But I only take—"

"You take cocaine, I suppose."

"Yes, and it's harmless."

"Is it?"

"Yes! Why, I know lots of actors who've kept up just because of cokey. For years! Their pictures go on and on, and they're fine."

"I wonder how fine they really are," Bishop said. "Although, with some concaine users, I'll grant you the ride lasts a little while. With others—what about Zelda Thomas?"

"What about Zelda?" Lillian was staring into his face as if

mesmerized. Again she was remembering the day the chic Universal star visited the Sennett lot and lunched with her and Mabel. Zelda had been less than fine then, distracted, trembling, searching with desperate eyes for the Count.

"She's very ill. Didn't you know? Has been for some time, although her friends have kept her secluded. Lately she's been hospitalized for toxic psychosis, and her symptoms have progressed to the point where her memory is failing, she has hallucinations—thinks bugs are crawling on her skin—"

"Stop! Oh, stop!"

"The end, by the way, is not at all pleasant. There are terrible convulsions—"

"I won't listen!" Lillian's hands were pressed over her ears. Her trembling hands.

"Miss French, you will listen, because for your mother's sake, I am giving you another chance. Continue as you are—and for the good of the studio—"

"What do you mean, the good of the studio? An addict, while she lasts, will work her heart out for you." Lillian had rallied enough for this bitter outcry.

"No." He shook his head. "Quite aside from the deterioration in your performance—which is a crying shame, by the way, as you could be good, very good. You might even give Rose a run for her money if you'd shake this nasty little monkey from your back. But..." He shrugged. "As it is, you aren't going to be much use to the studio for very long, and more important, we can't afford to have drugs found here. They are as dangerous from a publicity point of view as blatant immorality and drunkenness.

"We—Gus, Barbara, and I—believe that a day is coming soon when there will be so much public indignation that many of the film companies will be shut down, forced out of business, and we don't intend to be one of them. So, take your choice. You may remain with us or not. I have nothing more to say."

She could not guess that he had turned his back and stalked away so quickly because he was on the verge of betraying his genuine pity and concern. He admired her spirit now, and he had admired her courage in the fight with Mabel Normand. He had held his peace about the drugs as long as he had, in the faint hope that he was mistaken, or, if not, that she would decide without his interference to free herself. Cocaine didn't have the same stranglehold as heroin, and she was strong willed.

He hadn't the slightest doubt she could break the habit if she only wanted to, enough.

But the future was up to her. He had done everything possible to sway her, and he'd meant every word he said. However, the picture of Clara learning the truth about her daughter's addiction was not pleasant to contemplate.

Lillian sat alone for some time on the bench. She was feeling the lassitude that had plagued her recently, and it was an effort to contemplate going back to the set, which she must do in fifteen minutes or so. She'd force herself, but that hard-hearted Mr. Bishop—what a prig he was!—was right in thinking she hadn't much energy these days.

"Miss French—phsst!"

She looked out through the fence.

The Count. And just in the nick of time, too.

She gave a quick glance over her shoulder—no one around—and walked to the fence.

"I'm so beastly tired again," she said.

"I can take care of that. But have you the money? You didn't yesterday, remember, and I'm not doing this for charity."

"It used to be friendship."

"It's not now, believe me. Well, do you have it?"

"Not as much as you're asking. I can't pay so much! If I keep taking all that money out of my pay—it's practically everything I earn—my mother will get suspicious."

"Never mind then." He shrugged, and started to walk away.

"Wait! Oh, please wait!"

Turning, he stood considering her. There was something new and unpleasant in his usually bland expression, so that she wasn't surprised when he said, "Sometimes, very occasionally, I accept other currency. Which, of course, will have to be paid after you finish work. If we make a deal, however, I'll be generous, and you can have the coke now. Just say yes or no."

Lillian averted her eyes. It didn't matter that he was a reasonably handsome man. She understood at this moment how much she loathed him.

She remembered briefly the others she'd refused—the men at the parties and at the studios. Some she'd liked, and none had she disliked. Yet she'd evaded them all. This time there would be no evasion, and no escape. If she said yes, he'd hold her to it.

"Well?"

One final hesitation. But Mr. Bishop was wrong when he'd

said she had a choice. She didn't. If she went back to the set
now, without coke to help her, she'd never get through the
day.

"Yes," she said.

"Then come outside for your buy."

Chapter 49

October tenth, Joanna's birthday, and all the family invited
for the evening to the house on Los Angeles Street. All would
be there, too, except Aunt Flossie and Uncle Paul, for he
seldom left his bed these days, and Dell. Dell at the appointed
hour was striding along through the park, oblivious of the wet
and windy darkness.

Not far away, all along the street at the side, she could see
a row of lighted windows, and it was only too easy to imagine
the cozy suppers taking place behind the curtains. Against her
will, a vision of the happy gathering at her own old home crept
into her mind.

Then a gust of cold, wind-driven rain struck her in the face,
and the wistfulness was dispelled. She'd better get the tarps
on the machinery tied down, or there would be some expensive
damage. These strong swirling winds could whip off the heavy
corners as if they were tissue paper.

She avoided looking at the empty site where the ferris wheel
had stood for so many years. There was no use letting her anger
boil up again. She didn't agree with the others and never would.
A man who willfully destroyed someone else's property should
be punished, no matter what his reason had been. Everyone
who committed a crime had a reason, surely!

She always felt such a wrench, passing this spot and knowing the ferris wheel was gone for good. She'd loved the sight
of it soaring so high in the air. She would feast her eyes on

the brightly colored, gently swinging seats, and remember the good times, with Aunt Flossie, solid and sensible, planted on her straight wooden chair at the foot, and nearby, over at the carousel, Dell herself and Papa, working so hard and happily together.

The carousel, at least, remained, looming sturdy and re-assuring, even though several ties of the protective tarpaulin had, as she feared, come undone and exposed a section of the platform. On impulse, being unobserved, she reached through the opening, and in a rare betrayal of sentiment briefly patted the hard glossy head of one of the horses. Then, aware of wetness under her hand, she began to haul the heavy canvas back into place.

"Miss Adeline—" Olaf came tramping up, his feet in their big rubber boots sending little fountains of water spraying from the saturated ground. "Thought you might be out here needing some help."

"Of course I'm here. Somebody had to put back these covers." She was annoyed with herself for being so sure she'd be alone. She had thrown on an old discarded mackintosh of Ralph's, and her hair, uncovered, was wet and tangled by the wind. It wasn't that she cared what Olaf Mickelson might think, she told herself, but she had her self-respect. She was not a slattern.

"I think I'd better dry off the machinery first," he suggested. He never seemed to take umbrage at her sharp tone, and for some reason, while this made her feel ashamed, there was a queer little satisfaction in being so shrewish.

He had pulled a rag from his pocket, and without waiting for her agreement he set to work.

"When you finish that," she ordered, "there's the roller coaster to tend to. I'll go myself and check on the cars."

"You don't need to. I can take care of everything." He glanced at her. "Listen, Miss Adeline, haven't you heard about the Spanish influenza going around? It's bad down in San Diego, people say, and starting up here. You don't want to get chilled, and the way you're dressed, with no hat, you'd better get out of the rain."

"I'll do no such thing. This is my responsibility. Why do you call me Miss Adeline, anyway?" It was a question she'd intended to ask for some time. "My name is Mrs. Wilson."

"Is it?" He continued to wipe the exposed metal with care.

"Yes, you know it is!" In the dim, misty light from the lamp posts, spaced along the adjacent path, she stared at him.

He shrugged, then shocked her by saying, "Don't look to me like much of a marriage. Ever hear from him, over in Europe?"

"Why, you—what an impertinence! A hired man asking me a question like that! If you want to go on working here, mister, keep your curiosity to yourself."

"I don't need to be curious, Miss Adeline. I can see for myself you ain't happy."

Her lips were stiff when she answered. "Has Joanna been talking to you? Who has?"

"Nobody. I give you my word, Miss Adeline. Nobody."

"Hah! Well, think what you like. But if you hope I'll cry on your shoulder about Ralph Wilson, or about anything, you're dead wrong."

"I'd be surprised if you did," he said calmly. "You're a spunky woman."

"Thank you." The words came before she thought. Recovering, she asked tartly, "How could you tear yourself away from that fine birthday party over on Los Angeles Street?"

"You're right, it's going to be a fine party. Why don't you come?"

"Again, why I do something or I don't . . . is not your affair!" She certainly wasn't going to tell him how much it hurt her to see little Bunch, healthy little Bunch, toddling about. Oh, to be with Mama, who must always in her mind be comparing Dell with Lillian and Joanna. All of them in fact, telling themselves what a failure she'd been as a wife. She was a money-maker now, with a growing bank account, but that didn't matter a whit. To them she was still a nobody. Not a fancy movie actress like Lillian, with little to do every day but strut around in front of a camera. Not a wife and mother like Joanna, who didn't know what worry was and could sleep late every morning if she pleased. Those two were on top of the world, and she didn't want to be around them. Or Mama.

"It's not too late," Olaf was urging.

"*No*, I said! Mind your own business!" She added, "If you must know, I'm expected at Aunt Flossie's." It would have been sensible then to walk away, go on over to the roller coaster and start checking the covers on the cars. But instead she lingered, watching him work.

"What's it like on a farm?" she asked, breaking the silence. She really wanted to know. She'd never lived anywhere but right inside Los Angeles.

"What's it like? Long hours. Up before sunrise to milk the cows. And for a farm wife—cooking for a lot of hungry men, thirty or forty maybe in harvest time."

"I wouldn't mind that. I'd like it."

"I reckon you would. You'd be fine on a farm. You're strong and you don't mind hard work." After a moment, he added, surprising her because he was not a talker, "What I liked about it most was the animals. I like machinery all right, but I used to be plumb crazy about horses. It's a pity the way horses have lost out to autos. Horses are quieter, they're obedient, and they're beautiful, too."

She laughed, trying to sound scornful and not quite succeeding. "Haven't you ever seen a mean horse? Papa's horses weren't all quiet and obedient, I'll tell you. Some had a lot of spirit."

"Spirited and mean aren't the same. Even a mean horse can be quieted down and still keep his spirit." Olaf looked up at her, explaining, "He's only mean because of what happened to him. Something cruel. A foal isn't born wanting to give trouble. He just gets that way when he's been hurt. Been beaten, maybe, or ridden too long with spurs. He needs gentling then. That's all he needs."

Gentling. It was a nice word. It made her wonder what marriage would have been like if Ralph had known such a word.

Olaf covered over the carousel, and they ran together against the strong wind to the roller coaster, where they worked quickly and efficiently, not talking much, just a word now and then about what they were doing.

When they finished and returned to the path, she said gruffly, "You'd better get on back home. They'll be wondering if I'm working you to death."

"That would be hard to do," he said. They were standing beside one of the light posts, and gazing up at him, she noticed how his smile was twisted by the scarring. She wondered what he'd looked like before, and she experienced a sudden desire to try to smooth away the ugly puckering with her fingers.

"Come back with me, Miss Adeline. They'll be missing you," he urged. Then he said again, "It's not too late."

"For me, it is." She must have sounded less forbidding than usual, because after a pause he asked, "Would you like—would you want instead—some company this evening?"

She actually hesitated before she drew herself up and said, "Certainly not! Goodnight, Mr. Mickelson." What had she considered doing? Console herself with the hired man?

"Goodnight, miss."

Standing in the rain, which was coming down harder now, she looked after him as he walked away. He'd at least had the good sense not to press the idea. Company, indeed! That's what came of being pleasant to him.

But it was colder now and dreary, being out here all alone on Joanna's birthday. Adeline hadn't really meant to visit Aunt Flossie and Uncle Paul tonight, but she decided she wanted to.

She turned and hurried away through the rain, not guessing that Olaf, from the distance, watched until she reached Flossie's porch in safety.

Tony, with the ease of habit, balanced himself along the aisle. The speeding train was headed away from Santa Monica on its way back to Hollywood, and once it left Hollywood and reached downtown his shift would be over. Ordinarily he was in no hurry, because he'd come to enjoy this pleasant work Uncle Paul had suggested; but tonight, because of Joanna's birthday, he was impatient to get home. Besides, with this strange harsh cough he'd developed, and the achy feeling, he wondered if he weren't getting a cold.

"Ten cents, sir, if you're going all the way to Colegrove, Sanborn, or Elysian Heights." He rang up the amount by turning the brass pole running overhead, and the dial at the end of the car clanged an acknowledgment.

"Tell me," the customer asked, detaining him, "do movie stars ever ride this train?"

It was a familiar question, and Tony obliged. "Yes, indeed, sir, the Big Red Cars being the quickest and best way around regardless of cost! Tonight I'm afraid, with this rain, you won't see anyone famous. But only yesterday, Maurice Costello sat in that very seat with his little daughter Dolores."

"You don't say! This seat?"

"Yes, sir. And Gloria Swanson's aboard at least once or twice a month. Lily French, too—you know who she is, don't you? She rides us frequently." Tony grinned. He didn't add that Lillian only did so with grumbling protest, and only because her fine automobile for one reason or another refused to start.

He moved on down the aisle, his smile fading. This heavy fatigue was understandable, he supposed, quite aside from his not feeling so good today, because he was working a double shift. In a jeweler's window, there had been a sapphire ring that caught his eye. He'd never given Joanna a proper ring, and he had an idea that she'd prefer sapphires to diamonds. By working the double shift tonight and a number of times previously, he'd been able to justify the expense. The little box, wrapped in blue paper, was even now in his pocket.

"Evening, Mr. Knowland," he said. Paunchy James Knowland was a familiar figure. He was an official of the line.

"Evening, Mr. Bonnard. Looking forward to getting home to that little daughter of yours, I imagine?"

"Yes, indeed, sir."

Tony strode on. The last seat of the sparsely filled car was occupied by another regular, and as he collected the fare, Tony said, "Evening, Mr. Starr. Going in to the office so late in the day?"

The graying man in the bowler hat, the owner of a small printing business located downtown on Spring Street, gave him back a wry smile. "Believe it or not, Mr. Bonnard, I must meet a customer at this hour. Can't afford not to give him a bid, as he's publishing a pamphlet on government waste. Seems we've manufactured hundreds, maybe thousands, of airplane engines for the army, Liberty engines they call them, and they're still stored in warehouses somewhere. Wasn't time to use them, I suppose, and the war almost over, but there's always a grumbler around to jump on the government. I shouldn't criticize our author, however. It's bound to be a popular tract, with a big run."

"I always wondered what happened to those engines," Tony said.

"Did you? Soon you can buy a pamphlet and find out. Well, even if I don't get the business, the trip down tonight had to be made. I'm going to interview a couple more people as proofreaders. Almost certainly unqualified. All the others have been. But what can I do? The man I had for so long, fine young fellow, was killed last month in France."

"That's too bad."

"Proofreading is not the simple task everyone thinks."

"No?"

Tony, who had never heard of the occupation, steadied himself against the seat. He had a headache now, a bad one. Like a tight band around his head.

"No, indeed. One has to concentrate, look for errors, be sharp! Excellent eyesight is required, and a willingness to pass the day more or less alone. Few people are suited, and few, I might add, apply. Even though I pay as well as any printer in the business."

Mercifully, Mr. Starr resumed reading his newspaper. The train sped on, stopped, let off passengers, and rocketed away while the rain drove sheets of water against the dark shiny oblongs of the windows. Then Mr. Starr was gone, as well as the man who had hoped to see movie stars, and as the final stop at the car barns approached, only Tony and Mr. Knowland were left.

Suddenly the official, in an alarmed tone, exclaimed, "Mr. Bonnard—is something wrong? Mr. Bonnard!"

Tony—who had been leaning against one of the seats, suddenly so achingly weak that if it weren't for the presence of Mr. Knowland, he would have succumbed to the forbidden temptation of sitting down—heard those words. They were the last. The voice trailed away, the car darkened as if the electricity had failed, and he realized with horror that he was falling to the floor in a faint.

When he opened his eyes again, he lay sprawled on his back in the aisle, the lights overhead were bright, and his left leg hurt. His first concern was for his leg, then he understood he had hit it against a stanchion as he fell.

"All right now, Mr. Bonnard?"

Mr. Knowland's worried face hung like a moon above him. To approach him, Mr. Knowland had been forced to kneel on the floor between two seats.

"Yes . . ." Tony's spirits had never been so low.

He'd had one of his spells after all, when he'd thought— hoped—because the last one, occurring at home in the privacy of his bedroom, had been so many weeks ago, that the strange, embarrassing disorder was leaving him at last. Indeed, happy at finding work he enjoyed, he'd never really faced up to what might happen. As Uncle Paul had mentioned tentatively when they'd first discussed this job, he wouldn't be driving the train so there was no chance of injuring anyone—but, if a blackout should occur he'd be in full view of a number of strangers, and was he willing to take the risk? He had been willing. He'd been so optimistic, and so wrong.

"You fainted," Mr. Knowland said.

As if he didn't know! "Yes," he answered, unable to hide his profound depression. "I-I'm not well."

That was certainly true enough. His headache was worse, and was pounding, pounding, like an anvil. He tried to pull his thoughts together, to face the unfortunate fact that the one person present was an official of the line.

"I hope you haven't got the Spanish influenza!" Mr. Knowland exclaimed, rearing back and away as Tony's cough began again. "I've heard it's so bad in San Diego they've had to close that training camp near there, the Kearny Mesa Cantonment. Men are dying like flies! A few cases have shown up here, too, in the last few days—"

"No, no, it's nothing like that," Tony assured him wearily, as soon as he could speak. He was realizing he hadn't the heart for the effort of somehow explaining, of trying to keep his job. The ugly prospect, almost certain now, of falling unconscious in the aisle before a carful of gaping passengers appalled him. "But my health is to blame, and I shan't be able to go on doing this work . . . no, I'd rather not say any more." He struggled to his feet. "I'm giving you my notice."

"Hello, Lillian, Mama." Joanna, still in her apron, stood in the doorway, holding Bunch up to greet them. "Can you give Grandma a hug, Bunch?"

What with the kissing, Bunch's absurd attempts at words, and the warm sweet smell of baking redolent in the kitchen, all of them felt festive, even Lillian.

"Ummm," Lillian said, testing a small piece of chocolate cake. "Nice. I didn't know you were such a good cook, Joanna."

"I'm learning." Joanna was studying her sister. Lillian, in the newest of fashions, her blond hair expertly cut and waved, should have been prettier than ever. But there was a gaunt look about her, and an air of restless nervousness, both of which were disturbing.

"Is Adeline here yet?" Clara asked.

Joanna pulled her gaze away from Lillian's fingers, tapping rhythmically on the tabletop. "I'm sorry, Mama, but she refused to come. I don't know why it is, but we see less of her now than we did when Ralph was around."

Clara did not comment. Lillian, however, eyes very bright, asked carelessly. "Has anyone heard anything about him? What does Dell say?"

"We don't ask—" Joanna began, but then, thinking it was as well they knew, she added, "I'm afraid he's left her. She told us once that if he did come back, it wouldn't be to her."

"But she's still tied to him! What a rotten spot to be in. She should get a divorce." Lillian was speaking too loudly and sounded flippant, prompting the quick rebuke from Clara, "A divorce? Hardly! Dell is a decent woman."

Abruptly, Clara stopped. For the first time, in far too long, she was remembering her mother. Ma, who had divorced two men yet had herself been honest, courageous, and decent.

Lillian, not noticing her stricken expression, began to argue. "She's made her bed so she has to lie in it? Is that what you think, Mama? Ever faithful, if only to a nonexistent husband?"

Clara's lips pressed hard together. Picking up Bunch, she said to Joanna, "Where *are* Tony and Olaf? It's getting close to bedtime for this little one. She's rubbing her eyes."

"Olaf's gone to the park. He was afraid the rain might be causing some damage. And Tony isn't home yet."

"Speak of the devil," Lillian said with that new forced vivaciousness, "Don't I hear Tony now?"

"It's the devil himself, Lillian," Tony called. "Just let me hang up this wet coat."

He strode into the room and swept Bunch from Clara's arms. His back to them all, he said, "Dad's home, Antonia! Are we ready for the festivities, Joanna? Where's Olaf?"

"Here, too." His friend followed closely on his heels. "I saw you turn the corner, but you were walking so fast—"

"We're all of us home then! Ready to...celebrate—" Tony's voice, unnaturally hearty until that moment, broke.

Clara, from where she stood, could see his face. Silently, she beckoned to Lillian and Olaf, who followed her away into the parlor.

"Tony—what is it?" Joanna faltered. The tenseness of his shoulders, his bowed head, frightened her.

He set the child on the floor then, and turned. He said woodenly, "I've lost my job. I blacked out."

"Oh, Tony...dear Tony..." She ran to him, threw her arms around him. "I'm so sorry!"

His body lost a little of its rigidity. "It'll be all right, Joanna,

I promise you! I'll get other work. I've heard of something. Mr. Starr, the printer—he has an opening. He told me what's required."

He remembered with perfect clarity what Mr. Starr had said. *One has to concentrate, look for errors, be sharp!* How could any man endure just to sit and stare at printed pages, hour after hour, day after day? But at least he'd be alone when he blacked out.

Oh God, he was so tired. And he ached. Not just his head, but all over, how he ached!

"Tony, you're shivering. Are you ill? Dear heart, there's no need to think about work tonight—"

Tony stepped back. He'd been reminded, by the hard edge pressing into his side, of the little box in his pocket, and he drew it out.

"No, you're right. We don't want any unpleasant problems spoiling such a special evening."

"Tony! I didn't mean—"

"Here, Joanna, this is for you. With things as they are, you may not be able to keep it long. But happy birthday, my love!"

Chapter 50

The carousel had broken down again. All Olaf's ingenuity couldn't seem to keep it running for more than a few days. Adeline walked over from the roller coaster to watch him try again to repair the boiler which persisted in overheating.

He glanced up at her from his work, then, saying nothing, turned back to adjusting the valves. She told herself it wasn't the place of a hired man to comment on the new, shorter-length dress she was wearing. Nevertheless she felt unreasonably annoyed.

"You will be able to get the engine running again, at least by this afternoon?" Her voice was sharp.

"Yes, Miss Adeline." He was silent for a few minutes, then he cleared his throat and said, "You expecting much business today?"

"No. Very little. Otherwise why would I be standing here talking to you?"

He nodded. "Seems to me business has been getting worse."

She didn't answer for a moment and he expected she would tell him that if she wanted his opinion she'd ask for it. She'd been extra short with him all morning. But instead she remarked, "So you've noticed, too. Well, what's the reason, do you think?"

"Could be the amusement piers, down on the beaches. Another electric park opened just last week at Santa Monica. Trouble is, it's mighty easy to get down to those places. The Red Cars run fifty, sixty trips a day to the Venice pier, and they take you there faster than an auto can drive."

"Is that so?" She turned sarcastic. "Now how would you know that, I wonder?"

"I went down, a couple of Sundays ago, to have a look around. I wanted to see the Pacific Ocean. I've been here a long while now, and never once seen it. So I went to Venice, then to Ocean Park. They're the big ones." He stopped for a moment, remembering the marvelous sight of those long wooden piers, bearing their crowded cargo of amusement rides and jutting far out over the blue, white-capped water. He continued slowly, "A man could hardly walk around, there was so many people. Long lines waiting for everything. Ever been in the Haunted House, Miss Adeline? That's what they call one of those places you pay to go in, and it was something, all right! Ghost heads and screams and chains clanking. One room had a slanting floor, and everything just a little cockeyed, so you'd think you was drunk."

"Hardly a new feeling for you!" As she had never known him to take a drink, this was palpably unfair, but he showed no resentment. He never did.

She went on, saying what was really in her mind. "I suppose you went down there hoping to get a job that paid more."

He was engaged in a delicate adjustment and was silent for a moment, squinting into the mechanism. She watched his big hands move sensitively, surely, feeling their way.

Then he said quietly, "No, and you shouldn't ought to say that. Captain Bonnard's my friend. He'll be out of work, till he gets over this sickness he come home with, and maybe for a while after that, and they need their share from the carousel. I stay where I'm needed."

"Indeed, Mr. Mickelson. I had some idea the shoe was on the other foot. That you needed *us*. However, as you know so much about the amusement piers, tell me this—are they going to take any of our customers away for good?"

"You want the truth?"

"I do."

"Then I have to say, you've made all the money you're going to here. Look around you. Nobody waiting. The rides not working. No, Chutes Park won't be worth keeping open, not very much longer."

Adeline, who had expected to be reassured, glared at him. "I don't believe you!"

He shrugged. "You asked me what I thought. So I told you. There now, she's fixed again." He gave the engine a final swipe with a greasy cloth. "Let's fire her up."

Briefly the morning seemed to improve. The old equipment gave no more trouble and Olaf was free to run the roller coaster, sell tickets, and start the cars on their way. He should have been busy enough because, following her talk with him, Adeline prudently decided to let the other hired man go. When she suggested Olaf take over both duties there was no mention of a raise in pay, nor did he ask for one. All he said was, "I'll do what's needed," and Dell had the grace this time to hold her tongue.

However, the sparsity of the crowd, far fewer even than the day before, astonished Olaf, too. Neither he nor Adeline often read newspapers, or they might have understood sooner than they did. For an invisible specter had begun to stalk the amusement parks at the beaches as well as their own. The virulent influenza epidemic, which had raced across the country like a wildfire out of control and finally delved its burning, killing tentacles into California, had begun to spread up the coast from San Diego. The *Los Angeles Times* on that morning of October 13, reported the terrifying fact of its arrival.

Shortly after noon, Aunt Flossie appeared at the park, saying in an agitated way, "Adeline, I know you're busy—"

"No more than I'd expect to be, with no customers. I wonder what's become of Olaf? He went home for lunch and didn't come back. I suppose I was asking him to do too much!"

Aunt Flossie continued as though she hadn't spoken. ". . . but haven't you heard what's happening? It's the influenza—here in Los Angeles! Mr. Mickelson must have told you Tony is ill, has been for several days, but we didn't know what he had and it didn't seem to be anything to worry about. We didn't worry, except to think Mr. Starr, the printer, might be getting somebody else to work at his shop, with so much time going by.

"But Joanna and the baby both woke up feeling real bad this morning, and Joanna got worse, so feverish and sick to her stomach, that Tony called a doctor and got him to come. A big favor, as it turned out. The doctor is very busy and getting busier, with more and more of these dreadful influenza cases.

"He did come, though, and he told Tony that Joanna and the baby were—" She stopped, overcome.

"Aunt Flossie, what are you saying? Aunt Flossie?"

"Yes, yes. I just—well, he said they were dangerously ill, especially Joanna." Aunt Flossie, trying to recover her composure, blew her nose with a loud honk.

"But she's so healthy and strong! Surely—"

"That doesn't help. Not at all. He said it's the healthy young people who are dying, this time. Not babies or old people, but those thirteen or fourteen through their twenties. Tony is getting better—he must have had influenza, too, but Joanna . . .

"Now, Adeline, your Uncle Paul is very weak today and I must get back to him. But Mr. Mickelson is at home, helping, and later on, when we've been able to reach Clara, she'll come, too, I'm sure—"

"I'll go at once," Dell said.

"No, *Liebchen*! I knew you'd offer, but it's as I told you. *Young people.* That's why so many soldiers have died, they say. Queer and very sad, but there it is."

"Olaf's there—he's young!"

"Yes, but he's already been exposed to the infection over and over, what with Tony being sick. You haven't. You must return to your own house and stay there. Don't even go to the market. And you'll have to close down your rides, because you must keep out of crowds. That was what the doctor said— keep out of crowds! Do you hear what I'm telling you, Adeline? Mr. Mickelson said I was to make very sure you left here and stayed safe."

"Did he!" Adeline's anxiety turned to indignation but Aunt Flossie didn't notice.

"So, Adeline, are you going to close down? Right away?"

"Yes, Aunt Flossie, that's exactly what I'm going to do. You go on home, and don't worry."

Chapter 51

"Joanna? It's me. Dell."

Joanna's face turned toward the sound, but although her eyes were open they were glazed by fever, and she hardly seemed to recognize her sister. She finally said, wonderingly, "I ache so much. All over. I've never felt so awful . . . Bunch?"

"Bunch is fine," Dell said. "She's not nearly as sick as you are."

"But she's only a baby. So little. I hear her crying!"

"Tony talked to the doctor and he says the crying is a good sign. Don't fret. We'll take good care of her."

"You'll stay? Please—"

Dell said brusquely, "Certainly, I intend to stay. You have nothing to worry about except getting well. Aren't you thirsty?" Joanna's cheeks were like fire. Dell could almost feel the heat rising from the bed.

"Yes, but I can't keep anything down."

"You'll have to try." She urged in a softer voice, "Only a sip of this cool water . . . come now. . . ."

But Joanna had shut her eyes without answering, and already was tossing and turning in a restless doze.

Dell tiptoed out. She wondered about the baby, even though the fretful wail still sounded strong. Babies, she'd heard, went downhill very quickly. It would be important to keep offering milk and broth to her, too.

"What are you doing here?" It was Olaf, just issuing quietly from Bunch's room.

"Is Bunch all right?"

"Yes, although the cough keeps waking her. I said, what are you doing here? I told Mrs. Perkins to keep you away."

He sounded very angry, and it was the first time he ever had in the months she'd known him.

"She tried," Dell answered. "But this is my family. Besides, healthy as I am—yes, healthy! Just look at me! One doesn't have to be happy to be healthy."

He groaned. "You fool. Don't you understand? With luck, you hadn't been around anyone with this dreadful sickness, so you walk right into it. Well, maybe it's not too late. I want you to put on your coat right now, and leave this house."

"I've not the least intention of doing so."

"Your ma's coming. I just talked to her. So you aren't needed. Not at all."

Even in his anxiety, he saw at once that he'd hurt her. Her air of spirited determination seemed to fade before his eyes. "What I'm trying to say is—"

But Dell didn't let him finish. "You may be right, Mr. Mickelson, and later, if I'm in the way, I'll leave. Right now, though, I haven't time to talk. I'm going to try to bring Joanna's fever down."

"You won't be in the way. I didn't mean that—" he protested, but she had left him.

She worked hard all afternoon and he helped her without further argument. Tony, no longer very ill but still so weak he could hardly stand without assistance, must have nourishing food, and after he'd eaten, Olaf helped him bathe and change, and put clean sheets on his bed. Dell devoted herself to Joanna, sponging off her hot body, and coaxing her with spoonfuls of water, one swallow at a time. Frequently, Joanna would drift away into a restless stupor, and then Dell left her and tended to the baby.

She had dreaded entering the nursery. All these months, she had kept her distance from this child of her sister's, fearing to be reminded painfully of her own. She'd only been able to think of Bunch with the bitterest envy.

But the fretful crying that afternoon brought her running. Before she thought, she had picked up hot, cross, outraged little Bunch and was rocking her against her shoulder.

"All right, now. Auntie Dell's brought you something nice and cool to drink. No need to cry. Auntie Dell's here. . . ."

How easily the words came, and how naturally Dell held the overheated little body close to her. She looked into the child's flushed face and dulled eyes, and was suddenly terribly frightened. What if this baby died, too? No! No, she must not!

Patiently, Dell wheedled and cajoled while she held a cup of milk to the child's parched lips, and as Bunch at last settled down to drinking Dell crooned to her, a wordless, tuneless song but one that quieted the little girl and kept her from pushing the cup away.

"Is she taking milk now? Good!" Olaf had noiselessly entered the room and was watching.

Dell, annoyed at being observed in such an unguarded moment, said shortly, "We're going to run out soon. The milkman didn't come."

"He must have heard the news before we did, and walked off his job," Olaf commented grimly. "I'll go buy some later—there must be a grocery open—but right now we can get a little from the woman next door."

Although he didn't return empty-handed, he was visibly dismayed. "It's a different town, Miss Adeline, and all in a day or two. The neighbor barely opened her door, and when I told her the baby was ailing and needed milk, she acted scared—afeared even to hand it out to me."

"She didn't ask if she could help?" Dell was astonished.

"No. She was scared. People are dying, people who've been sick just a short time. I think for a while we can only count on ourselves."

Dell said, "And on Mama. I wonder where she is?" Olaf knew she hadn't forgotten what he'd said to her earlier.

Clara came just before six o'clock. Dell was in the kitchen, cooking supper for herself and Olaf, and tending a large kettle of chicken soup she was preparing for the others. At the sound of her mother's voice, she ran to the parlor, then stopped in the doorway, feeling the familar awkwardness.

"How good of you to help out, Olaf," Clara was saying. She must have been desperately worried about the three who were ill, but she smiled at Dell and added, "Something does smell good."

Dell barely heard. Noting Clara's immaculate coat and the hat that framed her face and her neatly waved hair, Dell abruptly became aware of her own disheveled appearance. Her hair, untended for so many hours, straggled on her neck. The new dress, worn for the first time that morning, was stained on the shoulder by milk smeared from the baby's lips, and on the skirt by specks of Joanna's vomit. A sour smell, unnoticed before, assailed Dell's nostrils. She wondered if it filled the room, wafting its way over to Mama who was so fresh and clean.

Clara, however, appeared oblivious to any repulsive spots or odors. "Please tell me quickly—how are they?" she asked.

"Asleep right now, all of them. The baby only just dropped off."

"I'd better not go up yet, then. Sleep is the best medicine. Dear me, you must have thought I was never coming! I had doubts myself. I started early enough, just as soon as I could after reaching Lillian at the studio, but the streetcars are running so seldom today. I had to wait and wait."

"What did Lillian say?" asked Dell.

"Say?"

"When you told her about the influenza."

"You know your sister. She merely said she wasn't worried. Even though, as even she must have realized, the entire city is suddenly terrified. In only a few hours, such horror stories have gotten around! But Lillian is unable to think about anything except this actress who has arrived at last from Chicago. Mr. Selig had decided to send everyone home, but the actress— Rose Bishop is her name—appeared at the studio this morning on schedule, so they kept on a small crew and they'll probably start shooting anyway."

"Lillian didn't offer to come with you?"

"No, dear, and just as well. You and Olaf are quite enough to be taking such a risk."

Clara was carefully hiding her bitter disappointment in her second daughter. It was true—Lillian hadn't offered to help. In fact, the idea quite clearly hadn't occurred to her. She had merely assumed Clara was calling to warn her, and said, "Mama, being here at the studio today means more to me than anything in the world. It's my chance! Can't you understand that?"

Clara, aware of the futility of any reproaches, had replied, "No, I can't understand. But do as you wish. Just try to stay out of crowds. Go straight home. And even if your car breaks down, don't ride the Red Car—"

Whereupon Lillian, much too excited to listen even to these mundane instructions, had ended the conversation as quickly as she could.

"Motion picture people are amazing," Clara added, trying now to explain to Dell and Olaf. "Actors, directors, it doesn't matter—they all seem to have one-track minds. Lillian is one of them, if I ever doubted it before."

You would say that, Dell thought sourly. *Go ahead, excuse her*. But then, looking at Clara's troubled face, she wondered suddenly if she weren't being unjust. If she'd done something thoughtless herself, she'd want Mama to excuse her to the others. There was nothing wrong with being loyal.

Mama was so poised these days! She was making a little money, so Lillian said, and she had a new air about her, one of confidence. Watching her and listening to her, it wasn't difficult to believe that all would be well now that she'd arrived. Joanna would have the best of care and if it were possible to save her, Mama would.

Already, to Dell, Clara seemed to be taking charge. She said, "Dell, why don't you come in here and sit down? I can just imagine how you've been flying around all day, trying to do everything that needed doing. Rest a little, and when Joanna and the baby waken, let me tend to them."

Dell, as she was bid, walked into the parlor and dropped into the big chair that had once been Papa's. Yes, she was beginning to flag, although she hadn't noticed it before.

She was about to say, with a glance at Olaf, "I don't suppose you'll need me here any longer—" but Clara hadn't finished.

"We can't have you getting sick, too, because then I simply don't know how we'll manage. Even with Olaf in the house to help, I'd be terrified to think of the next few days without your strength. Dell, it's such a relief that we have you to depend on. Thank you, dear, for dropping everything and coming. But of course you would!"

Dell stared down at her work-roughened hands, finding nothing to say. But then, hearing an ominous hissing from the kitchen, she jumped to her feet. "Oh, my! The soup's boiling over—"

"I'll fix it," Olaf offered, but she had scurried out the door ahead of him, no longer the least bit tired. She must have gotten, as Papa used to say, her second wind.

Tony was definitely on the mend. And the baby, though feverish and crying incessantly, was alert, taking liquids, and according to the doctor who came again because of Joanna, holding her own nicely.

Dr. Barnes was an exhausted man, a middle-aged, nondescript, unsung hero, who took his life in his hands every time he entered the room of an infectious patient. Not all doctors were willing to chance the disease, so Dr. Barnes had had no sleep for two nights running.

As Dell was busy in the kitchen again and Clara upstairs

with Bunch, Olaf spoke with Dr. Barnes after his visit to Joanna's bedside.

"How does she seem, doctor?"

"Not good. Not good at all. She's grown so weak in just a short time. They often do. Getting more liquids down may help, and of course keep her warm. She'll turn the corner back to recovery very soon—or not at all."

"There's nothing more we can do?"

"No. Just pray it doesn't turn into pneumonia. Now I must go. Will you cover what I've said with her husband?"

"Maybe later. He's feeling bad enough already, for bringing this home to her and the baby."

"He needn't. Sometimes I think this scourge is simply carried by the wind. It's showing up in places now where nobody's been!"

"That may be. But you're a brave man to face it so often."

The doctor studied him. "You were in France, weren't you? Mr. Mickelson, don't talk to me of bravery."

Clara sat with Tony at Joanna's bedside. With Dell caring for the baby, and Olaf doing whatever else was needed, Clara was spending most of her time here, watching over this daughter who was, in her mother's heart of hearts, the most loved.

Four days had passed, and she lay half-conscious, the terrifying spells of delirium rarer now but replaced by a torpor that was even more frightening. Her body lay curled, hour after hour, in a shallow-breathing ball. When she was awakened by a hard spell of coughing, they would speak to her, trying to distract her from the aching of her muscles and the soreness of her throat, and trying desperately, each in his way, to keep her with them.

Tony told her eagerly that he'd approached Mr. Starr on the telephone, and the printer had definitely promised to hold the proofreading position open until Tony felt strong enough to apply. Mr. Starr had a nephew, it seemed, who was a soldier, so he felt it a patriotic duty to assist a veteran if he could.

Joanna's nod, hearing this, was almost imperceptible, but Tony felt comforted. At least she understood that he would not fail her and Bunch, that he would be able to go on supporting them. Never, he swore to himself, would he let her guess how much he dreaded this new kind of work.

Clara, for her part, would talk as normally as she could about all manner of things, but particularly the subject in which

Joanna had been absorbed, the news from Europe, which even during this violent epidemic continued to occupy the headlines of the newspaper. *The war to end all wars* was virtually over. Although hostilities would continue until a peace treaty was actually signed, the Germans had capitulated.

"Look at this headline, Joanna," Clara would say. "See— UNCONDITIONAL SURRENDER SURE! Isn't that splendid?" She carefully covered the smaller item beneath with her hand, which reported for Los Angeles alone nine deaths from influenza in the last twenty-four hours, and almost five hundred new cases.

When Joanna did rouse, she always asked about Bunch, and they would tell her, "Fine! Almost well. When you're stronger we'll bring her in to see you."

"Couldn't she . . . come to the door?"

"My, I do believe you're better, don't you think so, Tony?" Clara would say, pleased, until she realized that almost at once Joanna had lapsed back into her strange restless sleep.

"The disease may be losing its grip on her," Clara told Tony worriedly. "But she's so dreadfully weak."

"Yes." He sat slumped in his chair beside the bed, his face in his hands. He said simply, "I will never forgive myself if she dies."

"Tony, she isn't going to die. Not after she's hung on this long. We won't let her."

He pulled himself to his feet and began pacing. Although his health was returning, after a minute or two of such anguished walking he would be forced to take to his bed, and Clara said soothingly, "It's a beautiful day. Why not go out in the backyard and sit in the sun for a little?"

"Yes, all right. Sometimes I just can't bear to see her like this, so pale, and every day weaker . . . first, though, Clara, I'd like to be alone with her, just for a little. Would you mind?"

"Of course not, dear. Call me when you want me."

She was gone. Tony took one of Joanna's inert hands in both of his.

"My darling," he whispered, "my dear, darling Joanna. You needn't answer, I don't even know if you hear me. But I must say this to you once more. I love you. So very much! If I hurt you with that silly business about your working, I'm sorry, truly sorry, and you must know I never meant to. We've always been so close, haven't we? Oh, Joanna, try to get well! Stay with me!"

She slept on. Gently he laid her hand back on the bedcover, then he rose, kissed her cheek, and tiptoed from the room.

Clara, hearing his footsteps on the stairs, rushed through the story she was reading to Bunch and went to resume her vigil. This time she shut the sickroom door before she sat down beside Joanna to wait.

At length her daughter stirred and Clara, lightly shaking her shoulder, said, "Do you hear me, Joanna? I've something nice to tell you. I've a message for you."

She hurried to the window and glanced out. Yes, Tony was safely lying in the sun. She did have a message, and because it was cheerful and would interest the invalid she intended to deliver it, even though Tony, with his prejudice against the newspaper, might prefer that she did not. Pit Tony's feelings against Joanna's good, and there wasn't much question what Clara's decision would be.

Joanna murmured, "Yes, Mama?" That she was rational was a good sign. If only she would fight harder!

"You had a visitor yesterday. I thought you'd like to know. Most people are afraid to come here, and I can't really blame them. But a man from the *Los Angeles Times*, Mr. McGowan, stopped by the house."

Joanna's thin, white face broke into a smile. Delighted to see this response, Clara went on, "He was very pleasant, and gave me several bits of news for you. Let's see . . . they're getting a new press—it seems one of the old ones broke down and almost kept the paper from coming out that day. Then, somebody named Tom Parker is retiring for the second or third time. And what else? Oh, yes—the newspaper's war correspondent, Charles Gold, will be coming home soon, perhaps before the Armistice is signed."

"I'm so glad!" The words were faint, but they were enough. Clara, seeing the unguarded expression of joy on Joanna's face, suddenly remembered Uncle Paul's story of a Charles, and was in consternation. This war correspondent was *the* Charles, undoubtedly.

"They expect to have a party for him," she finished mechanically. Then she turned away, and busied herself plucking the old blossoms from a faded bouquet on the windowsill. Thinking, *I should never have told her. Now, what can I do?* she said only, "I'll bring Bunch in today. I know you miss her."

Joanna was going to recover. She had hung on to the very edge for several days, and then, though she could have slid backward at the touch of a finger, she slowly began to climb, back to life.

Gradually, the house became less of a fortress, the inhabitants largely cut off from the city outside and grimly enduring. It had seemed strange that Aunt Flossie didn't call, but Clara and Dell had been so occupied they gave their old friend little thought. Consequently, when they did at last hear from her, they were stricken with remorse. It was they who should have inquired and offered hope and encouragement. Now it was too late.

"Paul died this morning, Clara." The deep, heavily accented voice managed this announcement, then broke. "I can't tell you how I—how I—"

"Aunt Flossie, I'll come at once with Dell. Please, just wait for us!"

A brief stop in the kitchen to inform Dell, then she ran up the stairs, deciding that she wouldn't burden Joanna, still so fragile, with this news just yet. Joanna, of the three girls, had been much the closest to Paul.

In her room, she paused only to snatch up a hat and bag, and then was out again and on her way. But on the landing, passing Joanna's open door, she looked in.

The girl lay very still, quietly gazing at the ceiling, and Clara was struck by her small, faraway smile. At any other time this suggestion of happy anticipation would have meant nothing, but Clara's sensibilities were sharpened by her grief.

She entered the room and said, "Daydreaming?"

"I guess I was." Joanna turned startled eyes on her mother. "What about?"

When Joanna didn't answer, Clara moved to the window. Tony was, as she thought, taking the fresh air again, his slender body stretched out in a lawn rocker, his face turned to the sun.

Clara returned, and said, "I haven't got much time just now. I must go out, but there's something I want to say to you."

"What is it, Mama?"

"This man, this Charles Gold—"

"He's a friend. . . ."

Clara was not deterred. If she needed any confirmation of her suspicions, the rush of color into her daughter's pale face was enough.

"Joanna, forget him! You're married to a good man who

loves you. Thinking about someone else, mooning over him as you're doing, is being unfaithful in your mind, which soon will lead to being unfaithful in body. That, my dear, for women like us, can only bring the greatest unhappiness." She paused, then added, "I know. I was weak, and it happened to me."

Joanna's eyes widened. There was shock in her face. What else was there Clara dared not guess, and she plunged on, wanting to finish while her courage lasted. She must, if there were any chance of swaying Joanna.

"Dearest, you and Tony have so much! Don't throw it away. You have Bunch, and a life to build together and good memories to share, as well as the delight I suspect you still find in his arms. Just as I did—in Sam's.

"There's this to think about, too. Don't ever imagine, if you are unfaithful, that Tony will forget or forgive. He doesn't accept that you're human and not perfect, although in his heart he's fearful that might be so. In so many ways, you see, he's like Sam—"

"Papa *knew*? Oh, no!"

"Yes. He knew." Clara wondered if she might be going to faint. She felt so wretched, so ill suddenly. She had never imagined sharing her shameful secret with anyone, least of all Joanna, the daughter she loved best, whose respect she most treasured.

"And that's why you simply stopped living—after he died?" Joanna's voice was inexorable. Her face betrayed nothing.

"Yes."

"I see . . . thank you, Mama. You said you had to go out somewhere?"

Joanna turned over in the bed, her back to Clara, her face to the wall.

Chapter 52

"What is it, Olaf?" Clara asked. She had stepped outside Flossie's house to answer the knock on the door, hoping not to disturb her friend who had fallen at last into a light sleep.

"Someone's been calling you, over at Los Angeles Street. I didn't want the phone to ring here and bother Mrs. Perkins, so I come to tell you."

"It can't be important," Clara said wearily. "But thank you." She took a step backward toward the house.

"Missus, he said it was! He called yesterday, too, and again this evening."

"All right, Olaf." His earnestness compelled her to listen. "Who was he?"

"He said to say Mr. Andrew Bishop. With some news about Miss Lillian."

"Oh, I see. Very well, then, I'll call him. You'd better get back to the house now, and Dell can go with you. Joanna and the baby may be needing something."

In the cool darkness she saw the rare smile soften his face. "They might," he agreed, "but there's no hurry. I think Tony will like being the only one there for a little, doing for them himself."

"I suppose he will." She managed to return his smile, but barely. It had occurred to her that she wouldn't be going back to the Los Angeles Street house tonight. Perhaps not ever. Facing contempt from Joanna would be more than she could endure.

"Olaf." Dell appeared in the doorway. "I'd like to stop by my house to get some things. Will you come with me?"

"If you want."

Clara watched them walk away together, the big man matching his stride to that of her sturdy eldest daughter. Worried and preoccupied as she'd been during this past terrible week, Clara had not been oblivious, and she silently wished him good fortune.

The tedious hours of tending the sick had given her plenty of time for thinking and remembering, the memories, perhaps not surprisingly, centering around the image of Ma, kind and cheerful, caring for *her* through some childhood illness. Defiantly, in light of Sam's firmly expressed opinion on divorce, Clara had decided that while divorce might be very wrong for some, it was right for others, and if Dell should ever want her freedom Clara meant to support her.

But would Dell want it? She'd spoken to Olaf as brusquely as always, and Clara shook her head.

"Olaf," Dell said as they walked along, "I've made up my mind. If things keep on as they are, I'm going to sell my rides—both the roller coaster and the carousel." She paused for a second or two, and he knew she was waiting for her voice to steady. Selling the carousel was for her a wrenching step. "There's an electric park down by the Long Beach pier that needs more equipment but can't afford the big price it costs new. This is a chance for me that might not come again."

"I think you're right," he said promptly. "You should sell."

"Oh!"

"Didn't you want the truth?"

"Yes. It's just—I've done this one kind of work all my life. For you, it's easy to change, but not for me. I don't know what else I can do."

"We'll think of something. Don't fret."

They finished the walk in silence. Then, as they reached the porch steps, she stopped and faced him.

"I have to thank you, Olaf. For all you've done in this terrible time. You didn't need to be there even, but you were. And you did so many nasty dirty jobs, emptying slops, changing soiled sheets. All that."

"I told you when you asked about the farm that I was used to hard work. Don't you think there's dirty jobs on a farm?"

"Anyway, I thank you. We couldn't have gotten through otherwise. And I have to say, too, I'm sorry for the way I've talked to you. I think I was just trying to hurt somebody. I'm not a very nice person anymore."

He gently grasped her arm, and turned her to face him.

"That's not so. You are a nice person, Miss Adeline. Now I'm going to say something to you this once. Then if you tell me, as I reckon you will, that you don't want to listen, that'll be the end of it. I'll go on working for you just the same.

"This is what I've been thinking. It don't look to me like you've got much of a husband. I hope he isn't planning to come back, because I'd like you to get rid of him, for good and all, and marry me instead."

Adeline gasped. But she said nothing.

"I'd treat you right," Olaf went on doggedly. "A woman to me is something so special that if I had you, I'd reckon I was the luckiest man in the world."

He stopped and waited. But she continued to stand quite still, looking up at him. After a moment or two of silence between them, he said quietly, "Unless, maybe, my face would make you pull away."

"Oh, no! Olaf, no!" she exclaimed. "I don't care at all about your face, except to be sorry you were burned."

"Well, then? If it's no, I want you just to tell me. I'm not made of stone, Miss Adeline. Please, just tell me."

"Olaf," she said, "I can't give you any promises, but I'm not saying no either, because I'm not sure. I've a favor to ask, sort of a strange one. I want you to kiss me. Will you do that— just kiss me?"

In the deep shadows of the porch, he complied, and when she didn't pull away, his big hands caressed her shoulders and after that gently sought her breasts.

Adeline had known desire before, only to feel it shrivel and die. This time, when the yearning began, she welcomed his breath on her skin, his lips, his hands, and felt the wondrous urgency grow and fill her. There was no fear this time. Not with him.

She reached behind her, opened the door, and drew Olaf into the warm shelter of her house.

"Andrew?" Clara, not wanting to wake Flossie, spoke softly into the telephone.

"Clara, I hate to disturb you at a time like this—but is Lillian with you?"

"No, she stayed in Hollywood. You can reach her at the studio, I imagine. Or at our bungalow. Is there some problem with her work?"

"Not with her work, no." He hesitated. "As I say, it's too bad to have to bother you, when you've had so much sickness to worry about—"

"Sickness, and a death." *And Joanna lost to me?*

"Oh, no, Clara! Not your daughter?"

"An uncle, who was very dear to us. He'd been ill for some time, though. So far as the epidemic went, we were fortunate."

"I'm glad for that. But Clara, I've some disturbing news. It's about Lillian. I'm making every effort to find her, but I thought you should know . . . she's disappeared."

"Disappeared? You mean she's gone off somewhere by herself?" Clara refused to take alarm. Lillian was such an independent sort. With Clara away from the bungalow, so that Lillian needn't account to her mother, any spur-of-the-moment plan could be carried out. "If a picture has just finished—"

"A picture hasn't just finished," he interrupted. "That's the point, Clara. The picture was just beginning, and she walked off the set and didn't return. Quite unlike her, I agree, but if you had seen her face, as she watched my sister Rose play Lilith . . ."

Chapter 53

So this, at last, was the great Rose Bishop!

Lillian, in her despised role of Eve, would not be making an appearance in the first scene, so she was free to stand at the side and observe. Realizing that her hands were trembling again, she clasped them together tightly out of sight, behind her back.

Why didn't they get on with it? But no, the famous actress first had to be introduced personally to all the crew, from cameramen and makeup artists down to the muscular young men who built the scenery. The English director, the highly esteemed John Eagleton, was bowing and kissing her hand as though she were royalty.

Enjoy it while you may, Lillian admonished her silently. Like all the others who had tried to break into the movies merely because they were illustrious, Miss Bishop would find her moment of adulation soon over.

Red-haired Barbara Gierek, her manner surprisingly formal, came now to take Lillian's hand and lead her up to be presented, and Lillian could only grit her teeth and bear it, murmuring something flattering with as much conviction as she could muster. Turning away, her eyes met those of Andrew Bishop and her heart plummeted. It was only too clear from his frown that he knew she hadn't given up cocaine. How he could be so certain, she had no idea, but he was. And before this day was over, she'd be fired.

All the more reason why she must show them quickly how good she was, how perfect for Lilith! He'd say nothing then. What could he say?

Miss Bishop and John Eagleton seemed in no hurry, though. They were talking about the influenza epidemic and the actress, in response to a question from Andrew Bishop, began telling them, in that rich resonant voice that carried well beyond the confines of the set, about the effect on her play in Chicago.

"One evening we had a full theatre, standing room only, and the next we were more than half empty. We hung on for two or three nights, then closed. A beautiful, successful production—finished! I didn't realize, coming here, that it was a case of out of the frying pan and into the fire."

"It isn't. Not exactly," Barbara said crisply. "There's an important difference. In motion pictures we aren't dependent on an audience, at least not until the film is finished and being shown, at which point success or failure is out of our hands. Regardless of what takes place beyond our gates today, we can still work, and I, for one, would like to. However"—she looked around the assembled crew, getting their attention—"while this epidemic is going on, I can hardly insist on anyone staying. Each of you is free to go home, and I will quite understand."

No one spoke.

"Very well, then. What I have said will be equally true tomorrow. And meanwhile, let's get started.

"Rose, you have read all the material we sent you on Lilith, as well as the scenario?"

"All of it. And I like it. Lilith is an intriguing character to play, which is the only reason"—she and Barbara exchanged a long glance—"that I'd be willing to come here and try motion pictures again. Especially with this studio. You understand that, don't you, Barbara?"

"I wouldn't have asked for you otherwise," Barbara said evenly. It was as though, despite the calm words, the two were fencing with rapiers. Obviously, there was no affection lost between them. Years later, Lillian would learn that at an early point in her career, Rose Bishop had been the object of adoration by Jan Gierek, who later married Barbara, and even then persisted in imagining himself in love with Rose. It was a measure of Barbara's compelling interest in the Selig Company that she would invite Rose to star in one of her pictures. It was also, had Lillian understood, a measure of Rose's talent.

Instead, during this exchange, Lillian was studying Rose, and her optimism grew. As revealed in the strong klieg lights, Rose was not far from being middle-aged. On the credit side, she had flawless olive skin that would photograph well; a thin, patrician nose; and extraordinary, large, sooty black eyes. Her eyes. Her face was surprisingly unwrinkled and her waist was slender as a girl's, but Lillian's sharp eyes noted with satisfaction a thickness through the hips and upper legs, faintly visible under the fine wool of her skirt.

Andrew Bishop was saying to his half-sister, "Rose, I'd forgotten that contralto voice of yours. It's a pity the screen is silent."

A pity indeed! Lillian exulted.

Rose only shrugged. "Acting without sound is a challenge, and I'm eager to try it again. Andrew, didn't I hear that Selig's has a remarkably talented costume designer?"

Andrew nodded. "Her name's Clara Fritsch."

"We'll see later what ideas she's had for me, but in the meantime, while we work out some of the action today, I brought something to wear which is a little more appropriate for Lilith than this traveling suit."

Lillian, listening, actually forgot herself and gaped at them. They were speaking of Mama—and not as a woman pottering with just another hobby but as a highly respected designer. Mama! All this time, Lillian had presumed that Mr. Bishop's visits to the house were primarily for personal reasons, the drawings merely serving as his excuse. Obviously she was wrong, as she should have guessed! For her mother, there would always be only one man—Papa—a fact Mr. Bishop must have quickly discovered.

"We haven't your dressing room arranged as yet," Barbara was saying to Rose. "We'll find something larger and more suitable later, but for today number six, if that will do, is free."

"Of course it will do. Dressing rooms aren't important," Rose answered coolly. "I've been in all kinds. Excuse me for a moment then."

As soon as she had left them, Andrew Bishop took a purposeful step toward Lillian, who at once became conscious again of the perspiration suddenly beading her forehead and the increased tremor in her hands. Surely he didn't intend to accuse her of drug taking here and now, not when Barbara was so busy and engrossed!

But no, to her relief he merely asked in a low voice, "Are you all right?" Although he was frowning, his tone, to her surprise, was concerned.

She nodded curtly and moved away.

"All ready to play Eve?" Barbara asked her.

"Oh, yes! It's such a marvelous opportunity, I feel!" Why did she sound so overenthusiastic? Lately, it seemed, if her spirits weren't down in the depths, she was bubbling in this phony way. Barbara must have found her response peculiar, too, because she was studying her thoughtfully.

But then the attention of everyone present returned to Rose Bishop, who in a short time had totally changed her appearance. She was no longer the well-preserved older actress dressed in smart though unremarkable plum flannel suit. This was a far younger woman, wearing a plain black chemise falling almost straight to her ankles, yet made of some soft material that clung and outlined her voluptuous bosom and slender waist. Her thick glossy hair, which had never been bobbed, lay in raven folds against her shoulders and down her back. Those enormous eyes and a red, full-lipped mouth were all one saw in her face.

Then she sauntered across the stage, and Lillian realized her original error. Rose's swinging legs and hips were, as she'd supposed, solid, no doubt always had been. They were also lithe, strong, and graceful, and in their earthiness highly seductive.

"You *are* Lilith." John Eagleton, the director hardest to please in all of Hollywood, said the words quietly.

Rose didn't answer, perhaps because, there being no voices in motion pictures, she disdained to add to the effect by using hers. But she smiled. It was an enigmatic, alluring, not quite human smile.

Eagleton, needing no megaphone on this small stage, said, "Ready, all. Adam, in this sleazy bistro in Paris, you're seeing her for the first time. She dances . . . you are drawn . . . you rise from your chair. . . ."

Lillian had stopped watching because her strength, in one of those abrupt switches that so appalled her, had drained away as quickly as sand from an hourglass. Her thin body felt so heavy she had to will herself to raise a hand.

Oh, God. How would she ever be able to play her part when the time came, and play it as well as she must?

The cocaine's effect should have lasted longer, much longer, but the intervals of boundless energy and well-being were getting shorter and shorter, and when she complained to the Count he only nodded and continued to ration out just enough to get her through a necessary few hours. She'd have to find him now, at once—and perhaps she could before her own first scene was called. He'd promised to meet her outside when this morning's session was over. He might well be at the gate already.

She backed away from the stage on which Rose Bishop held everyone's enthralled attention, and pushed herself to walk very rapidly toward the studio entrance. Hearing behind her a vigorous spatter of applause, and visualizing only too clearly what had evoked it, she began heavily to run.

Damn the Count anyway, for not giving her enough to last through this all-important day! Damn him. But please God, let him be here now.

He was. He was standing outside, coolly watching her approach.

"Finished already?" His tone was indifferent, but there was that queer new light of anticipation in his pale, flat, remote eyes.

"No. My part comes later—but I can't make it through! You've got to give me some right away, so I can go back and—"

"Sorry. I told you the rules. It's pay on delivery. But if we hurry, perhaps you'll still be in time."

What choice did she have? She pulled herself erect and nodded, walking on ahead of him, grimly determined that he wouldn't be able to sense her revulsion, which she suspected in some perverted way amused him. She'd seen how he gloated the first time he took her—raped her—and she wept because her flesh crawled so. She'd sworn that never again would he have that pleasure, at least. But now he unexpectedly caught up with her and grasped her arm. She could not help cringing, so when he spoke his voice was complacent.

"Don't think so badly of yourself," he said with mocking commiseration. "You aren't the only one chained to cokey, or heroin, or something. Most actors seem to have a fatal kind of weakness. They need a crutch to lean on. Some poor fools won't go outdoors unless their astrologer tells them the stars are right! Most of them though find it easiest to get fired up and full of talent on drugs. A poor lot, actors."

"You're one, aren't you?" Lillian snapped.

"Hardly. I'm too intelligent. My real business is taking over their paychecks. And if you look at the matter fairly, it's a pretty good deal for them. I provide a magic formula, and presto, they have talent."

"I'd have plenty of talent without your damned magic!"

"Come now, Lily. Where would you be if I hadn't been around when you said, 'Help me'? So drained! So tired! Where would you be?"

"I'd be better off than I am now," she said slowly. "I'd be back there on that set, and today I'd give Rose Bishop a real run for her money." She would, too. Wasn't that what Mr. Bishop had said?

I'm a fine actress! I know it and others know it. And I'm throwing it all away. . . .

What am I doing, going to bed with this slimy creep? Why am I even talking to him? I don't have to. I'm Lillian Fritsch, and I'm strong enough, smart enough—I can do anything, even get a cocaine monkey off my back. . . .

She jerked free and began to run along the street.

"Hey, where are you going? The hotel's around this corner!"

She didn't slacken her pace, and by a miracle felt a little of the old zest return to her step.

He ran up, caught her, and swung her roughly around.

"I asked you, where are you going?"

"Somewhere. Anywhere. But not with you. Never again. You smell too bad. Did you know that? You smell like something's rotted—"

He slapped her hard across the face, so that tears sprang into her eyes. But without another word she spun on her heel and left him. This time he didn't follow.

Chapter 54

"Where are you off to, so late in the day?" Tony asked. He had just gotten home. His eyes were bloodshot from the strain of searching for printing errors in closely set lines of text, and she noticed he looked tired and a little stooped, as he did every afternoon these days. Doing work you hated, feeling chained to a desk when you longed to be active, would exhaust anyone, Joanna thought with a stab of sympathy.

She said, wishing he hadn't asked, "I've been invited to a party—at the *Los Angeles Times*."

"Oh? Even if you don't work there?"

"Yes, because I know almost everyone who does. They are honoring one of the men who has just returned from overseas."

"A medical discharge, I guess."

"This isn't a soldier. He's a foreign correspondent," she explained.

"I see. That friend of yours, Charles Gold?"

"Yes." She was surprised that he remembered. The few conversations in which Charles had been mentioned had taken place long ago, before Tony left for France. Perhaps some instinct even then had warned him that Charles was important to her.

But whatever he knew or suspected didn't matter tonight. If he tried to forbid her going, she would simply defy him. Perhaps he sensed her determination because he merely said, "I'm going to be out myself. I'll take Antonia to Aunt Flossie's." He left her and went to find Bunch.

To Joanna it was like old times, driving her shiny black car down to First and Broadway. She parked in front of the editorial offices and ran happily up the stairs.

Although the huge cut-glass bowl almost covering one of the desks contained, out of deference to the powerful temperance movement, only fruit punch, there was an air of gaiety

343

in this usually staid, very busy newsroom. Mr. McGowan, catching sight of her, came striding from his private office and took her hand, saying, "This is a great day, is it not? The war is really over; we'll be hearing in a few hours about the signing. So Charles is only the first of my boys to come home." His face clouded for a moment, as he was reminded of those few who would never be back, and then the smile returned, restrained and somewhat wry, as it used to before the war. "Now," he concluded, "we can get on with our lives again."

He moved away to greet the publisher, Mr. Harry Chandler, and elderly Tom Parker took his place at Joanna's elbow.

"Mark my words," Parker said, "our Mr. Chandler may not swagger and bluster and make as much noise as his father-in-law, General Harrison Gray Otis, who ran this paper with an iron hand for so long. But it'll be one of the great newspapers of the world before Chandler gets through."

Joanna felt forlorn. One of the great newspapers in the world, and she was to be no part of it! "How are you, Mr. Parker?" she asked quickly.

"Too stiff and creaky to hang around here much longer. I'm retiring again, maybe you heard, just as soon as the young fellows get back. Although I guess that will be some little time yet."

"To bring so many thousands of men home will take a lot of planning."

"Making them wait very long, though, doesn't seem fair to the boys. Well, we'll see. Want a cup of that bilious punch?" When she refused, he went off to get some for himself.

Alone for an instant, Joanna stood savoring the familiar musty smells of paper and ink that always pervaded every nook and corner of this building. Against her will, her eyes were drawn to her old desk. One glance as she'd entered the room and she'd instantly spotted a new girl sitting there. A conscientious young woman, undoubtedly, because amid all the conviviality she was pecking away at Joanna's own typewriter.

"You needn't feel jealous of her," said a well-remembered voice at her elbow. "The poor girl will be lucky to be working on obituaries by next April or May. All the women will be losing their jobs when the men get back. Not you though, if you were still here. Ed thinks too highly of you."

"Hello, Charles." She'd spun around and was smiling up at him.

"You're looking far too thin and tired, Joanna."

"Influenza," she murmured absently. Surely he knew the same could be said of him! She was every day getting a little more color and fullness back in her face, but the years in France and whatever horrors he'd experienced had etched permanent deep lines around his mouth and eyes. Then she realized, with further shock, that he was leaning heavily on a cane.

Her eyes traveled down. He held his left leg stiffly, his weight resting on the right.

"Charles—what happened?"

"My ankle and knee don't bend anymore. Shrapnel." He was explaining quite calmly, as though discussing some stranger's disability. "But actually I feel very lucky. At least my leg is still mine, and I couldn't count on that for quite a while."

"Why didn't you let me—let any of us know? You were in a hospital, we could have written to you."

"Ed knew. But I asked him not to tell anyone. I was afraid Mr. Chandler might recall me, so as soon as I could manage it I went back to work."

She stared at him mutely, trying to imagine the pain he must have forced himself to endure once he returned to the trenches.

"I'd promised myself I'd finish out the war," he added.

"But in that case—the war isn't finished. Didn't you want to stay for the signing?"

A muscle twitched in his jaw, and for a moment he didn't answer. Then he said, "Do you remember my friend, the cook in San Pedro?"

"Peter Perkov."

"Yes. He was killed. In a late, pointless offensive, after the Germans knew they were beaten! Such a bitterly sad waste . . . his mother asked Ed, an old friend of hers, if I couldn't bring Peter's body home. It was an impossible request, but Ed agreed, pulled strings, and actually arranged it. He'd only needed an excuse. I think he wanted to see for himself how I was, and he has two other sources covering the formalities in Compiègne Forest."

Joanna said, "I'm so sorry."

She was only thinking of his friend, but he must have deliberately misunderstood her meaning, not wishing to dwell on Peter's death, because he said, "I did hate to miss the final scene. Professionally, though, it doesn't matter. I've proved I can work in the field with a bad leg, so I can be expected to do as well anywhere. There should be no problem in the future about my fitness."

"I suppose not."

"I just can't take you or any other girl dancing, or walking up in the hills when spring comes—and those were the things I looked forward to . . . please don't look like that, Joanna."

"How am I looking?" She tried to match his low-voiced composure, and failed.

He didn't answer. But the words "as though you care about me—" hung in the air between them as clearly as if he had spoken them.

Fortunately, the brief period of isolation, the two of them alone together, was at an end. Well-wishers were converging on Charles.

He said quickly, "There is so much time to cover, so many things I'd like to tell you about. I must see these old friends, but if you'll wait, later we can leave, go somewhere to talk. That's all I want, Joanna. Just to talk. We've been friends a long time, and I've missed you. All right?"

There was no time for deliberation. She nodded, then watched him hobble a short distance away to meet three of the reporters he'd known longest. She was pleased by their obvious respect as they gripped his shoulder and asked him questions. He spoke at length about the last battle he'd seen and about his voyage home, not so hazardous this time, although a stray U-boat might still sink a ship.

Joanna listened, wishing he'd been willing to talk as freely about the death of his friend.

"We'll have to take a Red Car," Charles said. "I sold my old Chadwick before I left."

"I don't mind. Where are we going?"

Just like old times!

"I thought, the beach—at Venice perhaps. There's a lovely wide stretch there, and benches. One thing I dreamed about in France was a quiet beach, without artillery tracing shells against the sky."

She'd never questioned any of his destinations, and she didn't now. They walked the half-block to the car stop, he limping but managing well enough with his cane, and were just in time to board a train for Venice.

The ride was a fairly long one, perhaps forty minutes, and for the better part of it, to her surprise, they rode side by side saying little. He, after a searching glance at her, gazed pensively out the window, while she, remembering vividly the other occasion on which they'd visited a beach together, felt a constraint that kept her silent. Finally, in an effort to end this unexpected awkwardness, she mentioned the book she was writing, saying how difficult it had been to make a start.

"Is it going better now?"

Encouraged by his evident interest, she said eagerly, "Oh, yes. At least I've discovered that a kind of structure has grown in my mind. I've a beginning and an end, but the middle is still hazy. Sometimes I think I should be a little older—"

"Older? Dear Joanna, you are older. You're married." His voice held a faint bitterness. "And, I hear, even a mother."

"Yes . . ." she said uncertainly. She glanced at him quickly, then looked away. "What I meant was, to write a novel, perhaps I should have seen a little more of the world."

"You always said that was what you longed to do, see the world. Paris—Tokyo—Timbuktu. I was so pleased that you and I had the same yearnings, the same dreams. But I suppose now, for you the world is contained here. You're happily settled, and don't mind missing Paris."

"But I do mind! I've been terribly jealous of you all this time—oh, not for being in the war, but in being so free to travel about. What a wonderful life, I've thought."

"Have you? Then I wasn't wrong . . . my word, Joanna, are we on the wrong train? It's stopping, and I see a ferris wheel—what a sight!"

Like children, they both had their faces pressed to the window. Although night had fallen, thousands of lights made the scene sharp and clear. A long pier jutted far out over the water, and on the pier and along the shore in both directions, against the backdrop of ferris wheel and roller coaster, were any number of brightly painted stalls, small buildings, and rides. Even here, inside the Red Car, pipe organ music could be heard, not quite drowning the raucous shouts of barkers.

"Venice—Venice—" chanted the conductor. "End of the line—Venice—"

"What happened to the beach, I wonder?" Charles said as they left the train. "All of this is new. I used to come here to fish. . . ."

"I remember now, I've heard my family talk about these amusement piers. But I'm sure the beach hasn't vanished," she consoled. "We'll find it."

Charles was limping swiftly through the crowds, still a tall and commanding figure, and he had taken her hand and pulled her along with him. He ignored the billowing canvas poster of an enormously fat lady, as well as the spiel of a little man in a checked suit, trying to lure them into his flea circus. But at the foot of the pier, there was a brown-painted, intentionally ramshackle little building, and Charles paused.

"I remember one of these from a boyhood festival. *The Haunted House*. Let's go in, Joanna. Do you mind?"

The rooms inside were dark except for a series of tiny blue bulbs showing the way. Grotesque heads leapt from cupboards, skeletons rattled, and now and then there was a rush of air from the floor, designed to blow a lady's skirt up as she passed. Both Charles and Joanna were laughing, and they laughed harder when they staggered across a tilted floor, then found themselves in a room lined with distorting mirrors.

They gazed at their images. Elongated, emaciated Charles; shortened, dumpy, face-askew Joanna. They were a comical pair all right and not to be taken seriously. Suddenly all the wariness between them was gone.

As if both wanted to prolong this interlude of innocent enjoyment they now strolled slowly, stopping at the various stands, even buying tickets to enter one of the tents and watch a lady trapeze artist, wearing a brief, revealing costume of spangles, perform high in the air on a fragile little swing. There was no net beneath her, and Joanna, hardly daring to breathe, could only think *How brave! I could never do that!*

A spirit-dampening moment came when Charles and she paused next beside the open-air dance pavilion, which was crowded with couples gyrating to the strains of "Oh Johnny, Oh Johnny, Oh!" Charles, however, pointing beyond, said, "Look there, Joanna—the Caterpiller. Strange name. Let's find out what kind of a ride that is."

In a moment they were climbing the steps to the platform and being directed to one of the high-backed, comfortably padded seats, just big enough for two. Shortly the string of little cars jerked into motion, picked up speed, and went circling swiftly on an undulating track.

Charles had just remarked, "Surely this isn't all?" when the meaning of the ride's odd name became clear. A heavy canvas, mottled green and yellow, lifted from one side and arched across all the seats, snugly enclosing them.

Outside, onlookers would be treated to a view of a giant worm, twisting and turning.

But inside, the bright lights had been cut off, and it was all too evident from the other riders' abrupt silence, broken only by the grind of the wheels and an occasional feminine giggle, what was customary and no doubt delightedly anticipated in those few seconds of privacy. In her amusement, Joanna's eyes sought Charles's and her smile faded as she found she couldn't tear her gaze away. Her body, thrown against his by the curving of the track, remained pressed close, his arm tightening around her. Charles, as though there had been no passage of time since they last kissed, murmured her name, and then his lips were on hers, on her throat, back to her lips again, and she, helpless to stop herself, returned his caresses, at first slowly, reluctantly, then with a fierce abandon.

But already the ride was ending.

The cars had slowed imperceptibly, and the green cover was lifted away, taking passengers by surprise.

"Yes," Charles said, "you have grown up, Joanna. And I think it's time we talked." She had stepped at once onto the platform, and he awkwardly hoisted himself out beside her. "The beach must be only a little further. I think I see empty sand, over beyond the carousel."

Although she walked in the direction he indicated, she didn't answer. She was marveling unhappily at the passion with which she had responded. Since her marriage, she had told herself she was fond of Charles as a friend. She'd told Mama he was only a friend. But it appeared she had deceived herself as well as Mama. And so easily—so easily! She, a married woman, had not only welcomed his kisses, she'd wanted more, much more.

Just beyond the carousel, gaily turning, there was a bench, and before it, just as Charles had suspected, lay a wide stretch of sand, bordering the dark blue ocean water. Waves crested in, white foamed, and receded, crested in again.

The stray thought came—*Would a heron appear tonight in the surf?* Then Charles was drawing her to sit beside him.

He said, his words clear even beneath the gay flourish of the music, "Back at the office, when I told you I wanted to talk, I wasn't being completely honest. Because what I want to talk about is us. You're a woman now. You don't need to be protected from yourself any longer, not by me, anyway.

"So let me say what I feel, just once. Because I do still feel it. I knew I had not stopped loving you the instant I saw you standing there, eyeing your old desk so wistfully.

"This is the girl who'll go with me, I told myself. Footloose. Fancy free. Enjoying every corner of the world.

"Then on the train, I was doubting again. You seemed different. The lovely young matron, cautious, uneasy. Joanna, which girl is you?"

"I don't know. Both perhaps."

He smiled. "The Caterpillar ride, I confess, gives me reason to hope. . . .

"My dear, you must understand. I have the life I wanted and I'll never give it up. My work has always come first. I even—God forgive me—resented being torn away from the Armistice meeting, the culmination of all those years of war, and hurried off home because of Peter. I confess it! Peter Perkov—and I loved him!

"So you see, that's the sort I am. I doubt if I will have children—they wouldn't fit into my life, and they wouldn't be happy there, always knocking about. But with those reservations, the rest of me is yours. If you'll come with me, I can promise you beauty and excitement—oh, Joanna, I have so much to show you!"

His arm was about her, and he was waiting, but Joanna, face turned away, was gazing at the revolving carousel.

This carousel, filled with young riders, was bright red, and except for being larger was extraordinarily like the one that had stood for so long in Chutes Park. There was even the same little black boy seeming to play the pipe organ, and as Joanna watched his finely carved hands lift then press the keys, as she watched the beautiful smiling horses and cats and tigers circle, rising and falling on their turned brass poles, she was imagining she could see the children she knew so well, those of the past. That boy, the agile one balancing himself while standing up in the saddle, grinning and soon to be reprimanded, that was Tony. There was Dell too, a little awkward and mistrustful of her own pleasure but enjoying the treat all the more for that. And Lillian—she was the pretty girl with the elfin face, so very determined to catch the brass ring. Joanna herself, not old enough to be put on alone, was riding sedately in the swan car with Mama.

But no, that mother and child weren't she and Mama. That was Bunch with Joanna. Bunch holding Joanna's hand, her eyes wide, her sweet mouth curved in an unconscious smile of delight.

And the man standing protectively beside the gilded swan, loving both the child and the woman, and loving them unselfishly, without any reservations at all—that was also Tony.

Charles said, "Joanna?"

He drew her closer, and she felt again the strong pull of desire. But this time she resisted. Desire and its fulfillment were important, but not to her, here, tonight. She could experience the most wondrous flights of passion with her own husband. Mama was right, of course. There was delight enough for her in Tony's arms.

Unable to find the right words, mutely she shook her head, and Charles drew away, no longer holding or touching her.

"It's too late for us, isn't it?" he said. "I understand you so well! I even know when it became too late. The day your daughter was born. Seeing her on visits home wouldn't be enough."

"No," Joanna agreed. "I could never leave her. Never!" But the truth, finally so clear, was that it had always been too late. Wander on foreign shores forever, just the two of them, Charles and she? That would never have been enough. Joanna wanted all of life! She wanted to be a part of what was happening, experience her own pain and happiness, not live as a spectator.

But she said nothing of this. She'd had a dream and Charles had had a dream. It wasn't his fault that their dreams were not the same.

He said heavily, "Well then, come along, Joanna. I'll take you home.

"No, please! I know the way. I'd rather go alone."

"That might be best." He managed a twisted smile, gave her a small wave of goodbye, then turned and walked stiffly away.

"*Auf Wiedersehen*," she whispered, watching his lonely figure disappear.

The house was empty.

So Tony was still out somewhere. She'd have to go to Aunt Flossie's to bring Bunch home.

But first there was the telephone call to make. She gave the operator the number of the little bungalow in Hollywood and waited nervously. Suppose Clara wasn't there? What Joanna had to say, she wanted to say at once.

But Clara answered.

"Mama, it's Joanna . . . I wanted to tell you I'm home again. You don't have to worry anymore about Charles.

"And there's something else. This is really what I'm calling about. It's just, I understand better now how—what you told me—could have happened.

"Mama, are you still there? Mama, I love you, very much."

Chapter 55

"Yes, Tony came back. He took Bunch and they went into the park."

"But the park isn't there anymore, Aunt Flossie! The grass going to weeds, no rides. It's depressing. Besides, Bunch should have been in bed long ago."

"Maybe he felt like seeing the lake for the last time. They're draining it tomorrow, I hear. And the path around it, and the pretty light posts, and the benches—all to be pulled out tomorrow. Well, as my dear husband used to say, 'Times change and we must change with them.'"

Joanna found them at once, near the old boathouse. Bunch, her dress wet and grimy at the hem, was playing as happily in a mud puddle left by a recent rain as if the sun instead of the moon were shining. On a nearby iron bench, Tony sat leaning forward, his face supported by his hands, gazing into the still water.

Joanna went to sit beside him.

"Remembering?"

"Yes. And daydreaming... it's sad to see everything go, isn't it? Hard to imagine the chutes torn down. But it doesn't matter, I guess. The lake won't he here either, a few hours from now... so you're back?"

"Yes." She was wondering how much meaning she could read into the simple question. Had he suspected how torn she was? Perhaps not. Or perhaps he'd known her better than she knew herself. "You said 'daydreaming.' Sounds pleasant. What about?"

"Joanna, I've a lot to tell you. I've made a decision." But then he fell silent, continuing to gaze away, and a small leaf of fear began to uncurl inside of her. Had she misjudged Tony's devotion? Was he so sick of that miserable job of his that he was giving up? Leaving her, as Ralph had left Adeline, to seek happiness somewhere else?

Not that she would blame him too much. She hadn't been the wife she should have been, trying to understand his worries and disappointments, truly cherishing him as she'd promised, through sickness as well as health. No, she'd thought only of herself and her own small frustrations.

"Then tell me," she said quietly.

"It's what to do for work. I can go on proofreading if there's nothing else, and I will. For you and Bunch—"

Such relief flooded her that she couldn't speak. He did still love her then.

"But I've had an idea. It's so wild that I'm afraid you'll think I'm crazy. But here goes. Remember that pamphlet I did for Mr. Starr? About the Liberty engines?"

She nodded, not comprehending.

"They're for sale, dirt cheap. The government can't wait to get rid of them, and they're beautiful. Absolutely the best. Joanna, I'd like to get money together and buy as many as I can, and build airplanes."

She didn't speak for a moment. The enormity of such an undertaking overwhelmed her. But his eagerness touched her, too. She hadn't seen him enthusiastic for so very long.

"Even dirt cheap," she said carefully, "for us, would be very expensive."

"I know. But there are loans. We could try to sell shares— to Dell, for example. Because I'd want Olaf in with us. He understands the construction of planes. I do, too, but from a different point of view. So it would take both of us. As for Dell—"

"If you let Dell get a finger in the pie, she'll want to run things. To protect her money."

"Then let her. We'll need somebody like that. A watchdog. Joanna, does that mean you don't think it's impossible? You see, I have to tell you this: I'd rather try and fail—I'd rather lose everything you and I have—than not to try at all."

"It's possible, I suppose. But Tony, aren't there a lot of people building airplanes?"

"Not nearly enough! You know how I complained because

America sent no planes at all to France. This is the right time, I'm convinced of it."

"Then, my dear, I think you should try. I'll help you—you will let me help you, won't you?"

"Joanna, maybe this is the time to say I'm sorry. About making you leave the *Times*, I mean. I knew I was wrong a long time ago, but somehow that first night, you got my dander up. I'm a ridiculously stubborn man. I had to prove to you and to myself that I was man enough to support us all alone. Once, when you were so sick, I confessed what a fool I was. I guess you didn't hear me."

"Tony, let's not talk about something that's over and done—"

"But you just asked about helping me. We were speaking of money, and it's true every nickel will count. Will you go back to work as a reporter? Now I'm asking you to."

"Then I just might consider it." They'd had enough, both of them, of solemn repentance, and she said in an exaggerated drawl, "Of course, I wouldn't want anything to interfere with this perfectly marvelous book I'm writing."

He was startled, but when he saw her expression, he too began to chuckle. Then, without quite knowing why, they were rocking in each other's arms, convulsed with laughter.

Finally Tony jumped to his feet. "What are we sitting here for when there's so much ahead of us to do? Let's get started. Come on, Antonia, want to ride on your dad's shoulder?"

The lilt was back in his voice. Tony was older, wiser, stronger now than the boy she'd always known, but he was still the Tony who delighted her, who needed her. And whom she needed.

"Yes," Joanna said, "let's go home."

Chapter 56

"I found her," Andrew said before he even entered the bungalow.

"Oh, I'm glad!" Clara answered calmly, even though more

than two weeks had passed without a word. She'd already noted that Andrew did not look as if he had anything tragic to disclose, confirming her original intuition that Lillian would turn up unscathed. Being safe physically didn't of course rule out some questionable escapade or other. Lillian's standards of behavior were not everyone's. But if this headstrong daughter of hers had been involved in something foolish, Clara for once felt blameless. Just as Sam would have wished, she'd tried hard to guide Lillian throughout these difficult Hollywood years, and she could think of nothing more she could have done.

Not that she didn't care. She did deeply, about them all. It was a delight to her, and a profound relief, that Dell was once again willing to take chances and risk her affections.

As for Joanna's call of the night before, Clara had never before experienced such a moment of pure happiness.

"Come in, Andrew," she said. "Lillian's all right?"

"Yes, she is. I told her I'd bring you to see her today. When I made that promise, though, I didn't realize the streets would be jammed with people. There's even a parade starting."

"You could hardly predict that the Armistice would be signed last night. Oh, isn't it wonderful! I've been listening to all the wild celebrating, bells, horns, whistles, singing. No one seems in the least worried about being in a crowd and catching influenza."

"I did see a few gauze masks as I came along, but actually, Clara, the epidemic is over, at least in Los Angeles. It's dying down almost as quickly as it struck, and soon will be forgotten."

"Except by those who lost someone," Clara amended. "And there are so many. Another funeral went by only a little while ago, pushing a way through the merrymakers . . . but tell me quickly, please, about Lillian! Where has she been?"

Andrew hesitated. He seemed to be eyeing her anxiously, in spite of his matter-of-fact manner, and Clara began to feel apprehensive after all. Then he said, "She's been in a small hospital, not far from here."

"A hospital? Oh, Andrew, has there been an accident? Or— surely not—influenza?"

"No, she's not sick or hurt. Listen just a moment, and you'll know everything. You see, the arrival of my sister Rose was not such a bad thing for Miss Lily French, as it turned out. Your daughter was stunned to discover that Rose is a great actress, truly a great one. But being as competitive as she is, as well as—in common with all the actors I've ever met—

supremely egotistical, Lillian rallied. She was certain she had it in her to be fully as good as Rose, if only—and again, as you will agree, she is a hardheaded realist—if only she would stop handicapping herself. Then and there, she swore she'd get rid of a terrible habit that was sapping all her strength and vitality.

"Clara, she took herself to a doctor, a very special man who has helped a number of other movie people get free of drugs."

"Drugs!"

"Yes. Lillian was a heavy cocaine user. Had been for some time."

"I can't believe it! She said she never would . . . she was so convincing. . . ." Yet even while she was protesting, Clara knew that what he'd told her was true. She should have guessed for herself. But the changes she'd noticed—the loss of appetite, the thinness, the nervous shaking—she'd attributed to the girl's frustration in not getting the *Lilith* part. "Then she was lying to me. And," Clara added, remembering, "to Mrs. Gierek."

"They all lie, Clara, to protect themselves. They can't help it. As for Barbara, I've persuaded her to give Lillian another chance. After all, one must recognize that to stop an addiction takes tremendous courage."

"And has she stopped?"

"The doctor says so. And I—knowing Lily French for a fighter—I say so, too. No, she's all right. Almost herself again, or will be soon. She wants very much to see you, even though you are the one she most dreaded knowing the truth."

He had his watch in his hand, and he added, "Clara, with these crowds, I'll have to drive very slowly. So, if you're ready, we should start."

His Ford was at the sidewalk. She only took time to get her hat and coat, then she was seated beside him.

He was right. To go anywhere at all today was difficult. The streets were thronged, people singing and hugging each other. Andrew's automobile was brought to a final standstill by the parade, organized jointly by a number of the movie studios, in which the participants, marching, skipping, dancing, proceeded abreast down the middle of Hollywood Boulevard.

The famous producers Mack Sennett, D. W. Griffith, and Cecil B. deMille, rivals and never the closest of friends, strode along in step, all grinning. And here was Charlie Chaplin, in derby hat and baggy pants, followed by hordes of children to whom he pantomined as seriously as though he were on camera.

Next came three vamps, together for the one and only time in their careers, all with a slinking gait and all ogling nearby men through their sinister black eyelashes: Louise Glaum, Virginia Pearson, and Theda Bara, the last declaiming throatily from time to time the subtitle that had made her famous: "Kiss me, my fool." Most of the cheers as they passed, however, were for the star a few paces behind them: Willian S. Hart, the most popular of all Western heroes. Astride his prancing horse, Pinto Ben, carrying sweet and pure Bessie Love before him in the saddle, he tirelessly waved his ten-gallon hat in sweeping salutes.

On and on they came—Mary Pickford, America's Sweetheart, with dashing Douglas Fairbanks; clowning Slim Summerville with his current partner, Louise Fazena. Every idol was trailed by his or her applauding admirers. It was plain there would be no driving on this street for many hours.

Oddly impatient, his fingers tapping the steering wheel, Andrew said, "As soon as there's a break and we can cross, I'll cut over to Venice Boulevard. We may be able to get through there."

Clara, assuming it had been arranged for her to visit Lillian at a certain hour, sat quietly while he maneuvered his automobile, first through the ranks of the paraders, then along Venice, which was barely passable, choked as it was with jubilant pedestrians. At length he angled to the side of the thoroughfare and parked.

He said, "Here we are, Clara."

"The hospital? No, why, Andrew, this is—" She was staring up at the lettering above a wrought-iron gate, which read SELIG STUDIOS.

"Yes. It's Lillian's studio, and mine. And yours."

"Andrew, I don't understand. You said, didn't you, she was in a hospital?"

"She was. Until yesterday, when she was released. As it happened, the actress who replaced her in Rose's film wasn't satisfactory, and Barbara told Lillian that if she could be ready—they're scheduled to start filming in only a day or two—she could have the role back. So, Lily being Lily, she insisted on rehearsing this morning, Armistice or not. Barbara, who dislikes parades anyway, agreed."

"But what am I doing here?"

He gave her an uneasy glance, then looked away. "I brought you for two reasons. The first, of course, is that Lillian wants you to see her acting. She wants you to be completely convinced that she's herself again. Your good opinion matters a great deal to her, Clara."

"And the other reason?"

"That's, well . . . Barbara mentioned to me that several additional scenes have been added, and therefore more costumes will be needed. One of the writers is on the set now, and you can talk to him yourself. Far better, don't you think, than just hearing about the new material from me?"

When she said nothing, he sighed and turned to face her. "I hoped, of course, that you might be enticed by Lillian's invitation to come inside. And once here, you'd find what we do so challenging and interesting, that you'd want to stay."

Clara said thoughtfully, "It occurs to me that I've been taking the studio's money all this time. Whether I liked it or not, I was working for the studio."

He gave a small unhappy shrug. That was the one argument he could never have brought himself to use. When she recognized her self-deception for what it was, she might give up the costume designing—and the meetings with him—entirely.

"All right, Andrew." She looked at him, smiling. "I will." The decision hadn't been difficult. Ever since Joanna's call the night before, she'd felt not absolved perhaps, but free. As if Joanna's understanding were Sam's.

Clara's shrunken, cold world was cracking further, letting in warmth and life, and she could no longer sit still. Not waiting for Andrew to come around to the car door, she threw it open herself, stepped out, and walked briskly through the studio gates.

ABOUT THE AUTHOR

Louise O'Flaherty was a senior at Wellesley College when her plans for a literary career were postponed by America's entry into World War II. She was taught to be a cryptographer, and as a lieutenant in the WAVES she worked a forty-eight hour week of swing shifts to break German codes. "A demanding, exhausting time," she recalls, "but one of camaraderie never to be forgotten." Married to a fellow Navy officer, she subsequently moved with him to Los Angeles, raised their three children, and at last devoted herself to the dreamed-of novels.

The locale of Ms. O'Flaherty's books is usually southern California, as she shares the enthusiasm of her husband, a historian, for the rigorous, little-known past of the area as well as its colorful and often controversial way of life. Her most recent novels include THE FARTHEST EDEN, POPPIES IN THE WIND, and THIS GOLDEN LAND.

Ballantine presents another series from the producers of *The Kent Family Chronicles* and *Wagons West*...

THE

AMERICAN PATRIOT

SERIES